Praise for the Guinness Girls novels

'A bright, pacy, readable account of the early lives of these extraordinary women . . . fans of *Downton Abbey* will adore this'   *Sunday Times*

'An utterly captivating insight into these fascinating women and the times they lived in . . . it's an absolute page-turner'   *Irish Independent*

'Masterfully and glamorously told . . . essential reading for history and gossip lovers alike'
Sunday Business Post

'The perfect glorious escape . . . the intimacy of a family drama, set against the most opulent of backdrops'
Sunday Independent

'A captivating and page-turning novel about a fascinating family. Fantastic'   Sinéad Moriarty

'Engrossing and page-turning . . . I loved it'
Louise O'Neill

'An enthralling tale that will dazzle and delight . . . If you loved the drama of *The Crown*, then you will adore *The Guinness Girls: A Hint of Scandal*'
Swirl and Thread

Emily Hourican is an Irish journalist and author. She has written features for the *Sunday Independent* for fifteen years, as well as *Image* magazine, *Condé Nast Traveler* and *Woman and Home*.

She lives in Dublin with her family. *The Guinness Girls: A Hint of Scandal* is her sixth novel.

Previously by Emily Hourican

The Glorious Guinness Girls
The Outsider
The Blamed
White Villa
The Privileged

How To (Really) Be A Mother (non-fiction)

The GUINNESS GIRLS

A HINT OF SCANDAL

..... ✳ .....

EMILY HOURICAN

A Novel

HACHETTE
BOOKS
IRELAND

First published in Ireland in 2021 by
HACHETTE BOOKS IRELAND
First published in paperback in 2022

1

Cataloguing in Publication Data is available from the British Library

ISBN 9781529352917

Typeset in Sabon LT Std by Palimpsest Book Production Ltd,
Falkirk, Stirlingshire

Printed and bound in Great Britain by
Clays Ltd, Elcograf S.p.A.

Hachette Books Ireland policy is to use papers that are natural, renewable
and recyclable products and made from wood grown in sustainable forests.
The logging and manufacturing processes are expected to conform
to the environmental regulations of the country of origin.

Hachette Books Ireland
8 Castlecourt Centre
Castleknock
Dublin 15, Ireland

A division of Hachette UK Ltd
Carmelite House, 50 Victoria Embankment, London EC4Y 0DZ

www.hachettebooksireland.ie

For my sisters, Bridget and Martha

Cast of Characters

London

Oonagh Guinness, now Oonagh Kindersley

Philip Kindersley, Oonagh's husband

Ernest Guinness, the girls' father

Cloé Guinness, their mother

Kathleen, former housemaid, now qualified as a teacher thanks to Ernest Guinness

Violet Valerie French, known as 'Valsie', Oonagh's friend

Victor Brougham, 4th Baron Brougham and Vaux, Valsie's fiancé

Nancy Mitford, the eldest of the Mitford sisters

Diana Mitford, Nancy's sister

Unity Mitford, Nancy and Diana's sister

Bryan Guinness, cousin of the Guinness sisters and Diana's husband

Bright Young People: Stephen Tennant, Elizabeth Ponsonby, Teresa 'Baby' Jungman, Zita Jungman

Evelyn Waugh, writer

Henry Channon, 'Chips', American diarist and politician

Oswald Mosley, British politician

Mary, Irish nursemaid at Bryan Guinness and Diana Mitford's home

Ned, Mary's brother

Luttrellstown Castle, Dublin

Aileen Guinness, now Aileen Plunket

Brinsley Sheridan Bushe Plunket, 'Brinny', Aileen's husband (nicknamed the Great Oouja by Maureen)

Annie, Cousin Mildred's protegée

Clandeboye, Co. Down

Maureen Guinness, now Marchioness of Dufferin and Ava

Basil Blackwood, 'Duff', 4th Marquess of Dufferin and Ava, Maureen's husband

Lady Brenda, Marchioness of Dufferin and Ava, Maureen's mother-in-law

Helen, housemaid at Clandeboye

Castle MacGarratt, Co. Mayo

Dominick Geoffrey Edward Browne, 4th Baron Oranmore and Browne

Mildred, his wife

A note from the author

This is a novel, not a history book. The characters are based on real people, but they are my imagined versions of these people. I have spent many years researching the Guinness sisters and family for *The Glorious Guinness Girls* and now *The Guinness Girls: A Hint of Scandal*. During this time I feel I have come to know these women. Because of that, for this novel I wanted to view each of them up close, rather than through the eyes of a single external narrator. The novel is built on real life events and people, (apart from Kathleen and her story), but my hope is that through my imagination and my interpretation of those events, I convey a sense of the girls' inner lives and go some way to bringing these three fascinating and enigmatic women to life.

Prologue

17 Grosvenor Place, London, 2 July 1930

'She won't come in, will she?' Oonagh looked nervously towards the door as though her mother Cloé might at any moment appear.

'Lord, no,' Maureen said. 'She never comes to this part of the house at all any more. Not since you two married.' She stretched out on her bed, the smooth pink of the satin counterpane bunching under her as she moved. One arm was bent under her head, the other waving an ivory cigarette holder lazily through the air in time to the music from the gramophone. Smoke from her cigarette zigzagged clumsily, then settled into a thick blue cloud around her.

'Stop jigging,' Aileen called sharply, from where she was propped against the headboard. 'You'll make me spill my drink.'

'How sad that sounds, Maureen. You must have missed us,' Oonagh said. 'You should have said.' She leaned forward in the armchair where she sat, feet drawn up under her, as though she might pat Maureen's head or hand, whichever bit of her she could reach.

'Not a bit,' Maureen insisted, twisting so she was out of Oonagh's reach and grinning at her. 'It was perfectly heavenly not having you two around.'

'All the more of Mamma to yourself,' Aileen said, which made Maureen laugh so loudly that Oonagh whipped her head around to stare at the door again.

'Oonagh, do stop behaving like a frightened mouse,' Maureen said. 'I tell you, she won't come in.'

'I believe you're still frightened of her, Oonagh,' Aileen said.

'Not *frightened*,' Oonagh said, 'not exactly. But you know . . .'

'I do,' Aileen said, pushing herself further up the headboard so that she sat straight. 'You think being married will mean you're suddenly frightfully grown-up, and won't mind about her at all. That you'll leave home and leave all that behind. And then you find that doesn't happen exactly as you thought it might. That she still stares at you as though you're a – a *marrow* in a guess-the-weight game.' They all laughed. 'And you find that it's just as bad as it ever used to be, being stared at so,' Aileen finished, fidgeting morosely with a diamond-drop earring.

There was a silence then, except for Fats Waller's 'Ain't Misbehavin'' drifting from the gramophone.

'I remember when I was a child—' Oonagh said.

'You're scarcely more than a child now,' Maureen interrupted, 'for all that you have a husband and a baby.'

'Well, I remember how I used to hold my breath when she looked at me like that, and I wouldn't be able to breathe again until she'd gone away. Like a fieldmouse under the eye of a hunting hawk – as though her eyes were *pins*' – she stuttered on the word slightly – 'to hold me in place.'

'Well, I'm not afraid of her,' Maureen said. 'I'm not such a poor little thing as you two.'

'And sometimes I think the effort of *not* being afraid is the very thing that has made you as you are,' Aileen said. 'Which, if you think about it, is rather the same as if you had been afraid.'

'Don't be absurd,' Maureen said. 'Oonagh, open a window, will you, before we all choke?'

Oonagh got up and threw wide the large sash window so that the cigarette smoke around Maureen was set writhing and billowing by the breeze. Outside, the sky was the colour of violet ink, the houses of Grosvenor Place and the walls of Buckingham Palace Gardens etched against it as though picked out in black thread. It had been a week of sultry weather, and the city had closed around them like a hot fist. But now a light rain fell and the smell of warm wet pavement rose up from below to mingle with the scent of night flowers from Buckingham Palace Gardens. A motor-car went by somewhere close, a hiss of tyres on damp road.

'How happy you must be for tomorrow, Maureen,' Oonagh said, leaning far out of the window to breathe in gulps of the night air. 'In . . .' she consulted the tiny gold watch that hung loose around her wrist '. . . less than twelve hours, you will be married.'

'Do you remember the night before your weddings?' Maureen demanded suddenly.

'Yes.' Aileen sat up and made herself another drink from the cocktail tray beside the bed, splashing gin into a glass and topping it up with Indian tonic water. She leaned back and pushed a strand of hair behind her ear.

'And? What did you feel?'

'Apprehensive,' Aileen admitted. 'As though I'd said yes to a party and suddenly realised I had no idea what kind of party, so I didn't know what to wear or what to bring.'

'You, Oonagh?'

'Relieved. I knew I couldn't live another week with Mamma in this house. All I could think was that the next day I would never have to sleep here again. And that my life was finally beginning.'

'I felt that too,' Aileen said. 'The life-beginning bit, not never sleeping here again.'

'Yes, that is a pleasant prospect,' Maureen said thoughtfully. 'Never ever having to ask anyone again if I may do something or go somewhere. My own motor-car, my own house, my own money. My own husband.' She smiled. 'No one to tell me no or insist I say yes. Instead me being the one to tell them.'

'But what do you feel? Oonagh asked curiously. 'Often, one doesn't know with you, Maureen . . . Always you behave as if you're so certain of everything. But if you are apprehensive, you can say, you know. Maybe we can reassure you.'

Maureen laughed, a little too much. 'No, thank you, Oonagh. I don't need your reassurance. I don't feel apprehensive in the slightest. I feel like I could burst with excitement.'

'You would, of course. And if you didn't, you'd still tell yourself that you did,' Aileen said, but she said it kindly. 'I must say, though, I'm surprised it's taken so long for you to marry. I would have thought you'd be out of the house like a shot, the minute Oonagh came down the aisle of St Margaret's as Mrs Kindersley. But I suppose you needed time to organise and have a dress made.'

'Not me,' Maureen said cheerfully. 'I'd have married Duff in my underwear, the very day after he asked me.' Aileen raised the thinly penciled lines of her eyebrows high, and Maureen rolled onto her side, reached down and slapped her sister's bare arm, a quick stinging slap that caused Aileen to wince. 'Don't bother making that boring shocked face because I know very well you aren't and only do it to seem grand and elegant.'

'My glass,' Aileen complained, lifting it high beyond Maureen's reach.

'Duff was the one who insisted on waiting,' Maureen continued, 'and on doing everything "properly".'

'And these days you do everything Duff wants,' Aileen said crossly, rubbing her arm against the satin counterpane to soothe it.

'I do,' Maureen said. 'Even when he wants to wait and be "correct", when I'd happily sneak him up here and tip Willis to say nothing to Mamma.'

'Maureen! You wouldn't.'

'I would. I tried, but he refused. Insisted it would be rude to Papa.'

'And so it would have been,' Oonagh said.

'That's all nonsense,' Maureen said. 'Why would Papa possibly care? Aileen, reach over and pour me another drink.' She waved her empty glass so vigorously that ash from her cigarette fell on the counterpane. She rubbed carelessly at it, leaving a harsh black smear.

'You can ask if you like,' Oonagh said.

'Ask what?'

'What marriage is like. Don't you want to?'

'No,' Maureen said, 'because my marriage, to Duff, will be nothing like either of yours.'

'I see,' – Aileen was nettled – 'and what does that mean? What will your marriage be like?'

'Perfect in every way, of course,' Maureen said, draining the glass Aileen handed to her, and passing it back. 'Pour another.'

'Oh, Maureen,' Oonagh said. 'I'm not sure . . .'

'Oonagh, don't bother. She won't listen. You know she won't. And in any case, maybe we all have to find out for ourselves . . .' She didn't finish and they all fell silent for a moment.

'The air smells so thick, I feel I could fall forward from this window and it would hold me up,' Oonagh said, leaning further out.

'Do you remember the doll's house we had as children?' Maureen asked suddenly. It had been the size of a tea chest, with a front that opened completely so that Oonagh, always small for her age, had been almost able to creep right inside. A perfect replica of the old house at Glenmaroon, made by one of the estate carpenters, it had been the most-loved thing in the nursery.

'What about it?' Aileen asked.

'You know how I used to hate when you played with it without me?'

'You hated anyone doing anything without you.'

'That in particular. It was because of the feeling I got when I opened it and found everything rearranged inside and not the way I'd left it. Flora and Mrs Patterson's lives' – those were their dolls – 'moved around and changed because you'd got there before me and rummaged through.' She made a face. 'And I'd have to take everything out, even those tiny brass candlesticks Nanny used to make us polish, and put it all back the way I wanted it.'

'I remember you doing that,' Aileen said. 'I thought you were just being tedious.'

'It made me feel ill and squirmy here,' – Maureen put a hand on her stomach – 'to know that you had changed it all around, that when I'd been imagining it one way, it had already been another.'

'How strange you are,' Aileen said.

'Well, that's what I feel now,' Maureen continued, ignoring her. 'Like you two have got somewhere before me and made it to your liking, not mine. For a time, you know, I didn't even want to be married because of you two doing it before me.'

'Maureen, this mania to be first in everything . . .' Oonagh said. But Maureen ignored her.

'Then, because of Duff, I changed my mind. And now I'm certain I shall be the best at being married of all of us.' Aileen and Oonagh exchanged looks and Oonagh started to speak but Aileen interrupted her. 'Don't bother,' she said.

'Turn the gramophone up,' Maureen called loudly. 'I want to dance.' She leaped off the bed, turned the volume high and began to dance around the room on her bare tiptoes. 'Oonagh, come and dance with me. And *stop* looking fearfully at that door . . .'

Part One

1930

Part One

1930

Chapter One

Rutland Gate, London

'Dr Gilliatt says you're to move about more,' Kathleen said, marching into Oonagh's room after the doctor had left. She hauled back the pale green curtains, the colour of lichen that grows on bark, so that the sun came spilling in and nudged at the end of Oonagh's bed as a dog might, head butting against a leg or arm when it wants something.

'Kathleen, don't!' Oonagh said, putting a hand up to shield her eyes from the brightness. With more light, she became conscious of the stuffiness of the room. A smell that was dense and inhabited – layers of Bois des Îles perfume laid one over another, last night's fresh scent mingling with an older, sourer memory, and beneath that a tired, fretful odour that reminded her of the bad night just passed. 'He didn't say any such thing.' She struggled to a sitting position, allowing Kathleen, who had a wiry strength, to help her up and settle her against the carved wooden headboard.

'He did. Only not to you because he knows you won't listen to him. He said it to me.'

'Because he knows I'll listen to you?' she asked wryly.

'Indeed.' Kathleen grinned. And you will, too. I'll ring for Burton to dress you and then we'll take a turn about the gardens.' Her grey eyes allowed no possibility of refusal.

'Must I?' Oonagh said. 'Oh, of course I must, if the doctor says so, but later. I'm so tired.' She put a hand to her stomach, and winced at a solid blow from within.

'Wait until the first time you feel it kick,' her mother Cloé had said many weeks before, when Oonagh had called to the house in Grosvenor Place where she had lived until her marriage to Philip almost a year ago. Cloé had peeled her lips back over her teeth in what was not a smile. 'Dreadful.' She shuddered. 'Quite the oddest feeling . . .' Oonagh had bent her head low over the tea tray so Cloé wouldn't see her lips twitch with laughter, and had thought how typical that was of her mother.

But the first movements had taken her by surprise. Gentler than the thudding of her own heart. Apologetic almost, as though the baby didn't wish to disturb her. And yet strange in ways that made her agitated. Somehow, she had not known that having a baby really meant, well, having it herself.

'You might have told me it would be like this,' she'd wailed on the phone to Aileen in Ireland, married a year longer than Oonagh and mother to little Neelia, which was Aileen's own name spelled backwards, so that Maureen, first hearing it, had rolled her eyes and said, 'What is it exactly that she hopes to undo with that?'

'Well, whatever did you think?' Aileen had snapped. 'That the maid could do it for you?' They had giggled a little, before Aileen stopped abruptly and demanded to know 'the latest' on Maureen's wedding plans. 'If I'm to come over to London, I want at least to know it will be worth it,' she had said, and Oonagh had been reminded of how Aileen liked always to behave as though she acted from duress and not desire; giving in, not taking part.

Oonagh had got used to the flutterings over the past couple of weeks, and come to feel fond, but even so, much about having a baby discomfited her: Dr Gilliatt's hands on her bare skin – hands he had carefully warmed in a bowl of water brought by Kathleen from the kitchen, just the way Mrs Taylor, the cook, when making pastry, would put hers in ice water to cool them. The way he moved those hands around, probing with his fingers across her stretched skin, like a blind man reading a face: that was obscene too. She had learned not to ask him anything more than the most basic questions – what must she eat, the date of her delivery – afraid that he would talk to her about what was happening within, and that she would be sickened.

'If he says "womb", I shall scream, I know it,' she had confided to Maureen just days earlier.

Maureen, unmarried, still lived at home in Grosvenor Place, for another couple of months anyway, and with both her sisters gone, was bored enough to visit often. Maureen had retorted, 'Surely the point of a man like

Gilliatt, physician to the royal family, is that he would never say such a thing.'

That morning, Gilliatt had repeated his advice that she not agitate herself. 'Babies like a quiet mother,' he had said jovially, patting her hand as though testing the bristles on a brush.

'Mothers like a quiet baby,' Oonagh had heard Kathleen murmur beside her, and had giggled.

'I am so tired,' she said again. 'Sit with me for a minute, Kathleen, before Burton comes, and then I promise, I will make the effort. Such a wretched night, you cannot imagine.'

'I don't need to,' Kathleen said. 'I can hear you very well from upstairs, tossing and turning and sighing.'

'Do I really sigh?'

'Yes, loudly too. It's like sleeping above stables.'

Oonagh giggled. 'I'm not used to being so much in bed,' she said. 'Why, before the baby, I spent more time in my bedchamber getting dressed than I did sleeping. Such parties, Kathleen. When we first came to London for Aileen's coming-out, it was like the whole city burst into a wild frenzy of merriment, like the opening number of a big show. Night after night, and always as though each one were the first.' Her voice was buoyant with remembered excitement, and she plucked at the bedsheet with busy fingers, as though keeping time with a distant beat.

'It's no wonder you're tired,' Kathleen said tartly. 'You must have worn yourself out before the baby ever started.'

'Oh, but the fun, Kathleen! Fancy-dress parties, with

everyone costumed as pirates, or babies, or circus people, scavenger hunts for a policeman's helmet or a napkin from the Ritz, dancing till dawn and gathering for lunch just a few hours later. Every day and night something new and delightful. Not always lying here, a slow and swollen creature that everyone's forgotten.'

'Hardly! There isn't a day goes by that that drawing room isn't full of your sisters and your friends. As giddy a bunch as I ever saw. *Baby, Zita, Valsie.*' She emphasised the names to show she thought them foolish. 'Stephen, Elizabeth – those Mitford girls, Nancy and Diana.'

'Well, *them*,' Oonagh said, making a face. 'Of course they come. What else are they to do? Anyway, even that is nothing to what it was. You've only been here a few weeks.' Kathleen had come for the baby, sent for by Oonagh's father Ernest as extra help for her as soon as he had been told this was to be what Dr Gilliatt called a 'complicated' pregnancy. For Ernest, every problem carried a solution, one to be executed by him quickly and neatly. 'I promise this is positively tame compared with what we were like.'

'You sound as though you long for those times again?'

'Only a little,' Oonagh said truthfully. 'Mostly I long for this baby. I cannot wait to hold him, for I'm sure it's a him, in my arms. Kathleen, you cannot imagine how much I simply long for that.'

'How you do exaggerate,' Kathleen said disapprovingly. 'Mr Ernest is downstairs. Shall I ask him to come up?'

'Is Philip here?' Oonagh asked.

'I haven't seen him this morning,' Kathleen said. 'I can ask Peters? But if I do, I know exactly what he'll say.'

'And what's that?'

'Neither yes nor no, but "May I carry a message to him, Miss?"' Kathleen said with a laugh. 'He guards access to your husband as though the man were a vault in the Bank of England.' Oonagh smiled at that, so Kathleen continued. 'Burton likes me even less, I think.'

'It's because you knew me as a child, back in Ireland, at Glenmaroon. Burton is rather jealous, I dare say.'

'I don't know what she has to be jealous of,' Kathleen retorted. 'All that means is that I've had more years of fetching and carrying for Guinnesses than she has.'

'Silly Kathleen! Why, at Glenmaroon we were practically playmates. You aren't that many years older than me, you know.'

'We were not friends! I was a maid, with work to do every day – fires and dusting and a great deal more besides. All made slower by you, following after me, asking could you help and saying, "Do I do it like this, Kathleen?" after I gave you a little brush of your own to do the grates.' Kathleen's voice was sharp but her look was fond.

'I remember,' Oonagh said. 'Often you were the only one in the house who was kind to me.'

'Nonsense,' Kathleen said, and Oonagh let her, even though they both knew it wasn't nonsense. That in a house full of servants but very often empty of their parents, the three Guinness girls, and Oonagh, the youngest most of all, for all they were rich and grand, had been no more proof against the moods of nannies and governesses than a puppy might have been. To be pinched and neglected when sour moods came upon them, to be locked into her room when they were angry, to be ignored when she cried because it didn't suit them to go to her.

She shifted in the high soft bed. 'Do you remember the time Gunnie found us and I was sweeping out the drawing-room fire while you did the brasses? She was scandalised. I don't know who she was more cross with – you or me?' She recalled the horror on her aunt's face. Gunnie held tight to all those responsibilities that Cloé ignored, so it had fallen to her to be shocked at finding Oonagh doing the work of a servant.

'I do know,' Kathleen said. 'And so do you, really.'

'Well, perhaps.' Oonagh shifted on the bed, uncomfortable, as always, at Kathleen's directness. 'Tell Peters to show Papa up. And see if you can find Philip before he goes to his office.'

Waiting for her father to bound up the stairs, Oonagh thought how often, now, she seemed to be silently tracking Philip through the house as she lay in bed or on the drawing-room sofa – listening for the sound of his footsteps or the closing of a door, sending servants to look for him while pretending to be casual in her interest. And how, a year ago, when they were first married, they had flown together through those same spaces, matched like swallows in the harmony of their movements, turning and wheeling and circling, always together. She wondered did Philip remember.

Ernest was shown in and Oonagh offered to ring for

coffee, then watched as he went straight to the sash window and pulled it up high.

'You'll let in a draught,' she said.

'Nonsense. The air will do you good. You're like your mother, believing fresh air to be injurious.' Because she wanted to be nothing like her mother, certainly not in Ernest's eyes, Oonagh allowed it, even though the greasy slick of petrol that lay across the soft smell of damp grass and leaves turned her stomach. And when Kathleen returned, she got up and took the high-backed armchair by the small round table where Ernest sat.

'What does Gilliatt say?' Ernest asked, when she was seated, draped in a pearly silk dressing-gown.

'You know . . .' Oonagh shrugged helplessly. 'That I must rest, but also I must take more exercise . . .'

'Well, never mind, he'll telephone me later and give me his report. Now, Kathleen . . .' – he turned around and fixed his bright dark eyes, like black beetles, Oonagh sometimes thought, on Kathleen, who leaned against the bedpost, arms folded comfortably behind her in the hollow of her back – '. . . you're settled in, I hope? I've hardly seen you since you arrived.'

'Yes, sir.'

'How did you like your studies?'

'Very well,' she said. 'They were interesting. Difficult too.'

'That's the ticket,' Ernest said, eyes twinkling above a brisk moustache. Oonagh recalled what he had said when he first proposed sending Kathleen to the teacher-training college at Carysfort in Dublin: 'A sharp mind like that must not be wasted on housework, and her father will never think to send her, or afford it.' He had, Oonagh had thought then, a need to do good that was like a twitch. But she was glad his scheme with Kathleen had turned out so well. Educated, and with the certainty that had brought to her, Kathleen at twenty-six was far more a force than she had been when she was sixteen and her duties were just fires and brass. With two younger sisters at home in the flat above the ironmonger's shop in Castleknock and a mother long dead, Kathleen had always had the habit of command, Oonagh thought with a grin, but now she had authority too. And a kind of determination that was given her by her education, but maybe by something else too – something that had to do with why she had been so quick to come from Dublin to London, to accept a position that really, Oonagh thought, was beneath a qualified teacher. But she had said nothing that would explain this, and Oonagh hadn't asked.

'What—' Ernest began, but Philip arrived to interrupt them.

'I can't stay long,' he said cheerfully, coming in and making so quickly for the open window that Oonagh wondered did the room still smell sour. She pinched her cheeks a little to bring colour to them and sat up straighter, turning her chair towards him. After the men had swapped pleasantries, Ernest left, saying he would return the next day, and Philip sat down in his empty chair, taking Oonagh's tiny white hands in his and rubbing them.

'Put your hand here,' she said, thinking how handsome he was with his shiny black hair, which he had taken to arranging so as to cover the place where it was thinning, although he was only twenty-three. He placed his hand where she showed him, where the baby erupted beneath her skin, then snatched it away, as though she had done something indecent. Oonagh felt offended on the baby's behalf. 'The kicks won't hurt you,' she said, 'only me.' She tried to sound light, amused, as she drew Philip's hand back towards her.

He let her bring it halfway, then pulled it back and made a show of consulting his watch, shaking his wrist from side to side, then holding it to his ear. 'I wouldn't want to do something wrong,' he said. 'To either of you.'

'You won't,' she said. 'You couldn't.' But he wouldn't give her his hand again. The way he had looked in wary fascination from her face to the round lump of her middle made Oonagh realise that he, too, had only then really understood what was going on. Like her, he had somehow thought that 'having a baby' meant something else.

'Any more names?' he asked then. It was a game they played, a way to talk about the baby that was not medical.

'Let's call him Celestin, because he will be as beautiful as an angel,' Oonagh said.

'Or Hermes because he will be born with tiny wings that grow from his ankles so that he flies where others walk.'

They talked nonsense, laughing and teasing one another, making silly jokes, and Oonagh thought how much more at ease Philip was with this than when she

had tried to have him put his hand on her to feel the
baby kick. How, she wondered, would he be when there
was an actual child to hold?

'Better get on,' he said then, and she nodded and
said, 'Of course,' even though part of her wanted to
tease that he behaved as though his job – stockbroker
in the City – was vital and urgent, rather than something
handed to him by his father as one might hand a parcel
to someone to hold, a parcel Philip held politely even
though he didn't know or care what was in it. She
forced herself not to ask if he would be home for dinner,
just as Aileen had told her. 'Do not be for ever clinging,'
Aileen had said, when Oonagh breathed a question
about why men, husbands, were so often busy, even
when that busyness involved a different room under
the same roof: a decanter, a newspaper and the refusal
of female company. 'Men must feel themselves free,'
Aileen had continued, full of the worldly wisdom of
her extra year of marriage.

And so Oonagh nodded and smiled brightly, but as
the door closed behind Philip, she felt her show of
energy fade too. 'Let's not go out, Kathleen,' she said,
when Kathleen came to her soon after. 'It's too cold.'

'You need air,' Kathleen insisted, and so they did,
although their walk around the tiny oblong of green
that lay at the centre of Rutland Gate, shared by all
the houses in that huddle, was slow.

'Could you not tell those friends of yours not to be
calling?' Kathleen asked, as they arrived back to the
house. 'Your date is soon now, and then Maureen's
wedding. You need your strength.'

'I couldn't,' Oonagh said. 'It would seem so odd.' What she didn't say was that without her friends to distract her – to demand her attention with their tales and antics, no matter how those tales pained her because she wasn't part of them – she felt entirely alone and forgotten, something trapped in the filthy mud of a riverbank while the water flowed swift and clean and far away.

Chapter Two

Cowes, Isle of Wight

The *Fantome* swayed and creaked as the crew piloted her around the Cowes breakwater and into harbour in a way that was, Maureen thought, both soothing and unsettling, like being rocked in a large, wood-panelled cradle that might tip over at any moment. She stretched out on the soft leather of the salon sofa, enjoying the way the low-ceilinged panelled room moved and shifted around her and the water danced in reflection on the wooden ceiling.

'Miss Maureen?' The knock was loud and firm. 'Miss Maureen,' the voice came again, 'we'll be docking shortly.'

'An hour later than expected,' she snapped back. The captain didn't respond, and Maureen was reminded of how, beneath the polite deference the crew showed her, it was very clear that she mattered nothing, was simply cargo and not the focus of their attention, which was the yacht, always the yacht, and not those who travelled on her. Unless Ernest was there. The reminder annoyed her, and she looked for comfort around the cosy room with its polished walls, the oil lamps behind their dusky pink tasselled shades already lit and glowing, for the windows were small and the late-afternoon light dim. She breathed deep the smell of leather, lavender beeswax and cigars that had sunk into the wood, overlying the tang of salt water, and watched light reflect off the decanter tops. 'It's like travelling in Papa's dressing case,' she said.

'Your move,' Duff said, putting down one of the ivory backgammon pieces with a satisfying clack. He took a sip of whiskey, then put his arms above his head and stretched. 'Will we dine on board, or go ashore?'

'Whatever you like,' Maureen said, looking over the small games table at him. Because Cloé wasn't there, she had shaded black pencil around her eyes so that they stood out more startlingly blue-grey than ever. On deck, on a clear day, they were, Duff had told her, the colour of the flax that grew around Clandeboye. Did he notice the make-up, or only the effect of it? Men, she thought, never much noticed anything unless you pointed it out to them. Not like women, who were made up of mostly eyes. And curiosity.

'I cannot wait to be Lady Dufferin,' she said then. 'And not "Miss Maureen".' She imitated. 'The captain may as well be saying "Miss Moppet" or "Miss Mouse".'

'You'll wear it well,' Duff said, smiling at her. Then, 'Do you mind that we won't live at Clandeboye?' This was the Blackwood family estate, some three thousand acres in the north of Ireland. 'Not at first, anyway,' he continued. 'I know my father would move from the main house if I asked, but I fear what such a change might do to my mother's nerves.'

'Lord, no. I'd rather it. I may be ready for the title,' Maureen grinned, 'but I am not at all ready for the responsibility. Let's have some years in London first, just you and me, where we can have fun, before settling down to all that.' She made a face. She didn't respond to the comment about Lady Brenda's *nerves*, because she didn't know what to say. They were much talked of, these 'nerves', but as yet Maureen had no real idea what they were, beyond a thing that must be said in hushed tones, as though 'the nerves' might overhear and be offended.

'The children will be brought up there, of course, regardless of where we are,' he said.

'Children?' She looked at him with limpid curiosity. 'What children?'

'Our children.' He took her hand across the tiny games table and squeezed it.

'Hmm . . . Yes, naturally. I mean, eventually. But some fun years first,' she repeated firmly. She didn't say it – Maureen never liked to express anything that showed her to be uncertain or uneasy – but it alarmed her how quickly everyone, even Duff, had jumped from congratulations on the engagement, to plans for the wedding and then, immediately further on, into a world of nurseries and weighty duties. And all this when the wedding was still well over a month away. 'You won't be doing that after you're married,' Cloé had said, with satisfaction, just days before, on hearing Maureen give minute instructions to her dressmaker for a costume to be created for a fancy-dress party.

'Why won't I?' Maureen had snapped.

'You simply won't have time,' Cloé had said, pleased. Maureen had thought of asking why not, what else would she be doing, but had thought better of it. She didn't like what she suspected the answer would be. 'Marriage is a job,' Cloé had said then, and Maureen had muttered, 'Not one you seem to be terribly good at.' But quietly.

'Do you love it?' she asked Duff now. 'Clandeboye?'

'I do. But I dread it too. All my life I have seen my father stooped under the fear that he will be the Blackwood to let it slip into ruin. That vast place – sometimes I see it like a millstone around his neck, holding him back, pulling him down, wherever he goes. And sometimes I wonder if the weight of it didn't bring on my mother's nerves. You cannot imagine how it consumes money.'

'I jolly well can! Papa has spelled it out to me more times than you can guess at. Sometimes I think the idea gives him physical pain.' Maureen laughed.

'I'm sure he doesn't at all approve.'

'He approves of you,' Maureen said, 'and that's what matters. So,' she leaned closer to him, '*do* you marry me for my money?' She smiled in all the lazy glorious certainty that he did not.

'No, I marry you for this.' He took her hand, held the palm up towards him and kissed the centre of it. 'And this.' He turned back her sleeve to expose the pale underside of her wrist, and kissed it. 'And this.' He pushed the backgammon table out of the way and moved to sit on the sofa beside her, leaning forward until the length of his body lay close against hers, then kissed her mouth. Maureen kissed him back, drawing him closer again. After a moment, it was Duff who pulled away.

'You heard the captain,' he said. 'We'll be docking shortly.' They listened to the *Fantome* as it creaked and groaned, moving efficiently this way and that as the crew directed it with their ropes and sails. The men called to each other from high up in the rigging, voices honed shrill to compete with the crash of the sea and the roar of the wind. 'And Gunnie will soon be up from her nap.'

'Gunnie!' Maureen said. 'She'll stay in her cabin as long as she's able. At least until we've stopped moving. How she begged not to come.' She laughed. "Every moment at sea is a torment."' She mimicked Gunnie's rather strained voice. 'But Mamma, for all that she hates to be deprived of her Greek chorus, wouldn't have let us travel together if she hadn't. And so Gunnie's feelings could not be considered. I did try to persuade Oonagh, but she was too mean.'

'Too poorly,' Duff reprimanded gently.

'Too selfish,' Maureen insisted. 'What did she have to do except sit around and radiate some of that married respectability of hers? No one was asking her to actually sail the *Fantome*! But isn't it funny,' she said, drawing Duff closer again and looking up at him from under her spiky black lashes, 'how Gunnie thinks only of how I must be watched at night, to make sure I go off to my cabin alone, and has simply no idea of what might happen on these long afternoons while she naps?' She shifted backwards on the leather sofa so that she was almost lying flat, and kept her arms around Duff's neck. Again, it was he who pulled away and sat upright.

'It's just another few weeks till we're married,' he said.

'Exactly, so why wait?'

'Aren't you afraid I'll lose respect for you?' he joked.

'No, my fear is that you will be altogether even more taken with me.' She smiled up at him.

'Maureen!' The yacht had stopped moving and they heard the sound of Gunnie's feet in the tiny corridor. 'Maureen!'

Maureen sighed and sat up, moving further along the sofa until there was distance between her and Duff. 'In here, Gunnie.' She raised a hand to her face and surreptitiously rubbed at the black pencil around her eyes.

Chapter Three

Dublin

The meagre bow windows of Jammet's restaurant did their best to light up the surrounding gloom of Nassau Street, but they had too hard a time of it, Aileen thought, as they walked towards the entrance. Dublin was a city for ever in twilight, even now, in late May, when the evenings were long. The contrast with London, where the streets were lit in a constant frenzy, was like walking from a bright, luxurious drawing room into an obscure and dingy hallway. She sighed and tucked her hand more securely into Brinny's arm, breathing in the thick smell of smouldering peat that sat between the tall houses on one side and Trinity College on the other. Dublin, she sometimes thought, was like a city sketched out, but not coloured in, as though the artist, having drawn an outline, had been called away or grown bored.

Inside Jammet's, the thick linen tablecloths and sparkling crystal, along with the magnificent deference of the staff, soothed her. 'Your party is this way, Monsieur et Madame Plunket,' the maître d' said, and Aileen thought how much more pleasant 'Madame' sounded compared with the paucity of 'Mrs'.

Their party – seated in the very centre of the room – were by far the most glamorous group there, she thought, looking with satisfaction at the other diners: doctors and their dowdy wives; civil servants who had once been on holiday to France. She took off the thick fur stole she wore and handed it to a waiter, conscious that all eyes were on her.

'Darling, you sit here,' their host said, 'and Brinny is at the other end.' It was, Aileen thought, as she smiled and sank graciously into her seat, entirely fitting that she and her husband should occupy the top and tail of the table.

'I can't possibly read that menu again,' she said to the man beside her – it was an old joke between them all that there was 'only one restaurant in the entire city'. 'You order for me.'

Still, half the room looked at her, so Aileen threw herself gaily into conversation, telling a story about a waiter the week before who wore a tie so dirty that 'I think he must have used it as a dog lead,' to much laughter. She knew what they said about her, that she was 'too grand by half' – she even knew that there was a story going around that she sent her underthings to Paris to be laundered, every day. Nonsense, of course – only certain very special dresses were laundered in Paris, and then only because no one else would do it quite right – but Aileen let it travel around. She enjoyed the distinction it gave her. 'Makes you sound idiotic,' Maureen had said, when she told her about the rumour, and perhaps it did, thought Aileen, but it made her sound something else too – original, daring, different.

'Where will you stay when you go to London for Maureen's wedding?' the woman beside her asked, leaning confidingly in, as though asking something intimate.

'We've taken rooms at the Ritz,' Aileen said. 'Sadly poky, but what can you do?' She shrugged.

'Not with your sister?'

'No, it's the wrong part of town,' Aileen said decisively. It wasn't, but she liked saying it. What she didn't say was that staying with Oonagh tired her. Oonagh's pleas that Aileen feel the same as she did were exhausting. It must be *wonderful* to be a mother, Oonagh insisted eagerly, continuing even when Aileen tried to say that, yes, it was fine and pleasant but wonderful? And Oonagh's brave determination not to be disappointed in her marriage – in marriage itself – was even more exhausting. The way she looked constantly for excuses for Philip's negligence, and found them, turning over his explanations like the women at the market barrows turned fruit, looking for bruising or rot. Only Oonagh looked for reassurance, not decay. It made her, Aileen thought, even less restful than the impetuous, impatient Maureen, who at least was only ever thinking about herself, not asking others to think as she did.

'Your *saumon*, Madame.'

Aileen ground out her cigarette on the plate beside

her, then watched as the waiter took that away and placed her food in front of her.

'*Merci.*'

He smiled fastidious approval of her accent and Aileen smiled approval of his approval. She looked down the table then at Brinny, who was uneasy as he always was when not outdoors and doing. The woman next to him was clearly bored, fidgeting with the watch strap buckled across her bony wrist, and Aileen wished suddenly that she could have seen Brinny where he shone, that bored lady: on a horse, driving a fast motor-car, getting up a game of tennis. As she watched them, Brinny raised his eyes and met hers and gave a shy smile. Aileen smiled back and gave the tiniest of eye-rolls, which he returned gratefully.

He didn't shine at parties or dinners. Aileen had known that when she married him three years before. It was why she'd married him. A half-decade of London parties where the only games played were the relentless conversational sparring matches that had only one point – the humiliation of one's opponent – had tired her to the point where Brinny's practical solidity and many silences had been a relief: like washing up on a stretch of warm sand after being battered by ocean waves, she had thought. She tried to remember the feeling now that relief gave way, so often, to exasperation.

'Do you hunt?' she heard him say to the lady beside him.

'Of course I hunt,' she snapped. 'What else is there to do in this country?'

They were so aggressive, these Anglo-Irish who had

stayed behind after the country's independence, Aileen thought, clinging to their crumbling houses like molluscs to a disintegrating rock. They banded together, battle-scarred and resentful of people like her who didn't know the hardships of their lives as intimately as they all knew each other's, the struggle to keep a foothold in a country that didn't want them – that had never wanted them, and now made no bones about showing it. But she knew enough, Aileen thought wryly: the cold bedrooms, the damp of stone walls that never fully dried out, sullen servants, miles of freezing corridor between bedroom and bathroom, the terrible food, and for ever looking over their shoulders in case masked men might come again, with their petrol and matches.

It was why she entertained so often. 'If we don't invite them, they might invite us,' she'd say to Brinny, with a shudder, 'and stay in one of those hopeless houses, I will not.' Luttrellstown Castle, in comparison with those sad old piles of the defunct Ascendancy, was warm, snug and dependable. The castle – 'More of a gate-lodge, really,' Maureen had sniffed happily when she first saw it – rose up from a flat bed of generous green parkland, and its compact form and burnished interiors made Aileen think of a jewel held out on the palm of Nature's hand. Inside, everywhere was warm and bright, wood and silver polished, windows sparkling.

Maureen, she thought then, with a sudden grin, would end up living in exactly the kind of crumbled heap she dreaded, by all accounts. The thought cheered Aileen greatly. 'Who wants to go on?' she asked, leaning forward. 'One of the nearly-nightclubs?' This was what they called the dark drinking dens that stayed open all night, where dockers and truck drivers were as likely as actors and debutantes.

'Good idea.' The woman beside Brinny perked up. 'I know a place . . .'

As they rose and began gathering bags and coats, deciding who would go in which motor-car, Aileen said quietly to Brinny, 'You needn't if you'd rather not. Someone will give me a lift later.' Someone would always give her a lift.

'Are you sure?' he said, and when she insisted, he didn't bother hiding his relief. 'Jolly good,' he said heartily, kissing her noisily. 'I'll see you later then.' He was gone even before they were, rushing out of the restaurant. She knew that he would have the top of the car down all the way home, feeling the cool night air whipping past, without her to complain of what it did to her hair. That he would smoke one of his cigars as he drove, faster than she would have permitted, singing loudly and slightly off-key, whatever popular song had caught his ear. He had a taste for the maudlin, she knew, and imagined him singing 'Am I Blue?' cheerfully at the top of his voice.

Really, she thought, half fondly, half in irritation, he was a man who would have done very well without a wife at all.

Chapter Four

Rutland Gate, London

That afternoon, her friends gathered as usual in Oonagh's drawing room, pushing impatiently past Peters, eager to see who was there, and who was not; men and women landing and taking off, like flocks of brightly coloured creatures. Feathers nodded in their hats, furs clustered at their throats, and diamonds sparkled on their fingers and wrists so that they were neither flesh nor fowl but somehow both. Chattering, laughing, gossiping. They were as careless of one another's secrets as birds are of spilling seeds, Oonagh thought, watching them all, plunging their beaks deep into the bowl and wantonly scattering bits of husk to the floor.

Stephen Tennant, eyelids shining glossily under a slick of Vaseline, trailing a yellow scarf around his neck and some floral cologne that mixed with the smoke from his Russian cigarettes, settled down beside her and crossed his long legs. 'You have company, I see,' he murmured, nodding towards Kathleen, who sat on a spindly chair at the edge of the room, looking around her with frank curiosity.

'She chats to me,' Oonagh said, patting Stephen's arm. 'When you are all gone to parties and lunches, and I am alone, Aileen in Ireland and Maureen away sailing' – she made a face – 'Kathleen is the person to rescue me from myself.'

'And what about Fliss? Felicity?'

'Busy and important with a job in publishing and a flat in Earl's Court. No time for little me.'

'She did give you a great deal of time, for ten years,' Stephen said wryly.

'Oh, I know. I don't complain. But isn't it sad when people one likes change, and one doesn't.'

'Well, couldn't Elizabeth chat to you?' he asked, as a woman with an eager, amusing face and a mobile mouth over too-large teeth threw herself down beside them.

'Why didn't you tell me you were leaving last night, Stephen?' Elizabeth demanded loudly. 'I would have come with you. That party was the most frightful bore and you knew it. I do think you're mean to dash off so, leaving one behind.'

'I see you're in the *Daily Express* again, Elizabeth,' Oonagh said. 'Driberg really excelled himself at the poetry of your life this time: "Elizabeth Ponsonby, leader of the Bright Young People, arrived dressed in spats and straw boater at an American party . . ."' she quoted. 'And a photograph of you in trousers and braces, looking ever so disdainful.'

Elizabeth ignored what Oonagh had said. Instead she

cast darting looks around the room, seeming to measure and weigh everything she saw. 'Tiffany?' she demanded, of a small lamp with a shade in bluey-green stained glass patterned with dragonflies, putting out a hand to run a finger along the tiny lead-edged squares of glass.

Oonagh had brought it home just the day before from Harrods on one of her few excursions, and had been pleased with it but now, unhappy at being quizzed by Elizabeth, she said, deliberately vague, 'It's pretty. Surely that's enough.' She felt as though she was playing a game of keep-away, holding something out of Elizabeth's reach that she wanted. It was a game that made her feel mean, but the eagerness of Elizabeth's curiosity repelled her.

'Oh, don't pretend you don't know,' Elizabeth said. 'Spare me that, at least.' After barely half an hour, she jumped to her feet. 'I must dash,' she declared, as though late for something, although to Oonagh it seemed that she went off like a stone from a sling because she could no longer sit still in that room, not because she had somewhere else to be.

'Always wanting to *know* everything,' Oonagh said, when Elizabeth had gone. Her words peeled off one another, like a napkin used to wipe her fingers, then dropped to the floor.

'You could be kinder to her,' Stephen said, taking a tiny nibble of a Florentine biscuit. 'She and Pelly have a rough time of it, you know. Not a penny between them. Neither of them can keep a job. Pelly's gramophone shop has closed, and now Elizabeth is so easily . . . *distracted.*'

'By whom?' Oonagh demanded.

'Well, almost anyone, from what one has heard . . .' He smirked. 'But broke as they are, it can't be easy for her to call here.'

'Well, I wish she wouldn't,' Oonagh said crossly. 'Now that I cannot go to parties, I find that we have no conversation any more. Elizabeth talks of nothing except what she has done and what she plans to do tonight, and I have no part in any of it.' She didn't say how left out and alone Elizabeth's talk made her feel. Nor did she mention Elizabeth's habit of putting Philip into her stories – of placing him, in the telling, always at the centre of a gay crowd, and always in company with pretty young women, sometimes adding. 'I say, you don't *mind*, do you?' and fixing Oonagh with her round eyes opened as wide as she could.

'What else is she to talk of?' Stephen asked.

'Who?' Diana, asked, joining them.

'Ah, the glorious Mrs Guinness,' Stephen said, making room for her.

'Once a Mitford always a Mitford, Nancy says,' said Diana, sitting down beside Stephen. 'So, who are you dissecting?'

'Elizabeth.'

'La Ponsonby? Bryan says she doesn't exist when she's not out,' Diana said, with a giggle. 'He thinks that when she goes home and is alone, she folds herself up flat like paper and puts herself in a drawer until it's time to emerge for the next entertainment.'

It was a cruel thing to say, and Oonagh wondered was it really her gentle, curious cousin Bryan, or Diana herself, who had said it. She looked, that day, Oonagh thought, carved of marble, her form cold and hard under a draping of silk and furs. While Oonagh watched, Diana took out a delicate gold compact and began to powder her face. It was as if the dust of the marble settled on her once more – an act of creation in reverse.

'What about Pelly?' Stephen said then, referring to Elizabeth's husband, a man none of them felt they knew, so much an appendage to Elizabeth did he seem. 'Tall and thin and mostly chin' was how Stephen described him.

'I doubt Elizabeth unfolds just for him.' Diana raised one thin, arched eyebrow halfway up her forehead. 'Here come Baby and Valsie,' as Peters announced them. 'I hear Valsie is engaged and soon to be Lady Brougham, yet she spends such a deal of her time here with you, Oonagh, that Victor must wonder where she is. I know she is your Best and Dearest Friend but, really, so much time?' Oonagh looked a question at her, but Diana gazed back limpidly. 'I must say, I do envy you, how well you all get on together,' she continued, whispering a little so that Violet – Valsie – greeting someone near the door, shouldn't hear. 'Bryan wouldn't like it one bit if we had company so constantly.' Her eyes, under heavy, secretive lids, were pale blue, with pupils so tiny they were the merest pinpricks. Nothing in those eyes gave away any meaning.

Violet, having taken a cocktail from the tray Peters held out, began to quiz too: 'Oonagh, you look tired. Doesn't she?' she appealed to Stephen. 'Look tired, I mean.' Stephen smiled in a way that could have meant anything and stayed silent.

'Well, I am tired, Valsie,' Oonagh said, raising a hand to indicate her swollen form.

'Yes, but you look tired,' Violet said, as though that were something different. 'What have you been doing?'

'Nothing, I swear it,' Oonagh said with a laugh.

But Violet wasn't to be put off. 'You need to rest more,' she said, with a mixture, critical and proprietorial, that Oonagh was coming to know, and quietly resent. Then, 'Where is Philip?' She glanced around. 'Why isn't he here?' There was a sharp little silence then, in which Stephen looked at his shoes and Diana at her hands, so that Violet added hastily, 'With you.'

'He's at his club,' Oonagh said.

'Oh, that club,' Violet laughed. 'We must try to drag him away from there more.'

'Must you?' Diana asked, leaning a little on the *you*.

'You said you would drive out in the afternoon yesterday.' Violet abruptly changed the subject. 'Did you?'

Oonagh felt tired and longed for them all to go so that she might rest, then wait to see would Philip join her for dinner. She looked an appeal at Kathleen, who stood instantly and came over. 'I can't recall. Kathleen, did we drive out?'

'We didn't,' Kathleen said, and the way she spoke snapped the lid shut on the next question already forming on Violet's perfect Cupid-bow mouth so that Oonagh was grateful.

When the drawing room was at last empty and Oonagh upstairs resting, Kathleen stepped out into Rutland Gate and began walking quickly away from the house, lest anyone come after her to tell her that Oonagh needed something else. The city called to her as the sea did when she was near it and could hear but not yet see the waves. The same urgency she felt when she was by Clontarf Bay on a sunny day now gripped her when she thought of London – all of it – out there beyond the fine houses of Rutland Gate and Grosvenor Place, where Ernest and Cloé lived, and Maureen too, until she married in just a few weeks' time.

As she turned into Knightsbridge, Kathleen speeded up, driven forward by the unfamiliar sounds of the city. There were so few horse-carriages that the dusty thump of hoofs was no longer the rhythm of the streets as it would have been on O'Connell Street or around St Stephen's Green. Instead there was the grumble of motor-cars, trucks and omnibuses, and she marvelled that the few horses there were did not take fright and bolt.

She stepped onto the road to cross with only the smallest hesitation. A motor-car, passing close by, honked at her and she felt the wind of its going *whoosh* past, but she found she wasn't afraid, only reminded to be more cautious.

The air was dirty, dirty like a factory floor, so that even after a short walk, her gloves were blackened with smuts and her face needed a flannel, but Kathleen didn't mind. If anything, she liked that she was taking on the colour of the city, even if that colour was made up of coal dust and engine fumes. It made her feel she was doing her job, even though she didn't know exactly what that job was – a companion of some kind, she supposed, although no one had ever spelled out her duties. But it must be something of the sort, because she was paid: an envelope with wages, good wages, appeared in her bedroom at the top of the house every Friday. And those wages, if she held them tight, would eventually be what gave her the freedom she had craved ever since leaving the teacher-training college with a degree that was so much less than it should have been. Less in a way that still stung her.

That disappointing degree? She still wondered at it. She had been a good student, eager to repay Mr Ernest's generosity and faith. Naturally curious, she had excelled throughout all the years, until the last. The Sisters of Mercy, with their calculated parsimony of words, said she had allowed herself to become 'giddy' and failed to study. But she believed that, because they had disapproved so much of her 'giddiness' and the form it had taken, they had painted this disapproval into her results.

Whatever the reason, her letters of recommendation had been lukewarm. The ways in which she had fallen short reared out of the bland words as surely as boulders from a river so no one reading it could have doubted the Sisters' true opinion of Kathleen. But neither could Kathleen point to any one phrase or combination of words and question it. That, she acknowledged wryly, was its brilliance.

At first, holding the disappointing degree and those inadequate letters, Kathleen had been crushed. She knew she wouldn't get the kind of school she wanted with them. Instead, she would have to make do with something small and rural and remote, out in the country where she didn't want to be, pushed deeper into a small life that she dreaded. And then Ernest's letter had arrived, and again he had been her saviour. A few years in London, he said, 'while my daughter learns to be a mother'. A few years, Kathleen thought, of a steady wage with no room or board to pay and, best of all, new references. She could come back then, with her saved wages and more promising acknowledgement of her abilities, and she could begin again.

And in the meantime, here was all of London to discover, starting with Rutland Gate. She thought of the house as she had first seen it: tall – five flights if you counted the attic – and all windows and white walls, inside and out. From the street looking up it was, Kathleen had thought, like one of the banks of white wax candles in church, all straining upwards to glory. Inside, it was so different from the rooms above the ironmonger's shop where she had grown up. She remembered how those rooms had smelled – of boiling bacon and cabbage water – and the way the steam ran down the windows so there was always a dampness in the air that you could almost rub between your fingertips. The rooms were dark, with ceilings so low they could touch them if they stretched their arms hard overhead. But how cosy too they had been on a winter's evening when the skimpy curtains were pulled tight and she, her two sisters and her da were all at the table together, knees jostling under the bare boards, piling butter onto the soft flesh of potatoes.

At Rutland Gate there was so much light she

wondered that anyone slept at all, that they were not like those city birds that the shining of streetlights had so disordered that they sang through the night and died in a season, because no welcoming cover of dark ever dropped down to bid them be quiet and sleep.

The colours of the house were pale blue and gold, and the furniture was delicate and spindly, like matchsticks. On a sunny day it was glorious and bright, but on a wet grey day, Kathleen missed the cosiness of a thick rug and a deep armchair.

There was a large basement with kitchen, pantry and servants' hall where Mrs Taylor, the cook, was disposed to be friendly, unlike Peters and Burton. She was small and vigorous and Irish, from Galway not Dublin – from farm folk, not the city traders and hucksters who were Kathleen's people – but being in a strange country meant they were more in sympathy with one another than they would have been at home.

On the entrance floor there was a dining room and Philip's study, although Kathleen couldn't see that he was ever much in there. On the first floor there were the main drawing rooms, front and back. Upstairs were bedrooms and Oonagh's sitting room. Above that again Kathleen's bedroom, what was to be the nursery, and a sitting room that was said to be hers but that she had no use for – nothing to put in it and nothing to do there that could not be done in her bedroom or downstairs. Her bedroom looked on to the little bit of green garden in the middle of Rutland Gate, and she could see the front steps of number twenty-six, the Mitfords' house, if she squinted to the side.

She had tried to make the room into something more like home, with a plaid rug over the bed that she found in a trunk and her few holy pictures, but in all that glossy elegance her little bits were adrift and did not add up to much. 'How pretty,' Oonagh had said, the night she arrived, picking up a small framed picture of the Virgin Kathleen's mother had given her before she died. When she noticed what it was she put it down, an expression of distaste tugging at her mouth.

No one, Kathleen thought now, thinking back to the envelope of money, ever said anything, so she didn't know who did the paying – was it Oonagh? Or Mr Ernest? She had tried to ask him, but all he said was 'The labourer is worthy of his hire,' with a twitch of his moustache. Guinnesses, she knew, liked to have people around them. All sorts of people, always around them.

Sometimes she worried that she was not useful enough, and that when Mr Ernest found out, he would send her straight home, and then she would once again be the person she had been in Dublin – humiliated and apprehensive, a person who had squandered an opportunity for education that had come unbidden, throwing it away for what? A few afternoon walks, cups of tea in Bewley's and serious conversation? The fantasy that she was someone special?

Here, so far away from her disappointment, and the foolishness that had led to it, she felt daring and certain again, filled with the same possibilities as the urgent, teeming city. She was, she supposed, still the same person, but she did not feel it.

Crossing Sloane Street, making for Green Park, she resolved that she would not let herself be sent home. That she would be useful and helpful and whatever else was required, because go back to Dublin before her time was up she would not.

Chapter Five

The minute Maureen entered the house, Oonagh knew it. The sound of her firm tread, impatient, on the stairs, a door slamming behind her and the echo of that door further along the hallway. A call of 'Hurry up, slow coach! I haven't all day. Come and see what I have for you,' came not just up the stairs and through the bedroom door, but through the very floor of Oonagh's room, propelled from below by the force of Maureen's personality.

She was back from a short trip on the *Fantome*, a pre-wedding jaunt that Oonagh had planned to join – they were to sail around the Isle of Wight – until Dr Gilliatt had expressed concern and Philip had forbidden it. She was in the back drawing room, standing by the window, when Oonagh came down, her hair set and gleaming, a shining ripple of close-set curls, cut short and pinned tight so that they sat like a gold cap against her white skin. She wore make-up – deep red lipstick defined her mouth, and even rouge on her cheeks – and was so carefully dressed that Oonagh wondered was she on her way somewhere, or was this simply Maureen knowing she would catch Oonagh off-guard.

The fashions of that year suited her better, Oonagh thought. There were waists again, and sharp shoulders, rather than sequins and straps and dresses that hung like shifts. Today she wore a dress of black with touches of white, tight at the waist with a slim skirt and a bodice that buttoned to one side with a row of white satin buttons and a crisp white collar. Her shiny conker-brown shoes had gleaming buckles.

She dropped her bag onto a small table and sat down. 'I can't imagine, Oonagh, why you have tea here when you could be at the other end of the room and watch the Mitfords coming and going. What is the point of their house being so close, and not watching it? They're better than a play.' She lit a cigarette and blew smoke in two quick thin streams through her nose, waving the cigarette around as she spoke.

The Mitfords, at number twenty-six, were a family of mostly daughters – six, to one son. Diana, of whom Oonagh saw a great deal so that they were, she supposed, friends, without being particularly cosy, had sisters called Pamela and Nancy who were the exact ages of Maureen and Aileen. There were younger sisters too, all of them charming and quarrelsome and impetuous – often Oonagh would watch the little ones tumble in and out of the house with their governess and dogs, always laughing and shrieking at each other, with so many nicknames apiece that it was impossible to tell who they called to. There was a mother who was vague and charming, and a father who roared so loudly with rage he could be heard right across the street. On days when Oonagh couldn't move much, these Mitfords were the closest thing to entertainment she had. She listened to their screams and calls – so much louder and more insistent than she was with either Maureen or Aileen – and tried to make sense of the silly things they said so that she could build a story out of it all to distract herself. But she wasn't about to tell Maureen how quiet her days could be, and how much she followed those exuberant doings.

'I see Nancy when she calls,' she said primly, 'and Diana, who calls too. That is quite enough. In Diana's case, more than enough.'

At that they both laughed and Maureen flicked her eyes upwards and said, 'Indeed.' But she wasn't to be distracted.

'But if you looked out of the window,' she continued, 'you would see who calls on *them*, and that is much more interesting. I hear Nancy and Hamish St Clair-Erskine . . .' and she was off, full of speculation and rumour.

'How are the plans for the wedding breakfast? You have just over a month now,' Oonagh asked, after a while.

'They don't progress at all,' Maureen said cheerfully, scooping up one of the fat little pugs Oonagh liked to have about her and kissing it energetically. 'Because I change my mind constantly. I do it on purpose, because of how funny it is to watch Gunnie agree first that one thing is the height of elegance, and then the very next minute that it's simply too vulgar, and all because I have led her to do so.' The dog in her arms put its tongue out, as pink as ham against the black of its snout, and licked Maureen's mouth. She put out the tip of her own tongue and let the dog lick that too.

'You are mean, Maureen. Poor Gunnie,' Oonagh said idly. 'And Mamma?'

'Oh, well!' Maureen said, putting the dog on the floor, where it began to lick its stomach, and snapping her fingers, like a whip-crack. 'She thinks as ever only about herself and how dreadfully ill this will make her. As if she is not always ill anyway, even when she's done nothing except lie down all day. In fact, I rather think you're becoming just like her.' She said it as though making a joke, but her eyes were a chilly grey-blue.

'I am not,' Oonagh said indignantly, tried to move herself off the divan until Maureen said, 'Lie still, won't you? You'll cause me to spill my coffee.'

'It's just this baby,' Oonagh said, sinking back with a sigh. 'Once he's born I shall be up and out again, you'll see. Dr Gilliatt says another few weeks, not more. By the time of your marriage, I shall be quite myself again. And then it will be your turn.' She laughed, rather meanly.

'Not for ages,' Maureen said calmly. 'I'll make sure of that.'

'But why?'

'Because not everyone sees joy beside the nursery fire, Oonagh. Some of us want to have a bit more excitement first.'

'But babies are such fun.'

'That they are not.'

'Does Duff know what you're thinking?'

'Oh, yes. We've had a delightful chat about it all.'

'By which you mean you've told him what you want, and he's pretended to listen,' Oonagh said tartly.

'My, hasn't marriage made you *cynical*,' Maureen said, in admiration. 'Anyway, how do you know it's a boy?'

'I know it. I'm certain.'

'If you're right, how strange that will be,' Maureen mused. 'A boy. We're all girls, and Aileen has a girl. Well, I shall have only boys. And I shan't be so jolly sick as you when I do!'

'If you do they'll grow up savage and wild in that forsaken place in the north of Ireland,' said Oonagh. 'I've heard Clandeboye is like a museum or barracks, where the butler and footmen wear wellingtons in the house because it's so damp, and guests must wear their overcoats to walk from one room to the next through the freezing halls. Live there and you'll slowly sink into savagery yourself,' she said, eyes lighting up a little at the idea.

'I will not,' said Maureen. 'For Duff will not permit it.' She said this with the pride of a simple and magnificent fact. 'There is simply no question that we will live there until he inherits, and that won't be for ever, thank goodness. His father is only fifty-five. And Duff has his career in politics to forge. We shall have *years* in London first. There is a house in Hans Crescent that I've told Papa he must buy for me, because it's over the road from Harrods and simply perfect for parties. I think we'll hardly go to Clandeboye at all. Why, I still haven't seen the place. Duff prefers that. It's hard for him, you know. Lady Brenda is mad – *quite* mad, I believe, not mad the way Elizabeth might say someone is mad, or the way many might say Elizabeth herself is mad when, really, they mean only that she's drunk.' She laughed at that, Oonagh too. 'She believes in fairies and thinks they speak to her. And Clandeboye is the place her madness keeps her. Just as well there is no need for us to go there beyond the most cursory visit as newly-weds. So, you see, we're perfectly in harmony, Duff and I.'

'Poor Elizabeth,' Oonagh said then. 'She was here again yesterday. I cannot see that her life is a joy to her.'

'Well, it certainly isn't a joy to me,' Maureen said. 'She's no fun any more. In fact, she was positively a bore last time I saw her at the Kit Kat Club. Nothing but moan, moan, moan about how too poor she and Pelly are. I told her "Elizabeth, darling, we're simply all poor now, after that dreadful stock market has let us all down so terribly. Such a blow, but one must be *brave*, don't you think?" Well, at that she gave me a most filthy look and rushed right out and away. So rude, I thought.'

'Oh, Maureen, you shouldn't!'

'That reminds me. I shall want you to call me Lady Dufferin once we're married,' Maureen said.

Oonagh laughed again, then clutched her side and winced. 'Do not! I haven't space to! No doubt you told Mamma the same?'

'I did.' Maureen grinned wickedly. 'I think she believed me for a moment.'

'I think you believed yourself for a moment,' Oonagh responded. 'No doubt you'd adore it. In fact, you'd probably like Duff to call you Lady Dufferin.'

'He can call me whatever he likes,' Maureen said, 'I shan't mind,' and she smirked at Oonagh. Peters announced, 'The Earl of Ava,' then, and Maureen leaped up, crying, 'Duff, you're too early,' in delight. 'We've only just had tea.'

He was, Oonagh thought, as she had thought before, a man as dense and dark as coal, with a glitter somewhere that you could see only from the corner of your eye, not if you looked directly at him. He had brown eyes, and towered over Maureen, even in her shiny heels. All of his features were large – his head too – so it was hard, she thought, to tell which dominated. Sometimes it was the eyes, wide apart, with heavy lids and rimmed with very clear whites. But then he would smile – not often, mind – and she thought perhaps it was his mouth: without any covering of moustache, it was firm and full.

Never had Oonagh seen Maureen anything other than the brightest point in any room, yet beside Duff she was almost overshadowed.

'I've just been telling Oonagh how we shall have years in London yet,' Maureen said with satisfaction. 'And all the parties I've planned.' Oonagh smiled automatically and nodded in a way she hoped seemed pleased. How hard it would be to live up to Maureen once she was married and Lady Dufferin, she thought.

Chapter Six

After they had left, Oonagh shifted around on the divan trying to find a comfortable spot. It was hours still till dinner time and she had no idea what to do with herself. Why did she so often feel like this after a visit from Maureen – irritable and full of tiny pinpricks? Even though her sister came 'to cheer you up, silly,' and always brought her something small – today it was a pretty silver seashell charm she had picked up – and even though they talked and gossiped and laughed together, when Maureen left Oonagh so often felt as though she had been slyly pinched. As though, beneath the gay chatter, an argument had been waged silently but with a strangling tightness. A jockeying for position, for assertion, between them that she had not asked for but could not ignore. And always, she felt she had lost.

It was a relief when Violet came in almost an hour later. They could, Oonagh thought, talk peacefully together, as they used to before she was married, when Violet had been so constant a companion at Grosvenor

Place that she had had her own space for clothes in Oonagh's wardrobes and a truckle bed that was all her own. Then it had been the two of them together constantly, but since her marriage, she realised, she had seen far less of Violet alone.

'How dull I am today,' Violet said fretfully, when they had exchanged hellos.

'I'll have Peters make you something reviving. A bull shot?'

'That would be dear of you,' Violet said. 'And then perhaps we could sit quietly, you and I? I am so very tired of always talking, talking, talking.' She sighed and leaned into the high-backed armchair she had chosen, almost disappearing behind the wings.

'Of course,' Oonagh said, and obligingly stayed silent once she had sent Peters for drinks.

But after barely a minute, Violet sat forward so that she was visible once more, resting her elbows on her knees and cupping her chin in her hands. 'How nice it must be to be you, Oonagh,' she said, with the hint of childish petulance Oonagh had once found charming. 'Able to sit here and simply order everyone around all day.'

'It's not the only thing I do,' Oonagh said, but she spoke gently. It was the nature of their friendship that Violet complained and Oonagh soothed. Had been since the beginning. Violet was temperamental, Oonagh was reassuring; Violet sophisticated and full of ennui, Oonagh gentle and hopeful; Violet drew attention to things Oonagh had that she didn't, and Oonagh, just seventeen when they had first met, felt guilt and gave them to her – dresses, furs, earrings, gloves.

'I dare say there isn't an order you could give that wouldn't be instantly carried out. Not a wish expressed that couldn't be gratified.' Violet said now, her teasing tone stretched tight over bare patches of resentment. 'It must be like having a handful of threads and knowing that by twitching any one of them, you can make something happen.'

'How is Victor?' Oonagh changed the subject. Victor was Lord Brougham, Violet's fiancé, whom Oonagh found endearing if tiring – his passionate interest in politics left her keenly aware of how little she knew, and made her wonder what he and Violet talked about together.

'He is well. I suppose.' Violet sounded weary.

'You don't sound terribly certain?'

'Not certain at all, to tell the truth.' Violet took a cigarette from her bag and lit it. 'He gambles very much more than I had supposed.'

'And how much is that?'

'Very much indeed. In fact, I'm rather wondering if I . . .'

'If you . . . ?'

'You know . . .' She shrugged her shoulders up and down, breathed out thin streams of smoke from her nostrils, like an impeccable blonde dragon, Oonagh thought.

'I see . . .' Oonagh contemplated her seriously for a while. 'But you said yourself you wanted to be married.' She didn't say that she, too, wanted Violet married, but she was conscious that she did. Mostly, she thought, because it would be more amusing if they both were, but also, a little, because then perhaps Violet would be too busy to make such a pet of Philip, and Diana would stop looking so consideringly at them all with those pale blue eyes.

'I do. Very much. I'm tired of being a single girl. I'm not modern the way Baby is. She says she has no need of any husband and cannot think of anything worse than to be married. I long for it.'

'Well, then,' Oonagh said. 'And Victor longs to marry you . . .'

'Longs . . .?' Violet said thoughtfully. 'Maybe not longs, exactly . . .'

'And after all, Valsie,' Oonagh continued, 'all men do something. If it isn't gambling, it will be something else as bad. Or they're bores, which is worse. Victor is not that at least.'

'No, I suppose not . . . I say, do all men really do *something*? Even Philip? No, not Philip, I'm sure of it. You are lucky, Oonagh, to be married as you are.'

'Yes, I suppose I am,' Oonagh said thoughtfully. Philip came in then and immediately Violet became gay instead of mournful, full of bright chatter and vivacity. All men had an electric effect on her, as though they were the switch to illuminate her, but Philip most of all. It was because, Oonagh reminded herself, they had known one another for so very long, since before Oonagh and Philip's marriage.

'Oonagh tells me all men are simply terrible,' Violet said, pouting at Philip.

'Did you?' Philip looked at his wife in surprise.

'Well, not exactly . . .' Oonagh said.

'And I said all men except you, Philip,' Violet said demurely.

'Did you?' he said again, looking delighted. 'Did you really?'

'I did.' She smiled up at him. And when Peters arrived with the bull shots she drained one in a gulp, then another. 'You were right, Oonagh,' she said, not looking at her but rather at Philip. 'Most reviving.' And she blinked slowly, lowering heavy lashes over her treacle-brown eyes and raising them again.

'See what I have for you, Oonagh,' Philip said then, and Oonagh saw he had something held behind his back.

'It's not my birthday,' she said, even though she knew how much Philip liked to give her little presents. The gift, unwrapped, was a camera. The size of a hefty cigarette case, she thought, turning it over and over in her lap, looking at it from every angle. It was like a tiny accordion, with a section that telescoped outwards, ending in a beady piece of round glass. 'What am I to do with this?'

'Take photographs,' Philip said. 'Then they'll be developed and you can bind them into albums. And when the baby comes you can take photos of him.'

'But I don't know how.' Was she really to learn how to take photographs, now, when all she wanted was to lie still?

'As for that, it's easy,' he said, sitting down beside her so that she had to shift up to make room for him while Violet leaned across to watch. 'The man I bought it from showed me, and I shall show you.' He fussed about, telling her how to hold the camera, how to point it, which button to push, that the beady piece of glass was the lens through which the image came, and must be kept clean and free of scratches.

And Oonagh forced herself to be enthusiastic saying, 'Philip darling, stand by the window and pose for me so I may practise.' The curtains were not yet drawn and the afternoon light, after a dull grey day, was a sudden brief blessing, as though the sky had given up the effort of holding itself so tightly closed, and relaxed enough to allow the grey to swing open, like a drab overcoat that reveals a rich lining.

'I must try to capture the light,' Oonagh said. Kathleen came in then with a pile of linen, and Oonagh made her and Philip move about, stand and sit in different spots so that the light might fall as she wanted it to. 'I have it, I think,' Oonagh said at last. 'Now Valsie can model for me.'

'Oh, I wouldn't know how.' Violet ducked her head modestly.

'Don't be absurd,' Oonagh said. 'There's hardly a magazine in town you don't appear in. What was it this week, the *Tatler*?' And she reached to the low table in front of her and took up a magazine. 'There.' She stopped at a page of photographs and there indeed was Violet, wearing a dress of shimmering white, high at the neck and cut into a low V behind. She was standing with her back to the camera but must have turned her head at the very instant the picture was taken so that she looked straight at the photographer with an expression of artless surprise. Beneath it was written,

Violet Valerie French, soon to be Lady Brougham, elegant in Dior, at the Savoy.

'Don't tell me you don't know how to model,' Oonagh said, 'when you seem to have been born to it.' And she enjoyed the sharp second that followed, watching Violet wonder whether Oonagh had insulted her, then deciding to assume she had not.

Violet shook her head and said, 'Oh, that,' flicking her eyes at Philip, who all this while had been looking from one to the other and back again – exactly, Oonagh thought, as if he were at a Punch and Judy show.

'Go and sit by the window,' Oonagh said, 'with Kathleen, and I'll take a photo of you both.'

Violet's mouth folded in on itself, like a rosebud so nipped with frost that it would never bloom, and Philip said smoothly, 'Why not take Valsie alone first? You could pose her in that chair there, with the lamp behind to light her?' And he was off, springing about the place, making jokes and disordering the room to bring all the finest things to where Violet was seated so that soon she was like a child at a birthday party surrounded by rich gifts. Oonagh obligingly picked up the camera and looked through it and clicked the shutter and smiled, and if her smile felt as mechanical as the camera shutter, well, no one knew that but her. There were pains that came and went inside her, like a piece of paper blown about on the wind, but she said nothing of them, although she saw Kathleen look carefully at her and knew she must have winced.

'I must go,' Violet said at last. 'I'm due at the Royal Academy where Augustus John unveils his portrait of

Tallulah Bankhead. There's all manner of scandal,' she continued, with great satisfaction, 'because they will not show John's portrait of that fat Italian, Mussolini. It was in the newspapers that he said he thinks there is something more beautiful than books and paintings, and that is guns and aeroplanes, and now they will not exhibit him.'

'The man's a fool,' Philip said. 'To talk of guns and aeroplanes!' Oonagh barely knew who Mussolini was, but she could see Philip was furious at the idea of him.

'Will you be at Lady Meredith's later?' Violet asked him, looking over Oonagh's head. 'She has yet another daughter coming out. I don't honestly know why she bothers. It's not like the last two took at all well. See me out, Philip, there's a darling?'

Oonagh lay still, arms wrapped around herself against the shifting pains inside, and listened to them going down the stairs, Violet's heels clacking on the marble with Philip's, brisker-sounding, beside them. 'When I knew her first she wasn't like that,' she said to Kathleen, when the sounds had died away. 'Really, she was quite an ordinary person, and sweet, you know, until she got engaged to Victor.'

She heard the front door bang closed, and then only silence – no cheery sound of Philip's footsteps coming back up the stairs. 'I think I'll dine in my room tonight,' she said quietly, when it was clear he wouldn't be coming back. 'I'm quite fatigued. I'll photograph you another time, Kathleen. I'm too tired now. But your face is much more interesting than Valsie's, for all that the *Tatler* cannot seem to have enough of her.'

Chapter Seven

But the next morning Oonagh could no longer pretend. The pains were so bad they woke her while the light outside was still thin and grey. Kathleen was already standing by her bed. 'I heard you from upstairs,' she whispered. 'I've sent for the doctor.'

'I'm sure it's nothing,' Oonagh said, biting her small white teeth together so as not to cry out. Dr Gilliatt had told her she had another week, maybe more.

'I'm sure it's not.'

Dr Gilliatt came quickly, and was calm. 'All is in good time,' he said expansively, 'so there is nothing to worry about.' His voice was deep and reassuring and he put a hand to Oonagh's forehead so that she felt like a child with a fever. Looking at him from the pinprick place of her pain, where everything was folded and condensed down and down, the more to hurt her, she watched as he swelled further into the importance of his moment. 'We call this phase the false dawn,' he said, with a reassuring smile all around.

'What must we do?' Philip said. He was careful to stand behind the doctor, Oonagh saw.

'Bring hot-water bottles,' Gilliatt told the midwife. 'And, Kathleen, bring no food, but a glass of lemonade might be welcome.'

'And I?' Philip asked.

'You may as well go to your club, for here you will only be in the way and distress yourself.' Philip looked relieved.

'I will give her something now, for the pain,' Gilliatt continued, 'and come back in a couple of hours to induce twilight sleep when she has progressed. There is nothing much to be done until then.'

But when he returned at the agreed time, he made no more mention of false dawns, and Oonagh, confused as she was, could see he was no longer soothing. In very little time there was an ambulance at the door and Oonagh was carried down the stairs, so pale she was almost blue. 'Come with me,' she muttered to Kathleen. 'Philip is not here so you must come with me.'

'Of course I will,' Kathleen said, and even though the ambulance men tried to bar her way, she pushed roughly past them, climbing in beside the stretcher that held Oonagh, and sat where Oonagh could see her, see nothing but her, as they drove fast through the streets to Portland Place, with the clanking wail of the siren around them.

At the nursing home, Oonagh was put into a narrow bed, Kathleen still beside her, and Gilliatt came.

'Where is Philip?' Oonagh cried, her arms wrapped tight around her. She was already confused by what the doctor had given her earlier, and frightened by the intensity of the pain that she could still feel, although Gilliatt's drops had put a shimmering barrier between it and her. It seemed, now, to come from a distance, like an echo, calling to her mockingly, offering to come and sit closer beside her. 'Where is Philip?'

'He will be here presently.'

'Then Papa? Is he here?'

'Presently, my dear. Now, Kathleen, you need to leave. And, Oonagh, hold out your arm.'

'No, Kathleen must stay!' Oonagh pleaded. Surely they would not leave her alone here, with Gilliatt and his needle, which looked as thick as a toasting-fork prong. 'Kathleen, don't go. Please don't.' But Kathleen, so resolute in the face of the ambulance men's attempts to remove her, was powerless before Gilliatt, and was sent out. Oonagh saw Gilliatt nod towards the nurse, who stood on her other side, and watched as if from a distance as the nurse took hold of her arm, removed it from the protective grasp of her own other hand, and held it out to the doctor as though asking his opinion of it. Gilliatt took hold of it, as though it belonged to him, not to her. She noticed his hands had wiry black hairs on the backs that disappeared into the starched white of his sleeve, and imagined him for a moment without that snowy jacket – shoulders and chest naked, covered with a thick pelt of those black hairs.

'Count backwards from a hundred,' she heard him say, and began to formulate 'ninety-nine' in her mind.

*

When she woke, she was in a different room. Prettier, with pale yellow curtains that were too short for the windows, and Philip sat in a chair beside her. Beside him was a spindly hospital crib on wheels with cream-coloured bars and a linen cloth spilling out over the sides. As Oonagh looked, the cloth stirred a little.

'A boy,' Philip said, his face breaking into a smile that chased lines of tiredness away. 'A fine fat boy.' Oonagh couldn't understand. She had been asleep for a short while. How was there now a baby? She remembered the pain, the fear she had felt, but no more. Where had this baby come from?

'May I get up?'

'You may not. Gilliatt was precise in his instructions. You've had a time of it, my dear. In the end, it was a caesarean section. By necessity, and only just in time. You are to lie still.' Only then did Oonagh begin to understand that the haze of pain that still wrapped her had a place where it all came together, a line that hurt more than everywhere else, and from that point her baby must have been taken. How strange, she thought, to remember nothing. To go to sleep and wake to find that someone has taken a baby out from within you, like a conjuring trick. She did not feel as though she had given birth. She had given nothing: it had been taken.

'But I must sit up if I am to feed him.'

'Gilliatt does not advise it. He says the effort will be too much for you.'

'But I have always planned to feed him. You know that.'

'You are not strong enough.' He said it as though

she were being silly and insisting childishly on something that could not be had: that a soufflé be made to rise again when it had already fallen, or an entertainment got up solely for her to enjoy.

'Diana gave a large cocktail party, just weeks after Jonathan was born, with the child at her breast and a wolfhound the size of a colt at her feet,' Oonagh said, knowing her comparison would do nothing to help her, 'and she had strength left over to look down on her guests. It cannot be so very difficult.'

'You are not Diana,' Philip said. 'She is as strong as an ox. You are not.'

And Gilliatt, when he came on his rounds through the nursing home, was, all over again, confident and firm. 'It's not to be thought of,' he said.

Even Ernest, who came at visiting time with sweets and fruit and a mechanical toy for the baby, sided with the doctor, saying Oonagh was too weak. 'Don't think of it,' he advised. 'Unnecessary trouble.'

'Let that be Nanny's job,' Philip added, once he saw that Ernest would back him and not Oonagh. 'And, in any case, how will you go to Maureen's wedding if you're feeding a baby?' And Oonagh, turning her head this way and that to watch whichever man was speaking, found herself agreeing, reluctantly, that Gay would be given the bottle, because she found she could not keep saying the same words, only to have them disagreed with by three different men, with their firm voices, who were not weak from birth as she was.

'Like this, you will be sooner back to yourself,' Philip said. 'Which is surely what you want.'

'Yes,' Oonagh agreed, although it was not, she realised, a question. She felt the picture she had created of herself as a mother – a mother utterly unlike her own – falter then, and even as her eyelids drooped with exhaustion, she thought how she would find some way to make that picture firm and true.

'Later, to celebrate, I will have de László paint a magnificent portrait of you.' Philip smiled, as though he had handed her a trophy.

Chapter Eight

'Has Oonagh said if she's coming yet?' Maureen demanded of her mother. It was the morning of the wedding, and she had been awake since before daybreak, counting all the ways in which her life was about to become markedly more pleasant. Lying against the heap of cream-coloured linen pillows, she had played her new advantages through her mind as though pouring a heap of sparkling jewels through her fingers, pausing here and there to examine one close up, turn it this way and that, before setting it back among its fellows.

By the time her maid, Willis, came in with tea, she was already at her dressing-table, trying on the famous Dufferin and Ava shamrock tiara over her tousled curls, and wondering if she might be able to keep it after the wedding. Surely Lady Brenda, with her nerves, wouldn't actually notice if the tiara was returned or not.

'She says she hopes to come for a while,' Cloé said

then. 'She's still very feeble.' Oonagh, Maureen knew, had become far more interesting to their mother since the violent birth of her son a month before, and her delayed recovery thereafter.

'Well, I say it's jolly annoying of her to be so undecided. Carrying on as if she's the important person today! I don't even care if she comes or not.' Which wasn't true. One of the many pleasant things Maureen had counted in her head earlier that morning had been the looks on her sisters' faces – especially that of Aileen, who had arrived from Luttrellstown a few days earlier with Brinny – as she walked into St Margaret's with the tiara holding a floor-length veil of Irish lace in place.

'I hope you will be kind to your sisters,' Cloé said, 'when you're married. They are the best friends you will ever have.'

'I have Duff now.' Maureen patted cold cream on to her face and began to wipe it with a Kleenex tissue. 'I don't need friends. Not like that.'

'That isn't what marriage is, Maureen. It's not a friendship. Or not exactly . . .' Cloé paused, unsure how to continue.

'I say, you aren't here to give me the Talk?' Maureen said suspiciously. 'I can assure you, you're a great deal too late for that.' She started to laugh.

'I worry that you're too impetuous.' Cloé stood behind Maureen, watching her in the mirror, and gently readjusted the tiara she was trying on her head so that the shamrock-shaped cluster of diamonds caught the sunlight that poured in through the open windows. 'You are always so very certain of what you want and don't want – that is a good thing,' she added hastily, as Maureen opened her mouth to object, 'but I fear you don't consider consequences.'

'Consequences are boring,' Maureen said.

'Yes, I thought you might say that. But, you know, you can't magic something away simply because it's boring.'

'Mamma, I need Willis to come and dress me,' Maureen said, looking pointedly at the pretty jewelled clock on the bedside table that stood at eight. 'And I have simply no idea what you're talking about,' she finished, under her breath, as Cloé left the room.

But she remembered the conversation later, after St Margaret's, after the crowds outside who stood in the hot sunlight and called her name and threw scraps of multicoloured paper confetti and shiny grains of rice, even as she clung to Duff's arm and wanted to whoop like a child who has won a race. And when they were back at Grosvenor Place in the ballroom, while servants carried trays filled with cool glasses of champagne and cocktails around, Maureen, hitching her cream silk dress in one hand, went to where Oonagh and Aileen stood with Nancy, Diana and Violet.

'I say,' she said, interrupting their congratulations, 'Mamma tried to have A Serious Talk with me this morning.' She started to giggle. 'Did she do that with you?'

'Oh, yes,' Aileen said. She stroked the muzzle of the silver fox she wore slung over her bare shoulders. Its eyes glinted amber. 'One of the most frightful moments of my life. Came to my room the night before the wedding and simply wouldn't go away. Determined to tell me about A Wife's Duty.' Aileen was laughing. 'In the end I had to pretend to call Burton for a sick bowl to get her to go away.'

'You?' Maureen asked Oonagh.

'No,' Oonagh looked sad. 'She barely spoke to me before my wedding, remember? Everything between us had become so strained by then . . . We've been better friends since, though,' she added eagerly. 'And especially since Gay.'

'Do not start talking about that child,' Maureen threatened.

'Muv tried to have the Talk with me,' Diana said. 'And then, when I told her I had simply no idea what she was trying to say, she wrung her hands and said, "If only Nancy and Pamela were married as they should be, they could explain to you," and then Nancy put her head through the door and said—'

'I said, "Stand aside, Muv. I'll do the honours,"' Nancy interjected, 'and Muv said "Nancy, what could you possibly know?" and when I tried to tell her what I knew, she almost *ran* from the room.' She and Diana went into peals of laughter.

Violet laughed too, shaking her head slightly so the perfectly coiffed golden curls danced, until Diana raised her thin eyebrows high and said, 'I say, you're still a Single Girl, Violet. Perhaps you shouldn't listen.'

'Or, perhaps, now that you're soon to be married, you need the Talk too. I'm willing to oblige.' That was Maureen, her tone mocking – as it usually was when she spoke to Violet – head slightly tilted.

'Well, Nancy isn't married,' Violet blurted out. 'Perhaps she shouldn't listen either.'

'Nancy isn't listening,' Diana said. 'Nancy, as I have already explained, is *giving* the Talk,' and they all laughed, rather meanly, until Oonagh changed the subject by asking, 'What did Mamma say?' and patting Violet's arm sympathetically.

'Something about *consequences*, and how marriage isn't a friendship. Aileen,' Maureen demanded, 'you're married the longest of us. Would you call Brinny a friend?'

'Well, not a friend, exactly,' Aileen said.

'What, then?' Maureen said. 'I think Duff is a most terrific pal.' She looked over to where Duff stood with Ernest and some Oxford friends. As she looked, he caught her eye and grinned. 'You, Oonagh?' Oonagh shook her head very slightly. 'Diana?'

'No,' Diana said thoughtfully. 'Bryan is a dear. But not a friend. I have my sisters, though.'

'I rather think that's what Mamma was trying to say,' Maureen said, 'but I told her I had no need of sisters, with Duff,' and she walked away, enjoying the sound of her heels on the polished wooden floor of the ball-room, towards where Duff waited for her.

Oonagh looked after her. 'Some people become diluted with marriage,' she said. 'They become less themselves. Maureen, I imagine, will be more Maureen than ever.'

'Dreadful thought.' Aileen shuddered theatrically.

'The honeymoon?' Diana asked, flicking a fingernail idly against the side of her glass.

'Burma, so they can visit the Kingdom of Ava, and gloat over Duff's title, then India, so they can walk in the footsteps of Duff's grandfather, the great Viceroy, Frederick,' Aileen said.

'Not so much a honeymoon, then, as a victory lap,' said Nancy.

'Precisely, Nancy. Now, come and see my new puppy,' Diana said. 'The dearest little dachshund you ever did see, called Jacob and simply heaven. I've left him with the coats and he'll be crying, so you see I must get him.'

After they were gone, and Violet had drifted after them, Aileen pulled over a spindly gold chair for Oonagh. 'Here, sit, you look ready to drop,' she said.

'Thank you.' Oonagh sank gratefully into it.

'I see you found something to wear,' Aileen said, pulling in another chair for herself.

'Eventually. Burton had to let out my largest gown, and even so I feel I'll be snapped in two at the waist, it's so very tight.'

'When I saw you yesterday, I didn't think you'd come at all.' Aileen had called to Rutland Gate the day before, with Brinny, both blowing clouds of blue smoke, Aileen demanding 'news' and Brinny nodding solemnly beside her. When Gay was brought down, dressed in layers of white frills with his round face under a crochet bonnet, Aileen had said, 'What a pretty little dumpling he is,' but waved him away as though he was a dish she didn't care to try when Oonagh offered to let her hold him. 'They're all the same really at that age,' she had said firmly, and Oonagh, though bursting with the desire to tell her the million ways in which Gay was different – so very different – from all other babies, had said nothing. Later they had gone to Grosvenor Place together, to see Maureen on 'her last night', as they said, and Oonagh had to be nearly carried home, so exhausted was she.

'I thought of it,' she admitted now, 'but Philip would have been disappointed.'

'Philip?' Aileen asked. 'Not Maureen?'

'You know what I mean.'

'Yes, I suppose I do. Maureen wouldn't have been disappointed at all if neither of us had shown up.' They giggled at that, and Oonagh felt it was mean. But also irresistible, to gang up just a little on Maureen on her day of triumph.

'I won't stay long,' she said. 'I must get back to Gay.'

'Oonagh, you are very much in danger of becoming a bore about that child.'

'I fear that's what Philip thinks,' Oonagh admitted, in a small voice. 'He says I need to fuss a jolly lot less.'

She remembered Philip's face when he had come upon her bathing Gay a few evenings earlier, while Nanny stood looking on, arms crossed tight in disapproval. 'I must have my nursery to myself,' she had said to Philip, and he had agreed instantly.

'Yes, Oonagh, best leave the boy to Nanny.'

But Oonagh, still smarting from being told she mustn't think of feeding her own child at a time when she was too weak to disagree, stood firm. She had found that motherhood was a place where she could be joyful, where the love with which she looked was looked back at her in return from Gay's blue eyes. And because of that, she found a stubbornness and a resolve that were new to her. And so 'It's not *her* nursery, it's mine,' she insisted, first quietly, then more firmly, ignoring the sharp intake of breath from Nanny, and the confusion on Philip's face.

She had tried then to tell him how she could not be a mother like Cloé, able to bear her girls only in the drawing room for an hour after tea and before dinner when they were changed into pretty clothes and played quietly with a book or puzzle. But she saw that, although he nodded and mmm-ed along with what she said, he didn't listen. 'As long as the boy is healthy and Nanny doesn't mind too much,' he said eventually. Then, 'I must dress for dinner. Are we going out?'

'You go,' she had said. 'I'll dine here.'

And he had said very well, and gone to dress, but his tread was heavy on the stairs and when he looked in again before leaving the house, he tried again. 'Café de Paris?' he said. 'Sure you won't change your mind?'

'No, thank you,' Oonagh had said, and Kathleen, who had brought fresh towels, must have noticed his face too, because she said, 'They're only small for a short time,' comfortingly. Though whether it was to Oonagh or Philip she spoke, Oonagh wasn't sure.

'I think I bore him,' she said now, to Aileen. She had never said those words to herself, let alone out loud.

'I should think you do,' Aileen said. 'You'd bore anyone just now. But don't worry,' she said kindly, 'I'm sure you'll be much less dull once you stop fussing over the baby.'

Stop fussing over the baby, Oonagh thought. How

could she? She wanted only to be with Gay, always with Gay. Being away from him was a matter of waiting, patiently, pretending to be diverted, until she could be with him again, flying up the stairs to the nursery, ignoring the look on Nanny's face, and throwing herself to her knees before his cot to scoop him into her arms and press her face into the warm spot where his sweet neck met his delicious shoulder.

'Perhaps I will,' she said.

Ernest walked across the room to join them then. He was, she could see, agitated. 'Were you at that ridiculous White Party at Faversham?' their father demanded, and when Aileen said no, he continued, 'It seems there has been a tragic accident – a young man, Gordon Russell, has been killed. It will be in all the papers tomorrow.'

'He's an actor, isn't that so?' Oonagh said. 'Whatever happened?'

'He and Elizabeth Ponsonby were on their way home at five in the morning and the car overturned. The fellow Russell was driving. Elizabeth managed to climb out of a window and has only a fractured rib. Russell died on the spot. I've had poor Arthur Ponsonby on the telephone from early.'

'Goodness, how terrible,' Diana, back with a tiny dog in her arms, said. 'Isn't it, Jacob diddums?' And she kissed the little dog.

'Where was Pelly?' Oonagh asked.

'He didn't go with them.' Ernest paused. 'It seems the car that contained Elizabeth and Russell was being pursued by another chap, owns a garage. John Ford.'

'Ludy,' Oonagh says.

'You know him?' Ernest turned sharply towards her.

'He's one of Elizabeth's young men . . . No wonder Pelly wasn't there,' Oonagh said, with a roll of her eyes towards Aileen. 'But why was Ludy pursuing them?'

'It's not clear yet, although it seems there was a row of some kind. That, too, will be in the newspapers. Arthur is beside himself. It seems there is no way to keep Elizabeth's name out of it.'

'If I know Elizabeth, she won't want her name kept out of it,' Aileen said drily.

'How perfectly typical of her,' Oonagh said. 'She wouldn't come to Maureen's wedding because she's in a pet, always, about how poor they are, and although Maureen has done nothing . . .' Even as she said it, she wondered at the loyalty to Maureen, dried hard like icing, that compelled her. 'And instead she goes off and gets herself mixed up in something like this.'

'But what has any of it to do with us?' Aileen asked.

'It's a time for restraint, not excess,' Ernest said. 'I would rather not see any of you written about in newspapers for any reason.'

'Because it's July?' Oonagh asked. 'I agree, rather late in the season.'

'Because the country is in quite shocking disarray,' Ernest said. 'Nothing has been the same since the crash of the stock market. There are well over two million men unemployed, and growing all the time. That's an army. Give them a good general and they could take London in the morning.'

'But whyever would they want to? We're not their enemies,' Oonagh said placidly. 'I'm sure we wish them all that's best.'

'Well, I'm not sure they wish us all the best,' Ernest said. 'These are men without money or prospects, whose womenfolk must take in washing, and worse,' – he looked grim – 'to bring in a few shillings. Their children have rickets and stunted growth. If they don't wish us well, it's hardly surprising. These are not good times for showing off and frivolity.' Oonagh wondered what he meant, but Diana seemed to understand.

'That's exactly what I think,' she said excitedly, but was stopped from saying more by Duff rapping a cake fork against his champagne glass and moving to the centre of the room.

'May I have your attention . . .' he said, and it was a measure of his charm, Oonagh thought, that even though he spoke quietly, the room fell immediately silent.

Later, Oonagh tried to gather her things quietly to go home, but Violet saw her and came over. 'Let me help,' she said. 'You sit there and I'll fetch whatever you want. Cake? Champagne?' She made a great show of helping Oonagh back to a chair.

'No, nothing, thank you,' Oonagh said. 'I must get home.'

'Oh, but you can't,' Violet said, triumphant. 'We've all decided to see Maureen off properly and will drive as far as Croydon with them. We're to bring champagne and toast them once more before they go. Philip will drive the car round in a moment.'

'No, really, I can't,' Oonagh said again, but Violet wasn't listening.

'Philip,' she called, 'do come here and tell Oonagh not to be so dull.'

Philip came over then, full of geniality. 'What's this?' he cried. 'You don't think of going home?'

'But Gay . . .' Oonagh began, then stopped when she saw his face.

'Tell her she must come to Croydon,' Violet said.

'Valsie is right,' Philip said. 'We're all going!'

'Is Victor?' Oonagh asked, knowing she was being spiteful, but Violet simply looked at her and said, 'Yes, as I said, we're all going.'

'I'm sure it will be delightful,' Oonagh said, trying to keep her voice light, not to let loose the exhaustion and pain, 'but I must go.'

'But how will you get home?' Philip said. Oonagh could see the slight downward pull of his mouth in case she asked him to bring her, and thereby spoiled his fun.

'Kathleen will take me,' she said in relief, catching sight of Kathleen's thin, energetic form on the other side of the room. Then, 'Kathleen,' as she came closer, 'what are you doing here?'

'I came to get you,' Kathleen said, putting an arm out for Oonagh to lean on. 'I thought you might be tired.'

'I am,' Oonagh said gratefully. As she left, leaning against Kathleen's capable shoulder, she watched Violet slip lightly into the coat Philip held out for her, then fold up the fur collar close against her cheek, turn her head and smile warmly at him. Oonagh paused, as though she would go back, then set off once more towards the front door and Gay.

Chapter Nine

Rutland Gate, London

It was several days after the wedding that Aileen arrived at Rutland Gate to visit Oonagh and, still standing in the drawing-room doorway, pulling at her gloves, demanded abruptly, 'Can't you ring up Mamma and ask her here too?' She knew she was being rude, but she was irritated by her failure to convince Brinny to stay in London longer. 'We're due to travel home tomorrow, and I don't wish to call to Grosvenor Place as well but rather do all my farewells here.'

'I can try,' Oonagh said. 'But you know Mamma . . . Is Brinny coming?'

'No, he's determined to buy a new motor-car before we leave. I've tried to tell him they aren't like dresses, he doesn't need one in every colour, but he assures me they're exactly the same and that a man in his position cannot be seen in the same car twice.' She sat down abruptly in an uncomfortable straight-backed armchair, dislodging a cushion.

'And what position, exactly, would that be?' Oonagh murmured.

Aileen chose not to hear her. 'We were at the Kit Kat Club last night. You should have come, Oonagh.'

'I did so long to. But Dr Gilliatt is terribly strict.'

'I imagine that is barely half true,' Aileen said, watching her. 'Philip came in, very late, with Valsie and Brenda Dean Paul – who thinks she's an actress now, imagine! – just as we were leaving. Brenda was shrieking about being arrested again. Sometimes I think that girl is quite deranged.' She ran a hand through her hair, newly set, and turned a foot this way and that, admiring the shine on the buckle of her patent shoe. 'I say, you don't mind Philip being about so much without you, do you?' she asked, unwilling to look Oonagh in the eye, but feeling compelled to ask.

'No,' Oonagh said. 'It's much jollier for him than staying at home.'

'Well, that's all right, then,' Aileen said in relief. 'Pass me a gasper.' Oonagh handed her the cigarette box and she peered in. 'Is this all you have? What about those Russian cigarettes you usually smoke?'

'Dr Gilliatt disapproves of smoking. He says just three or four a day.'

'The man sounds a total bore,' Aileen said. 'My own doctor, Wilson, positively encourages it. To calm the nerves.' She exhaled slowly and luxuriously, or in a way that was intended to seem slow and luxurious. In fact, she felt agitated. When not waving her cigarette about she pulled at her skirt and jacket, although both were so perfectly fitted there was nowhere that needed pulling. She found a thread in the hem of the skirt and began twitching at it, only stopping herself when she realised she was about to unravel the entire seam. 'You can't imagine what heaven it is to be in a real nightclub after Dublin,' she continued, 'where there are only the pokiest of places and they always smell queer, as though when we're not all dancing in them, someone might actually live there. Someone not terribly clean at that . . .'

'I don't know why you don't live in London,' Oonagh said 'Papa could buy you a house and you could be close by and Gay and Neelia could play together in the square and it would be so much more pleasant.'

'Brinny won't have it,' Aileen said. 'He says London chokes him after a couple of weeks. And I know what he means. One does always rather feel as though one is scrambling somewhat to keep up here . . . Always a new nightclub, a new exhibition of paintings, a new place one simply must go or new person one simply must be friendly with . . .'

'Whereas in Dublin there's never anyone but you to keep up with,' Oonagh interjected with a laugh. 'Better to reign in hell than serve in heaven?'

'Something like that.' Aileen lit another cigarette. 'And I doubt it's so very different for you.' She thought then how she enjoyed being able to complain that Dublin was dull and provincial, compared with the restless feeling in London that she was at the heart of a million things that must all be done and seen to be done. 'In Dublin, the best parties are all mine,' she said, trying to explain. 'I give them, decide on them, invite everyone who comes to them. And if I choose not to, there is nothing else to replace them, so I never feel I'm missing out on anything.'

'Yes, I can see that would be nice,' Oonagh said vaguely, 'if one cared about that sort of thing. But surely you don't. I mean, how can anyone, when there are so many other things, more interesting and important . . .'

'If by Other Things you mean that child, I warn you, I shall scream,' Aileen said.

'I just meant . . . other things, you know.' Oonagh shrugged. 'Not just parties and keeping up. I mean, does it matter if I wasn't at the Kit Kat Club, or that you won't be at Lady Meredith's next week?'

'I happen to think it does,' Aileen said stiffly. 'Although, of course, everyone will know that I'm not there because I'm not in the country, so that's all right.'

Diana was shown in then before Oonagh, brows drawn together in a puzzled frown, could respond. 'Darlings, I was with the Old Pair and thought I would just look in and see how you are. You must be so terribly flat, after the wedding. I remember Muv, after Bryan and I, said they were all simply dismal. Except Farve, of course, who said he felt as though he'd struck gold, so much did he hate all the fuss and bother.'

She stood in the doorway to say all this, glittering like the first hard frost of winter, the little dachshund, Jacob, in the crook of her arm. For all that she spoke the same as any of their friends – the same ridiculous exaggeration and absurdity – she did so without emotion, so that she might just as well have been reading the shipping forecast, Aileen thought. 'It's her top lip,'

Maureen had said, when Aileen remarked on this. 'Watch the next time. It doesn't move, or at least hardly at all. She's like a horse nibbling at a hedge. Only the bottom lip moves. And then not enough to give her voice any expression.'

'Let's go for a walk about the gardens,' Diana said then, making Aileen feel a flash of irritation at how much she took over. 'Jacob needs the air. Such a waste to be inside on such a day,' she continued. 'And, indeed, to have gardens that are never used except by the children. Unity told me this morning that she plans to dig up the entire square and plant strawberries, then sell them for sixpence a punnet at the gates. We'd better go before she begins.' Aileen had seen this Unity, Diana's sister – a ferocious child, some fifteen years, whose middle name was actually Valkyrie – just that morning as she arrived, stumping along Rutland Gate, glaring out from under a pale blonde fringe that looked as though she had cut it herself, and had no doubt that she planned to do exactly as she said.

'Very well,' Oonagh agreed. 'Besides, Dr Gilliatt says I must walk more.'

'Darling, we are so very sick of Dr Gilliatt . . .' Aileen said, with a frown. 'You make me feel I'm visiting a nursing home.' Then, 'Mamma?' she asked.

'Lying down,' Oonagh said. 'Peters telephoned. But Papa is on his way.'

Ernest and Brinny arrived together as Oonagh, Aileen and Diana clustered on the front steps. 'You're early,' Aileen said to Brinny. 'I'm not ready. We're walking about the gardens.'

'Shall I come with you?' Brinny asked eagerly.

'No,' Aileen said. 'You go to the club and I'll send word when I'm ready.' She took Ernest's arm to descend the steps.

'Jolly good,' Brinny said, but without his usual cheer. He was like a dog that leaps up when the door opens, only to sink down again when it is clear the master is going out alone, Aileen thought, wishing he could seem more energetic. 'Sir Arthur Conan Doyle has died,' he said then, still standing at the top of the steps. 'I call that bad show. What, no more Sherlock Holmes? No more Dr Watson? What am I to read now?'

'Something new?' Oonagh suggested.

'But I have no wish to find new friends when I'm happy with the old ones,' he said wistfully. 'Aileen tells me I must exert myself and make friends, but I never know what to say and, besides, I like only those I've known for a long time. Is that so bad?' he appealed to Oonagh, but Aileen cut in irritably, 'I asked you to make an effort, to talk about something other than horses and cars. Is that really so difficult? Now, do go on. I'll come and find you when I'm ready.'

They walked about the gardens of Rutland Gate, Aileen's hand through Ernest's arm, even though she could see Oonagh was struggling to keep pace and looked chalky white.

'Diana, do give us more of your political opinions,' she said with a laugh. But instead of looking discomfited, as Aileen had expected, Diana stepped forward eagerly.

'Why, yes,' she said, 'for I'm sure that unemployment is the one problem that really matters. And that Britain, now, can only survive by vigour and by action.' She sounded, Aileen thought, as though she was reciting something learned by heart.

'Is this what Bryan is saying?' Ernest asked in surprise.

'Oh, Bryan! No,' Diana said. She bent her head to Jacob in the crook of her arm and rubbed her cheek against the dog's silky ear. 'Bryan cares for nothing except writing his stories and diaries.' She straightened up, brushing her hair from her face where it had fallen forward. 'And his friends, I suppose,' as if even that much praise were hard for her.

'He's a good fellow,' Ernest said sternly.

'Yes. But he's not serious about anything. And these are serious times. You say it yourself.'

'They are.'

'I have heard that the people no longer trust politicians, who know how to talk but not to act.' Again, she sounded as though she was reciting a lesson learned and Aileen longed to quiz her – which politicians did she mean? Who were the people who didn't trust them? – but Ernest got there first.

'Who have you heard that from?' he asked.

'That chap Mosley. I went to one of his assemblies.' She spoke with pride. As though an assembly were some daring new entertainment. 'You've heard of him, I suppose?'

'I have,' Ernest said. He laughed. 'A man who started with the Conservatives, crossed the floor to Labour, then left to set up his very own New Party, before that floundered under him. A man who fails at everything, it seems.'

'Not everything,' Diana said. Her face had more colour in it than Aileen had ever seen, and she wondered was it the July breeze that blew brisk through the garden. 'Because it sounds as though you agree with him.'

'I didn't say that,' Ernest said stiffly. 'And I happen to think our politicians very capable.'

'Oh, I don't mean Walter,' Diana said hastily, and Aileen knew how much Ernest would dislike this mention of his younger brother, Diana's father-in-law, who had been minister for agriculture until the last election when he was voted out. 'He's too brilliant for words, of course. I mean the others,' she said, making a vague waving motion with her gloved hand and smiling reassuringly at Ernest.

'This has nothing to do with family,' he said abruptly. Aileen could see that Diana had annoyed him by assuming that his only interest was personal. 'It is far too serious for that. Nothing has been right since the Crash, and matters are only getting worse. There is not the mood for tolerance of such excesses as there were. Why, the Prince of Wales himself has been told to show more restraint, him and that set he entertains at Fort Belvedere.'

'He is the last person to listen to anyone who tries to restrain him,' Diana said, with smug familiarity. 'He says he will go to no more court balls, that they're tedious and irrelevant, that he'd rather play the drums at the Kit Kat Club.' She laughed. 'But I've heard him agreeing with Mosley, that the people desire a new creed and a new order, that they're weary and disgusted with the present way.' The same excitement was in her voice.

This time, Oonagh must have noticed it too, for she said slyly, 'So, you're bored of art hoaxes and fancy-dress parties, and have decided to try Ideas?'

Diana blushed – a thing Aileen had never seen her do – but was spared answering by a shout from behind them. 'Off the path!' a furious voice called. 'Off the path!' They turned and Unity was hurtling towards them in a rickety go-cart made from a wooden crate, pulled by a fat black Labrador going at a clip. 'You have to move,' she shouted again, laughing wildly. Her hat had fallen off and her hair escaped its bands so that it streamed out behind her. 'Move!' she screamed. 'Labby has seen the gate for home and I cannot stop him!'

Sure enough, the dog rushed past, panting and straining, with Unity laughing and making great play of pulling at a pair of leather reins she had tied around his back, which he ignored entirely.

They scattered, and when they came back together, Oonagh and Diana moved ahead and Aileen dropped behind with Ernest. 'Is it really so bad as all that?' she asked.

'I'm afraid it is. This will be the devil's decade if we can't address these problems.' And even though Aileen had only the vaguest understanding of what he meant, the look on his face, the twitch of his moustache, were enough to tell her that he was worried.

Chapter Ten

A few days later, Ernest arrived so early at Rutland Gate that Oonagh, hearing his step on the marble tiles of the hall long before she was ready to go down, was alarmed. 'What is it?' she called, from halfway down the stairs.

Ernest, handing his hat to Peters, said, 'An accident. Come down and I'll tell you,' and Oonagh grabbed the peignoir Burton had followed her with and went straight down to him. They went to the morning room where Philip was having breakfast. 'Duff's father is dead,' Ernest said, waving away the cup of coffee Peters had poured for him and gesturing instead towards a dish of kippers. 'An aeroplane crash. Last night. He and Maureen, somewhere in a jungle in Burma, cannot be found to be told.' He pulled out a chair and sat down, so Oonagh did the same. 'Frederick was coming home from Le Touquet. You'll remember he went there after the wedding, for a few days at the casinos. He decided to leave a day or so early, because he was worried about Lady Brenda.' Everyone, Oonagh recalled, worried about Lady Brenda.

'Good God, what happened?' Philip asked, white coffee cup suspended halfway from the table so that the gold rim glinted like a tiny smiling mouth, Oonagh thought.

'An air-taxi,' Ernest said. 'Fell apart over Kent. All five passengers, the pilot and co-pilot. All dead.'

There was silence as they took in what he had said. Oonagh tried to remember the man she had seen at the wedding, just over two weeks ago, because she felt the need to fix him clear in her mind now that he was no more. But all she could call up was a bristling moustache and a pair of deep-set eyes. There had been little hint of Duff's restless energy. In fact, Frederick – fussing over his wife – had seemed to her like a man whom life had left sodden with disappointment, but who had decided he would never say so. Would take his dreary secret to his death. And now he had.

But it was too hard to call him to mind, so vague a person had he been, so obscured by his preoccupation with Lady Brenda – nervous, always, for what she might do.

'Efforts are still being made to find Basil and Maureen who are somewhere on their way to India,' Ernest continued. 'And, indeed, to gather the pieces of the plane together. Bits are strewn across a five-mile radius.'

'The passengers?' Philip asked.

'Fell into an orchard,' Ernest said. 'Cherry trees.' Oonagh made a choking noise before she could stop herself, thinking of bodies tumbling from the sky, seven of them, crashing through trees that must have looked soft, even yielding, from a distance, then the green leaves turning, too fast, into branches, and the shocking finality of solid trunks. Were the trees the late-bearing variety, with ripe red fruit still heavy on the boughs? But it was too much. She shuddered and tried to turn the picture from her mind.

'They say tens of thousands of pounds' worth of jewellery is scattered across the countryside,' Ernest continued.

Through the windows of the breakfast room she saw that it was a beautiful day outside, fresh and blue as though painted in watercolours. Not the sort of day for death. She thought of the countryside winking with jewels, flashing their own desperate Morse code into the sunlight. Except that whatever distress call they signalled, it was too late.

'I wonder what happened to the plane,' Ernest said. His delicate fingers twitched on the bone handles of his knife and fork, and Oonagh could see he was turning over possibilities vigorously in his mind, considering failures of engines and mechanics, diverted by that from realisations of death and destruction.

'Will they cut short the honeymoon?' she asked. 'When you find them? Maureen and Duff?'

'I imagine so,' Ernest said. 'Duff will have much to do.'

'So, Maureen is a marchioness already,' Oonagh said. And even though she knew Maureen had expected more time to be young and married, without the ferocious care of Clandeboye, she found she was more envious than sorry.

Chapter Eleven

London

August was sultry, with a kind of sullen heat that Kathleen, brought up in a city by the sea, forever played on by brisk winds, had never known. The days piled heavy, one upon another, like, she thought, feather bolsters laid out and stacked. The streets and parks emptied as anyone who could fled to the country or seaside. Oonagh, well but unwilling to leave her doctor, stayed put, so the family did too, but because she spent much of her time lying in her room with the curtains drawn against the heat, or in the nursery watching as Gay grew fat and round and happy, Kathleen was free to go about.

She had found a corner of Hyde Park that seemed to trap what little breeze there was so that it was nearly always cool, and took to going there on the hottest afternoons with a book, or what few letters came from home. She would take these from Peters, who handed them over as though they might carry some contagion, and store them in a pocket or purse until she was alone on that shady bench. That was how she kept up to date with the doings of her sisters and father, and the very few friends she had still. And it was at the end of one of those letters, from her elder sister Margaret, or Peggy, that she learned, *The master you were friendly with is gone from Carysfort now. They say he is in a different teaching post but no longer in Dublin. I wonder do you hear from him at all?*

It was, Kathleen knew, Peggy's way of trying to find out what Kathleen had never told: what exactly had been the nature of the friendship with Mr O'Loughlin? The nuns had assumed the worst – instantly, without asking, without question – and Peggy had tried to assume the best, but when Kathleen wouldn't give her anything much beyond 'It was a friendship, and a slight one at that,' she had been left suspicious, Kathleen knew.

And maybe, Kathleen thought now, she should have been more forward with her explanation. But by then it was too late. The anger within her at the whispers and suppositions had been too great, so she couldn't, any more, try to give her side of a story that shouldn't have needed to be told. In any case, she knew no one – except Peggy – wanted to hear her side. She didn't, in their eyes, have a side.

It had been, she thought now, just as she had told Peggy, a 'friendship', nothing more. Mr O'Loughlin had discovered her interest in history and been approving of it. From that had grown a friendship, or what she told herself was a friendship. A half-dozen walks around Blackrock Park or by the sea after lessons were done, tea in Bewley's café while he talked about reform and the penal laws. Kathleen, older than the other girls in the teacher-training college, and without friends, had been glad of company, interested in hearing his ideas. If anything, she had thought of these walks and cups of tea as an extension of lessons. She didn't know where he lived, didn't know his first name, had never asked him a thing about himself or he about her. And yet even that little was too much.

He was married, and his wife was pregnant and had miscarried a baby. That was when the whispers began. In a town as small as Dublin there were always whispers. They said it was Kathleen's fault, even though Kathleen had never met her. The whispers said that the strain of knowing what her husband was doing, going about with Kathleen Murphy, was the cause. And what could Kathleen have said to that? It was as if Kathleen was a witch, with the power to ill-wish a woman she had never seen.

Even Mr O'Loughlin, when he said, 'Better we don't speak any more,' that last afternoon, had looked as if he might half believe what they said, so that she had wanted to shake him and remind him that he knew the truth, remind him of his own proud boast that he was a 'rational man'.

She had been defiant at first – head high in the knowledge she had done no wrong – but when she saw what the whispers had cost her, her defiance grew much less. Even though the shame wasn't hers, the consequences were: the shoddy degree, the sparse, almost mocking, letter of recommendation, the slamming shut of possibilities.

She wondered now, Did Mr O'Loughlin leaving mean there had been consequences for him too? She doubted it.

The letter finished 'fond wishes for your good health, Kitty'. Kathleen sat and watched people walk by – blessing the hurry and indifference of every one; all these people who knew and cared nothing for her. She stretched out her arms in the luxury of that as though it had more power even than the sun to warm her.

Close to her now a girl was wheeling a giant perambulator, with a boy of maybe six months sitting high in it. The child was screaming so that his poor face was brick-red and his legs, beneath a white crochet blanket, stiff, beating a tattoo of distress against the mattress. As they passed, Kathleen heard the girl implore him, 'Oh, stop it now, please, please, stoppit.'

She sounded close to tears herself, so Kathleen said quietly, 'I think he's strapped too tightly in, and that's why he screams.'

'I thought so too, but Nanny Harris said to be sure he wouldn't fall out. He gets that excited when he does see the ducks that I pulled the straps extra tight,' the girl said breathlessly.

'Loosen them a little and he will be fine,' Kathleen said. 'Let me help you.' She tried to adjust the straps, which were indeed cutting into the child's chubby arms. 'See can you calm him a moment that I might get at the straps.'

'Now, Jonathan,' the girl said, 'let me sing you a little

song.' She began, '*Sleep, O babe, for the red bee hums / The silent twilight's fall . . .*' in a remarkably sweet voice and the child quieted enough that Kathleen freed him of the reins that held him. The girl – who looked to be a few years younger than Kathleen, smaller and rounder – lifted him out and bounced him in her arms while she finished singing: '*A leanbhan O, my child, my joy / My love and heart's desire / The crickets sing you a lullaby / Beside the dying fire.*'

'You didn't learn that in London,' Kathleen said. The child, silent now, looked about him with round, astonishingly blue eyes.

'I didn't,' she said. 'My mother taught it to me at home in Dublin.'

'What part?'

'Dún Laoghaire.'

'I know it well,' Kathleen said. 'What brought you here?'

'This little fella.' She jiggled the child in her arms so that he laughed. 'I know I should put him down,' the girl said. 'Nanny Harris says it is bad for him to be carried so. That his back will not grow straight unless he is sitting upright.'

'Our nanny says the same,' Kathleen said with a laugh. 'But little Gay's mother disagrees and says there is nothing so good for a baby as to be held and shown the world. Keep him out a while longer? I'll push the perambulator while we walk. Where is your house?' she asked. 'How long have you been in London?'

'Six months. I came when this little fella was born. We live in Buckingham Street, number nineteen, and

Jonathan's father brought me over because he said he wanted his son to have the kindness of an Irish childhood.' Now that she had an address and a name – Jonathan – as well as the child's startling blue eyes, Kathleen found herself putting pieces together. 'I think I can guess?' she said with a laugh. 'A Mr Bryan Guinness?'

'It is. But how did you know?' The girl looked terrified, as though Kathleen might be a spy sent to watch her, so Kathleen explained her amateur detective workings, and how her family connected with Jonathan's. 'I'm Kathleen,' she finished.

'Mary,' the girl said. 'So you are a nursemaid too?'

'No, not exactly. Though I have to do with the baby sometimes.'

'Then what are you?' Mary asked.

'You know, I'm not sure,' replied Kathleen.

'Well, let's work it out so,' Mary said. 'Where in the house is your bedroom?'

'There.' Rutland Gate now lay in front of them and Kathleen pointed to the window on the third floor that was hers.

'Not the attic?'

'No.'

'Do you take care of Gay every day?'

'No, there is a nanny for that, but I play with him and help Oonagh to bathe him because she insists on doing that every night.'

'Do you write letters for her?'

'Sometimes. And I make telephone calls. I go to Harrods and Fortnum's.'

'You talk like them,' Mary said. 'Or not exactly like them. Like us too, but your words are more like their words.'

'I trained to be a teacher.' But she knew Mary was right – it wasn't just that. Living with Oonagh, being so constantly with her, with her friends, with Philip, with Ernest, she was starting to sound more like them. Her words had begun to snip themselves off at the ends now like theirs did, and emerge distinct and discreet, not running into one another. She didn't yet know what she thought about that.

There was a pause. 'I suppose you're a companion of sorts,' Mary said at last, but Kathleen could see she was discontented by her failure to be any one thing. 'But you're like my brother Ned. He won't be one thing either.'

'What several things is he?'

'He is a labourer, at the docks, unloading ships, but now he is a painter too, he says, and when I said that house-painting was a decent profession he laughed and said, "Not houses, pictures." Whatever that means.'

'Does he live in London too?'

'Yes, in a place called Soho that is close to Covent Garden. A dirty, noisy place, but he doesn't mind. Our ma is right about him. She says he was born to sup sorrow with a long spoon.' She sounded disapproving.

'What a strange expression,' Kathleen said. 'What does it mean?'

'I don't know for sure, but it suits Ned. If you like, come with me next time and you can meet him and see for yourself.'

Kathleen, realising that here was a chance perhaps to have friends of her own, said yes, and she came to meet Ned barely a week later. He was older than Mary but younger than Kathleen by two years, with curly hair and eyes that tilted up at the corners so that the bright blue of them ran towards the brown curls. He looked about him as though he found everything amusing, and as though he believed it had been made so for his own self.

Having met him, Kathleen thought she could understand what their mam must have meant when she said he supped sorrow with a long spoon: he was one of those born to light. He looked for laughter and he found it, he looked for fun and he found that too. And others found those things when they were with him. It wasn't that he was foolish or irresponsible, she thought. It was that responsibility seemed to come to him with ease rather than as a burden. And he was as quick to throw it off as he was to assume it.

Mary and Ned's London, she found, as they went about together, was more populous than Oonagh's – perhaps, Kathleen thought, because wherever she went with Oonagh, people stood back to give them room. If they alighted from the motor-car outside Claridges or the Ritz, the uniformed man on the great doors sprang forward, as though someone had hurled him from a sling, to smooth Oonagh's path. Passers-by paused, holding back, until she was gone by, with Kathleen in her wake.

With Mary and Ned, she was jostled and bumped constantly, mostly with good humour. In turn, they jostled and bumped back, so everywhere they went felt crowded and busy.

Ned, she discovered, had learned all sorts of strange things about London, and loved to tell them. Like, since the time of Charles II, there must always be six ravens in the Tower of London, and the first plan for the Tube was to have covered canals filled with water and boats to carry people along.

In turn Ned asked a great many questions about Kathleen's life, interested in how it differed from Mary's. 'You're like a house dog,' he said, when she was done describing, 'rather than a kennel dog.'

'That's very rude,' Mary said.

'I don't mind,' Kathleen said with a laugh. 'I know what he means. I'm like one of the pugs.'

'Exactly. You have the freedom and fondness of the drawing room. It's because you are educated,' and he looked at her with respect, 'but don't you wish for more?'

'Like what?'

'To mix with different people, to see and hear different voices and places and customs.'

'What do you mean?'

'There is a market on the street where I live, Berwick Street, and the things on sale – I don't even have names for half of them, or understand the languages they are offered in. But there is more energy in the people and the stalls there than I have ever seen. Next time, I will bring you a thing called salt beef to try.'

'Surely you don't eat that.' Mary sounded disgusted.

'I do, and more besides,' Ned said. 'Pickled herrings even. I'll try anything.'

'I don't believe you, Ned,' Mary said. 'You couldn't.' She made a face. 'That's not our food.'

'It's better than our food. If you'll come with me some day, I'll see that you try the best of what there is. But you'll have to be off during the week. They all stay indoors on a Sunday around there, and there isn't a soul on the streets.'

'I'm never free during the week,' Mary said, proud of the regularity of her life. 'And' – piously – 'I should hope indeed that they take the day of worship seriously. I go to mass at Our Lady Queen of Heaven every Sunday and I hope you do too.'

'My Jewish neighbours take it more seriously than ever we did,' Ned said with a laugh. 'I thought Catholics were God-fearing, but we're nothing compared with those lads. Even Mam with her decades of the rosary has little on them.' He did not, Kathleen noticed, answer the question about his mass-going, and when he looked at her, he gave the ghost of a wink.

'I could come during the week,' she'd said in a rush. 'I can be free most days, if I know that Oonagh doesn't need me.' He smiled at her, his eyes sliding upwards, and she smiled back.

Chapter Twelve

Rutland Gate, London

'**D**arling, stop talking!' De László spoke politely but sternly. Philip had been true to his word and had commissioned a portrait of Oonagh to mark her twenty-first birthday, and Oonagh had been delighted. But after the early thrill of importance, she quickly found herself bored and weary. At first she tried to have Gay with her, but he distracted her and made her move about, so de László banished him. And Philip, after watching him make the first sketches, rushing excitedly from Oonagh to de László and back again to see what had been done, realised how slow the painting would be and lost interest. De László wouldn't allow her friends to call in the first days of sketching her so it was Kathleen who sat with her.

Oonagh had been arranged on a chair, in a shadowy corner of the drawing room, with nothing else in the portrait. 'With others, I must distract, maybe use a looking-glass, flowers, even a headdress, but with you,

Oonagh, one needs no such distractions,' he said smoothly. He was full of such compliments, which made Oonagh giggle with their practised air, but behind all that, and even despite a preening moustache, his eyes were clever and quick, flickering back and forth, missing nothing, so that at first she felt as though she were under a hot bright light trained too long upon her. 'It's like being back with Mamma and Gunnie,' she confided to Kathleen. 'To be looked at and considered from every angle, as though I were a diamond, which might yet prove to be false. You must stay with me, because I cannot bear it otherwise.'

Oonagh wore a white muslin dress with a turquoise-green sash, and held a straw hat in one hand, as though she had paused for a moment on a hot day. The other hand she rested delicately on her collarbone. Around her neck she wore a necklace of hefty emeralds that was to be another twenty-first birthday gift from Philip, given early so that it might be included – and that the world might see the solid value he was able to place upon her.

The dress was the one she had worn to be photo-graphed with Gay for the *Sketch* some weeks before. That day, the photographer had looked at how she was with Gay and said, 'You are to be congratulated, Mrs Kindersley. I have photographed so many children who hardly recognise their mothers. They cry for Nanny and are afraid of the woman they must call Mamma. But I see that your son positively worships you.' Oonagh, thrilled, had decided there and then to wear the dress for her portrait. But she was glad Philip hadn't heard the compliment. He still found her devotion excessive – 'ostentatious' was the word he had used – as though she did it for show when the truth was she tried to restrain herself.

Mostly, she sat on a Monday and a Tuesday to be sketched, mornings drifting slowly by while she and Kathleen waited for de László finally to put down his pad or pencil and announce, 'I think that is all for today.' And as they waited, they talked quietly, the enforced stillness of body causing Oonagh to reveal more than she otherwise would, as though her mind raced to make up for sitting immobile.

'How much I want another child,' she said one morning, voice low. 'Not now, of course, with Gay still so tiny, but soon. And they say I can't. Philip is alarmed by Dr Gilliatt and says he does not think it wise. Gilliatt has told him I must be careful. That he cannot be sure another baby might live, or even that I might. But he's wrong, I know he is.'

'And what if he's not?' Kathleen said. 'It may be that Philip is right to be cautious.'

'They're wrong,' Oonagh insisted. 'They must be. I've never wanted to be anything more than a mother, and always, in my mind, a mother of many. I see them all about me, in my imagination, and it's such a happy scene.'

'Seeing it doesn't make it safe,' Kathleen said tartly.

But Oonagh ignored her. 'It simply isn't possible that I'm to have one child and no more. I miss them, Kathleen, the children of my mind's image. I see them so clearly, and then, when I look up, they're not there, and I feel the pain exactly as if they had been, and were taken away.'

'How you exaggerate,' Kathleen said, as she had said before. 'You are very young. There is plenty of time yet. And Gay barely an infant. Enjoy the child you have rather than hastening to have more. There's no hurry.'

'You don't understand,' Oonagh said. What she didn't say was that there was a hurry, that she could feel Philip drifting away from her now that Gilliatt was so determined she be the mother of just one child. She felt Philip accepting this, and altering the image of his family accordingly. And she felt her place in his mind dwindle. She thought how the rest of his life would expand around her, growing larger and stronger, while she was obscured and left behind. If she had more children, her place in his life would be bigger.

'Aileen thinks I should spend less of my time with Gay,' she said. 'She thinks my child gets the affection my husband should have.'

'Perhaps he does.'

'But how can it be right to raise a child without showing proof of affection?' Oonagh demanded.

'No one is asking you to raise Gay without affection. Just try to be moderate.'

'Kathleen, I remember well – too well! – how much I longed for some crumb from Mamma, and how cruel the nannies were who brought us up. I cannot bear that Gay should ever know what it is to look to his mother's face for some sign of love from her, some soft word or caress, and find nothing. People think we don't remember our childhoods but we do. I remember every bit of mine. Every cross word and kind. Every time Nanny or Mamma was harsh, and every time you, Kathleen, were not.'

Useless for Kathleen to try to tell her that Gay's childhood was different, and her vigilance unnecessary. 'I must make sure of it,' Oonagh said, agitated and almost fretful.

When the first sketches for the portrait were finished and de László had grown less strict, gradually those put off by his sternness began to drift back, and soon a little gang gathered almost every morning. Stephen Tennant, Diana and Nancy, occasionally Bryan, over endless teacups and plates of Mrs Taylor's delicious biscuits.

'At least we know where you are, Oonagh darling,' Stephen said, pursing his lips. The cupid's bow of his mouth was enhanced with a slick of red and he wore a gold shirt with extravagantly ruffled sleeves that entirely covered his long, slender hands so that he had to keep shaking them back every time he wanted to lift a teacup or light a cigarette. 'Reliably in your anointed place, thanks to de László. Everyone else seems to have vanished. That or, like poor Elizabeth, given in to some terrible gloom. You'd think she might have thrown off that ghastly incident by now.' Elizabeth was still in hiding after the car crash and the death of the young actor.

'Well, these are gloomy times,' Diana said vigorously. 'Only a fool would ignore that in favour of dressing up and going to parties. What was it last week? Another Black and White party?'

'Delicious fun,' Stephen drawled. 'And don't pretend you weren't there, Diana, because I saw you, wearing that fabulously expensive Mainbocher, too. I do quite see why you must try to seem all serious, to try to impress A Certain Someone, but look around, my poppet, he isn't here, so there is no reason to be dreary with the rest of us. You do seem to lead a double life these days. Giving parties to beat the band with Bryan, then sneaking round to see Mosley deliver his tedious speeches.'

'Diana doesn't sneak,' Nancy said. 'Wherever she goes, she has to be the centre of attention.' Oonagh wondered was she being loyal, or catty. With sisters, it was hard to tell.

'How is little Jonathan?' she asked, to defuse.

'Well, I suppose,' Diana said.

'And, Nancy, how are the dogs?' Nancy had two new French bulldogs, Dominic and Lottie.

'And I suppose you're going to ask me, "How are the parties?"' Stephen said peevishly.

'She could ask you how is the book?' Nancy said mischievously. '*Lascar: A Story You Must Forget*? Is that it?'

'It's *A Story You Must Remember*, but yours is a better title. Perhaps I'll steal it . . .' Stephen said gloomily. Then, 'You have no idea how terrible it is still to be forced to be a Bright Young Person when I'm neither Young nor Bright. Everyone with any sense is so terribly tired of it all. Everyone except the Prince of Wales, and he is neither Young nor Bright either, except he doesn't seem to know it. Or how to be anything else, for that matter. Ever since Waugh wrote that book, everyone thinks they know all about me and have me so very figured out.'

'Well, how do you think I feel with my name on the front of it,' Diana said, 'like I'm the high priestess of parties?' Oonagh bent her head to hide her smile, causing de László to tut, and wished that Maureen were there. Only she would have dared to laugh out loud.

'You were perfectly thrilled when it first came out,' Nancy said. 'Almost as though you'd written it yourself. Prouder even than of baby Jonathan.'

'I shouldn't worry.' That was Stephen. 'The book is mostly dedicated to Bryan. Your name is only there to be polite. Waugh told me so.'

'How much better you do make one feel, Stephen,' Diana said crossly, picking up Jacob, and playing with the diamond collar around the dog's slim throat. 'When will Maureen and Duff return?'

'After Christmas. They'll spend Christmas in India, where they're deep in the jungle because Duff wishes to hunt, yet they dress for dinner with every formality each night. Maureen says they make a play of it, dressing as though for a court ball.'

'I thought they would come back after his father died.'

'I thought so too, but Maureen said what was the point? By the time Papa found them, and then by the time they travelled back, the funeral would have been over. So they went on to India as planned.'

'Let's have a look at what you've done with Oonagh,' Stephen said. 'I've yet to see the ugly woman you haven't managed to make beautiful. Even the most hideous of the Spanish princesses are rendered glorious by your brushstrokes.'

'Not until everything is finished,' de László said. It was one of his rules: no peeking.

'No cheating, Stephen,' Oonagh said. 'I shall plan a magnificent party after Christmas to reveal the painting, and to celebrate my twenty-first birthday. I know it's months away, but it will be something to look forward to, and celebrate Maureen and Duff's return. I'm sure they will be feeling as flat as we are.'

'Have you taken a house?' Nancy asked.

'No. Philip says we may visit his parents in Sussex. They have a place called Plaw Hatch Hall. Try saying that after one too many.'

'Well, aren't you lucky?' Nancy said, with her sly malice. 'A month of playing daughter-in-law.'

'Sounds dreadful,' Diana said. 'How will you stand it?'

'Violet will come with us. Victor will be at Brougham Hall but Violet says Cumberland is too far, so she will stay in London and plan her wedding, and visit us.'

'Too far? From what?' Nancy asked. 'Not too far from Victor, one supposes?' She and Diana looked at each other – sometimes Oonagh thought they were telepathic, those sisters, more so even than she was with Maureen or Aileen – and then at Oonagh.

'What?' she demanded.

'Nothing,' Diana said.

'Not a single solitary thing,' Nancy agreed, looking a sly challenge at Oonagh, who held her gaze for a moment, wondering would she dare insist on an answer, then turned away.

'Tilt your chin down a little, Oonagh,' de László said then. 'We need to see those wonderful eyes, darling. And do stop talking.'

Chapter Thirteen

Plaw Hatch Hall, Sussex

The first Friday-to-Monday at Plaw Hatch Hall happened a week later. Philip drove, with Oonagh beside him and Violet in the back. Kathleen followed with Gay and the luggage. Nanny was left at home. 'She'll be coals to Newcastle,' Philip said. 'Mother will adore looking after Gay.'

They chattered and gossiped as they drove, lush fields flashing past, occasionally singing along to songs that came on Philip's new car radio. Oonagh thought how jolly it was, the three of them together like that. Violet was at her most charming, laughing at everything Oonagh said, reminding her of small but pleasant triumphs – 'Do you remember that time at the Café de Paris when the Belgian count . . .' and admiring everything that caught her eye – 'Lovely brooch, darling. Cartier?' – but without the needling tone she sometimes had. Philip looked approvingly from one to the other, laughing at every joke and saying, 'Capital idea!' to everything they proposed, no matter how absurd. Oonagh wished Nancy and Diana could have seen them then – how well they all did together, how happy they were, the three of them.

Plaw Hatch was an untidy house that Philip described as Arts and Crafts, which seemed to mean a lot of small rooms with small windows, even smaller windowpanes, and too much woodwork. 'It looks like it's made of gingerbread,' Oonagh said, as they drove up to it. 'Like I could snap off a windowsill and eat it.' She laughed. Philip did not. Violet, who had first smiled at Oonagh's observation, saw Philip's face and stopped.

The house had windows and chimneys everywhere, the former small and the latter tall. And pointed roofs all set at a right angle so that the house seemed to double back protectively on itself, like a sleeping dog curled up to guard its flank. The front door was in a jutting-out bit that would have been the muzzle if it were indeed a dog, so that walking through it, Oonagh thought, was like entering the dog's mouth.

A butler stood in the doorway and looked over all their heads as he announced, 'Sir Robert and Lady Kindersley are in the morning room.'

'Very good, Thompson,' Philip said, and then, 'I can find my way,' irritably when Thompson turned to lead them into the house.

The morning room was darker than Oonagh had expected for such a bright day – the many small panes of thick glass that made up each window seeming to repel the sunlight rather than allow it in.

Sir Robert and Lady Kindersley – Gladys, as she

insisted Oonagh call her – welcomed them from two high-backed armchairs on either side of a yawning empty grate. Over tea and shortbread biscuits, Sir Robert talked about his National Savings Committee and how tough he'd had it as a boy when his father had lost his money and had to take him out of school. 'It was the making of me,' he said repeatedly, 'the making of me.' He stirred his tea aggressively. When Philip failed to respond beyond a vague 'Was it?' Sir Robert showed his displeasure by mocking the lack of hardship in his son's life: 'You've had it too easy,' he said. 'You and Dickie.' At the mention of her favourite son, his wife's head whipped up and she looked eagerly around. But Sir Robert ignored her. 'Far too easy,' he continued. 'Silver spoon, what? That's my fault, of course,' he continued, but not as though he meant it, rather as though he believed it was Philip's own fault. Oonagh, at first bored, began to feel rather sorry for Philip. What, she wondered, was he supposed to say? That, yes, he was spoiled, a ruined person? It hardly seemed fair. Dickie – 'Daring Dick' as they called him, Philip's younger brother – was certainly rash and excitable, perhaps a little spoiled, but Philip?

'If anything, I find Philip too conscientious,' she said loyally.

'Conscientious?' Sir Robert said. 'About what?'

'Well, his job,' Oonagh said, thinking of Philip's long hours at the office. Beside her, on the ugly shell-shaped sofa, he shifted uncomfortably and placed a hand over hers to bid her be quiet. Perhaps he was embarrassed to have his wife defend him, she thought.

'Conscientious!' Sir Robert said again, but quietly this time, looking at Philip from under his heavy brows.

'Oh, yes,' Violet chipped in, 'he's deeply serious about things that *matter*,' and she smiled around at them all. Philip, Oonagh noticed, was properly blushing now.

Gladys, meanwhile, was good and sensible, and asked questions constantly without listening to the answers, so that after half an hour in her company, Oonagh wanted to scream.

Nancy was right, Oonagh soon decided. Gladys – indeed the entire house, and Philip, while they were there – seemed determined to treat her not as a wife and a mother and a Guinness, but as a daughter-in-law and scarcely a grown-up. Someone to be indulged and ignored, whose oddities might be pointed out and criticised or laughed over. One of these oddities was her devotion to Gay, and another was the friendship with Kathleen.

'I suppose it's from being brought up in Ireland,' Gladys said crossly. 'This confusion over people and where they belong. Valsie, I understand – I've put her in the Chinese bedroom.' She looked approvingly to where Violet was talking gaily to Sir Robert. 'But Kathleen, I do not. Is she someone who sleeps beside the nursery, or a friend who has a bedroom close to yours?'

'By the nursery, please. That way she can listen out for Gay.'

'Very well,' Gladys said, and thereafter clearly filed Kathleen away under the heading of nurserymaid, because no sooner had she and Gay arrived, an hour after Oonagh, and Gladys had kissed her grandson and queried whether he was looking 'a bit peaky', she said, 'Perhaps Kathleen would like to take Gay to the nursery.' She showed few signs of 'adoring' to look after him, Oonagh thought.

'She can take him in a moment,' Oonagh said. 'I'll go with them when I've finished my tea.'

'And in the meantime, Thompson would be happy to show Kathleen up to the nursery,' Gladys said again.

Immediately Kathleen stood up and said, 'Yes, of course,' scooping Gay from Oonagh's arms.

Later, one of Philip's sisters arrived with her children, and they were swiftly given to Kathleen too. 'Sorry,' Oonagh muttered, when they crossed on an upstairs landing. 'I didn't . . . I don't . . .' She shrugged. 'I didn't expect this.'

'It's nothing,' Kathleen said reassuringly. 'Truly, I don't mind.'

'No, but I mind for you,' Oonagh said. 'Only I don't know what to do. It isn't my house . . .' She sounded feeble, she knew, but other than make a scene, she didn't know what she could do. 'If only Maureen were here,' she said. 'She is so very good at standing up to people. She never minds a row.'

'And you do,' Kathleen said. 'About as much as other people mind some deadly disease.' She smiled and Oonagh smiled back, but she twisted her hands in nervous indecision until Kathleen had to tell her firmly, 'Go down, Oonagh. I'm perfectly all right.'

Downstairs the house was quiet, even sluggish, like a silted-up stream, Oonagh thought. Philip flicked through a newspaper, then stared out of the window, and seemed to find the whole thing as dull as she did. Oonagh wondered why he had insisted they come. But then he stood and said he would go out riding. 'Will you join me?'

Oonagh, who disliked riding and was looking forward to a cosy chat with Violet, said no and was about to suggest she and Violet take a turn about the gardens, when Violet said, 'I'll come. May I?' as though she was a child asking to go on a treat.

'Of course,' Philip said. 'We might even try a spot of fishing later.'

'I don't know why you stay indoors, Oonagh,' Violet said brightly, 'when there is so much to be done outside.'

'If you like killing things or charging about on horse-back,' Oonagh said, but she said it quietly. She wished Violet didn't always feel she needed to exert herself to be pleasant and placating. She knew that she was a coward about rows, but at least she didn't feel, as Violet did, that everyone must be charmed by her. It was, Oonagh thought, a habit left over from their younger years, when Violet had been so much in the house at Grosvenor Place. She had been a favourite with Gunnie but less so with Maureen – who declared her 'sly' – and Aileen and Cloé, who both ignored her. She had learned, then, Oonagh thought, to be always diplomatic, never rising to Maureen's barbs or Aileen's dismissal, instead rushing to smooth the way if a disagreement threatened to break out. And she did it now with Philip, jumping in if it ever seemed he might feel wounded or neglected, coaxing him into a better humour and jollying him if he became gruff. It was both useful, and irritating, she thought.

Oonagh longed to tell her to be less busy about such things, but now was not the right time. Instead she helped Violet get ready, lending her a tweed jacket – 'It's warmer than yours' – and waving them off as they rode out.

Late that afternoon, Kathleen did join them, when the children were brought down to the drawing room and made to sit quietly under her watch. This was a large room where the small windows didn't matter so much once the curtains were drawn and a good fire was going. Light flickered like a grin, bouncing off the engraved silver tea set and highly polished tray so that flecks danced on the rather low panelled ceiling. The children sat quietly with picture books and even Gay was still, dozing in Kathleen's arms, tired after playing with his cousins all afternoon. Violet and Philip came back, both smelling of wet leaves and the smoke from bonfires. Violet threw herself into an armchair and said how exhausted she was and how a night of dancing in town was 'nothing so tiring as a day out on a horse'.

'The woods will need to be thinned before next season,' Philip said, waving away his mother's offer of a teacup and pouring gin into a glass. He added a twist of lemon, ice and a splash of soda – a small splash – and handed it to Violet. 'The trees are so thick there is no getting through at some points. Violet and I had to force our way at times. Drink, Oonagh?'

'Not yet,' Oonagh said. 'I must take Gay up for his bath.'

'Surely you don't mean to bathe him yourself,' Violet said, 'when Kathleen and the maids are here to do just that?'

She sounded, Oonagh thought, just like Philip's mother. 'I always give him his bath,' Oonagh said. 'You know that.'

'Valsie is right,' Gladys said. 'It's unnecessary when there is a household of people here to do it for you.'

'But I like to,' Oonagh said. There was a pleading note in her voice that mortified her – why could she not throw down her words like a gauntlet, as Maureen would?

'Wrong time of year for thinning,' Sir Robert said, taking a pipe from his mouth and blowing out a cloud of thick blue smoke as though he were a chimney not properly swept. 'Have to wait a few months.' Oonagh hoped his late response to Philip's remark would allow the bathing of Gay, and her part in it, to be left behind. But Violet made sure it wasn't.

'Goodness, you are modern, Oonagh,' she said, with a little laugh. 'Next you'll be wanting to bring the child everywhere with you, as though he were a companion. Or a dog.'

'It's a piece of foolishness,' Gladys said confidently. 'One of these new notions. It's not good for the child, you know. He needs to grow up strong and manly, and you'll spoil his chances if you allow yourself to mollycoddle him. Philip, don't you agree? You don't wish to see your son spoiled, I suppose?'

And Philip, who never actually interfered with anything Oonagh wished to do with Gay beyond saying,

'Must you dote so excessively?', looked harassed and said, 'Indeed, Oonagh. You're perfectly silly about the boy. Let someone else bathe him.'

Oonagh looked desperately at Kathleen, who said, 'I'll do it,' quickly, so that Oonagh gave her a grateful look.

'What a monstrous to-do you do make of it all, Oonagh,' Violet said then, with an exaggerated yawn. 'You'd swear you were the only person ever to have a child. Why, the rest of our acquaintance seem to manage it with perfect ease.' She said this with a smile and a rise of her sharply arched eyebrows that she may have intended to seem fond, but she could not entirely hide the flicker of spite in her words. And perhaps even she heard it, because she moved closer to Oonagh then and said placatingly, 'But tell me now about the portrait. How does it progress?'

And Oonagh, rather than snapping at her, let Violet sit down beside her, and took the drink Philip handed her, and clinked it with the one Violet held out. She smiled as Violet said, 'Bottoms up, darling,' and clinked back and even told her a little about the sessions with de László. And then, as soon as everyone's attention was elsewhere, she slipped out and made it upstairs in time to catch the end of Gay's bathtime.

'I know you say she used to be a sweet person,' Kathleen, ever blunt, said as they knelt together in front of the porcelain baby bath, 'but it seems to me she likes to make mischief.'

'She's just nervous about her wedding,' Oonagh said, determined to be loyal. 'Also, she cannot be expected to understand. She is not yet married, not yet a mother.' She poured water gently over Gay's head, careful to avoid his eyes, and rubbed sweet-smelling shampoo gently into his scalp. 'When she has a husband and a baby of her own, she'll settle down. It's a terrible time in a girl's life, when you're grown-up but not married. I remember it well.'

'Is it?' Kathleen said quizzically, so that Oonagh looked at her and laughed.

'Not in your life, of course. But you're different from the rest of us, Kathleen.'

Chapter Fourteen

London, Autumn 1930

Watching Oonagh's small humiliation – her relegation to a lowly place within the Kindersley household – Kathleen felt sorry for her. But she couldn't help rejoicing when Oonagh began to leave her behind in London when they went to Sussex. It meant she could, at last, explore the market Ned had spoken of.

They met at Piccadilly Circus on a dirty cold Tuesday morning that already spoke of autumn although it was only September. It was the first time they had met without Mary, and Kathleen wondered would he feel strange, as she did. But he didn't seem to.

'How was the Tube?' he said, coming up behind her.

'I still dislike it,' Kathleen said, surprised and pleased that he remembered, 'but I'm learning to be less afraid. Or at least to show my fear less.'

'It's not a horse,' Ned said with a laugh. 'It makes no difference to the Tube whether you're afraid or not.

Now, come along, and I hope you're hungry.' He took her hand in his – she was surprised at how rough it was, then surprised at her surprise: had she so quickly forgotten that most hands were worn and calloused from work? – and pulled her towards him.

The first sign they had come close to the market was the birds circling overhead. They were not like the city birds Kathleen was familiar with – the sparrows, thrushes and blackbirds of the Rutland Gate gardens. They were larger, dirtier creatures with ragged wings and arrogant heads – ravens, crows, even gulls, although they were far from the sea. They wheeled about overhead, calling loud and harsh. 'Why so many?' she asked.

'Leftovers,' Ned said. 'Scraps. More birds come every week, and they grow more aggressive. I've seen one fight a child for a spoiled bit of meat. The child won, but only just.'

'Do the children really fight for scraps?'

'So doggedly there can be no doubt how badly they need them.'

Closer to, the birds' cries were drowned out by the shouts of traders so that Kathleen felt they might walk around the corner and into a wall of noise, and then they were in Berwick Street. There were stalls that sat close to each other, side by side in rows as far along as she could see. They were positioned under shop awnings that stretched out into the centre of the road, each one almost meeting the awning of the shop opposite so that it was nearly a covered market, with only thin gaps between the brightly coloured sheets of canvas. Waves of people pushed up and down between the stalls, weaving in and out and around, calling to each other. Beside where she and Ned stood on the corner a stall was selling flowers, bunches wrapped in waxy white paper. On its other side there was a stall for meat and she wondered how the flower owner could bear to have his wares tainted by a smell of blood that was like rust. Across the way, a man with oranges heaped into piles like fat gold coins was shouting, 'A wine glass of juice in every orange,' which made Ned laugh. 'He pumps them full of water every morning,' he said. 'He has a physician's syringe to do it with.'

Kathleen didn't know if it was the din, or that there was nowhere to hide from all the things on display, but somehow even the grimy light seemed too intense, and she found she was screwing up her eyes against the glare and the chaos. By turning her head only slightly this way and that, she could see stalls offering jugs of milk, bolts of cloth, strange, ungainly fish that lolled accusingly, eggs, glassware, highly polished brass lamps, saucepans so big you could have bathed a baby in them, knife grinders and a shoe mender. Foods she didn't recognise, bowls of spices that made her wrinkle her nose because she couldn't tell if the unfamiliar smells were enticing or disgusting, and raw sounds made by the cries and calls of the stallholders who seemed more determined to outdo each other in pitch than to say clearly what it was they had and did.

'What language are they speaking?' she asked Ned.

'Many languages,' he said, taking her basket,

switching it to his other hand and taking hold of her arm. Immediately she felt reassured by the warmth through the cloth of her coat. 'There are people here from Russia, from Poland, from many countries in the eastern part of Europe, as well as those from this corner of London.'

Russia. Poland. Kathleen could see these countries on the map when she called it to mind, but she found she knew nothing useful about them, except that they were large – very large – and far away.

In the window of some of the shops, men sat cross-legged on the floor with tape measures around their necks, as though they were mannequins, except they nodded and smiled at passers-by. One, who had a thin sprinkling of teeth, grinned and waved at Ned as they passed. 'Tailors,' Ned said. 'Blessed with great talent. If you ever need something made, Kathleen, tell me, and I will bring you to the very best among them.'

They walked all the way to the end, and gradually Kathleen relaxed her hold on Ned's hand, which was still tucked through her arm. She grew easier with the strangeness, the noise, the heat of so many pressed close together, the unfamiliar foods on display and the smells that lurched from good – warm bread, cinnamon – to bad – blood-drenched sawdust, partly cured leather – and back again. As she settled and began to feel less overwhelmed, what she noticed most was not the new things around her, but Ned, and how he was. Instead of being wary of it all as she was, he was giddy with it. He called a greeting to a bearded man who had old books for sale, and waved at a woman in the window of a fabric shop. Others clapped him on the back or shoulder as they walked by, and every place they stopped – 'Because you must try this, Kathleen . . . and this,' giving her pieces of meat, cured fish, cheese – the people at the stalls knew him and had a smile or a kind word.

'You are so at home here,' Kathleen said in wonder.

'These are my neighbours,' he said. 'Many of them are as new to London as I am, or only a little less so. They came from countries that will no longer welcome them, and hope to make a way for themselves, a life for their families, just as I do. Many are running from religious persecution because they are Jewish, and somehow we have all ended up here, together, in this square mile of London. We live so close, almost one on top of another, so that it is not possible we are not friends. It is a bond, of necessity first, but of fondness too.'

Kathleen knew herself to be brave and curious – she'd been told so often enough – but Ned outdid her by far. He seemed to feel no terror of this newness, only interest. 'Weren't you afraid of them all, in the beginning? Even a little?'

'More interested than afraid. Curious, I suppose. Everyone at home in Dún Laoghaire was so familiar – I knew them all as well as I know myself. The look, the sound, even the smell of them, and how that varied from the Sunday when they had a bath, to the Friday when they went to church with a dirty collar and hoped no one would notice.' He ran his finger reflexively around the inside of his own collar. It was, Kathleen saw, worn but clean. 'I knew their days, their plans. Even the secret things they wouldn't tell were always the same secret things: the ones who liked a drink more than they should, who spent the money they earned on the dogs rather than their children, who were sick with envy of a friend's good fortune, or had a yearning for a wife who wasn't theirs. Even the hidden contents of their hearts were no mystery to me. Here, it's all new. These people think in a different language from us, and I like that. Even what should be familiar here is different. Like that.'

He pointed to the pavement across the street and Kathleen saw scribbles in thick white chalk on the uneven flagstones. Ned crossed and bent to look closely at them.

'Got it,' he said. 'Back of Truman's pub, tomorrow, eight p.m.'

'What?' Kathleen asked.

'A meeting,' Ned said.

'Of whom?'

'British Communist Party,'

'What are they?'

'People who believe in equality, decency, dignity, a fair wage, an end to colonialism,' Ned said. 'In other words, all the obvious things that somehow aren't obvious to everyone.'

'Are they like those who fought for independence at home?' Kathleen asked, trying to fit what Ned told her into what she knew, remembering the men with revolvers who would sometimes spill onto the streets of Dublin, the sound of their boots on the cobblestones as they ran from the policemen who pursued them. And the children who would run behind again, fingers cocked like guns, playing at being IRA. Then had come the years where the men, instead of fighting the British, fought each other, and even the children had split so that angry shouts of 'De Valera' battled with 'Michael Collins' over the cocked fingers.

'Sometimes. Not exactly,' Ned said. 'Though those at home would have been the better for a bit more Communism and a lot less Church.' Kathleen was shocked at what he said. One thing not to go to mass – she didn't go much any more, not since the Sisters – but quite another to speak against the Church. She didn't say what she thought. 'And the chalked scribbles?' she asked instead.

'It's how they tell us about meetings: chalk on pavements and walls with the details. It's cheaper and faster than printing leaflets, more reliable than word of mouth, and more secret.'

'It's written in the middle of the street,' Kathleen said, laughing. 'How can it be secret?'

'Only those of us who know, the Comrades, will be able to read them. The rest of the world walks past and sees nothing. Except those who hate us, who will try to work out what the signs mean so as to come and break up the meetings.' His excitement seemed to be as much at the concealment and cunning – maybe even the chance of a fight – as the meeting itself.

'Who are the Comrades?' Kathleen asked.

'I'll tell you all about them,' Ned said, 'but not now because I'm late for work. Afternoon shift. I've the SS

Clareisland to unload. A Guinness ship,' he said, with a wink at her. 'I'll walk you back to the Tube.'

'And those?' She pointed to the jug of eggs he carried, a dozen, given by a man at a stall that had a sign saying, 'Bick's Eggs'. Many were broken, spilling their insides so that the unbroken sat unpleasantly on a mess of yolk and slimy white, but Ned carried them carefully, quite as if they were whole.

'I'll leave them on the doorstep. No one will take them when they can buy Bick's Eggs themselves for half nothing.'

'What will you do with them?' she asked, as they walked.

'Pour in some brandy and drink them.' It sounded disgusting.

'You could make an omelette,' she said. 'They're easy.'

'How?' He turned eagerly towards her.

'Shell them all. Add a splash of milk and salt and beat. Put a bit of butter in a pan and when it foams up hot pour in the beaten eggs.' She described the swirling of the mixture to him, so that he nodded thoughtfully, and how to tell when the omelette was cooked enough underneath.

He listened carefully. 'Thank you,' he said, when they arrived at the station. He gave her the jug to hold for a moment while he buttoned his coat. She looked back towards Berwick Street. The birds were fewer now, and plunged with less intensity. The market must be packing up. Perhaps they would go with Ned, she thought, to the unloading of the SS *Clareisland* that had sailed from Ireland right into the heart of the city, and throw themselves with beady ferocity at the bits that fell from boats or washed up against the greasy docks. She liked that they, like Ned, had a pattern and a purpose to their days.

'I'll see you soon,' Ned said, and touched her lightly on the cheek with his hand.

Chapter Fifteen

Clandeboye, Co. Down

The train from Belfast pulled into Helen's Bay, where a small brick station house was dwarfed by the extravagant turret that rose above it. Set against the bare winter branches, it was exposed and grandiose, and forlorn in the way such things often were, Maureen reflected; the idiocy of man's vanity exposed by the fastidiousness of Nature's retreat.

She sighed. She had anticipated this visit for so long – and had always imagined it as short: a swift, energetic swooping down, a few days of being shown around and taking the measure of the place, then a flurry of goodbyes. After which she could retreat to her London life, her proper life, as she thought of it. She had imagined coming here as a daughter-in-law, almost a casual guest. Instead, she was now mistress of the place.

'How long will we stay?' she had asked Duff, as they planned the journey.

'It's our home now,' he had said and then, 'I'm sorry,

I know this isn't what you expected,' so that she had felt obliged to reassure him that she was thrilled, squashing down her apprehension even as it rose, rancid, inside her – *what was she to do, so far from everywhere and everyone? What did people do, when they lived on such estates?* She had never really thought about it, believing she had years in which to find out. And when he offered to have Lady Brenda moved to a smaller house on the estate she had said, 'No, please don't. I'm sure there's space for all of us,' and was rewarded by the relief in his face.

The platform was empty and the train stopped with a lurch before Duff got up and began to gather his hat and coat. 'Shouldn't we hurry?' Maureen said, watching him slowly fold a newspaper.

'No need,' he said. 'The driver knows we're aboard and will wait until we have alighted.'

'The master has returned home,' Maureen said with a grin.

'Yes,' he agreed, but solemnly. 'If I'd permitted it, all the tenants would have been here to greet us. It's my first time returning as marquess. Perhaps I should have allowed the fuss,' he said thoughtfully.

'Well, I'm surprised not to see a double row of house servants in livery, at the very least, to hail your new bride.'

'I thought of it,' he said, taking her mink coat and draping it, dark and glossy, over his arm, 'but I know how much you hate that sort of thing.' He grinned. He knew well how much she loved that sort of thing. 'Truth be told, I doubt any of them has livery any more.

Nothing the moths haven't got at anyway. I warn you, darling, this isn't what you've been used to. Clandeboye is a pretty wild place for someone raised in comfort like you.'

Maureen thought of all the ways she had heard Clandeboye described – *a museum or barracks, where the butler and footmen wear wellingtons in the house because it's so damp*, according to Oonagh; *a great baronial barn of a place*, Waugh had called it; even Duff referred to it as *that vast place*, and *a millstone* around his father's neck. Well, whatever poky ruin it might be, she was able for it.

'You've already warned me of that,' she said patiently, as they stood on the empty platform watching the stationmaster hand down the carefully lined basket in which the dogs had travelled. 'Several times. And I'm not such a hothouse creature as you think. Why, all those nights in the jungle in India, and did I ever complain?'

'You slept in a silken tent and were served off silver plates. What was there to complain about?' He laughed.

'I do hope they weren't too sick, poor darlings,' Maureen said, as the basket was brought towards them. It juddered and twitched and she could hear the dogs yapping inside.

'You're welcome back, m'lord.' A man in a cloth cap approached them, bobbing in a way that was not quite a bow but seemed to want to be. His accent was thick but his words, with a singsong lilt, were clear enough.

'Tommy. Very good to see you.' Duff put a hand out and clasped the other man's, squeezing it tight. Tommy's was large and square with thick gnarled fingers, yet Duff's, Maureen saw, did not disappear entirely into it. She was glad of that.

'This way,' Tommy said. He led them into the station house, through what Duff said was a private waiting room for the family and guests of Clandeboye, and along a short tunnel to where a fat pony and an old-fashioned carriage waited. The Dufferin and Ava arms were carved on the carriage door, but almost buried under a thick coat of yellow varnish so that Maureen could only just make out the eagles and lion passant.

'How very feudal you are,' she said, as Duff helped her in.

'The avenue is too narrow and overgrown for a car,' he said, settling first the dog basket, then himself beside her. Tommy clicked to the pony and they set off down a narrow lane with high grassy banks on either side so that she could see nothing except tattered autumn greenery. 'This is the family's private road.' They drove under a thick stone bridge with another coat of arms carved deep into it, then out onto a broader sweep of parkland.

Suddenly the house was visible in front of them. It was bigger by far than Glenmaroon, Maureen saw. She counted ten large windows across and the same again above them, with a great many chimney stacks. It sat comfortably in a wide expanse of smooth lawn; trees had been cut back all around the front of the house but allowed to mass behind so that it seemed to lean into that deep green embrace.

'Ah, Clandeboye! "Thy friendly floor/Slieve-Donnard's

oak shall light no more,"' Duff quoted mockingly. 'Though the floor is vastly less friendly than it was.'

'What?'

'Sir Walter Scott wrote it. And he wasn't the only one. Tennyson had a go too:

> *'Helen's Tower, here I stand,*
> *Dominant over sea and land.*
> *Son's love built me, and I hold*
> *Mother's love in letter'd gold.'*

'Rather sick-making isn't it?' She made a face.

'Utterly,' he grinned, 'but I say that only to you!'

Instead of drawing up to the front of the house, the trap continued around to the rear. 'The servants' entrance?' Maureen said. But the carriage stopped before a hefty door of plain wood, set into a low blank wall painted a dull red. A butler in dusty black opened it, nodding in a deep incline and said, 'Welcome.' Maureen, conscious of Duff just behind her, walked through the door, up four broad and shallow stone steps into a large hall, and began to laugh.

'Not the servants' entrance I see,' she said, looking around. And then, with a loud laugh that echoed, 'More like the nursery or playroom of a particularly bloodthirsty child.' By the door to her left a rhinoceros head was mounted on a stone block, its two horns raised to the roof in an expression of agony. On the other side of the door, a giant iron bell stood by a telescope poised delicately on its stand, while above, on the wall on either side, swords were fanned out in violent sun shapes. Ahead, a pair of red velvet curtains led deeper into the house and were held apart by two baby bears, stuffed and set upon their hind feet, each holding a silver salver in its paws, as though proffering, or begging. Through them she could see, further on again, above a staircase that climbed into mystery, a vast stained-glass window that cast blobs of yellow, pink and blue light down on the preposterous collection of objects.

She turned slowly about, looking around her, sometimes breaking into another laugh. There were weapons everywhere, pieces of artillery mounted and set in angular designs against the walls. Pikes, axes, cruelly curved swords and daggers, muskets and pistols. On the floor lay a tiger-skin rug, the beast's head yearning towards the two standing bears as though it would crawl up to them to beg for companionship in that strange room.

Around and about stood Indian and Burmese celestial figures, including a meek-looking Buddha, side by side with classical statues. Chess sets jostled with bowls made of china, silver and copper that were placed on top of cabinets and sideboards, and everywhere were chairs. Chairs with squat, stout arms and chunky, curved legs; chairs with delicate, spindly backs; chairs with embroidered seat covers and scratched leather arm rests. Looking sternly down on all of this glorious cacophony of objects was a large portrait of a man in brilliant scarlet robes.

'Grandfather Frederick, I presume?' she said, pretending to curtsey.

'Indeed. The first marquess, Viceroy of India and

friend of Queen Victoria,' Duff said. 'He's responsible for all this . . .' and swept out an arm that seemed dismissive and admiring at once. 'Manning, we'll have tea in the Georgian drawing room.' And he set off, through the red velvet curtains, past the staircase and along a corridor panelled in dark wood with a thin strip of red carpet running along the centre of a dark wood floor, like a tongue through a toothless mouth, Maureen thought, as she followed him, the dogs nervous and close at her heels.

They passed rooms, some with open doors so she could see into them. A study, a library entirely walled with books, a billiards room. As they walked, the house shifted around them, progressing in ornamentation so that after a while they were no longer in a cabinet of curiosities, but rather in a more conventional country house, like Glenmaroon or any of the many houses of Maureen's friends, large, filled with comfortable if shabby furniture taking advantage of various pretty views. It was, she thought, like travelling miles and years in just a few steps.

The 'Georgian drawing room' turned out to be a large room facing the direction they had travelled – she could make out the station turret – with a fine view over the parkland. Maureen flopped onto a dusty pink sofa and looked around. The dogs piled onto her lap, squeezing close for comfort in that strange place. 'Home at last,' she said, with a touch of irony, taking in the stained carpet and scuffed furniture. She looked out through the many-paned glass doors to where evening was pressing hard on the afternoon, consuming the parkland in steady gulps. This was the time, she thought, when streetlights would come on in London and the city swapped the broad glow of the day for the hard dazzle of night. Not here, though. As dusk fell, it simply blotted what was before it, so that soon, she saw, there would be nothing but the gathering black pressing up against the windows. There were no lights to be seen. No town or hamlet to gleam brightly, not even the twinkle of lamplight in a cottage, or lantern over a stable door. It might, she thought, with a shudder, have been the very last house in all the world. She turned towards the fire, a poor thing, and poked at it to stir some semblance of life.

Manning arrived then and Duff said, 'Have you seen Lady Brenda?'

'Not recently, m'lord,' Manning said.

'I see. Well, we won't wait. But do bring an extra cup.'

'Who's that?' Maureen asked, when he had gone, pointing to a portrait of a lady with clever, amusing eyes and a mouth set against the laugh that looked ready to escape it.

'Helen Sheridan. My great-grandmother.'

'Helen's Bay, the railway station?'

'Yes, and Helen's Tower. And there's another Helen's Bay, an actual sea bay, by the beach. Sometimes I think the whole house is Helen's still.'

'So what did she do?'

'Crashed into a long line of incredibly dull Blackwoods and changed them for ever.' Duff settled himself in an armchair opposite her, and Maureen took a moment to delight in this, the very first time they had sat as husband and wife in a place that was to be their home. It was too soon by far, but still. She looked around at the parade of Blackwoods and nodded solemnly.

'Until Helen,' Duff continued, 'generations of them wanted nothing more than a house to shelter them from the cold northern winds after a day's hunting, and to entertain their neighbours a few times a year with dishes of mutton or pheasant.' He pointed upwards to the portraits that hung about. Frugal-looking ladies in mob caps, canny men in ruffs with ramrod posture. 'Then, after generations of pleasant dullness, one of them, Price Blackwood, took a strange fancy and brought home this most unusual bride, Helen, granddaughter of Richard Brinsley Sheridan.'

'The playwright?'

'Precisely.' He steepled his fingers together with mock-pomposity. 'Helen had one child only, Frederick, and raised him for greatness. And, in the doing, destroyed the family appetite for pleasant dullness for ever.'

'Which is why you've married me.' Maureen got up from the dusty pink sofa to perch on the arm of his chair.

'It is.' He smiled.

She smiled back and he leaned forward to kiss her. She held herself perfectly still in anticipation, waiting for the press of his lips. But before his mouth touched hers, a second door at the far end of the room opened and through it came someone Maureen took at first to be a child: tiny, with hair teased into long ringlets that hung about her pale face, wearing a white satin dress and grubby white satin slippers. She came in on a kind of pirouette and rushed forward to where they sat, stopping short, like a startled woodland creature. Maureen got up from the arm of Duff's chair, and the figure swayed towards her, reaching for one of her hands and pressing it.

'Welcome,' she trilled. 'Welcome.' Only up close did Maureen see that her face, under a thick dusting of white powder, lips drawn on shakily in red, was not that of a child but of a woman in middle age. It was Duff's mother. Lady Brenda. Maureen remembered her from the wedding, but had paid scant attention at the time to the tiny woman clutching her husband's arm. Now, she looked closely. And saw that behind the blank questioning of the round blue eyes ran a tremor of fear.

Maureen said something about being glad to be there and Lady Brenda released her hand and turned to Duff.

'Mother,' he said, getting up so that he towered above the tiny figure. She stepped lightly out from under him, as though he had cast a shadow that blocked her warmth, and said, 'So you are come at last.'

'I am sorry, Mother,' he said, 'not to have been here sooner. You understand, I'm sure. It was too far, and we were not found in time. Maureen's father had a job to track us down at all.'

'Your father would have wanted to see you,' Lady Brenda said.

'He would have wanted us at the funeral,' Duff corrected her, with a note of pedantry in his voice that Maureen hadn't heard before.

'I suppose you won't stay long?' Lady Brenda said

brightly, looking about her as though ready to hand Duff his hat.

'We'll be back and forth a great deal between here and London, Mother,' Duff said, with the same heavy note of pedantry.

'Well, I don't suppose we shall trouble each other much,' Lady Brenda said. 'I'll stay out of your way and you'll stay out of mine.' She sang it almost, in a nursery-rhyme voice, then went to perch on the edge of a hard chair near the wall.

Tea arrived and it was cold, so Maureen sent Manning back for hot water. 'Won't you wait?' she asked, as Duff poured himself a cup anyway.

'Hardly worth it,' he said, passing a cup to his mother.

Maureen took a sandwich from a pink-and-white willow-patterned plate. The bread was thicker cut than she was used to, and denser than London bread, but the sandwich – cucumber with some herb that might have been chive but was more lemony – was delicious. Duff must have seen the surprise on her face because he said, 'Anything cold is all right. It's hot food that's impossible. Miles to the kitchens, and no one at all used to hurrying any longer. There is, I tell you, a great deal to be done.'

'I think I'm beginning to understand,' Maureen said, looking about the tired, scruffy room.

'Until you have seen the bedrooms and tried to have a bath, you cannot possibly,' Duff said wearily.

Brenda nibbled daintily at a Florentine biscuit, looking around her with the alert, pleased air of a child at an amusement. After a few bites, she cocked her head, as though listening to something far away, put the biscuit down and went back out through the far door.

'Not one of her good days,' Duff said. Maureen watched her go, then picked up one of the little dogs and hugged it close to her, suddenly wanting the comfort of its warm, familiar body.

'Does she have good days?' she asked.

'Yes. Though not many.'

'At least my mother, in her peculiar moments, shuts herself away in her own rooms and fusses with Gunnie about food.' She kissed the little dog on the nose and it stuck out a pink tongue to lick her mouth, and whether it was the journey, the neglected chill in the air of Clandeboye, the dwindling light or the strange exchange with her mother-in-law, Maureen, who never cried, felt, just then, a little like crying. *You're tired from the journey*, she told herself sternly, even though journeys never tired her.

Chapter Sixteen

Maureen soon discovered that Duff was perfectly correct when he had said she couldn't understand the privations of Clandeboye until she had seen the bedrooms and tried to have a bath. Within weeks of their arrival, she knew a great deal more. The weather turned much colder, and the limitations of the house grew stark around her. Although her money had already installed a new heating system while she and Duff had been away, it turned out not to be equal to the vast and labyrinthine demands of Clandeboye. Outside, the trees shook themselves free of the final clinging wisps of leaf and stood, bleak and bare, against skies that were more bleached of colour than any she had seen before. And where in London and Dublin, Maureen had always felt as though there was an inch, a minute, a pane of glass between her and the weather, here it was the opposite. Weather prowled around the house and scratched at the doors and windows. Rain rotted the frames, sun blistered the wood, and wind shook the panes as though it had sworn it would get inside. It felt personal, and as she lay in bed at night, listening to the sounds from outside, she imagined all the wind, all the rain, whipped up from every surrounding part, bundled together and hurled in fury at Clandeboye, bludgeoning the wooden shutters of her bedroom repeatedly so that at night the curtains stirred and shifted, heavy velvet though they were.

And yet, she found, she did not care. Not for the damp, the chill, the stained surfaces and mottled walls, because all this was made nothing by the joy of watching Duff in the childhood home that was now his. To hear him talk of the plans he had for it, the changes he would make, all the ways in which he would transform this unyielding pile of frigid stone into a place of comfort and delight and, best, that he would do it for her. That the money for this transformation was hers, she cared nothing – the energy and the impetus were Duff's, and his love for her. That was what mattered.

While once Maureen had decided where they would go, who they would see, what play to attend, now it was Duff who told her what to do because they were in his home, on his land. And Maureen, who hated anyone to tell her to do anything, loved it. 'Hopeless,' he said, one wet morning, looking at the shoes she had put on to walk about the parkland with him. 'You can't wear those.'

'But these are Harrods' finest.'

'And useless in the damp earth of Clandeboye. But it's no matter. There's heaps of stuff all over the place.

Help yourself to anything you find.' He was right. In between the savage, beautiful objects of Clandeboye were all the ordinary clutterings of a country life, only more abundant than she had seen them. Piles of walking sticks and wellington boots, hard hats for horse riding, and waterproofs hanging in great heaps on pegs beside the back doors. Some seemed decades old, and none looked as though it belonged to anyone in particular. Indeed, Duff simply caught up the nearest jacket and threw it over himself when he went out, so Maureen did the same, soon acquiring a store of warm, waterproof things that mostly didn't fit – Duff's family were all clearly larger than her – but were practical.

'If my friends could see me now,' she said, decked out in a heavy green Barbour and cap, 'they simply wouldn't recognise me.' She wondered at how pleased that thought made her. Whatever gloom had grabbed her on the first night at Clandeboye, she had shaken it off, finding energy in the crisp mornings and the constancy of Duff at her side.

'They would think you eminently sensible,' Duff said, taking her hand and tucking it into his own pocket.

'Pooh, your jacket smells of dog,' she said, drawing closer as they went through one of the many small side doors and out into a blustery morning.

'Everything here smells of dog,' he said. He was right. Along with Maureen's pugs there were the house dogs, spaniels and pointers mostly, gun dogs, who lay around the library and drawing rooms, getting fat, heads heavy on their paws.

'They seem so glum,' Maureen had said of them.

'Why, my little Wiggins nearly frightened one to death, and he's less than half the size.'

'They miss my father,' Duff said. He had never said he missed his father, and Maureen had never asked. He had read the telegram, which had waited well over a week for them at the Hotel Britannia in Mysore, in their bedroom with its ceiling fan going *whump whump* above their heads and the double balcony doors open to the sounds of children in the hot dust below, and handed it to her without a word. 'I'm so terribly sorry,' Maureen had said, reading the words Ernest had sent, spaced out so coldly even though she could feel his concern: FREDERICK DEAD STOP PLANE CRASH STOP CONDOLENCES STOP ERNEST STOP

'Do you want to go back?' she had asked, pushing aside her own feelings of regret. 'We could start at once.'

'There isn't any point,' he had said. 'The funeral will be long over.'

'But we could—'

'There isn't any point,' he had repeated, and had begun to talk of practical things – a letter he must send his mother, more letters he must send his bank – so that Maureen had not been able to move the conversation to a point where she could ask, 'Are you unhappy?'

But perhaps now she could, she thought. After all, it was he who had mentioned his father. She opened her mouth to speak, but— 'And they miss the hunt,' Duff continued, cutting her off. 'They aren't used to being so long without, but I haven't time to go out shooting. In the spring I'll have a shooting party and they'll cheer up.' So she didn't ask. There will be another moment, she thought.

Ever since their arrival, Maureen had explored, following the house as it turned about in unexpected ways, with strange corridors and staircases that didn't always lead where she thought they would. Even after weeks, the geography of the place defeated her, and on rainy days when Duff was busy with the estate, she sometimes explored for the sake of it, allowing herself to wander wherever the flow of rooms wished to take her. Even then, she wasn't at all certain that this did not change from day to day – a staircase that led to one part of the house seemed capable of leading somewhere else entirely a few days later.

There were rooms that looked as though no one had been into them in decades. Dust thick on the floor, windows blackened with streaks and dirt, the acrid smell of animal droppings and occasional heaps of feathers that suggested some poor bird had flown in, become trapped and died. Walls were mottled with damp and bulged in strange places. Wallpaper that appeared patterned would, on closer examination, prove to be mildewed, while some of the wooden floors were warped, and sloped in strange ways that caught at her feet as she walked across them, threatening to trip her. There were sighs and creaks and whispers in corners, always out of sight.

In fact, very soon the house appeared to her almost as a person, a living creature with prejudices and whims, even breath and heartbeat all its own. No matter what systems she tried to implement, the food never arrived hot in the dining room and there was never hot water when she wanted it so that she took to bathing at odd hours – Manning, tipped off by some mysterious means, would appear to inform her solemnly, 'There is *water*, m'lady,' and Maureen would abandon whatever she did and go straight to have a bath drawn.

Soon, she narrowed the circle of her inhabiting to a set series of rooms – the better drawing rooms downstairs, a small library on the first floor, her bedroom, the dressing room that stood between that and Duff's room. She never once ventured into the kitchens. 'You'll need a map, and a pair of galoshes,' Duff said, when she asked should she pay them a visit. 'A dictionary if you are to understand Mrs Samuels, and a thick skin indeed if you are to withstand the stares. Better deal with Manning.'

'I must appoint a housekeeper,' Maureen said, 'for clearly Manning is not up to the job.' But she didn't and, after a while, lazily, changed to 'Perhaps I can send for Kathleen,' to which Duff said, 'Certainly, if you wish.'

'If Oonagh will let her go,' Maureen said, over dinner one evening in the small drawing room. They ate at a tiny round table pulled up before the fire so that their knees bumped. Usually it was just the two of them, because Lady Brenda rarely came down, so these evenings felt, Maureen thought, cosy and intimate, like the days of nursery suppers that were, after all, not so long behind her. 'She clings to Kathleen as though she were herself a bird in an ornamental cage and Kathleen the one branch. But, then, Oonagh never could do a thing for herself.'

'And you, my darling, do far too much,' Duff said, his face warm in the firelight. 'You should rest more.'

'How feeble you must think me.'

'Hardly,' he protested. 'More ferocious than feeble.'

Those evenings, they sat long before the fire, not moving as the table was cleared around them, tarnished silver plates taken away and replaced with coffee, a decanter of brandy, bowls of nuts and sweets. She had brought a gramophone player with her from London, and would play records, the sound on low, while Duff read. They talked over India and Burma, and these nights, Maureen did not remind him of the grand stories she had told to her mother and Oonagh when they had first arrived back to London – 'They all simply worshipped us,' she had said then, 'everywhere we went, crowds of people chasing after us and calling, "*Bhavyate*", as we passed. It means "magnificence", you know.'

Instead, during evenings in Clandeboye, they spoke together of smaller moments, an elephant with its calf sighted at dawn, the colour of the sky above the jungle before the light faded entirely from it, in voices that were low because they had drawn so close together, Duff's arm about her shoulders.

And then, early – so much earlier than in London – it was time for bed and they would go up together, his hand in hers, into the dark and quiet reaches of the house. And even though he was always gone by the time she woke in the mornings, she knew that he had spent the night in her bed rather than go back to his own room, and that evening he would return to it. And because of that, she rang for tea and accepted a cold cup from Ellen, the elderly housemaid, and smiled and sang snatches of song as she dressed, knowing that when she went down, he would leave whatever he did and join her.

Aside from Ellen, and the rumbling rumours of the cook, Mrs Samuels, it was, Maureen found, a very male household. There was Manning himself, various footmen to do his bidding, men to sweep and lay fires even though that should have been a woman's work, men again in the grounds with ladders and rakes and buckets, although more often than not when she saw them they were sitting or leaning or otherwise idle.

'An estate like this requires a lot of maintenance,' Duff said, when she asked him.

'It is themselves they are maintaining,' she said, but he chose not to listen.

While the footmen did not actually wear wellingtons, as Oonagh had predicted, when Duff was not around they often appeared in pullovers. And Manning, when not in the drawing room or dining room, was to be seen in an overcoat. She could hardly blame them, Maureen thought. As the weather got colder, she slept with two extra rugs thrown over her bed. When Duff was not there – and after a while he was more in London, often for a week at a time: there was talk he would be appointed as private secretary to the under-secretary of state for India – she allowed the dogs into bed with her, thinking how horrified Cloé would be.

Without Duff, Maureen felt herself to be smaller than she was in London. When she was alone, there never seemed very much to do – games of patience, solitary walks through the leafless landscape, lonely meals. The servants, she found, rather ignored her – in a house so big, there were plenty of excuses not to have heard her bell. She felt as though she had to fight, hard, to be the equal of a place so vast and full of rooms. That she must fight, too, to be the equal of the family ghosts, who were numerous, and grand, and some still active. The spirit of the first marquess was everywhere, and his mother, Helen, was evident too, chiefly in the tower that bore her name, and could be seen, like a beacon, from every corner of the estate, but also throughout the house and even in dishes produced from the vast kitchens, recipes devised for and by her and passed from cook to cook since.

And then there was Lady Brenda, drifting about like a living ghost. She ate barely enough to stay alive, Maureen discovered, and slept fitfully. Often she kept to her room for most of the day, then emerged after dark to wander the house, a shawl about her shoulders and dirty slippers, or nothing, on her feet. She stayed away from the rooms Maureen had chosen as her own, preferring the darker, lonelier corners of the house, parts of which were so neglected as to be positively dangerous. At night, Maureen heard her humming snatches of song or muttering under her breath, punctuated by the scuffing sound her slippers made on wooden floors.

'Is it because she lost her husband?' she asked Duff, on one of his returns from London, wondering why she did not say 'your father'.

'She's always been like that,' he said. By then Maureen knew he hated to talk about his mother. 'But before, her bouts of strangeness were more predictable, and she had bouts of sanity too. Now, well, the tranquil times don't come as often. There is no one now to manage her in the way my father did.' He described how, when he was at Oxford, he would bring friends home. 'We had a secret den in the attic. We dragged up a couple of chairs, a gramophone, a rug. We had a store of apples too, and a decanter of brandy. But we had to play the gramophone very low, and be right out of her way – in case the distant sound of music led her to our den. She thinks she hears fairy gatherings, you see, and goes about looking for the Little People. Music from far away causes her to sink into a kind of enchantment, and she will keep seeking and seeking till she finds it, certain that the Little People are teasing her, likely to pop up at any moment, but not to be trusted.'

'Like a tricky kind of upper house servant,' Maureen said with a laugh.

'Yes, but frightening too. When in those moods, she is gripped by deep alarm as well as fascination.' He sounded, she thought, sad and weary. 'I used to hear her walking about, looking for us, and feel sorry that we shunned her.'

Christmas approached, and although the weather was cold, it was mostly dry and clear. On fine days they walked miles across the estate, as Duff took note of everything that needed to be done, and he marvelled at her energy, saying, 'Nothing ever tires you,' in admiration. And Maureen, who had always been told she was too loud, too boisterous by those closest to her, was happy. They would come back for a cold lunch served in the library, then read or play backgammon, and although India and Burma had been their official honeymoon, Maureen thought of those early days at Clandeboye as the real honeymoon. All the more when they ended abruptly. She began to feel tired in a way that was new to her – an exhaustion that coiled itself around her and squeezed tight so that the prospect of their long tramping walks, which she had loved so much, dismayed her.

'Is there a doctor who might call out?' she asked Duff sleepily one morning. 'I find I need a tonic prescribed. I know the one Mamma's doctor used to recommend, so he need do nothing but order the making of it.' But when the doctor came, he turned out to be a stuffy older gentleman who refused to prescribe without first asking her a great many questions and examining her.

'I can't prescribe that tonic,' he said at last. 'It wouldn't be suitable.'

'Why not?' Maureen demanded, ready as always to do battle for what she wanted.

'Because it is not suitable for women in your condition.'

'What condition?' she asked, as though he had insulted her.

'You are having a child,' he said gently. 'That's the reason for the dizziness. Have you really noticed nothing more?'

Maureen thought back. Yes, she had been a little tired, but people were often tired, or so they said. And the tears that had threatened to escape once or twice were unusual, but surely not significant. 'Nothing much. Are you sure?'

'Quite sure.'

First Duff's father dying, and the move to Clandeboye, now this. Maureen put her face in her hands. *This was not what I planned*, she wanted to say. *Not what I wanted*. But he was a doctor: she couldn't say such a thing to him. And she couldn't imagine saying it to Duff either, because he was her husband, or to Oonagh or Aileen, because they wouldn't understand. There was no one she could say it to. No one she could tell how perturbed she was, had always been, at the idea of motherhood.

It wasn't that she was afraid. That, she thought, might have been easier. It was more complicated. Brought up by Cloé, noticing with the sharp eyes of a child the various expressions that had played across Cloé's face any time she contemplated her daughters – anxiety, mistrust, apprehension, even a certain fastidious revulsion, a reflexive drawing back and away from them if they approached – had left Maureen with feelings she didn't understand but were uncomfortable. But perhaps, she thought, her own child would be different. Perhaps a boy would be different. She was certain it would be a boy.

Chapter Seventeen

Rutland Gate, London

'**O**onagh, you're not listening.'

'I'm looking at preserves,' Oonagh said. Kathleen, she knew, was trying to tell her about some sort of market in a place called Berwick Street she had been to with a friend called Ned, but Oonagh had little attention to spare. Now that Christmas was done with, there was a large birthday party to plan.

'Diana and Bryan gave a party last week, and Diana served quails' eggs dipped in celery salt,' she said thoughtfully. 'I don't see the point, so tiny they're hardly worth the effort, but everyone else seemed to think it rather wonderful. I wonder how I might outdo her. I want everyone to forget about her party entirely when they come to mine. What do you think of whole quail stuffed with foie gras?' she finished. 'Too disgusting?'

'Yes, much too disgusting,' Kathleen said snappily.

Oonagh looked sideways at her and said, 'And when

have you ever had quail stuffed with foie gras, may I ask?' with a grin, and then, 'Oh, go on, I'm listening.'

'At Berwick Street, Ned made me try salt cod and I was certain I'd hate it, but I didn't at all. And everything there was tumbled into great heaps, together, nothing like here, where each item is displayed so carefully and singly, like they're chosen to be precious, not necessary.'

'I wonder should you really be going about with Ned so much?' Oonagh asked. 'You know how people talk.'

Kathleen gave a shout of laughter that caused a woman near them, dressed in the same type of slim-fitting fur-trimmed jacket as Oonagh, to stare at them. 'About you, maybe,' Kathleen said. 'No one talks about people like me. Or if they do, it isn't in that sort of way. Why, the length of the street, in and out of all the stalls, and no one said or thought a thing except to welcome me as a friend of Ned's.'

'And are you?' Oonagh asked slyly. 'A friend of Ned's?'

'I am.'

'And is he a friend of yours?' Oonagh asked. 'Because they're not at all the same thing.'

'I believe he is.'

'Well, in that case, you may invite him to my birthday party.' She handed Kathleen her gloves and picked up a tin that she turned over and over in her hand. 'Cherries glazed with blackcurrant syrup?'

'Will Maureen come to the party?'

'Yes. She and Duff will come over from Clandeboye a few days before, the same day as Aileen. Their London house is ready now, and Maureen says she cannot spend another minute in the countryside. She's lucky,' she said wistfully. 'Duff adores her. You only have to look at him and you see it. And now a baby on the way too.'

'She must be pleased?'

'Triumphant, she says. As though no one has ever been so clever before. Insisting constantly how thrilled they both are. And even though at first she said they would wait a while, now she says it is the perfect time.'

'Well, you have Gay,' Kathleen said.

'I know. But all the same . . .' Oonagh made a face. 'And now Aileen has written to say she will have her second baby just a month or so after Maureen.' She didn't tell Kathleen how that news had dismayed her: how could she have said such a thing about her own sister? And it wasn't that she was not pleased for Aileen. She was. Only that Aileen's news – the happy expansion of her family – seemed almost to mock Oonagh, to leave her stuck somewhere behind her sister. 'Gay should have a little brother or sister too.'

'What does Dr Gilliatt say?'

'The same as ever.' She sighed. 'That it could be dangerous. But he can't say that for sure – even he admits that.'

'And Philip?'

'Well, Philip . . .' she said, pausing before a display of a peculiar green fruit '. . . Philip doesn't say so much. About this or anything else.' It was the closest she had yet come to admitting that all was not well between them, even to Kathleen – who must know very well how little he was at home, and that when the portrait was unveiled at the party in a few weeks' time, Philip would be among those who were seeing it for the first time.

'I prefer to see the finished piece,' he had announced after his first few visits when there was still nothing on de László's canvas but a few lines. 'I have not the imagination to fill in the blanks, and would rather see it when the artist says it's ready.'

Nancy, there at the time, had laughed and said, 'Darling, no one is looking for imagination from you. Leave that to de László. You bring the money.' And indeed Philip, Oonagh knew, had paid over fifteen hundred pounds for the portrait. But he was true to his word and didn't come again. And when it was finished he had shown no impatience to see it, only a banker's interest in the cost of framing it, so that Oonagh had felt somehow insulted, as though she had offered him something, and he had declined.

'I must stop at the chemist,' Oonagh said, as they climbed back into the motor-car. The inside was warm and the driver tucked woven plaid rugs over their knees so it was nice to look out at the damp of the day. 'Philip left my photographs to be developed. I'm sure they must be ready by now.' She had become clever with the camera – taking it around with her and photographing friends and parties, 'Such a boon on boring evenings,' she confided to Kathleen. 'When I simply can't bear to talk to someone dull any more, I take out the camera. I can both hide and watch behind it.'

She leaned forward then and tapped on the glass for the driver to stop. 'You stay here, Kathleen. It's too filthy to get out.' She stepped out onto the pavement and walked the few steps to the chemist's door, treading neatly around the worst of the puddles. Beyond the clutter of bottles and potions in the window, the shop was well lighted, spilling a creamy bounty into the gloom of the afternoon. Opening the door caused a bell to ring somewhere in the back, a deferential tinkle. Inside, the shop smelled of rosewater and the beeswax that had been used to polish the wooden counter. A man appeared, wiping his hands, and Oonagh handed him her receipt.

Waiting, she moved about the shop, touching things gently with her gloved hands. A dispensing jar, a packet of hairpins. She picked up a bar of soap and raised it to her nose. Lily of the valley. She put it on the counter beside her purse and dusted off her gloves with a hand-kerchief. The man returned with a square yellow packet that said *Holiday Time is Kodak Time*, above a sketch of a smiling young woman holding a box camera in front of her.

Back in the car, rug over her knees, Oonagh opened the package and began to flick through the contents, holding up one photograph, now another, to the light, then passing any that were interesting to Kathleen. She hoped always to improve, and was critical of her efforts, looking closely at the sharpness of the pictures, the shades of light and dark. She never minded too much about likenesses – 'After all, people look different all the time' – but rather what she liked to think of as the 'technical aspects'.

'Isn't this dear?' She gave Kathleen a snap of Gay that had turned out well – silhouetted against the sharp light of the nursery window, his face was almost entirely in darkness. 'And here are a few from that too-boring dinner we went to.' She flicked through a selection of couples in elegant black and white evening dress staring glassily into the lens.

'They look like show ponies,' was Kathleen's verdict on one of the photographs, taken from the bottom of a heavy staircase and showing two women descending, holding their skirts carefully out before them.

'Yes, but look at him,' Oonagh said, pointing a finger. Behind the women, so they could not see him, a man was captured in the very moment of laughing, mouth wide, so that he looked as though he would swallow them whole. 'That's a good photo,' she added. Then came one of six people seated casually around a low table. She had caught the light well, she thought approvingly. The way it hit the slashed crystal glasses and ashtrays, throwing it off like so many slender spears in a way that was harsh and impatient and seemed to hold the entire group prisoner without their knowledge – locked into a spell they didn't yet know needed to be broken. Philip was there, beside him Violet, and to his other side two couples whose names she couldn't remember. None of them was looking at the camera lens, Oonagh was glad to see, feeling she had managed to snatch something. She went to pass the photo to Kathleen, then took it back. There in the darkness that had gathered in the bottom left corner, down below the chairs, almost below the low table, Oonagh saw something. Philip's hand. And in it, Violet's. Their two hands intertwined and half lost in shadow, as though they had something precious they were keeping hidden, cupped within their joined palms.

'Look,' she said, handing the photo over.

'Very nice,' Kathleen said.

'Look more closely.' Obligingly, Kathleen peered in, squinting in the shoddy light of a day that was darkening already.

'Oonagh?' She looked up, seeming unsure of what she had seen.

'Mmm.'

'But . . . ?'

'Oh, it's not such a surprise,' Oonagh said, taking Kathleen's hand in hers and squeezing hard. She wasn't nearly as calm as she pretended to be. Inside, her heart was butting against her ribs in a way that made it hard to breathe properly. But she was determined not to show it. Not to admit to it.

'How is it not?'

Oonagh shrugged, turning away her face to stare out of the window. 'I have suspected . . . I didn't know, of course. Or at least,' she said carefully, 'I didn't know that I knew, if you see what I mean? But I find that, after all, I am not so surprised. In fact,' she said, face hardening, 'I am already thinking how this might be useful.' And if it could be useful, she thought, that would lessen her humiliation.

'Useful how?'

'I'll show Philip the photograph, so that at least he spares me his denials.'

'You think he will try to deny it?' Kathleen asked carefully.

'At first, yes. He has always said they're simply friends and have been for a long time and I knew that before I married him. And perhaps that's true . . . You know that Philip was Valsie's friend before ever I met him?'

'I did not.'

'Well, he was, although I have never known the extent of it . . . And perhaps I was too quick to believe him when he told me it was nothing . . . In any case, I married him when I knew there were reasons why I should not, if I had looked for them.' She was silent a moment. 'But he cannot continue to deny when I have this.' She twitched the photo out of Kathleen's hand. 'And then I will tell him that I can tolerate it, but would tolerate so much better if I had another baby.'

'Oonagh,' Kathleen was shocked, 'you can't say that. Why, it's . . . How can you say you will tolerate something that is not tolerable, that should not be tolerated?'

'Because there's no point in making a fuss. Of course I won't say quite that to Philip. I will say only that I can no longer pretend I don't know what half of London knows – and what they must both be perfectly at ease with everyone knowing because they do so little to hide it. And that perhaps a new baby will be a chance for us to start again. He cannot ignore me now, with this.' She was silent for a while and they continued to move, slow and smooth, through the foggy streets. 'And maybe it will be.'

'What?'

'A chance for us to start again. I would like that,' she said sadly.

'If . . .' Kathleen began, and then fell silent.

If you survive, Oonagh knew she had stopped herself saying.

'And her?' Kathleen asked. 'She is to be married in just a few months.'

'To her I shall say nothing. What could I say?'

'No "making a fuss"?' Kathleen said gently.

'No. You know how I can't bear scenes.'

'You hate scenes and will do anything to avoid them, yet you can plan all this to get what you want? You're a funny mix.'

Part Two

1931

Chapter Eighteen

Clandeboye, Co. Down

'You can't ask someone to take the boat and train just for a Friday-to-Monday. Especially not Stephen and Baby and that lot. They must stay at least a week,' Maureen said to Oonagh, ringing her up in Rutland Gate one morning. 'So, you see, I must have Kathleen, because how am I to manage where to put people? And there is no housekeeper here to do it.'

'So you must get one.'

'I can't possibly. You know how tedious I find such things. And I can't ask Manning. He's most peculiar, Oonagh. Sometimes I think he's more heron than man, picking his way about the house.'

Oonagh's peals of laughter reminded Maureen of how she missed having someone to chat to. Duff, for all the delight his company brought her, was not, she thought, a *chatter*.

'How is "thy friendly floor"?' Oonagh asked then.

Maureen had told her about the poem and Oonagh had immediately turned it into a tease.

'Perfectly fine, but I need Kathleen.'

'In a month, after my party,' Oonagh promised, 'then you can have Kathleen. If she'll go. She's making quite a life for herself here in London.'

'Is she now?' Maureen was disapproving. 'I thought her life was to look after you.'

'Well, if it was, it isn't now.' Oonagh sounded amused. 'She has friends. One in particular. A *man* friend.'

'How unsuitable.' Maureen imagined Kathleen – stern, straight-backed Kathleen, swift and decisive in everything she did – and began to giggle.

'Yes. More than you know, even. A *Communist*, Kathleen says. I think she's rather pleased.'

'Well, never mind that. What am I to do?'

'Ask Aileen to join you. You know she never can resist telling everyone what to do. Why, she would have your household organised in no time.'

'Yes but I would have to put up with her company. And the Great Oouja. And I'm sure I cannot.'

'Well, perhaps if you stopped calling him that . . .' Oonagh said. 'Poor Brinny. In any case, I'm not so sure you would have to bear him—'

'I say, do tell!' Maureen pounced on the hint in Oonagh's voice, the way a cat will pounce on a dusty sunbeam.

'Nothing. Only that I think she likes to go about by herself more now . . .'

'I see.' Maureen paused, taking this in. 'Well, I would too if I was her. I wondered how long it would take her to catch on that the Great Oouja doesn't exactly scintillate . . . But perhaps it's not a too-terrible idea. Aileen, I mean. For I must have someone. I can't invite Baby, Stephen, Zita as we are, and in the meantime, there's a friend of Duff's who comes, Betjeman, some kind of a poet. He knows Duff from their years at Oxford. He has been coming to Clandeboye "for ever", and misses no chance to let that be known.' She sounded plaintive, she knew, but couldn't stop herself. 'He's for ever talking about "the old days" with such a proprietorial air, like he *owns* them. And reminding Duff of things they did when they were on vac from Oxford. I cannot bear him. And when he's here, I find I cannot bear Duff either.' Which wasn't exactly true, she reflected. What she couldn't bear was how much attention Duff paid to this Betjeman. How concerned for his comfort he was. All the time he spent with him, walking about the grounds or sitting before the fire in the library, talking about books and history and the India Question. The way Duff said, 'You must feel free to join us,' to her, but seemed not to mean it, so that Maureen felt as she imagined Lady Brenda must have felt when Duff and his friends had made their little room in the attic away from her. Shut out. Shunned.

And it wasn't just Betjeman. As if news of the baby had broken the spell that had held her and Duff suspended alone together, now people came constantly. Duff's friends, clearly feeling they had allowed quite enough time for a honeymoon, began to visit, men who called him Ava with gruff intimacy, or – considered a great joke – 'Mindless', a nickname from Oxford. They cared nothing for the lack of comfort at Clandeboye, declaring themselves well used to it with a familiarity that insulted her. They rode hard to hounds and disappeared with guns and dogs for long days, coming home only when it was dark. There was a game room where the birds they killed were hung, row upon row of them, hooked through the neck so that their heads lolled to the side, the bright glory of their feathers dulled and stained with blood that was thick like dried mud. Surveying the spoiled bodies, Maureen, never usually squeamish, was surprised by how much she minded that they had been dragged from soaring glory to lumpen ignominy. She wondered was it the baby making her feel queasy in unexpected ways.

At night, after dinner, these men and Duff disappeared together into one of the smaller rooms and played cards – often till the sun came up. Maureen knew, because there were mornings that she was up as they were going to bed, passing Duff in a hallway or on the stairs and seeing his bloodshot eyes as he greeted her politely.

They drank as they hunted – seriously, in near-silence. The shuffle of cards and flare of a match to light the cigars they favoured were sometimes the only sounds. When they did talk, they addressed themselves to the talking with intent. They gathered in armchairs, passing around a decanter, and devoted themselves to conversation as if it were something to be wooed.

Maureen felt excluded from this group of men who had known each other, many of them, since childhood. They banded together as though making a last stand, and spoke in a bizarre shorthand, littered with nicknames and private jokes that were nearly unintelligible to anyone outside. Like Betjeman, they referred constantly to events long past that no one other than themselves recalled.

Some made efforts to include her; others, such as Betjeman, did not. But what Maureen really could not stand was how those men adored Duff, and the obvious pleasure he took in their company.

For those men, Duff had magic, just as he had for her, and what Maureen couldn't bear was that in their company he had less need of her. Their adoration was as familiar to him as a glove – he wore it lightly but fondly – and while they were there, Maureen knew that she receded a little for him, her reality diminished by his early closeness to theirs.

These men did not flirt with her, or pay her the kind of attention she was used to. They tolerated her, for Duff's sake – and that made her feel as Cloé did: as though she was under scrutiny, something to be assessed and reassessed.

She didn't tell Oonagh any of that, or that she was certain Manning, and the footmen, drank Duff's wine when he was not there. She knew Oonagh would disapprove, and knew, too, how impossible she would find it to understand that Clandeboye was not like London. Or Dublin. Not like anywhere Maureen had ever lived. And that the idea of wrestling the house into her control was so daunting that she had decided not to do so. Not now anyway, when, four months into her pregnancy, she was still tired with the baby. This last she did tell Oonagh, mainly because she hoped it would make her more sympathetic about persuading Kathleen to come over.

'Perhaps *you* are becoming just like Mamma,' Oonagh retorted smartly, and Maureen remembered guiltily how she had teased Oonagh when she was expecting Gay. 'Feeling exhausted when you've done nothing except lie down all day!' But her voice said she was joking and quickly she added, 'Only wait till the baby comes. Everything will be wonderful then. And in the meantime, you have my party to look forward to next month. Can you be content till then?'

'No,' Maureen said. 'If Duff can have his Greek chorus, then I shall have mine. I'm going to ring up Aileen.'

Maureen telephoned Luttrellstown Castle, and waited while someone went off and found Aileen, who was, apparently, overseeing renovations to the basement. 'Aileen, if I sent a car for you, would you come straight away? It's only four hours, less if you don't stop for lunch. I need you to help me or I cannot invite my friends.'

'And why should I?'

'Because you're bored, and because you're curious. And because I need you.'

'Very well. But not for a few days. I am busy, you know.'

'A local pony jumping competition that absolutely must have you to judge?'

'Don't sneer. I have responsibilities.'

'You'd better pack sensible clothes. It'll be a busman's holiday, I'm afraid.' But the idea of Aileen was cheering, and the certainty that she would help shake Clandeboye into some semblance of order even more so.

When Aileen arrived three days later, drawing up in the ancient silver Rolls Maureen had sent, and had been shown into the drawing room, she said, through a cloud of cigarette smoke, 'Exactly as grand as you said, and even more extraordinary. That rhinoceros. The poor creature.'

'I know,' Maureen agreed. 'One expects it to moan, or low, or make whatever noise it is that rhinoceroses make. Or is it rhinoceri?'

Aileen ignored her. 'Where have you put me?'

'Difficult to decide. So many rooms to choose from. How funny it must be just to have ten. Can something really be considered a castle, with so few bedrooms?'

'Twelve,' Aileen corrected her. 'And from what I can see, choice here is limited to those that are not falling down.'

Maureen laughed. 'Let's go to the library,' she said, now that the necessary hostilities were out of the way. 'I'll have Manning send tea there. It'll be cold, I warn you, but at least we run less risk of Lady Brenda . . .'

'I must have visitors,' she explained, once they were settled by a fire that didn't smoke, with tea that was almost warm. 'But I can't be bothered with all the arranging, and I have no one to do it for me. You've seen Manning . . .'

'Indeed . . . But you look marvelous. I expected something more, well, rustic. But you look . . . happy?'

'Oh, I am,' Maureen assured her, just as she assured everyone. 'You know how I like things to be neat?'

'Do you?' Aileen asked, with exaggerated surprise.

'Yes. And even though I didn't plan on a baby, not at all, I see now that it is just the right thing.' It was what she told herself, firmly, repeatedly: *Just the right thing*. Because what else was she to do? Give in to the alarm she felt? Perhaps the alarm was unjustified. Perhaps motherhood really would be, as Oonagh swore it was, the answer to everything. Maureen didn't even know what kind of 'everything' Oonagh could possibly mean, what obscure questions they were that Oonagh answered with motherhood, but believing that was more comfortable than doubting it.

'I never knew you to do something, no matter how unwillingly, that you didn't then firmly decide was *just the right thing*,' Aileen said wryly.

'What else is one to do?' Maureen asked, and they were silent for a moment. Maureen thought of all the many many things that must be made *just right* because there was nothing else to do, no way to change them, only accept and absorb them. 'Isn't married life wonderful?' she asked then, to turn the conversation. Let Aileen answer that, she thought, recalling what Oonagh had said. Sure enough, there was a pause.

'Yes, I suppose so,' Aileen said thoughtfully, sounding as though she was asking a question rather than answering one. 'But are you sure you should be entertaining?'

'If Duff can have his friends, I must have mine too.'

'Duff's friends are used to this place. And, besides, they aren't delicate flowers like Stephen and Baby.'

'Stephen may look delicate but he's tougher than us all.'

'There's nothing here for them, though.'

'I am here,' Maureen, supremely self-confident, said. 'But I need you to help.'

'Need, is it?' Aileen asked, with a wry smile. 'One doesn't hear that so often from Maureen Guinness.'

'I'm Lady Dufferin now,' Maureen retorted. 'And, yes, I really do need . . . Be a darling, will you?'

And Aileen said she would. 'Leave it to me. I will arrange it all.'

By the next day, Aileen had found a local girl, sister to one of the gardeners, to help Ellen, the ancient house-maid. The girl, she told Maureen, who was yawning over a pile of magazines, was young and clever and brisk about dusting and changing sheets, and understood that shaving and washing water needed to be hot. 'The only problem is her name,' Aileen finished.

'Why?'

'It's Maureen,' Aileen said, shoulders heaving with laughter.

'I'm only surprised it isn't Aileen,' Maureen said. 'Or indeed Oonagh. What was Papa thinking, naming us all after serving girls?'

'We can call her something else,' Aileen said. 'What would you like?'

'Call her Helen,' Maureen said mischievously. 'She'll fit in ever so well. When can she start?'

'She's already started.' Aileen said. 'And,' giving a defiant look, 'she's cleaning my bedroom first.' When Duff came in, minutes later, he pulled Maureen up out of her chair by her two hands and kissed the top of her head. 'I have married a perfect little doll,' he said fondly, contemplating the height difference between them, and then, 'Churchill and Pakenham are coming for a few days, to shoot.'

'I didn't realise they'd left,' Maureen said sweetly. 'Well, I'll invite some people too.'

'And who are "some people"?'

'You know – the usual. Baby, Zita, Stephen, Waugh. Whichever hangers-on they forget to turn back when they get to the boat, along with whoever else they pick up along the way.'

'The house will be groaning at the seams,' Duff said. 'I doubt we've had as many people in ten years as you'll invite in ten weeks.'

'Your friends don't count as people, of course,' Maureen said, and grinned up at him.

Aileen, watching them, saw the way they struck fire from one other, raising flashes and sparks on contact, like bits of flint will. And how, deeper down, below the exchange of words and smiles, something smouldered. She compared what she saw with the way she and Brinny behaved together – his careful politeness that was almost deference, her own concealed impatience. And later, up in her room, she slammed the book she carried so hard onto the bedside table that a small Chinese figure of a lion with lolling tongue fell off and smashed. She kicked the pieces under her bed. Let Helen – Maureen! – deal with it after she was gone.

Saturday came and Aileen, having overseen the thorough cleaning and making ready of rooms, insisted on meeting the guests' afternoon train at Helen's Bay, even though Maureen said, 'I don't know why you bother. I wouldn't think of it.'

'I want to see the station,' Aileen said. 'Remember, I arrived by motor-car. I want to get a look at it before you rename it "Maureen's Bay".'

'Now, that's an idea,' Maureen said with a laugh. 'Very well, then. You can go in the carriage with Tommy.'

The carriage made several trips along the dank green avenue, picking up people, dogs, trunks and travelling cases from the station and depositing them at the house. Aileen rode back with the first group, all claiming to be 'exhausted! Such a trip. A boat, and a train, and a place called Belfast in between. Honestly, how *can* Maureen . . . ?' but all chattering furiously.

'Where might I find embroidery thread to match this section of sky?' Stephen Tennant demanded, holding out an exquisite piece of tapestry he was working on.

'Don't!' Evelyn Waugh said loudly. 'He insisted that tapestry have its very own seat on the train.'

'He tried to buy it a ticket,' Baby said, 'only the ticket man forbade him. Can you organise a subscription to the *Bystander* while I'm here?' she asked. 'Or is it altogether too godforsaken? One does want to stay in *touch*.'

'By which you mean see how many photos they include of you,' Stephen snapped.

They were, Aileen thought, with a giggle, like schoolchildren playing at being grown-up – posturing for each other, striking attitudes – no more adult, really, than little Neelia at home in the nursery. She wondered was it just her few years extra in age or something else that made her feel so much older.

At the house, they greeted Maureen warmly, eagerly accepting her offer of drinks. 'One may as well,' Waugh said. 'We've been up all night so it's not the same as starting early.'

In the drawing room, the chatter continued, with Baby giving a lengthy account of a party: 'A Red and White party,' she said, throwing herself onto a sofa so that a cloud of dust blew up around her and hung in the late-afternoon sunlight. 'Even the cigarettes were red and white, and the food – lobster and strawberries, too disgusting. The police came on a narcotics bust, and were so adorably polite, barely came inside, just asked that "Miss Brenda Dean Paul" be handed out to them. So of course we did just that and I must say Brenda was a brick, went out to them like a lamb once they agreed to give her time to find her bag.'

'She seems to pop in and out of court and jail with the regularity of a clockwork toy, these days,' Maureen said, settling down beside Zita and lighting a cigarette. She leaned back and breathed two jets of smoke out through her nose. 'Is she really such an addict?'

'Hopeless,' Baby said. 'Fonder of drugs than some mothers are of their children.'

'Even the *Bystander* is disgusted.' Waugh took up the story. 'It seems the party coincided with a hunger march, and the *Bystander* have a large editorial, comparing the two most unfavourably and saying these are delicate times for England.'

'Sounds like Ernest,' Aileen said. 'Convinced we're hurtling towards revolution in a gin glass.' She remembered Ernest, *This will be the devil's decade,* and hoped Waugh would contradict her, say it was all nonsense and Ernest fussed too much, but he didn't. Instead he began to read from the magazine:

'". . . such ill-bred extravagance was flaunted, as too many hungry men were marching to London to get work . . ."'

'The *Bystander* . . .' Maureen said thoughtfully, 'not standing by so much now.'

'No. *Quite* committed,' Waugh agreed. 'So much so that one wonders . . .'

'Wonders what?' Aileen asked.

'Well, one doesn't want to be on the wrong side,' Waugh said thoughtfully. 'And it does rather seem as if sides are being drawn.' Aileen thought then of waves of hungry marching men, moving grimly forward, only to founder on the sharp, glittering frivolity of Maureen's friends. She winced a little.

'Our lot don't exactly get to choose, though,' Baby said, with the kind of unexpected insight she sometimes showed – usually just when Aileen had given her up as entirely foolish. 'We must go, or stay, where we're welcome.' She yawned, putting her arms straight up above her head, and looked around the grand and shabby room with a small smile.

'Which reminds me,' Maureen said. 'Violet's wedding in April? Are we all welcome at that?'

'Oh, yes,' Baby said. 'Violet is keen to show her new in-laws just how very popular she is.'

'I suppose that means we'll have to be nice to her, then,' said Stephen.

'But not too nice,' Maureen said, with a look at Aileen.

'Certainly not,' Aileen agreed. They didn't mention Oonagh. They didn't need to. All the things Oonagh didn't say they knew with as much certainty as if she had written them in letters a mile high.

Maureen's friends did not mix well with Duff's, she saw immediately. They were too different. It was, she thought, like watching a flock of small birds pecking, at food, at cocktails, at conversation, while around and between them lumbered solid, purposeful beasts – boars or badgers – that occasionally startled the birds so that they flew upwards in a crowd, chattering in alarm, and alighted elsewhere, watching accusingly, before drifting back in ones and twos.

They all drank, but even their drinking was different. Her crowd drank cocktails, accompanied by constant music, the gramophone playing loudly from morning to night. They took trays up to their rooms as they dressed for dinner, coming down in their evening gowns and jewels, hair perfectly coiffed and make-up done. Their slender white arms and bare backs were exposed to the icy draughts of Clandeboye, protected only by the collars of fur these women seemed to wear as though they were themselves half animal, huddled inside something deep and warm and soft, draped about their necks or shoulders, sometimes with the feet or head still attached, glassy eyes staring balefully out above an ornamental clasp. Exquisitely turned out, they sat there, amid the damp-stained walls, tattered rugs and rattling windowpanes, indifferent as sea birds perched on a rock.

Duff's friends, on the other hand, drank solidly and often silently. Starting early and finishing late, rarely betraying by anything more than the dwindling levels in the decanters how much they had consumed. They did not become gay or bright or giddy. If anything, she realised, they became ever more serious, huddling over their talk as though it were a fire that might go out and leave them all in darkness if they stopped tending it with words and thought. And Duff must have found her lot just as mysterious, because after the first night, when they were alone together in her bedroom, he asked, 'Do you not tire of the endless chattering?'

'Do you not tire of the endless politicking?' she countered.

He described her friends as 'brainless twits' then, while she retaliated that his were 'dry-as-dust old sticks-in-the-mud'. But they traded these insults almost luxuriously in the weeks that followed, as the house filled and emptied and filled again, as a form of teasing they both enjoyed, and often as a kind of warring prelude to love. One minute they were snarling at one another, and the next she was in his arms, and the ferocity of his mouth on hers was all the more because there had first been anger where there was now passion. She had begun to understand that this mix – of anger and passion – was like a drug to her, as necessary as whatever Brenda put into her arm with that silver syringe of hers, so that she provoked him more, and more often, with greater insults and jeers.

'You are like Salome,' he said, one dark night, after a particularly terrible row, wrapping his arms around her as they lay tangled in bed, the row, and the passion, finished.

'Why?' she asked sleepily, trying to remember who Salome was.

'You will never be happy until you have my head on a plate,' he said, and pulled her closer, so much closer, and wrapped his arms so tightly around her that she could scarce breathe. She couldn't tell if he joked, or was serious.

Chapter Nineteen

Rutland Gate, London

Who else knew? Oonagh wondered, when she woke. It was her first thought every morning now, as reliable as the sound of the milk float. Diana? Nancy? Stephen? All of them, no doubt. But why hadn't they said? They didn't say – that was the thing. They gossiped, hinted, made sly jokes. But they didn't *say*. And, after all, she'd done the same.

'Who knows what really goes on?' Diana had said wisely at a lunch one day, when someone – not one of their lot – said 'I don't know why no one tells poor Pelly what Elizabeth gets up to.'

'If he has any interest in knowing, you may be sure he knows all about it,' Diana had continued. 'And if he doesn't, well, then, he doesn't.' And Oonagh had nodded vigorously and said, 'Yes, indeed,' thinking how polite and civilised it all was. But it was very different, she thought now, when you were the one they gossiped and joked about.

For a moment as she lay in bed, listening to the house begin to stir around her, she imagined being far away from them all – back in Ireland where the air smelled of turf and wet grass and there was no one to look at you and whisper behind their hand, then pushed it from her mind. Soon, maybe.

Anyway, she supposed they had tried to tell, in their own ways. All those looks and pointed remarks. And she had ignored them. Just as she had ignored the intimacy of the way Philip and Violet spoke to one another. Until she couldn't. Until the photograph – if she shut her eyes she could still see the two hands entwined in the gloom beneath the table – forced her to acknowledge what all those sideways comments and pointed jokes had meant.

Confronting Philip took many days of nerving herself, forcing herself to go against all the bits of her that wanted her to say nothing, to honour the code and pretend she'd seen nothing, simply carrying on as before. But finally she put the photograph gently before him one morning when he came into her bedroom to say goodbye, and she said, 'Please don't say anything now because you will only lie, and I couldn't bear it.'

He looked at her, brown eyes wide and dark, and eventually said, 'Very well. We'll talk later.'

'It's like waiting for Papa, when you've done something terribly naughty,' she confided to Kathleen, halfway through the day. 'I feel positively sick.'

'Except you haven't done anything at all,' Kathleen said, 'and he has. Remember that.'

'I'll try.'

Oonagh thought about ringing up Maureen or Aileen and talking it all through with them, but pride stopped her. She knew they knew: if Baby and Diana did, of course they knew. But she couldn't bear to say it to Maureen – so newly married, so triumphantly in love. Couldn't admit that her own marriage had painted itself into this sad little corner. Aileen, she thought, would understand. But she didn't want Aileen's understanding either. And neither did she want the rush of confidences that might come with that understanding – a description of the state of Aileen's own marriage that Oonagh might have guessed at, but wasn't ready to hear confirmed.

No, she decided, she would say nothing to her sisters. She had Kathleen. That was enough.

She wondered had Cloé ever had a conversation the like of which she was soon to have. And, if so, how had Ernest responded? But she couldn't imagine it. Cloé had no words even for the parts of her body that ailed her – beyond a vague 'here' and 'there'. How was it possible that she could summon up enough directness to name things like infidelity? Oonagh paused on the word, considering it. Considering what it meant to her. It meant Philip's wrongdoing, yes, but more than that. It wasn't just that he had betrayed her: he had diminished her. Allowed her to be an object of pity and gossip, a foolish figure, the Wronged Wife – Oonagh drew back her shoulders and sat up straighter at the thought – rushing about to try to make him happy, planning little parties and entertainments, ordering Mrs Taylor to prepare dishes he liked, striving for his comfort, and he, meanwhile, had taken the protection of his regard from her and given it to Violet.

Violet. Oonagh, to her own surprise, felt far less anger towards Violet than might have been expected. Violet, she thought, was exactly as Violet had always been: charming, irresponsible, covetous, wanting what Oonagh had because Oonagh had it, expecting to be given what she wanted because she wanted it.

But Oonagh couldn't have been Cloé's daughter without examining her own part in all of this. Cloé, so quick to blame, had instilled a belief in *fault* in her youngest daughter. *So where did I fail?* Oonagh wondered. But, really, she knew well. All those hours in the nursery, the care lavished on Gay, the way she snuck out of her life to be closer to his – everything she had stopped doing with Philip in order to be more with Gay. That was her fault.

'Kathleen,' she asked then, 'your friend Ned . . .'

'What of him?'

'Well, if you needed to say something difficult to him, how would you go about it?'

'That would depend on what it is,' Kathleen said. 'With Ned, nothing is difficult if it is an idea. I could propose any impossible scheme you can imagine for "Society" and he would welcome the discussion.'

'How nice Ned sounds!'

'But try to talk to him about anything more . . . personal, and it is as if he isn't there.'

'How not there?'

'In his mind, he's gone. He might nod politely as

though he listens, but he doesn't. Personal things bore him. Sometimes I think people bore him. Individual people, I mean. What he likes are lots and lots of people, with the kinds of problems lots of people together have, not small personal problems. Like where someone might go or what that someone might do.'

There was something in her voice that made Oonagh say, 'I see,' in a comforting tone.

'But at the teacher-training college, there was someone . . .' Kathleen continued.

'Yes?'

'The history master. We were close for a while. Maybe because I was older than the other girls – almost his age – maybe because I cared more for history than they did. I don't know. But we would have walks, and conversation.'

'And?'

'And no more than that. But it was enough.'

'Enough for what?' Oonagh said gaily. 'Did you fall in love with him?'

'Heavens, no!' Kathleen sounded shocked, so that Oonagh was reminded how very differently they thought of some things. 'He was married. And, anyway, not . . . But he was an easy person to talk to, and I liked his company. I remember him saying "The shortest route is always the direct one. Just say it, Kathleen. Whatever it is, just say it."'

'Good advice.'

'Hmm. I don't think he took his own advice, but, yes . . .'

'How did he not take his own advice?'

'There was some trouble. The Sisters at the teacher-training college didn't like the friendship. People talked – in a city like Dublin, people always talk,' Kathleen said bitterly. 'And when it came to it, I don't think the master was as direct as he might have been because that friendship was of his making. He sought me out, not I he, and when there was trouble about it, he didn't stand with me but let the Sisters make out there was something sinful, not decent, about a few walks and talks, so that they wouldn't give me the letters I needed to get a good position. He was weak, when he should have been strong.'

'Would a few letters really have made such a difference?'

'More than you can ever imagine. You cannot have any idea, Oonagh, the way you were brought up, what such things mean.'

'I suppose not,' Oonagh said humbly, then swiftly changed the conversation. 'And so you came here?'

'Yes. And very glad I am too.' Kathleen put her book down and gave Oonagh a broad smile.

'Are you really?'

'Yes. I cannot think of a better thing to have happened.'

'Does Ned know about the history master and the Sisters?'

'I told him, and he said,' – she imitated Ned's voice – '"It's the System that's wrong, Kathleen. Not him or you or even the Sisters, but the System."'

'I see,' Oonagh said. 'How infuriating of him.'

And Kathleen gave her a grateful look. 'Infuriating,' she agreed.

When Philip came back that evening, he and Oonagh dined alone together for the first time in many weeks, and when dinner was finished and Peters had led his troop of footmen out of the dining room, Oonagh chose the shortest route.

'You've seen the photo, Philip. We both know what it means. I hope you'll spare me denials.'

'Very well, no denials,' Philip said.

And then, because he didn't seem to know what else to say, Oonagh took the lead: 'Do you wish to divorce?' she asked, working hard to keep her voice from trembling.

'Good God, no.' His eyes flickered around the room, taking in the many beautiful and precious things in it, and Oonagh felt he was counting the cost of such an action – everything he would lose if he lost her. And she was glad of it.

'Good,' she said. 'I don't want that either.' From there it was, she thought, almost easy. They both made promises – her as much as him – to do better, be more often together, be as they were in the early days of the marriage. She spoke of another baby and instead of rushing straight to invoke 'Dr Gilliatt says . . .' he listened to her and nodded thoughtfully. Neither of them mentioned Violet's name until the very end, when Philip asked, 'Will you say anything to Violet?'

'No. But I expect you to.' He hung his head. 'She is to be married in just a few months,' Oonagh continued. 'I expect she will settle down then and there will be a natural end to all this anyway, when she has a husband.' *Of her own*, she wanted to add, but didn't. Philip looked unhappy. 'Philip, for all our sakes, his too, this must be an end to it.'

'You're right,' he said. 'I know it. I'm glad of it.' And he took her hand and pressed it tightly, and Oonagh let him and thought, gratefully, of how she had forgiven him, and of the relief this forgiveness was.

Kathleen, listening to the rumble of their voices from the dining room late into the evening, thought about Mr O'Loughlin as she hadn't in a long time. Not since meeting Ned. She thought back over Oonagh's questions that afternoon – *Did you fall in love with him?* – and how she had felt as she said, 'Heavens, no!'

She remembered her own humiliation – she always remembered that – but now she remembered something else too. The bleak look on Mr O'Loughlin's face when he passed her in the hallway of the teacher-training college unexpectedly on a day he shouldn't have been there. He had a bundle of books under his arm, taken from his classroom, she supposed, and they had come face to face round a corner. Kathleen, still smarting from the shame of her conversation with the Sisters, and the way the Sisters had painted something filthy into what had been a friendship only, with their raised eyebrows and carefully inflected tones, hadn't known what to say. And so she said nothing, turned her face towards the other wall and walked past him. But not so quickly that she hadn't seen how his arm had twitched as though to stop her, and the look on his face that said he wanted to pause, to talk. For a long time, she had wondered what he might have been about to say.

Sorry? I didn't mean . . .? Could we . . . ? Somehow, even in the freedom of her own mind, she never could finish that sentence for him.

She didn't wonder any more – what did it matter? – but now she found herself thinking for the first time about Mrs O'Loughlin. What had she made of it all? And when she lost the baby, had that really anything to do with Kathleen? She had always been certain that it had not, but listening to Oonagh earlier, watching the play of mortification, reluctance, determination on her face as she nerved herself to speak to her husband – to seek a scene rather than avoid one – Kathleen had suddenly found herself thinking a lot more about Mrs O'Loughlin, a wife, as Oonagh was a wife, and how that might be something vulnerable too.

Chapter Twenty

Luttrellstown, Dublin

Sitting in the back seat of the old silver Rolls-Royce, on her way home to Luttrellstown from her weeks at Clandeboye, Aileen looked out at winter fields scraped bare and drab, waiting patiently for their first delicate covering of green – the tender spread of new shoots that would lie across them, like a fertile mist, until it strengthened enough to be the new season's crop. It was a relief to be gone, she thought. Too much proximity to Maureen was exhausting. Always had been. Everything, always, a competition, a game that must be won. Or lost. Even the simplest conversation could be a dance: Maureen asserting herself and Aileen forced to either confront or submit, even when they pretended it was just about clothes, or food, or which part of the woods to walk in. Maureen's company, though funny and stimulating, was tiring in the way a day's hunting would be.

Maureen was different since her marriage, or maybe

since starting a child, Aileen thought, but not by much. Whatever softening had taken place was around the edges, not at the centre. To be in her company was hard. To be in her house, impossible. Certainly for long. And even though the house was slipping through her fingers – Aileen had seen immediately that the household was set up for one person's convenience only, and that was Manning – still Maureen had managed to create parts of it in her image. Manning was clever enough to understand that as long as the trays of drinks kept coming, as long as the decanters were kept topped up, and food appeared at regular intervals, inedible though it often was – Aileen shuddered, remembering the endless greasy reheated lumps of hard pheasant – Maureen was content to leave the rest of the house to carry on operating within whatever shadowy system best suited Manning, and the mysterious Mrs Samuels in the kitchen.

There were, she thought, as the Rolls neared Hillsborough and slowed to trundle through the town behind a tractor, two Clandeboyes. There was the surface, which was mostly illusion – fantastical masks and curios and flashes of grandeur – and seemed mutable: a question of a new roof, a better system to get food from kitchen to dining room. And then there was the heart of the house, which was deep and secret and unyielding, where nothing could be done that was not already being done. And in a way, Aileen thought, the house reminded her of Duff – that sophisticated, even elaborate surface, and the stubborn, primitive core. She had seen, one morning as she breakfasted alone, a pile of menus handwritten in French offering suggestions of meals such as *galantine truffée*, followed by *timbales de filets de soles cardinale, poulet sauté châtelaine and so on,* down to a *gateau de mille-feuilles.*

'Who are those for?' she asked Manning.

'Lady Brenda,' he said. 'It is the custom for her to choose the menu from these cards each week. I have suggested to Lady Dufferin that she might like to take over these duties, but she has declined.'

'And does Lady Brenda choose?'

'She does,' he said proudly. 'As you can see, she has made her mark beside several of these dishes.'

'And what happens when she has made her mark?'

'The cards are brought to Mrs Samuels in the kitchen.'

Aileen turned away so he wouldn't see her laugh. The idea of these menus travelling up and down the broad staircase of Clandeboye every day, following Lady Brenda as she tripped about in her filthy white slippers until she made her marks upon them, only for them to be returned to the kitchens and languish, unread, was hilarious. Because day after day, no matter what the cards said, the only food to reach the dining room was thin soup and pheasant cooked in a selection of unpleasant ways.

'What are the kitchens like?' she had asked Maureen, when she came down that morning.

'I don't know, I've never seen them.' Maureen had said. 'If you want to go, ask Manning to show you because I shan't.'

Thinking about this now, Aileen laughed again. And

yet something about her visit had left her discontented, she thought, staring out at the fast-moving countryside, had loosed within her a little secret spot that was sore and irritable to the touch.

Aileen had always enjoyed describing Luttrellstown as a Fabergé egg – somewhere small but exquisite. But now, driving through the gates, she looked again and it seemed to her almost like a doll's house, a toy for a child to play with, in comparison with the creepy, spoiled magnificence of Clandeboye.

'How did it go?' Brinny asked, coming upon her where she sat in the prettiest of the downstairs rooms, the wooden panelling warm around her, a dish of hot crumpets to revive her after her journey, and a copy of the *Sketch* to leaf through.

'Ghastly.'

'Why so?'

'Rotting, falling down, unmanageable. She'll never set it right,' Aileen said, with satisfaction, looking around at the elegant comfort before her.

'Were you able to do much?'

'I did what I could,' she said, conscious that in the end, Maureen having bidden her come up, she had quickly decided that, after all, it didn't matter how ramshackle the place was. 'Part of the charm,' she had decided – though only after Helen, as she was now, had thoroughly cleaned and dusted some of the bedrooms. Aileen had felt like a servant, to be sent for, and then dismissed.

'Who do we have for dinner tonight?' Aileen asked then.

'Teddy and Dotty.' Teddy was Brinny's older brother, Lord Plunkett, and Dotty his wife, Dorothée. 'And Lord Castlerosse.'

'Not Doris?'

'Good God, no,' Brinny spluttered.

'Pity, she's lively at least,' Aileen said. 'Even if she has been around the world in eighty lays.'

'Lively is one word for it,' Brinny said. 'But I don't want her anywhere near Neelia.'

'Luckily, for all that she's his wife, Castlerosse doesn't seem to want her anywhere near him either. I suppose he will write about this dinner in the *Sunday Express*.'

'I suppose he will.'

Aileen made a face as though revolted, but secretly she was pleased. She had begun keeping scrapbooks into which she pasted every newspaper cutting that mentioned her, Brinny or Luttrellstown. *It's simple record-keeping*, she told herself. *Part of my duties towards the family*. But it wasn't that, or only partly. Turning those pages, reading back over Castlerosse's Londoner's Log or the *Irish Independent* or the *Daily Sketch*, and seeing her name in hard type, gave her a sense of *mattering* that was absent in so much of the rest of her life. As if only when she saw written proof that she had been at the races, the horse show, a hunt ball, could she believe it. *Ah, yes*, she would think. *I wore the grey chiffon and the MFH said what an honour it was to have us attend* . . . And she would be comforted by the memory – proof, for any of her London friends who thought to wonder whatever had happened to Aileen Guinness that she was still there.

'And we have had a letter to say that your Annie will be arriving this evening.'

'Too frightful! You can't be serious.' Aileen groaned.

''Fraid so.' Brinny slapped a riding crop absently against the side of his leather boots, then looked at it as though surprised to find it in his hand.

'Anyway, she's not my Annie.'

'Well your Mildred's Annie, then,' Brinny said, peaceably.

The girl was a protégée of Cousin Mildred. Mildred, after years with the Guinness household as one of Cloé's companions, was now 'too frightfully busy' for any of them – engaged in what Ernest called 'a rather clever racket', with admiration. It was, Aileen understood, something called 'flipping': she and Lady Colefax would buy up London houses, generally on their last legs, and convert them into three or even four smart little flats, beautifully decorated, and sell them for a great deal more than they had paid or spent. It was, Ernest said, 'a very sound business proposition, at a time when no one can afford the great London houses any longer'. He had described the flats as 'pieds-à-terre', which translated, Aileen knew, as 'foot on the ground', and really meant no more than a bedroom and bathroom and somewhere to hang clothes. She supposed such a poky little place might do for some.

Annie was a young relative of Mildred's, and apparently Mildred had plans for her. 'I am sending her to you for some polish,' Mildred had written, many weeks ago now. 'She is a dear thing, but sadly shy and gauche and you will know exactly what to do with her. I hear you entertain most beautifully, these days, everyone from Hollywood actors to near-royalty. And I know you are the soul of kindness and will do what you can for such a sweet but friendless creature.' Mildred certainly did *not* know she was the soul of kindness, Aileen had thought, with half a laugh. She was nothing of the sort. But the flattery had worked even though she saw through it. The fact that Mildred had written to her, not to Oonagh or Maureen, the image she had conjured of Aileen as a Lady Bountiful with the smartest access, these things had won her over so she had said a grudging yes. And having warned Brinny – reassuring him that it all might yet come to nothing – she had promptly forgotten about it, until now.

'What time does she arrive?' she asked.

'The letter said the four o'clock train. I have sent a car for her.'

'I'm sure she will be very dreary,' Aileen said.

Mildred's description had been accurate, Aileen decided, when the girl was shown in to her later that afternoon. She was barely out of her teens and indeed 'sadly shy and gauche', something that, rather than make Aileen feel protective, caused her irritation.

'You must stop twisting your hands together,' she said, after just a few minutes, during which Annie stood awkwardly in front of her, and Aileen looked her over from head to toe. 'It makes you look gormless.'

The girl gasped and pulled her hands apart as though they burned, and thereafter let them hang limp by her sides in a way that was almost worse. She was thin, with shoulder-length red hair parted at the side and left to hang about her face, and a face as pale as any Aileen had seen.

'You are like the whey left over after milk has been skimmed,' Aileen said, watching her and noting the way a tiny muscle pulsed under her right eye. 'Freckles too. But maybe there is something we can do about those.' The hair she didn't mention, considering herself wonderfully tactful. Mildred had red hair too, but a deep dark red that was striking, not these orangey wisps. 'You must be tired,' she said then, having decided she couldn't spend any longer talking to the girl. 'Someone will show you to your room where you can rest and we will meet again at dinner. Be down for seven sharp.'

And the girl, who had said nothing at all beyond 'Hello' and 'Thank you so much for having me to stay,' nodded and blurted out, 'What marvellous views you have.'

'Yes. Everyone says so,' Aileen agreed. She felt mean, knew in fact that she was mean, but the irritation of the Clandeboye visit was with her still – like dirt you can't get out from under your nails, she thought – and with it an urge to lash out and wound. *I'll be kinder later*, she thought.

Lord Plunkett and Dorothée were the first to arrive for dinner, already standing with their backs to the fire, glasses of whiskey in hand, by the time Aileen was dressed and came down.

'Well,' Teddy asked, coming forward to kiss her, 'you survived?'

'Just about,' Aileen said, smiling, as she always did when confronted by Teddy's vigorous energy and good humour. It wasn't the *title* she envied him, whatever Maureen might say, it was his vivid personality. The way he always had a plan in mind – something he wanted to do, often involving a large gathering or a small plane, and how much his cheerful determination reminded her of Ernest.

He was, she often thought, so different from Brinny. And she thought this even though she knew, knew well, how much she hated to be compared with her sisters. Teddy had purpose in everything – the way he buttered a roll or put on his coat or argued a point – as much as in his hunting so that Brinny seemed always, even now that he was a man of twenty-seven, to be trotting behind, saying, 'Wait for me, Teddy.'

What do you expect from a younger son? Aileen heard Maureen in her head and shook it. In fact, she hadn't understood these things about Brinny at first. In the early days of their courtship, she had gone where he wished to go – to race meetings and motor tracks – so she had seen him where he flourished. His confidence in such environments had obscured from her the hesitancy he showed everywhere else. And by the time she had understood that he would never shine in company, or behave towards her with anything like the certainty he showed with his horses, dogs and cars – that he would tiptoe around her as though she might shatter at a look, when what she wanted was for him to reach out and take hold of her firmly and tell her what he wanted of her in a way that would make her want to give it to him – well, by then they were already married.

'I can't imagine Maureen's honeymoon in the jungles of India was any more savage than that place,' she said then, moving forward to the fire, accepting the drink Brinny held out to her.

'A baby?' Dorothée asked, with her usual frankness.

'Yes. July.'

Castlerosse arrived, and Aileen had to tell her stories all over again, and this time she embellished them so that Clandeboye stood on the very edge of ruin, walls and roof ready to rot and fall inwards at any moment, while Maureen perched amid the decay defiantly playing her gramophone and surrounded by loutish servants. Which, Aileen thought, was close enough to the truth. She was conscious, as she spoke, of the exact and careful choreography of Luttrellstown – the precise moment the curtains were drawn across the windows to shut out the manicured parkland, which was the moment that the dusk outside went from alluring charcoal to the flattened black of night. The size and shape of the ice cubes in the frosted-glass-and-silver ice bucket, the modulated temperature of the room so that they stood evenly spaced out, rather than huddled before a smoking fire. So pleased was she with it all, and with the elegance of her guests in their eveningwear, that when Annie shuffled silently in and stood by the doorway, she waved her forward gaily. 'Come and meet everyone,' she cried. 'Everyone, this is Annie who is come to stay with us for a few days.'

But when the flurry of hellos was finished, and before dinner was announced, Teddy, picking up on the earlier conversation, said, 'They say Duff's star is rising fast in

Westminster. I don't imagine they'll be much at Clandeboye,' Aileen felt a hot needle of irritation prick at her. She turned to Annie, who was seated at the furthest end of the room, and said, 'What shall you do while you're here?' knowing full well that Annie had nothing to do that wasn't organised by her, no plans that weren't Aileen's plans, no friends to meet that weren't Aileen's friends. And when the girl blushed and stammered and finally said, 'I like to walk,' she smiled fixedly at her and said, 'Well, you'll find some lovely walks around here,' and the petty meanness of that, while it shamed her, gave her satisfaction too.

After dinner, and even though she could see her guests were happy to linger at the table, or return to the drawing-room fire, Aileen said, 'Let's go downstairs, to the Boîte.' The Boîte was what she called the basement nightclub she had had put in, in place of what had been a cold storage room.

'Won't we rattle around down there rather?' Brinny asked, looking around the table at the small, quiet group.

'Don't be dreary,' Aileen said. She wanted Castlerosse to write about the nightclub so that everyone reading his column would know that even so far from London there was a lively, sophisticated scene, with Aileen at the heart of it. She wished Brinny had thought to invite more people and wondered who they might get to come out at short notice. But that would require telephone conversations and she didn't want to bother. Descending the stone steps to the basement, she kept up a flow of chatter that almost hid the fact that no one else talked much. Once inside the Boîte, she put a record on loudly and demanded Teddy dance with her. Brinny obligingly asked Dorothée, which meant Castlerosse should have asked Annie, but he didn't. Instead he stood watching the others. Perhaps he was too fat to dance easily any more, Aileen thought. But he could at least have talked to the girl.

The room was dark and low-ceilinged, with walls upholstered in deep red satin, low lighting and a small bar at one end. The effect, she always thought, was rather like being on a yacht, or in a small hotel. But it needed more people to make it work. That night, with just six of them, she was conscious that it felt rather forlorn. There was a faintly musty smell, as though the air had been breathed in and out too many times, and a chill that hinted that under the red satin the walls were not quite dry.

It was, she decided, Annie's fault that the evening was a failure. In a party so small, everyone needed to play their part, and the girl simply wasn't making the effort. 'There's nothing pretty about a wallflower,' she hissed, as she passed close to her, propelled by Teddy, who was a jolly good dancer, 'except in a garden on a summer's day. Can't you make an effort?' The girl flushed miserably, and Aileen, instead of feeling bad, decided that this was all part of the polish Mildred had asked her to apply.

Annie, she saw, moved closer to Castlerosse, clutching her empty glass and said, 'Do you hunt?' in a small voice.

'Do I look like I hunt?' Castlerosse said irritably. Aileen interrupted Brinny and Dorothée, sending Brinny to dance with Annie, which he did, even managing to bring a scared smile to her face with his genial conversation, and letting Dorothée deal with Castlerosse, which she did with her usual cool humour so that now he was the one scrabbling to amuse, while she stayed detached. But even so the evening never really took off and Aileen was conscious of the discontented feeling, a quiet suspicion that, after all, her nightclub was the thing she dreaded most of all – provincial. The feeling lasted until the guests left and Annie, looking exhausted and still frightened, had gone to bed.

'I think I'll go up,' Aileen said.

'I might look in later?' Brinny said, a question in his voice as he pulled fretfully at his moustache.

'Not tonight,' she said. 'I'm tired.'

'Very well,' he said. And she knew he would sit in the library with the dogs and the decanter and drink, alone, until late. That the next day he would be sullen with her and they would avoid one another about the house and grounds, until forced by whoever the evening's guests were to come together as hosts.

As she changed for bed, deliberately enjoying the warmth of her room, the thickness of the white carpet and upholstered four-poster bed after the threadbare comforts of Clandeboye, soothed by the speed and deference with which a maid brought her hot milk and cinnamon when she rang, Aileen thought about how quickly she had answered, 'Not tonight,' to Brinny's half-question. It wasn't that she didn't care for him, she thought. But it wasn't that she was tired, either. That, too, was part of the prickle of irritation: the way his uncertainty was most noticeable when he spoke to her. Give him something practical to do and he had an unreflecting self-confidence that was very appealing. But he couldn't seem to carry that through to the other parts of his life. In conversation, he was always a step behind those with the quickest wits, still politely puzzling out a joke when everyone else had moved on. And when he spoke to her, put his arms around her, asked for her time and company, always it was as though he approached something that was too fragile, too delicate, that he was scared of as much as he was compelled by it. How diffidently he had suggested he might 'look in'; how easily he had accepted her 'Not tonight.'

The way Brinny spoke of being 'terribly fond of you, you know', and the embarrassed duck of his head as he said it – those things had always faintly irritated Aileen. And now that she had heard Duff talk of love to Maureen, talk of it proudly, openly, the way she had never yet heard a man say the word, her irritation was greater than ever.

'Preservation at a price,' she had heard the Betjeman fellow murmur into Duff's ear one afternoon as they watched Maureen conduct an orchestra of her friends playing homemade instruments – beating the backs of chairs and upturned bowls with their hands and impro-vised batons. 'I suppose it *is* worth it?' Betjeman had continued, gesturing out of the window towards a group of men with ladders who were about to make a start on replacing some of the main roof.

And even though Maureen's humiliation was Aileen's too – how could it not be, when their money came in the same quantity from the same source; when they had the same blood, the same upbringing, the same way of walking and talking and standing? – Aileen had been secretly pleased. Happy to hear Maureen insulted and belittled by this man with his poetic aspirations and uncertain mouth, and she had looked at Duff without turning her head, hoping to see him acknowledge the humiliation of those words.

Instead, 'Wrong tree, old chap,' Duff had said loudly and amiably, and Aileen was surprised at how tolerant his voice was. 'I love her, sorry to say.'

'But does she make you happy?' Betjeman had asked.

'I hope to make her happy,' Duff responded, watching Maureen who stood then on a chair, the better to wave her baton – a folded ivory fan – at the musicians.

'That's not what I asked,' Betjeman had said. And Aileen, listening to him, had felt the same frustration: a need to hear something snippy about Maureen that Duff could not or would not meet.

She thought of Duff's face earlier that same day, when Maureen had told him about the new maid and how her name was Helen. 'She wouldn't be the first country girl around here to be called Helen,' he had said, in some satisfaction. 'It became quite popular.'

'Oh, she wasn't really called Helen,' Maureen had said, 'at least not when she arrived.'

'What do you mean?' Duff asked.

'I had to rename her,' Maureen said. By that stage, Aileen listened carefully. 'Her name wouldn't do.'

'And you picked Helen?'

'I did.' Maureen looked sideways at him. 'I thought

it would help her fit in.' And Duff, instead of being angry or pompous or quietly insulted, as Brinny would have been, just laughed and said, 'Well, well.'

Everything, Aileen had seen, was a challenge between them, a contest, but one they approached willingly, with enjoyment, so happy in their arena of two that everything outside it was faded and reduced, and they were perfectly content to have it so, because within, the arena was vibrant and vital and enough for them both.

Aileen got into bed, trying to find the satisfaction she needed in the crisp, cool, heavy linen sheets and even distribution of goose feathers in the eiderdown, so unlike the lumpy damp of beds at Clandeboye. But the prickle of irritation stayed with her, just as if it were the frog in the fairy story who climbed onto the princess's pillow and squatted there, foul and dripping, beside her.

Chapter Twenty-One

London

The first time Ned took Kathleen to the place where he lived on Berwick Street, he warned her so many times of what she would find – 'It's not even a flat, it's a room, half a room, in half a house, less than half, which should have been torn down long ago' – that eventually she told him she didn't care if he lived in a tin can, she wanted to see it. With that, he fell silent, but she could see he was nervous, and knowing that made her feel more relaxed than she would have otherwise been, to be going alone to a young man's lodging place.

Without the market to lend it colour and energy, Berwick Street on a chill winter day was the stringy, lonely grey of a city pigeon. They squeezed past a grocery store on the ground floor, which breathed out lye soap and rotting apples, to a side door that needed a good push to open. Ned put his shoulder to it, motioning her to stand back. Inside, the hall was narrow and dark – and once the door was shut, the only light came through the grubby half-moon-shaped pane of glass above it. Too close to the door, and seeming to hurtle downwards in a rush to get out, was a steep flight of scuffed wooden stairs. 'Up here,' Ned said. 'First floor.'

Their footsteps clattered mournfully into the empty space. The walls were yellow and the wood was yellow, even the ceiling above, as much as she could see of it, was yellow, so the stairs seem to float unanchored, like a cigarette butt in a spittoon.

By her side, Ned was conscious, she could tell, of the dust underfoot, the crumpled news-sheet that had come to rest in a corner of the return, and the sour pinched smell on the landing of the first floor. That had no carpet either, just more bare boards, some that wobbled and shifted as they walked across them.

'Here we are.' He opened a door and stepped aside to let Kathleen through first, lingering behind as though he didn't want to see her face as she took it in. It was a square room with mottled white walls and a large window, filled entirely with the grey forms of the houses opposite, so that they seemed to peer in, while at the same time drawing back in disdain. The room had been clumsily partitioned – a new wall, not even painted, ran through the middle so that the window, which presumably had a twin on the other side of the partition, was set wrong, too far over, and the room seemed to tilt to one side.

A brass bedstead stood in the far corner, with two or three neatly folded blankets at its foot – fawn-coloured, edged with faded blue. Beside it was a white enamel jug and basin on a small table. The basin, she saw, was half full of cold water and a thick scum of suds floated on top, like clumps of clotted cream. A razor and a bar of soap sat on a chipped saucer, and the smell of Imperial Leather battled with the damp she could see staining the wall above the bed where the window frame let in rain. A cramped grate facing the partition had a few lumps of coal in it but no kindling. Kathleen knew about fires, and she wondered how he ever got it to light. Between the bed, the small table on one side and the grate on the other, there were bare floorboards. No rug, not even a hearth rug, to bring the corners of the room closer together.

'Not much like Rutland Gate, is it?' Ned said.

There was no possible answer to that. 'Those houses across the road blocking your light,' she said instead. 'They're like long-faced maiden aunts looking over, unhappy with what they see but determined not to turn away.'

'It's their duty to observe,' he agreed solemnly, and they both laughed, the awfulness of the room made better as soon as they did. 'Sit down,' he said, pulling over a chair with legs that buckled outwards like those of a fat man.

'But where will you sit?' There were no other chairs.

'On the bed.' And he did, springs twanging and groaning beneath him so that she thought he must be sunk deep into a steel cradle under the thin mattress. They tried to talk as they usually did – Kathleen asked who was beyond the partition, 'A Polish man, his wife and two daughters,' and where he kept his clothes,

'Under the bed, in a suitcase' – but it was cold in his room, no benediction of sun got past the disapproving houses opposite, and they couldn't find much to say that didn't seem false. Soon, Kathleen was ready to leave.

'Shall we go?'

'In a minute. I want you to stay long enough that I have the picture firm in my mind, of you here, in my room.' He looked so long at Kathleen that she started to blush. It was the first time she had known him turn all his attention to a person – her – and not an idea. He leaned over, awkwardly because the bed was lower than the chair and a little too far away so he was off balance, and kissed her.

He wasn't the first man to kiss her, but the first in a long time, and the first she wanted to keep kissing her, partly because she could see he did it in defiance of the terrible room, but mostly because his mouth on hers felt nice. Mr O'Loughlin had never kissed her and she would never have let him, but once or twice she thought it might have been in his mind. She pushed away the thought.

Beyond the engine oil on Ned's trousers and a breath of coal dust that sat lightly on his jacket, he smelled of warm bread. A nice smell, she thought. But all the same, after just a moment, she tilted her chair back further so that he must stop, or fall forward on his face, and stood up. 'I should go,' she said.

'Stay a bit?'

'I can't.'

'Should I say sorry?' he asked then, eyes slanting up at the corners in that laughing look.

'No, you should not.'

And then he smiled, with his mouth as well as his eyes. 'It's too cold here anyway. We'll go out and buy a lemonade. The shop on the corner has bottles we can take with us if I promise to bring them back.' On the way back down the stairs and out of the front door – the same wrenching tug to get out as get in – he whistled and his boots made a cheerful clattering sound. He was, she thought, as glad to be gone from there as she was.

The street was empty except for a couple of children kicking a ball back and forth. At the corner shop Ned went inside and Kathleen waited. A boy, maybe eight, left the game and came towards her. The sole of one of his boots was loose and slapped against the cobbles, echoing alongside him as he walked. He came close up beside her, so close she could smell the unwashed sourness of him, and asked, 'Got anything for me?' His face, Kathleen saw, was pinched by poverty, pinched as surely as if someone had taken clay and, with bony fingers, pinched it here and there, pinched hope and brightness out of it, pinched it hard to make it thin and hollow and wary. Pinched it free of any expectation except a hard word.

She couldn't keep looking at him. 'What kind of thing?' she said, bending her head towards the purse over her arm.

'Anythin'. Anythin' at all.' She was wondering whether to scrabble for a ha'penny, or if it was something else he was after, when Ned came out with the lemonade in stone bottles. Kathleen waited to see would he shout at the boy, the way Philip would have, or give him money and send him off, as Ernest might. He did neither. 'What do you want?' he asked him.

'Got anything for me?' the boy said again.

'Here.' Ned handed him one of the lemonade bottles. 'Be sure you share that now. And,' as the boy made to run off, 'give the bottle back to Mrs Levy when you're done. Don't break it, or put it down and forget about it.'

'Do you think he will?' Kathleen asked, when the boy was gone, the slapping echo of his broken shoe keeping pace with his steps. The dull sound was taken up by the twin rows of houses and thrown back and forth, back and forth between them, until a yell from the gang of younger children greeted his return and drowned it out.

'He might.' Ned shrugged. 'He knows he'll get nothing from me next time if he doesn't. And,' he laughed suddenly, 'he also knows very well that he'll get something the time after. That I can't stay off with him.' Kathleen thought how different it was to be with Ned, who made jokes more than he was serious, compared with Mr O'Loughlin, who was more serious than he was anything else. He had liked to talk, long and earnestly, about bits of history he said others had got wrong, and he had right. Sometimes Kathleen had thought he liked her company so much because she listened to him. And she had listened because she was fond of him, but mostly because she had no one else to talk to, and had felt flattered that he cared to tell her these things. With Ned, she listened because she couldn't not.

'Does he ask often?' she asked, of the boy.

'Always.'

'Don't his mother and father stop him?'

'If he can't get a few bits from people like me, his little sisters will go home so hungry there's no hope the evening meal – jam and bread and not much of either – will fill them. His mother and father rely on him to scrounge where he can and share with them. It's how they survive.' They were both thoughtful then. The day seemed even darker than before. Kathleen passed her bottle of lemonade to Ned. 'Here, you take it.'

'Certainly not.' He motioned it back.

'Well, then, we can share.' And they did, passing it back and forth between them as they walked through Soho Square gardens. But Kathleen couldn't shake from her the dull look in the boy's eyes – as though he had never seen anything bright or lovely and known it to be his, so that he had given up believing that any bright or lovely thing ever would be. There was poverty in Dublin, she knew it well, but maybe, she thought, she had lost the habit of seeing it, being so much wrapped within the luxury of the Guinnesses, because she couldn't free herself of the boy's face. Like eyes too accustomed to light that are suddenly turned towards gloom and defeated by it, unable to pick out anything distinct within it, living with Oonagh had made her forget what the lives of others looked like.

'Can his family not be helped?' she asked, after a while.

'Whose?' Ned was thinking of something else.

'The boy?'

'We try.'

'Who is "we"?'

'The Comrades.'

'Those meetings you go to?'

'The very same.'

'They are like the Church then, giving alms?'

'They are nothing like.' Ned sounded harsh. 'The Church give out of despising pity and only ever a handful at a time. The Comrades try to give a life made better by the rebalancing of society. Theirs – the Church – is charity. Ours is dignity.'

'How do the Comrades try to rebalance society?' Kathleen asked, wondering what that even meant.

'You should come to a meeting with me. Hear for yourself.'

'Maybe I will. And you should come to Oonagh's party with me.'

'Maybe I will.'

Chapter Twenty-Two

Luttrellstown, Dublin

The morning after her return, Aileen sent for Neelia and the nanny before she got up. The child was placed at the end of her bed, propped against a cushion, so that her short legs dangled high above the floor, and Aileen asked her questions about what she had done in the days when Aileen was away. But Neelia, just turned two, had few words still and confined herself to saying, 'Mamma,' in surprise, and 'Dat?' about the various bottles and jars on Aileen's dressing-table, so Aileen gave up talking to her and quizzed the nanny instead. What had Neelia been doing? What had she eaten? Where had she been? Who had she seen? The answers gave her a picture of her daughter's life that she approved of. Order, routine, careful interaction with suitable fellows.

'It will be nice for her to have a little cousin in Ireland,' Nanny said, knowing where Aileen had been.

'I don't suppose she will ever spend much time at

Clandeboye,' Aileen said firmly. 'It is not a house for children.' Although it would be a house for Maureen's children, she thought uneasily. Maureen had shown her the nursery on their tour. As bleak a room as Aileen could imagine: north-facing, with tattered linoleum on the floor and wallpaper that bulged with damp. In front of the fire stood a screen made by some child of a previous generation – pictures and poems cut from books and newspapers, pasted one on top of another: a cacophony of smiling children, wistful mongrels, garish flowers, everything held down by a layer of gluey varnish turned yellow and thick with age. It was a screen that spoke of generations of Blackwood children and hours of idle neglect.

'You will redecorate, of course,' she had said.

Maureen had shrugged. 'Eventually,' she had said, indifferent, already on her way back out of the door. 'Come and see the tower room.'

'But perhaps Maureen's children will visit here,' Aileen said then. 'Now, Neelia,' she turned to her daughter, who was sucking one of the ribbons on her sailor dress, 'you must be very good and do exactly as Nanny says.' She scanned the child's face, searching, as she always did, for evidence of whom she would look like – Aileen and her sisters, or Brinny. Sometimes she thought she saw herself in that chubby face, but then Neelia would turn suddenly, and in profile Aileen would see, with alarm, the unmistakable swell of Brinny's nose.

After breakfast, Aileen went to look for Annie, and found her in her bedroom still, sitting on a straight-backed chair before the window. 'Whatever are you doing?' she asked. 'Have you breakfasted?'

'I wasn't hungry,' Annie said.

'You didn't know where to go, did you?' Aileen asked, amused. 'Well, never mind, it's not long till luncheon. You won't starve. Come and walk about outside. You said you liked to walk.'

They walked about the gardens closest to the castle and Aileen quizzed her. What had she thought of last night's guests? Of the conversation at dinner? The hours in the Boîte? But Annie seemed overwhelmed, unable to feel she could have an opinion on them. 'They seemed very old,' she said at last.

'Only because you are very young,' Aileen said. She made sure 'young' sounded, if not quite an insult, certainly a disadvantage. Then, 'Walks aside, what do you think you're doing here?' she asked.

'I'm not really sure,' Annie said, twisting her hands together until she caught Aileen's disapproving eye and stopped. 'I finished school and there didn't seem very much for me to do, and Mother hasn't been well, and then Aunt Mildred said I should come here. And, well, you know Aunt Mildred.'

'I do indeed,' Aileen said. 'What did you do at home?'

'You know, the usual sorts of things, I suppose.'

'Tennis, walking the dogs, baking scones, making pot-pourri with dried rose petals?'

'That kind of thing. Swimming parties in the summer, sometimes picnics. Making sure the little ones didn't get into mischief.'

'I remember it well,' Aileen said. She thought back

to those terrible days between the schoolroom and coming out. The boredom, the impatience, the dread sense of time passing by and gobbling up one's future before one could even get to it – as if, she had always thought, the future, her future, had been a box of biscuits that one of her sisters had got to first. Because of remembering that, she suddenly felt a little more kindly towards Annie. 'Was there anything you liked at school?'

'I liked German.'

'German?' It wasn't at all what Aileen had expected.

'Yes. Instead of a *mademoiselle* at school, we had a *Fräulein*, and studied German. And I was rather good at it,' Annie said defiantly. It was the first hint of spirit she had shown, and Aileen didn't know whether to be amused or annoyed. 'It's a language that makes sense,' Annie continued. 'It has rules and reasons and everything has a place.'

'And you like that?'

'I do. Maybe it's from being the eldest. I like things to be orderly and as intended.'

'I am the eldest too,' Aileen said.

'Well, then, you know what I mean.' Again, that flash of spirit. 'I cannot stand when they are out of place.'

'You sound like Nanny making one tidy the nursery cupboard,' Aileen said, because she wasn't going to agree with this red-haired child. 'Which is very nice, I suppose, but what on earth is one to do with German? No,' she said thoughtfully, looking Annie up and down, 'that won't be any good. We'll have to do something about the freckles, and the hair, and see if we can't introduce you to some nice young men.'

'Aunt Mildred never bothered with nice young men,' Annie said. 'Instead she started a business.'

'No, I suppose she didn't. But we can't all be Aunt Mildred.' Aileen had always felt so sorry for Mildred – too tall, that fiery hair, no money, a domineering personality that meant she wouldn't, couldn't, perhaps, stoop and draw herself in and down so as to be appealing and fragile, someone a young man would want to protect and care for. Aileen had only ever seen the ways these things made Mildred a bad proposition for marriage – had, indeed, added up to 'unfortunate' circumstances when they were all young. But now? She remembered Mildred the last time she'd seen her, in London, negotiating the speed of a building renovation over the phone while making notes in the margins of some kind of contract, neat columns of figures that, when Aileen asked, Mildred snappily explained were 'our percentage of the deal'. Around her was an air of busyness, vitality, of important decisions that awaited her input, men ready to do, who first needed her orders. Aileen had been prepared to sit and chat for at least half an hour before she was expected for lunch, but Mildred had said, without much regret that Aileen could see, that she couldn't stop, she had a 'site visit', whatever that was. So Aileen had said, 'Of course, I only dropped by for two minutes to see that you're all right,' and Mildred had grinned at that and said, 'Well, aren't you kind,' as though she knew exactly what had just passed through Aileen's mind.

'We can't all be Aunt Mildred,' she said again. 'But if we can lighten your hair a little, you might have more luck with a husband.' As if that was the key to Mildred – lack of luck with men.

Annie looked mutinous, but didn't say anything. 'Will that man really write about last night in his newspaper?' she asked after a moment.

'"That man" is Viscount Castlerosse,' Aileen said, 'and, yes, he will. He has a column in the *Sunday Express* where he records all the most interesting people and parties. It's called Londoner's Log, but he makes occasional exceptions for happenings outside London. Why, he might even mention you,' she said, as a joke, in order to enjoy the preposterousness of Annie being mentioned in such a widely read column.

'Oh, I wouldn't like that at all,' Annie said, and Aileen wanted to slap her. How dare this child say, *I wouldn't like that at all*, as if there was the slightest chance of it?

'There are some people coming for lunch,' Aileen said then. 'I'll need you to make a much greater effort than last night. Now, you'd better go back to the house and get ready. You can't wear that dress.' And as Annie walked away, Aileen hoped that the girl wouldn't have another dress to put on, except for the evening one she had worn last night, and would be confused about what to do, and uncomfortable.

Briefly, Aileen wondered why she was still being what Maureen would have called 'so mean' to Annie. It was to do with still feeling cross about Clandeboye, and tired after last night's party, but it was more too. Sometimes she suspected that her meanness was caused by Maureen, in the same way that a badly fitting door will cause a worn patch on the floor. Ever since she could remember, she had been on her guard for one of Maureen's barbs, or her habit that was almost instinct for taking light and attention away from everyone else, and drawing it to herself as surely as if it had been a shawl she wrapped around her shoulders. If Aileen was indeed 'so mean', it was partly at least because Maureen had made her that way.

'It doesn't matter so much for you,' Aileen used to say to Oonagh, 'because you are the youngest and must naturally be eclipsed by both of us. But I am the eldest, and it isn't bearable that Maureen should overshadow me so much.'

'She doesn't intend to,' Oonagh had tried to say.

'If she doesn't, that's even worse,' Aileen had replied glumly, 'but in any case, I don't believe that. She knows very well what she does.'

She checked her watch now, tiny and delicate, the numbers picked out with diamonds, and knew she should turn back to the house, but she didn't. Even though her shoes pinched her and were wrong for walking such a distance, she carried on. She thought of a story Gunnie used to tell them when they were small. It was a story their aunt had delighted in, about a young girl who was dressed for church one Sunday morning and somehow her nanny had put a pin through the child's flesh as she was dressing her. The girl tried to say something, but the nanny was in a hurry and ordered her to be quiet. And she was quiet, saying nothing then, or when she was in the carriage on her way to church, nothing in the church, where she stood and knelt and sang her hymns just as everyone else did, with no hint that she was in agony with every move. And afterwards when the family got back to the house, the girl fainted dead away and only then did anyone notice the stain of blood gathering and deepening on her petticoats.

How Gunnie had loved that story, Aileen thought now, seeing in it everything that was noble and sacrificing and proper for children. How often she had told it to them, and been disappointed that they didn't see it as she did. Oonagh had been petrified – 'What if she didn't faint and no one ever realised she had the pin in her and it stayed there?' she had asked, at an age when the absolute power of nannies was complete and terrifying.

Maureen, of course, had mocked the girl: 'I would have taken out the pin and stuck the nanny with it,' she used to say.

Aileen insisted that the girl was a fool not to have loudly told the nanny, or her parents, that there was a pin stuck in her. But inside she had thought, *Perhaps the girl liked the pin. Perhaps it reminded her that she had something that no one else had, a secret pain that made her important, and that gave her something to think about that was sharp and real and sore in a way that made perfect sense because it came from a pin. And the girl knew that to remove it would be to remove the pain, so that, really, knowing that was almost as good actually removing it. At least with a pin, you know where you are.*

Coming towards her on horseback she saw Brinny, the only moving spot in all that green and placid parkland.

He came close, then pulled in his horse and jumped down, holding the reins in one hand. 'What are you doing?'

'Walking.'

'Walking?' He was, she saw, inclined to be stiff with her after the rejection of the night before, and so she held out a hand and saw the spark leap in his eyes.

'Walking and thinking.'

'Let me walk with you?' He switched the reins to his other hand and took her arm.

'Please do,' Aileen said. 'Though I don't ask you to think with me.'

He blushed a little at that, but answered gamely, 'No, not my strong suit, I suppose.' And she took hold of the arm he held out and drew it close to her, liking the warmth and solidity of it. The horse blew gently into her hair from behind, and the smell of the animal, hot in the morning sunshine, mixed with clean sweat and the sweet smell of straw from the stables was comforting.

Chapter Twenty-Three

Rutland Gate, London

The morning before her party Oonagh called Kathleen early to her bedroom. 'I need to send myself out of the house,' Oonagh said. 'Or at least Peters says I must be sent out, that they will never get everything ready otherwise. I thought we could take a drive.'

'Of course,' Kathleen said. 'Or a walk?'

'Foul day,' Oonagh said. 'There's a fog brewing. A real London Special. Let's ask Mrs Taylor to make us a flask of coffee and some pastries, and we can have a picnic in the car and drive about and look at all the people. We might even do a spot of shopping.'

'Just as long as it's not flowers,' Kathleen said. 'I heard them complaining in the kitchen that there aren't enough vases and they'll have to stand the flowers in milk jugs.'

'That might be quite chic,' Oonagh said with a laugh.

The morning was indeed filthy: so dark it could have

been before dawn although it was after ten by the time they left, with the choking smell of sulphur and soot that meant fog coming down in greasy sheets to settle across the city, sometimes for days at a time. The streets were almost empty as they drove about.

'Bleak enough, isn't it?' Kathleen said, as they looked out at the sad grey streets. 'I hope it won't stop people coming to the party.'

'Of course it won't,' Oonagh said. 'I say, there's Diana.' Leaning forward, she asked the chauffeur to stop, and rolled down her window. 'Over here,' she called, waving. Diana crossed to the car. 'Can we give you a lift?' Oonagh asked.

'That would be kind. Bryan set me down. He's gone to his chambers and is to pick me up afterwards from Asprey's. But I realise I can't possibly go there today. Too gloomy, don't you think?'

'What is too gloomy?'

'Oh, everything.' Diana got in and sank down into the car seat, drawing her collar close up to her chin. She wore a dark fur coat so thick and squashy she took up half the back seat and Kathleen had to move close in to Oonagh to make space for her. Her hair was untidy, almost dishevelled, and for many minutes she said nothing, shaking her head distractedly when Oonagh offered her coffee from Mrs Taylor's flask. Oonagh gave Kathleen a raised-brow look but said nothing either so they travelled in silence.

'Bryan has bought a house in Wiltshire,' Diana said at last. 'A place called Biddesden House. He wants to spend more time in the country. He says a more pastoral life will be good for Jonathan. And the next little one.' She didn't look at either Oonagh or Kathleen as she said this, but straight ahead, and there was no softening of her perfectly moulded features. She did not, Oonagh noticed, even raise a hand to her middle or fold an arm protectively across her waist, as women everywhere will nearly always do.

'Such happy news, Diana,' Oonagh said, and shifted restlessly beside Kathleen. 'When?'

'Yes, I suppose it is,' Diana said vaguely. 'September. And in the meantime, I suppose I should be glad it's only Wiltshire. His first notion was Ireland.' She shuddered.

'How I would love to go home to Ireland,' Oonagh said. 'Only Philip won't hear of it. "A God-forsaken place" he calls it.'

'And I agree entirely with him. But even so, one will miss one's friends, buried down there in Wiltshire.'

'We'll come and visit,' Oonagh promised.

'How kind,' Diana said, even more vaguely, so that Oonagh, swallowing a laugh that threatened to escape, thought it wasn't her friendship Diana was afraid of missing. But she didn't say that.

'When do you go?'

'Bryan would go immediately,' Diana said, with a thin spine of bitterness. 'But I've persuaded him to stay for a little longer. Now, tell me everyone you've invited to this party.'

Kathleen could see Diana wasn't pleased at the idea of Biddesden, but she didn't realise just how it had upset her until that afternoon, when Mary told her as they walked about Rutland Gardens with Jonathan and Gay.

'There's been shouting and everything,' Mary said, 'and that never happens. He doesn't raise his voice, a softly spoken man, and sure she hardly speaks to him at all. I'm surprised he had it in him.' She dropped her voice, although Jonathan was hardly likely to understand. They had reached the bench in the centre and, by silent accord, sat down. Mary took Jonathan out of his perambulator and sat him on her knee, bouncing him gently as she held his two hands in hers. Gay was asleep and Kathleen knew Nanny would be furious if she found out because it wasn't his designated nap-time. But Oonagh insisted that he be allowed to sleep if he was tired. 'Too cruel to keep the poor sweet awake when he wants to nap, don't you think? Only don't tell Nanny,' she had said, and laughed her guilty, hiding laugh, the one that almost folded in on itself, which meant she had no intention of confronting Nanny, but no intention of doing what she said either.

'How do you mean?' Kathleen asked.

'He never goes against her,' Mary said. 'I've heard him try sometimes but always he gives in. I think he's afraid of her.'

'Does she raise her voice?'

'She does the opposite.' Mary almost shuddered. 'She speaks very slow and very clear, and it's like a stone statue – one of those that sit high up around the city – has taken to scolding you. He can't stand up to that at all. None of us can.'

'He's too gentle, I suppose,' Kathleen said.

'I heard you!' a voice called then, loud and harsh from behind them. They turned quickly and there was Unity Mitford, who had, Kathleen thought, shot up alarmingly in the last few months so that she was taller than Kathleen now, stepping out from the bushes. She had, Kathleen could see she, the Mitford face, but an untidy version. The lines were less finely drawn, the hair coarse and dry rather than sleek, rising up from a broad brow. 'If I didn't agree with you, I'd tell Diana just exactly what you say,' she said, scowling at them. 'Only it happens I do agree. Bryan's like butter, he's so soft.' She said it scornfully, and was gone, running heavily over the new grass, before Kathleen could say that was not what she had said, and not what she thought.

'Do you think she'll tell?' Mary was distressed and began to ready herself to go, strapping Jonathan back into the high-wheeled perambulator and pulling the hood up so that he was quite hidden.

'She said she wouldn't. Besides, she's only a child. Who would listen to her?'

'Diana, that's who. She has great fondness for Unity, these days. And less so for Nancy, for all that they used to be such friends. With Nancy, she quarrels, whereas she and Unity are tucked up in the small drawing room for hours, talking and talking.'

'She won't say anything,' Kathleen said again. 'She'll forget by this afternoon. Certainly by the time of the party. Oonagh has invited her and the little Mitfords to come early so they can watch the guests arrive. She said she would have loved to do that when she was a child, that she was always banished to the nursery with Nanny guarding the door when Cloé and Ernest had parties. But I will keep an eye for Unity, Mary. I'm to go to the party too – Oonagh has given me a dress of green silk by someone called Schiaparelli; it arrived too long for Oonagh, and in the taking-up, lost its shape, so she gave it to me. It doesn't really suit me because green isn't my colour, but it is the most beautiful thing I ever owned.'

But Mary wasn't listening: 'Oh, I know she'll tell, and there will be terrible trouble,' and it was all Kathleen could do to calm her down. 'I suppose you'll be leaving soon,' Mary said, after a while, when she had been persuaded not to head straight for home. 'Back to Dublin. You said you'd stay a year and that year is soon up. I'll miss you, when you're not here. And,' slyly, 'Ned'll miss you even more.'

'I might not go when I said I would, after all,' Kathleen said.

'Really? And why not?' Again, Mary looked sly.

'The time has passed more quickly than I thought it would. A year always took so long in Dublin, but has galloped past here, and I think I'd like to see a little more.'

'A little more of who?' Mary nudged her sharply with her elbow, grinning, but Kathleen didn't answer. It was true that she couldn't imagine saying goodbye to Ned, not now when his company was bright and vital in a way she had never known, and couldn't willingly step away from. But she wasn't going to say that to Mary. She had no idea what her friendship with Ned might become – she didn't even know what it was then, only that she wanted to find out.

'Besides,' she said, 'Oonagh needs me to stay. There's things still to be done at Rutland Gate.' She wondered would Mary ask, 'What things?' in that snappy way of hers, and if so, what Kathleen could tell her – she certainly couldn't say *Philip is not faithful*.

But Mary had turned her attention again: 'What if that Unity has gone already to Buckingham Street, and is even now telling Diana what she heard?' She looked terrified. 'Why, she might be waiting for me when I go back, this very afternoon.'

'She won't be,' Kathleen insisted. 'She'll have gone out shopping or be having tea in a hotel, same as all those friends of Oonagh's. And even if she was, what could she do only scold you?'

'You don't know Diana . . . Anyway, she can turn me off.'

'For that?'

'For less.' Hearing the terror in Mary's voice, Kathleen realised that she, with her ill-defined but affectionate relationship with Oonagh, had no real understanding of the wretchedly insecure life of a nurserymaid. Ned, she thought, had tried to tell her, but she hadn't really listened. Mary picked Jonathan out of the pram and clutched him as though someone might snatch the child from her arms. Held too tightly, he started to cry.

Chapter Twenty-Four

For the party, Oonagh decided on the white muslin dress de László had painted her in, to have her hair done in the same style, and wear the emerald necklace. She liked the idea of replicating the portrait, imagining herself as a kind of visual illusion, as though she had stepped out of the canvas to walk among her guests.

'Well?' she said, coming into the drawing room and turning about so that Philip might see her from all angles.

'Beautiful,' he said with a smile, 'exquisite,' and he kissed the top of her head.

'Let's sit here and have a drink and wait for the first guests, just the two of us,' Oonagh said, pulling a low embroidered footstool close to the armchair where Philip sat. 'I'm sure Peters will be only too happy to think I've stopped "helping".' She laughed and he laughed with her, which made her heart feel light and fast within her, as though it danced to a beat that only he could set. They sat close together on the sofa and he put his hand over hers as she leaned a little against him.

'Cigarette?' he asked.

'No, thank you. I'm happy just to sit and enjoy the calm before the tempest.' She leaned more heavily on him.

But no sooner were they happily settled in friendly silence than Violet was shown in. Oonagh looked a question at Philip, who shrugged his shoulders slightly and shook his head. He even rolled his eyes just a fraction, so that Oonagh felt a swoop of pleasure that allowed her to greet Violet cordially. She had barely seen her since confronting Philip with the photograph, but she knew that he had in turn told Violet, and Violet had suddenly departed for her parents' house in the country. She had known, Oonagh presumed, to let some time go by. But now here she was, clearly feeling enough time had gone by.

'Don't be cross, darlings,' she cried, coming in, sinking onto the sofa opposite Philip and fitting a cigarette into a long holder. 'I simply couldn't keep away a minute longer. I'll help, I promise. Pretend I'm not here, and I'll be so good and quiet you won't even notice me. Victor will be coming later but I decided not to wait for him.' She wandered about a bit after that, offering suggestions about the laying out of the heavy crystal ashtrays Peters had brought up and fiddling with flower arrangements. Then, as Oonagh was called away to see to something Peters needed, she heard, with a pang, Violet say, 'Mix me something delicious, darling,' to

Philip and pat the seat beside her. 'Then come and tell me what you've been doing.' As Peters closed the door behind her, Oonagh's lightness of heart faded.

First to arrive were Diana's sisters, whom Oonagh found standing in the hall huddled in a little knot together, Unity in front with two younger girls half hidden behind her. 'Thank you for saying we might come,' Unity said stiffly. She seemed uneasy, ready to run away, Oonagh thought.

'To see all the people,' one of the younger girls said.

'The ladies in their evening dresses,' the other chimed in. She had a hint of a lisp: *dwetheth*.

'This is Jessica,' Unity said, tugging the older of the girls out from behind her, 'and Debo.' They stood and stared, all three of them, with those Mitford eyes that were always intently focused.

'Come up to the nursery,' Oonagh said, 'and you can stay with Nanny. If you look over the banisters, you'll be able to watch everyone arriving. And I'll send you up something delicious.'

As they reached the nursery, Kathleen joined them and Oonagh heard her say to Unity, 'Were you really listening, in the gardens?'

'I wasn't *listening*,' Unity said mutinously, 'but I heard what you said,' and Oonagh wondered at the hand of Fate that had dealt charm in such abundance to every one of those girls, even Diana, and withheld it so spectacularly from Unity.

'I won't tell,' she heard Unity whisper furiously. 'I'm not a sneak. And in any case I told you, I agree with you.'

'Won't tell what, Unity?' Oonagh, curious, paused on the corridor and looked from Kathleen to Unity. 'Agree with what?' Oonagh could see that Kathleen didn't know whether to thank Unity or scold her, but neither answered, and before she could ask more, her guests began to arrive.

They poured up the steps and through the doors of Rutland Gate so fast that Peters no longer bothered closing between waves, but stood like a sentinel, door wide, nodding low in welcome and murmuring names and titles as people passed by, as though whispering a lullaby: 'Your Grace', 'My lord', 'Sir . . .' Even the mere Mr and Mrs were injected with a new dazzle that evening. Outside was a night so dark and thick that it clogged the throat like treacle, and all those who entered did so in a rush, hurrying up the steps and into the bright hallway, grateful to leave behind the dense fog that was so dirty the white gloves the ladies wore were changed immediately once they were inside.

'A London Special,' they said, laughing, shaking foul drops from hat brims and putting aside the handkerchiefs with which they had covered their mouths for the short walk from motor-car to front door. 'Good to be inside,' they agreed, as though congratulating each other on being there. And indeed, thought Oonagh, they probably were. For in all of London that night – that week even – there was nowhere else to be except her birthday party.

The house was ablaze. Lamps glowed, fires were lit, looking-glasses sparkled and threw bright reflections back and forth, as though playing their very own secret game of catch. And her guests glowed almost as brightly. The men were uniform in their evening suits with starched shirts, and a perfect backdrop for the plumage of the women. There were dresses of pale silvery blue, dusky pink, creamy golden yellow, and grey in every hue from silver to gunmetal. Burnt orange and copper and purest gold. All weaving this way and that in rooms where furniture had been removed or pushed back so there was space for people to mass and mass, the crowd deepening so that soon the rooms were full, with the overflow to be found on the landing at the top of the stairs, even sitting on the stairs, balancing glasses on the floor beside them and all chatting, chatting, as if they were desperate to tell all the news of the world fast, before time ran out.

Oonagh saw Nancy leaning against a recess in which stood a large blue and white urn, with the man she was engaged to marry, Hamish St Clair-Erskine, stooped over her. He had a childish face, Oonagh thought, that did not fit with his height and the width of his shoulders. It was as if he was a very young man looking through one of those face-in-hole boards at the seaside painted like a much older man. And he pressed so close to Nancy, talking intently down at her, that Oonagh worried she would stumble backwards into the urn, and looked around for Peters, thinking she must tell him to have the urn removed. Nancy, usually so full of chat and laughter, was silent, she saw, and as Oonagh passed them, she saw Hamish put his hand on her upper arm and lean closer. 'You haven't known a single happy moment since we met, have you?' he said, with satisfaction. *No wonder her family don't favour the match*, Oonagh thought.

It wasn't long before her jaw ached from smiling and her neck from nodding. How tiring this party was. How many times had she said 'Hello' and 'Thank you, you are kind,' she wondered, nodding at a friend of Cloé's in a deep purple gown who put her face too close to Oonagh's when she spoke. She wondered what Gay was doing, and if he had noticed that she hadn't been in to him this evening. *If I went now, he'd still be awake*, she thought suddenly.

'I must see to something,' she said to the lady in purple, who stepped back with a disapproving look and said something irritable about 'young people' that Oonagh didn't catch.

Talk to no one, she thought, as she moved quickly through the room. Stop for no one. From the corner of her eye she saw Peters move towards her, and side-stepped to avoid him. She wasn't quick enough to avoid Violet, however.

'Darling, what a clever choice,' Violet said. 'To wear the same dress as the painting.'

'You've seen it?' No one was supposed to see it until the unveiling, Oonagh thought. How had Violet seen it?

'Philip showed it to me,' Violet said casually, but with a look that wasn't casual.

'Well, you should have had the decency to say no,' Oonagh snapped. 'What a vile, sneaking thing to do when you knew I wanted to reveal it properly.' Violet, used to a mild and compliant Oonagh, looked surprised and took a step back, which gave Oonagh the space she needed to run upstairs.

She slipped into the nursery where the table was laid with sandwiches and bowls of ices. 'Eat them quickly,' she said to the Mitford girls, 'before they melt.' The girls looked at her with round eyes. Oonagh knelt on the floor and with relief took Gay into her lap. Once the door was shut, the sounds of the party were almost lost, muffled in the thick, soft carpet that was the pale pink of peony roses. Under the sharp pinch of the pine cones Nanny kept to burn – she had Kathleen pick them up all over London, Oonagh knew – she could make out the clean chalky smell of talcum powder, and the cologne they patted onto Gay after his bath.

'You know you don't need to be here,' Nanny said, as always faintly offended that her kingdom was not her own.

'I know, but I like to be. Just for a little while.' She tried hard to seem certain, not as if she was asking, but when the door opened again, she started in a way that was almost guilty, and looked across at it.

It was Diana, in a gown like a column of silver, hair piled high on her head so that her long neck was exposed. 'I came to see my little sisters. You had the same idea, I see,' she said, coming in and closing the door behind her. 'To escape. Much easier for me, I should have thought. Won't you be missed?'

'Not for ages,' Oonagh said, wondering if Philip had noticed her absence. 'Everyone's too busy congratulating themselves on being here, and looking to see who isn't.'

'When *did* you get to be such an idealist?' Diana said.

'Honks! Play cards with me,' Debo said, climbing down from the table. Immediately Diana tucked up her gown and knelt on the rug, and soon she and Debo were playing some fast and complicated game that Oonagh couldn't follow. It involved slapping playing cards out of one another's hands while Jessica, whom they called Decca, yelled encouragement and advice. Diana was laughing as Oonagh had never heard her laugh and a strand of her hair had escaped the complicated knot at the back and hung loose. As she watched, Debo rolled onto her back and kicked out with her feet, catching Diana in the stomach, but Diana just laughed all the more.

Gay, on Oonagh's knees, stretched out his hands towards them, as if he, too, would have joined in, and even Unity's face was soft in the glow of the fire.

'There you are.' The door opened again and Kathleen slipped in. 'I've been looking all over. It's time for the unveiling. You'd better come down.' Oonagh looked at Diana, who sighed and got to her feet, the silver dress falling to the floor in a glowing cascade.

'It's Gay's bedtime anyway,' Nanny said, holding out her arms for the child.

Oonagh kissed him several times on his fat cheeks, which were flushed rosy and warm, and handed him over, whereupon he began to cry, clutching at the neck of her white dress. 'Don't cry, little angel,' she said in distress. 'Don't cry.'

'I should have known you'd be up here.' It was Philip, impatient in the doorway. 'Everyone is waiting.'

'Let them wait,' Diana said grandly. Gone was the

playful creature of a few moments ago; she tucked the loose hair back in, and was her marble self again.

'No, let's go down,' Oonagh said, standing up. 'We may as well. I'll look in again later,' she said to Nanny, patting Gay's outstretched hand and trying not to see the tears, round and heavy, in his eyes.

'You will not,' Philip said. 'It's your party, Oonagh. You have duties.'

'Perhaps Violet can perform them for me,' she hissed at him, as they walked out after Diana. 'Now that you've shown her my portrait, she'll be able to match me exactly.'

'I didn't offer,' Philip said. 'She asked. What was I to say?'

'No. You could have said no.'

'I'm sorry, darling.' Only then did Oonagh realise he had never apologised before – not when she showed him the photo, not when they'd had their long talk. Because of that, she let him put his arm around her bare shoulders, and they walked down to the crowded drawing rooms together. 'I tried to say no,' he said. 'I really did.'

'Violet can be hard to refuse,' Oonagh said, suddenly ready to skip with relief. 'I know that.'

Downstairs, she stood beside the very same green and gold chair on which she was painted, smiling at Philip as he made a speech in which he complimented her beauty in a series of wooden phrases that were received with more enthusiasm than their originality deserved. She looked across at Maureen and raised an eyebrow. Maureen pretended to ignore her. Then Philip wished her 'Many happy returns, darling,' whisked the white sheet from the portrait that was hung high on the wall behind her, and everyone clapped.

The portrait, unveiled, was undoubtedly beautiful, Oonagh thought – faithful, but without the heavy flattery de László usually employed. The figure on the canvas seemed to hover, delicate, unsure even now if she would alight upon it, or drift elsewhere. Looking at it, Oonagh forgot all the tedious hours of sitting in one spot, and found that all that now existed was this perfect depiction of the person de László had created.

'What do you think?' Ernest appeared beside her.

'It's jolly good,' Oonagh said, 'isn't it?' She had no idea how to describe what she really felt – a kind of intense relief, the certainty that, from now on, the painting could be the place she looked when she no longer knew who she was; and the place everyone else looked to first when they wondered about her. De László had answered the question in a way that Oonagh herself could not.

'A little chocolate-box in colour for my taste,' Maureen said, coming to join them, 'but I'll allow he has caught your likeness very well. I suppose now Philip has the portrait, he need hardly bother with the real thing any more.'

She smirked at Oonagh, who felt a fleeting chill, then forced herself to smile, and said, 'Just what I was thinking. Now there is the portrait, *no one* need bother with the real me any more, and I shall be entirely free.'

Ernest gave her a curious look. 'What kind of freedom would that be?' he wondered. Then, 'Where's Aileen?'

'She and Brinny just arrived. Late. I don't see why they come all the way from Ireland and then can't be on time,' Maureen said.

What kind of freedom indeed? Oonagh looked around at her noisy crowded rooms full of people she called friends. It was a question she had no answer for. Not yet. But one she began to understand she must consider.

Brinny hadn't wanted to come, Aileen reflected, looking at him standing awkwardly in a corner. Of course he hadn't. 'I don't see why we should go all the way to London for a party,' he had said. 'We have plenty of parties here.'

'It's my sister's coming-of-age.'

'A married woman with a child. I should think she's rather come of age already.' He had laughed at that, looking to see would Aileen laugh with him. She had, but briefly.

'We have to be there,' she had said. 'It would look terribly odd if not.'

And he had sighed and said, 'Very well,' but when she suggested they go for several weeks, he had balked and negotiated her down to a few days. As she watched, she saw her father cross the room and go to him. Well, that was a relief. She was about to go over to Bryan when she felt a hand on her elbow.

'There's a man here who would like to be introduced to you.' Stephen Tennant interrupted her thoughts. 'Baron Hubert von Pantz. No, darling,' sternly, 'don't be silly,' as Aileen started to giggle. 'I think you'll like him.' He waved in the direction of the man now standing beside him – Aileen caught sight of heavy dark eyebrows, shiny dark hair and expressive dark eyes, before the man bowed low over her hand.

'I saw you from across the room and thought, *There is a most elegant and beautiful woman,*' the baron said, straightening.

'Not from here, are you?' Aileen asked ironically. But she was flattered.

'No. I am from many places, but originally Austria, although I do not now live there. And you?

'I live in Ireland.'

'Do you? A beautiful country that is like stepping a hundred years back in time. And what do you do there?'

What did she do? Aileen cast around for something that would make sense to this man. 'I have a racehorse,' she said. 'A few actually, but one in particular.'

'I see.' He looked disappointed. 'The horsy crowd. I know it well.' He waved his cigarette around. 'Hunting, race meetings, the Fridays-to-Mondays in a freezing castle. Tea in front of a smoking fire in a damp drawing room. Last week's news, last season's fashions. You see, I know Ireland.'

It was so exactly what Aileen had always feared her life had become that she was silent for a moment. 'Our castle isn't freezing,' she said automatically. 'I made sure of that.'

'I stand corrected.' He bowed again but didn't look at all contrite.

'Anyway, what's wrong with all that?'

'Nothing, nothing at all, for most people. But for

you? I confess I didn't suspect it. You don't look the part. The dowdy gowns, the baggy tweeds. Vionnet?' He took in the creamy-yellow silk of her evening dress, which draped itself crossways from waist to shoulders, then fell in a sleek waterfall, rushing to the floor past her feet so that when she walked, it was as though she moved through a pool of gold. When she had put the dress on that evening Brinny had laughed hoarsely and said, 'Be careful a cow doesn't try to eat you. You are the exact colour of a buttercup.'

'Yes,' she said.

'And bought direct from the Avenue Montaigne, fitted by Madame herself?'

'Yes.' She basked in the hot light of his attention.

'One can always tell,' he said in satisfaction. 'So you are sometimes in Paris?' the baron continued.

'Yes, and London too. I'm not always in Ireland.' She sounded defensive, she knew.

'I'm glad to hear it. A woman like you needs activity, attention, excitement.' Again he examined her carefully, up and down, and Aileen stood, brazen in his gaze, and let him. '*Impeccable*,' he said then, emphasising it in the way the French did, and smiled at her. 'You are a triumph.' It was, Aileen thought, with a sudden giggle, as if he knew the silly rumours – that she had her underclothes laundered in Paris – and approved.

'I amuse you?' he asked tolerantly.

'You seem very interested in women's clothes,' she said, with sudden suspicion. After all, Stephen had introduced them . . .

'I'm very interested in women,' he said smoothly. 'And

now, I must leave you. I see our amusing friend Stephen signalling most wildly.' Normally, Aileen thought, as she looked after him, it was she who did the leaving.

'Who was that funny-looking fellow you were talking to?' Maureen, coming upon her, demanded.

'Just some friend of Stephen's.'

'Stephen has the oddest friends. Now, you'd better come with me. Oonagh has just been terribly rude to Violet and I need to find out why.'

Chapter Twenty-Five

At first Kathleen hung about the hall, unwilling to go up to either of the drawing rooms – opened now to their full size, the double doors between them pulled wide so that they formed one large, high-ceilinged room – because even the few people she knew, like Bryan or Ernest or Maureen, looked so smart that she felt shy of them. The green Schiaparelli dress, so glamorous when she had first put it on, felt faded and dull beside the relentless intensity of colour and sheen all around her.

But after a while, when the flow of people through the door calmed enough that Peters closed it more and more often, when the entrance hall had emptied of guests giving up coats and patting their hair, she dared go up.

At the far end of the room, Oonagh was still receiving congratulations. To Kathleen, who knew every movement of hers by then, she looked tense and tired. Above her, the portrait stared down at them all with an abstracted benediction. It was, Kathleen thought, almost like the inner essence of Oonagh, stripped of the daily concerns that weighed her down, set free in paint to be her most glorious self, as she sometimes was when absorbed in playing with Gay, or staring at him while he slept. And because of that, she thought, it didn't belong in that room with so many to stare at it. It was too vulnerable. The ˜white dress looked, from the distance of the doorway, like a shift or nightgown, and the hand posed lightly on her collarbone seemed suddenly fearful, as though raised to ward off a blow.

Supper was laid out and cleared and no one, that Kathleen could see, ate a thing. There was a bar set up in the study and waiters with trays of drinks – champagne, cocktails called Sidecars and French 75s in broad V-shaped glasses – moved through the crowds like dancers, their trays emptied and refilled, emptied and refilled in dizzying succession.

She stood out of the way in an alcove by the window that looked on to the street because she wanted to watch the front steps. The arrivals were fewer now, so she could see who came and went. Oonagh had insisted she invite 'any friends you wish' so she had asked Mary and Ned. Mary had refused, terrified – 'I couldn't, what would Mrs Guinness say?' – but Ned readily agreed, and said he would be late. Kathleen watched for him because she knew he would be dressed wrongly, and that he would not care.

Bryan came to stand with her. 'Do talk to me,' he said. 'Your voice makes me think of home.' Together they watched Diana, who danced with a man with shiny blue-black hair. 'Marriage has made a beautiful woman of her,' Bryan said thoughtfully. 'With lovely young girls, it is impossible to tell. Some fulfil their promise, many don't. Maybe they become pretty. Or elegant. Few have the character to become truly beautiful.'

'Surely it's a question of face,' Kathleen said, 'not character.'

'Not so. It is character. A willingness to accept what being beautiful means. To take that responsibility.'

She had no idea what he was talking about so said politely, 'I am sure it is being happy that makes her beautiful.'

'I think it might be the opposite,' he said, turning away from the sight of Diana, away from Kathleen, and looking out towards the street, one hand caught in the heavy velvet curtain that was pulled back and held in a thick gold tassel. 'She is still waiting to be happy so her beauty is expectant, not settled. Some women find joy in motherhood and marriage, but I don't believe Diana is one of them.'

'Is there anything more tragic than a man in love with his own wife?' Stephen came to stand beside them and handed Kathleen a glass of champagne.

'No thanks,' she said. 'I do not like the taste.'

'Very well.' He drained the glass himself. 'Now, how much do you think this party cost?'

'Don't be vulgar, Stephen,' Bryan said.

'Only those with money think it's vulgar to talk about it. And they don't mean that it's vulgar, they mean that they wish others wouldn't draw attention to how much of it they have. You should hear Elizabeth. Talks about nothing else, these days.'

'Well, perhaps if Pelly got a job they might have more.'

'Ah, yes, a job,' Stephen said with soft maliciousness. 'And how is your "job" going, Bryan? You have an office now I hear?'

'Chambers,' Bryan said, 'but I confess no one ever briefs me. They think I don't need the business.'

'You don't.'

'True. But they think I'm not interested.'

'You're not.'

'That's true too,' Bryan admitted. 'Come and meet someone. A new American someone has brought,' he said then. 'He's called "Chips", would you believe? Chips Channon. From Chicago. He was up at Oxford with Prince Paul of Yugoslavia. He fell so in love with titles that now he won't go home.'

'With titles, or with princes?' Stephen asked.

Kathleen went with them, for lack of anything better to do. They passed Elizabeth, who danced unsteadily towards them. And Kathleen watched everyone sidestep her approach, unwilling to be drawn into conversation because Elizabeth, now, was repeating herself too often and laughing too loudly.

The American – Chips – was in the study with Ernest and some of Ernest's friends. He was younger than them, but older than Bryan and Stephen, tall, with a smooth, almost cherubic face and eyes he turned on each with perfect certainty. Kathleen was impressed by his assurance, and his refusal to admit there was a single thing about America he missed.

'The lobster?' Ernest asked.

'Much better here.'

'Music. You will admit there's better jazz?' That was Stephen.

'The music at the Kit Kat Club is as good as anything you'd find in New York,' Chips insisted.

'There must be something?'

'Not a darn thing,' he said, adding 'my apologies,' with a bow to Kathleen because she was the only woman present. 'Have you read my novel, *Joan Kennedy*? I think that says pretty clearly what I think of our two nations.'

'I thought the only polite thing to do with that novel was never mention it,' Stephen whispered in her ear, and Kathleen had to stifle a laugh. Clearly no one had told Chips so, because he continued to talk about it in loud, assured tones.

Kathleen took up her post by the front window again, and was in time to see Ned arrive. She ran downstairs, dodging knots of people, to open the door before Peters could terrify them. Ned was wearing his usual suit, exactly as she had expected, although she could see he had put on a clean shirt and combed his thick curls.

'Well, look at you,' he said, with a wide smile, taking in the green dress. 'Don't you look wonderful!'

'It's Schiaparelli,' she said, then blushed because what could that possibly mean to Ned?

In the drawing room, they stood and watched what had become a very rowdy party. A jazz band played 'Just a Gigolo' and more people were dancing. A girl glided by dressed like a medieval page in a short pale blue tunic and white tights. She had taken off her shoes and walked lightly on her toes, a fixed smile on her face and her eyes vague. A group of others, Stephen Tennant among them, had found a hot-water bottle and were pouring the ends of glasses into it and swirling it around.

'Just like Mother used to make,' one said, forcing a slice of lemon through the neck.

'That'll put hairs on all our chests,' said Stephen, 'even mine.'

'Who shall we feed it to?' asked a girl with black eyebrows and shining dark hair. Elizabeth had fallen into a heap on a chair that was too small for her in a corner of the room. As Kathleen watched, Diana picked up a coat from the arm of the sofa and, with a sigh, draped it over her. Elizabeth, she knew from Oonagh, very often ended nights out like this – dead drunk in a corner. But this wasn't the end of a night, it was barely the middle.

'Are you hungry?' Kathleen asked Ned. She knew he had come straight from unloading the ships.

'Starving,' he said.

'Come to the kitchen. They have cleared dinner but there will be plenty of food there.'

There had been a call for bacon sandwiches from the guests – how typical, Kathleen thought, that they wouldn't eat supper when it was served, but now must have this food of lorry drivers when it was after midnight – and downstairs Mrs Taylor was busy frying masses of bacon in hot fat while the housemaids stood at the oak table in the centre, buttering mountains of bread that they piled up in thick slices at either end.

Ned had a bacon sandwich, and then a second, along with a cup of tea poured from the brown earthenware kitchen pot by Mrs Taylor, who took an instant liking to him when she found his father was from 'out west, Carraroe in Galway'.

'What happens to the leftovers?' he asked then, looking at the many platters of cold meats, fish, terrine sliced thin with a border of gelatine shining wetly in the low kitchen light, cheeses, apple and plum tarts, trifles, a giant syllabub in a crystal bowl that was beginning to sag at the edges, dissolving into a sticky puddle.

'First pies, soups, stews, fricassées – as many as I can – and then an awful lot of waste,' Mrs Taylor said. 'I can make you up a bundle to take home, if you'd like?'

'I know a dozen men who would come in the morning and take this away to be distributed among those who need it,' he said. 'I cannot think it will fill the bins of Knightsbridge while they starve.'

'Well, I don't know . . .' Mrs Taylor hesitated. 'Mr Philip wouldn't like it.'

'He needn't know,' Kathleen said in a rush. 'If the men come early, and in by the back, he will never know. I will be responsible,' she said grandly. If she had drunk the glass of champagne Bryan had offered, she thought, she could not have felt more reckless. It was Ned's presence that made her feel so, as intoxicating as a glass of golden bubbles would have been.

'Will you dance with me?' Ned asked, when the question of leftovers was settled. On their way back upstairs, they met Duff coming out of Philip's study.

He was smoking a cigar, and a dense cloud of blue smoke followed him.

'Kathleen,' he said politely. Kathleen nodded. She was shy of Duff, whom she had met only a handful of times, in Rutland Gate and Grosvenor Square. Shy of how little he talked. Shy, too, of how clever he was, and how, when he looked at her, it was to look, and not to be seen.

'Who's this?' He indicated Ned. Ned stepped forward and Kathleen introduced them. Duff shook Ned's hand and then said, 'What do you do?'

Kathleen was trying to think what to say, when Ned said, 'I work on the docks for now, but I want to write for the newspapers.'

'Write what?' Duff asked.

'What I see,' Ned said, a shade defiantly.

'And what is that?'

'How the children of the flats around Berwick Street live. How the men who can't work are barely more miserable than those who do because the living wage is no such thing. It's not a living wage, it's a starving wage.' Kathleen held her breath, ready for Duff to demand that Ned leave. But he didn't.

'Go on,' he said, lighting a cigar.

'Take a night like tonight – that pea-souper of a fog outside. Here, you shut the door, draw the curtains, and it's like it isn't there.' It was true, Kathleen thought, that there was something almost cosy in knowing that the dank grey nothing that surrounded the house was held at bay by the warm fires and bright lights inside. 'In Berwick Street, and all the streets like it where there are tenement flats, on a night like this they plug the holes in the walls and windows with rags to stop the fog creeping in because it makes the children sick. They cough so hard they shake. But the only rags they have are the ones they wear, so they have to sit in blankets, or naked, their clothes stuffed into the windows, until the fog has passed.'

Duff looked at Ned steadily all the while he spoke, and Kathleen thought in terror of what Maureen would have said to such a speech. But when Ned was finished, Duff said only, 'Well, and can you write all that?'

'I can tell what I see,' Ned said. Instead of squirming under that gaze, as Kathleen knew she would have, he let Duff look, and looked back himself. 'I have done some reports for the *Daily Worker*, but what's the point in writing for those who think like I do? It's the ones who don't that I'm interested in.'

Around them, men and women clutching glasses and waving cigarettes pushed past and jostled, so many that it would have been easy, very easy, for Duff to allow himself to be caught up and moved on, away from this conversation and back into the flow of the party. Kathleen waited for that, planning how she would console Ned and explain to him that these people weren't like them. Instead Duff stayed, planted firmly, watching Ned. And then, when Kathleen could almost bear it no more, he said, 'I know a man at *The Times*. I'll get you in to see him.'

'Since when?' Kathleen said to Ned, when Duff was gone. 'Writing for newspapers?' She was astonished, again, at Ned's faith in himself.

'Since I stopped seeing how different and exciting London is compared with Dublin, and started seeing all the ways it lets itself down. A great city, lived in by desperate workers and their starving children, men who can't get jobs whose wives scrub sheets for ha'pennies while their children paw the dirt of the streets for scraps and beg strangers for charity. Or worse.'

'You sound like Ernest,' she said in surprise. The band were playing 'On the Sunny Side of the Street' and beside her Ned started to hum the tune. 'Come upstairs,' he said, catching her hand. She could smell Duff's cigar smoke on him, and thought suddenly that the smoke clung longer than Ned's sombre mood.

On the other side of the room by the window, Stephen was deep in discussion with the photographer Cecil Beaton and a man called Francis Bacon who was a painter, 'and a frightfully ugly one at that', according to Oonagh. Kathleen watched as Maureen approached them. The shape of the baby visible beneath her evening gown, Kathleen could see Maureen was slightly unsteady in her gait, although you might also think that the room was full and hard to navigate, or indeed that it was tilting with so many in it. That, she thought with a smile, was the effect of Maureen's sense of herself – to make you question gravity faster than her, even when she had drunk a trayful of cocktails. As Kathleen watched she stumbled, so Kathleen moved forward, closer to her, Ned with her.

'Isn't it sweet, Kathleen?' Maureen said. 'Cecil wants to photograph this fellow Bacon, and in return hopes Bacon will paint him. Really, I do not know who has the worst of it.' She laughed, loud and harsh, looking from one to the other. The cigarette between her fingers was pointed like a needle.

Bacon gave a twisted grin so that Kathleen couldn't tell if he was amused at what Maureen said, or at the audacity of her saying it, but Beaton stayed silent, then muttered, 'You really are the biggest bitch in London, Maureen Guinness.' His voice was choked, as if it couldn't believe its own daring, and he looked terrified.

'Lady Dufferin to you . . . *Cecil*,' Maureen responded, lingering on his name to emphasis the paucity of it. He turned and walked away, and Kathleen could see his hands were trembling. Maureen looked after him with a complicated expression. Not easily wounded herself, she had always found it hard to understand the more sensitive feelings of others, Kathleen thought. Remarks she threw out – aiming for a laugh, a flashing response – so often, especially now, seemed to land not as she intended, but as a grievous insult. And, of course, Maureen could not take back something once she had said it. Could not apologise, or even explain. And so, Kathleen knew, she could seem crueller than she intended to be.

'What was that about?' Oonagh asked, coming over with Aileen.

Stephen filled her in and Oonagh started to laugh. 'Did he really call you that? Who would have thought old Cecil had it in him.'

'I don't see what you find so funny,' Maureen said. 'He called you London's Oldest Teenager, only not to your face.'

'No, I suppose he doesn't need to. Not when you're

so sure to tell me,' Oonagh said, and the two glared at one another.

'Where's Duff?' Maureen said then. 'I think it's time we left.'

'In the library, *Lady Dufferin*,' Cecil said, coming up behind her and speaking loudly. 'Losing again at cards. In fact, I don't know why you don't just give all your money to a bunch of sharks, rather than let him do it piecemeal. Not that the *pieces* are so very mealy from what one hears.' He looked beadily at her. 'Rather *large* pieces, in fact.' And then, affecting surprise at Maureen's face, he added, 'Oh, I'm sorry, didn't you *know*? I assumed everyone knew. But perhaps, when there is so very much money, one doesn't notice it trickling away.' And, kissing Oonagh, he said, 'I just came to say good-night, dearest, and thank you for a delightful party.' And he was gone.

'Perhaps you deserved that,' Aileen said quietly into the silence that followed.

Kathleen saw Maureen's face darken. She opened her mouth to retort but Chips arrived, loudly insisting he wished to dance with all of the girls. 'Such glorious Guinness girls,' he said. 'The Three Guinness Graces. If only I had met you before you married.' He put his arms out wide and encircled all of them. He spoke fast and his eyes were so bright that Kathleen wondered did he have a fever.

'Which one of us?' Oonagh asked, pulling away from him a little. But he wouldn't let go.

'Any.' He beamed, turning his head to one side then the other. 'Any.' Ned looked revolted.

'Funny,' Maureen said, 'I would not *exactly* have thought *you* the marrying type. But I suppose marriage takes all sorts, these days.' And she smiled at him with outrageous sweetness. There was a horrible silence, then Stephen, beside Ned, sniggered and muttered 'two for one' under his breath. Kathleen wondered would Chips behave as Cecil had, telling anyone who would listen that Maureen was that ugly word, a bitch. But he didn't. He laughed. Broad and loud.

'You,' he said, dropping his arms from Aileen and Oonagh's shoulders and taking Maureen's hands in both of his, 'are a tonic. And now I insist you come and dance with me and tell me *everything*' – he swept his free arm wide – 'about these people.'

'There you are, darling.' It was Brinny, who looked exhausted. 'Shall we go?'

'You go. I'm going to stay a little longer,' Aileen said.

Kathleen watched as she waved Brinny a brisk goodbye, then disappeared to the powder room. After a few minutes, she emerged, face powdered and lipstick newly applied, a rich dark purple slashed across her mouth as though, Kathleen thought, she had been eating plums. She remembered Glenmaroon then, when the girls were small, and how greedy Aileen had always been about fruit stolen from the orchard and glass-houses. Maureen and Oonagh would take a bite or two then discard the rest, but Aileen would eat and eat, even unripe fruit, until she had stomach pains that Kathleen would have to hide from Gunnie.

Chapter Twenty-Six

Rutland Gate, London, Spring 1931

As the days stretched and skies brightened, London emptied. Summer came quickly, as though it had been watching for an opportunity.

It was fortunate that she had Nancy, Oonagh thought. Stephen was in Spain, Maureen and Duff at Clandeboye, Ernest sailing on the *Fantome*, and Cloé had closed herself up at Grosvenor Place with Gunnie, saying she did not wish to see anyone. Bryan and Diana were mostly at Biddesden, where Diana had discovered with satisfaction that 'There is after all a great deal to do. A whole house to furnish and decorate, just as I want it to be,' so that Oonagh complained to Nancy, 'She now talks of nothing but paint and furniture. It's like having tea with the man from Hogg's General Stores.'

Nancy became a frequent visitor, calling almost every day. She had moved home, to number twenty-six, because the couple she had been living with – Evelyn Waugh and his wife, also Evelyn (Oonagh was never quite sure they hadn't married for the 'fun' of being, as they called themselves 'He-Evelyn' and 'She-Evelyn') – had decided to live apart, so Nancy, still unhappily engaged to Hamish St Clair-Erskine, came home, and took to early-morning visits.

'Unmarried daughters at home are not encouraged to lie in bed,' she said the first time, when Oonagh commented sleepily on how early it still was. In her voice was an echo of complaint. 'Just one of the many joys of being back with the Old Pair,' she continued. She sat on the end of Oonagh's bed, drinking cups of tea and chatting, and soon, on these mornings, Philip began to join them before he left for his office – drawn, Oonagh supposed, by the sounds of laughter and merriment that were always to be found where Nancy was, as much as by the greater kindness now her husband and herself.

He would sit in the chair by the window and accept a piece of toast or a cup of tea, which Oonagh pressed upon him, and carefully share out sections of his newspaper with stories he thought they would like – 'HMS *Tiger* has been decommissioned, you might tell Ernest. They don't build warships like that any more' – and Oonagh and Nancy together teased him, but gently, in a way that was careful to be admiring and even flattering. In this, they worked together, as though they were ants or bees or other hive creatures, Oonagh thought. Without ever exchanging a word, they, women, banded together to make him, a man, feel himself magnificent. And it was so easy, she marvelled.

For Nancy, when not being cruel, charm was like breathing. She couldn't turn it off or even modify it very much. The slightest favours were asked for as though they were heroic undertakings. 'I say, you wouldn't, would you?' she might begin, adding, 'No, I'm sure you wouldn't.'

'Wouldn't what?'

'No, no, never mind. It's too much.'

'What's too much? Wouldn't what?'

'Be a darling and pour me another cup, would you?'

The first time, Oonagh had thought she was mocking her and wondered had there been something in her manner that had been ungracious. She searched her mind, as you might a coat pocket when something has dropped through a rip into the lining, but could find nothing. And then, when Nancy did it again, she understood better. This time was over an umbrella – Nancy wanted to borrow hers while she dashed across the road to number twenty-six, saying, 'Are you absolutely positively certainly certain you won't mind?'

'It's not a family heirloom, Nancy,' Oonagh said, half laughing, half exasperated, 'just an umbrella,' and Nancy gave her a wicked look as if she knew very well she was being absurd.

Philip, however, seemed unable to discern the fine edge of mockery that ran a border to Nancy's extravagance, and he stretched out as she heaped flattery upon him, like a cat before the fire. Oonagh was glad he did, glad that Nancy bothered to cajole and charm him, and glad to help her, merrily returning the darting looks of mischief Nancy threw at her as she did so. It made

Philip happy, and being happy kept him more often with her. And even though she knew Nancy was marking time, keeping her hand in, as it were, until a more vital purpose for her charm came along, or perhaps distracting herself from the sorry turn her own life had taken – 'I am twenty-six, the eldest, and live at home with three little sisters. All I need is a few peculiar habits and a cat,' she said mournfully to Oonagh, in an unguarded moment – her presence in the house made everything more fun.

Violet called far less since the night of the party. Something had shifted between them, and Violet responded by keeping her distance. Besides, her wedding was just a month away and she was busy. 'She is to have eleven bridesmaids,' Oonagh told Nancy one morning, 'and is ordering such quantities of mono-grammed linen that there is no sewing being done anywhere in the country except the stitching of the letters "VB" in embroidery silk.'

She spoke to Nancy, but it was at Philip she looked. He had been cleaning the tips of his shiny black shoes by rubbing them against the underside of the armchair opposite him, but he stopped as she spoke, and she could see the way his face twitched a little at the story. She knew he missed having Violet around, but she didn't know if it was Violet herself, or the attention she heaped upon him, that he missed. Violet had always treated Philip like someone magnificent and delicate all at once. She deferred to him, listened to him, asked his opinion as though his were the voice of record, but also fussed over him, suggesting little things for his comfort – a drink, a cigarette, a cushion – all of which he affected to disdain but clearly loved.

Watching Philip with Nancy, seeing how he responded to her teasing and her absurd cajoleries – 'Will it be fine today, Philip? I swear I will believe no one but you' – Oonagh was inclined to think it was the attention he missed, and she was more than ever grateful to Nancy, on her own account, but mostly on Philip's. They were happier together now, and she swore to herself that she would spare him more of her time, would stop running to the nursery every moment she had. If theirs was to be a good marriage, as they had promised one another it would be, then they needed time together. And so, when Philip suggested a few days in Le Touquet the morning after the conversation about Violet's wedding, she forced herself to say, 'What a delightful idea,' and not to think instantly of Gay and how she couldn't bear to be away from him.

Within a week they were gone. They stayed at the Hôtel du Monde, where there were enough of their friends to make it 'very companionable', as Philip said with approval, but none so close that they couldn't avoid them if they wanted. He was relaxed in her company as he hadn't been in the nine months since Gay was born, she thought – even before, when she was so ill, and every moment she was not lying flat in bed was a trouble to her so that their dinners and afternoons together had been a monumental effort of pretence. Now, he joked with her as of old, teasing her about how carefully she avoided the sun.

'Is the parasol to come with us everywhere we go?

I can't wait to see you play tennis. Racquet in one hand, parasol in the other.'

And Oonagh felt herself expand in the warmth of his full attention, no longer indistinct everywhere except with Gay, and became solid and confident.

They breakfasted late together on the terrace outside their bedroom, swam or took drives in an open-topped car, climbing high into the hills and looking down at the sea below, which was like a piece of blue satin ribbon stitched to the fawn edge of the sand. At night there was dinner, and dancing, with other couples they knew from London, and enough cocktails to be gay but not so many that they woke with headaches every morning.

'Isn't this bliss?' Oonagh said, as they lay on warm sand under one of the hotel's umbrellas one afternoon, the sound of the sea congratulating them with smooth repetition. 'No office, no callers, no dreadful house-keeping and questions about "Would Madame like the duck in a roast or a pot roast?" As if I have any idea?' She laughed, and Philip laughed too, and looked down at her, his face tanned and happy so that Oonagh wondered if there was a different sort of life they could lead together.

'Imagine we got rid of everyone,' she said thoughtfully. 'No Peters, no Mrs Taylor, no Nanny. Just Kathleen. We could live in a hotel – people do, you know, Aileen does when she's in London, and says it's ever so restful – and go wherever we wanted. We could follow the sun and Gay could grow up playing in the water and on the sand, and we could teach him everything he needs to know.' It was a new version of the game they had played before Gay was born – suggesting names for him like Celestin and Hermes and other foolish possibilities. But either Philip had forgotten the game, or he didn't want to play.

'But Gay must go to Eton,' he said. 'A boy needs an education.'

And Oonagh, who couldn't bear to think of a time when her son would be taken from her, his trunk packed and stowed aboard a train that would take him away for so long while she stood on the platform and waved him off with a breaking heart, changed the topic abruptly. 'Did you see that couple at dinner last night, the quantity of pudding she ordered?'

The night before they were due to leave, while Oonagh was at her dressing-table packing her jewels into their travelling case – something she liked to do herself, so that Kathleen had once teased her she must believe they could tell the difference between her and another – Philip, in evening dress, wrestling with a cufflink, said, 'Why don't we stay longer? I don't need to be back yet – Father himself has said I can be spared a few days more.'

Oonagh, who had counted every day and had begun to count every hour, till she would see Gay again, felt as though something inside her had been pulled, hard and unexpectedly, like the communication cord on a train, so there was a sudden deep pain. Not daring to mention Gay but desperate to stop him making new plans, she blurted out, 'What about Valsie's wedding? It's in less than a week. She'll be so disappointed.' And she saw Philip's face snap closed so that suddenly, too late, she realised that the wedding was the very thing he hoped to miss, even to ignore the very fact of it.

'Very well,' he said immediately, and refused to talk any further about it, even when she hurriedly said, 'Well, maybe a few days. Or Kathleen could bring Gay out and we could stay much longer . . .'

'No,' he said, 'you're right. It was a foolish whim.' And because neither of them could say what they really wanted, they said nothing, and went back to London as planned.

And Oonagh, even as she buried her face in Gay's neck and kissed him over and over again until Nanny said, 'Be careful, you'll overexcite him, madam,' wondered at what she had done, and what it would mean.

Chapter Twenty-Seven

Hans Crescent, London

'Is it just me or has this city become the biggest bore?' Maureen asked fretfully, as she watched Duff get dressed.

'You're just not used to the soft living any more,' Duff said with a smile. 'Too long at Clandeboye.' They were in London for Violet's wedding, staying at their house in Hans Crescent, had arrived with the first warm days.

'It is heaven to be in such comfort again,' Maureen said, stretching luxuriously and putting her hands above her head to feel the upholstery of the satin padded headboard. 'I can't get used to there being no howling draughts. And for April to mean spring, rather than more winter.' She laughed and sat up, looking approvingly around the cream and gold bedroom. 'Now, why don't you come back to bed?' She smiled at him and fluttered her lashes exaggeratedly. 'Surely you don't need to be at the House this early.'

'It isn't early,' Duff said. 'Only you could think that.'

'Well, you would, too, if you'd been out with Chips at the Café de Paris half the night.'

'I wish you wouldn't go about with that fellow so much. I don't trust him. He's a sight too nosy. In fact, if you ask me, he's a spy. No one who goes on about how much he despises America and Americans could be anything else. How can you trust a man who denies where he comes from?'

'If he's an American, you can applaud him.'

'All the same, I'd rather you had a lot less to do with him.'

'Wonderful fun, though.'

'Because he flatters you.'

'Everyone flatters me,' Maureen said. 'They know how I adore it.'

'Well, just be careful,' Duff said, shrugging on his jacket. 'Don't, for God's sake, *tell* him anything. And be careful who you introduce him to.'

'He says he'll call later. But he can't come to much harm with Oonagh and Mamma, who will visit too,' Maureen said, wriggling further down under the eiderdown. 'Neither of them knows a thing.'

'And try to remember you're having a baby,' he said, leaning down to kiss her goodbye. 'In less than three months now. Do take it a little bit easy.'

'As if I could forget,' she said, making a woeful face. But after he had left, she fell asleep again so that it was late indeed by the time she was up and dressed, wandering about the house with the discontented feeling she had begun to know too well. It followed her about all day, from the time Duff left in the morning – always early, no matter how late they had been out – until it was time for drinks and dressing for dinner. The first cocktail banished it, like magic, replacing discontent with the giddy excitement Maureen lived for. Indeed, sometimes she didn't bother with tea at all, but today, because of Mamma and Oonagh, she held herself in check. Oonagh, she had noticed, had all sorts of theories about drinking being 'bad for the baby', and Maureen, brought up on Cloé's endless conversation about diet, knew that she couldn't bear to begin on what should, and shouldn't, be eaten.

'How was Le Touquet?' she asked, when Cloé's litany of ailments had been exhausted.

'Lovely,' Oonagh said. 'We thought about not coming back, but one couldn't miss Violet's wedding.'

'Couldn't one?' Maureen asked, watching her carefully. 'I should think *one* very well could. Especially if *one* was you, Oonagh.'

'Your teacups are getting smaller,' Oonagh said, instead of answering, walking to the window of the drawing room that overlooked the street with one in hand. 'This is so tiny it could belong in a doll's house.'

'Mamma gave us those,' Maureen said.

'I do hate clumsy cups,' Cloé said. 'And large plates. Like troughs.' She shuddered.

'No one could describe this as a trough,' Oonagh said, taking a plate so slender Maureen imagined it might shatter just by her holding it. On it she placed a biscuit like a communion wafer. 'Or this as food. More like a sacred offering. Maureen, now that you're eating for two, you'll need to pile on at least six, one on top of another.'

'I have never thought there to be any excuse for making a pig of oneself,' Cloé said disapprovingly. 'You're having a baby, not a calf.'

'You never think there's much of an excuse for eating at all,' Maureen said. 'Now, what do you think of the house?' It was their first visit since the decorators had finished.

'All that marble,' Oonagh said. 'It puts me in mind of Harrods food hall. This could double as the overflow for the poultry and fish.' She laughed, then saw Maureen's face. 'But beautiful, darling, and so convenient,' she added hurriedly. 'You could run a string from one of the windows and a Harrods assistant could make up a little basket of goodies and send it back over to you.'

'Essentials,' Maureen agreed.

'Caviar, tea, a few bottles of gin.' They both giggled. Then, 'What about children?' Oonagh continued. 'Is there anywhere to play? I suppose Hans Place has a garden, and Hyde Park is not too far.'

'The children won't be here,' Maureen said. 'They will be at Clandeboye.'

'But only while you're there?'

'No, all the time. Much better for them.'

'So you won't be often in London,' Oonagh said.

'I know what you're getting at,' Maureen snapped, 'and we jolly well will. You sound like Duff now.' She put on a mocking voice: '"What about the children?" Whatever children there are will remain at Clandeboye, as they should, and we shall divide our time. As we should. I did not expect to be living there so soon, but I'm damn—' – she saw Cloé's face and changed to – '*determined* not to vanish into that old wreck of a place. Country living is all very well for a while, and not for any more than that.' One thing to fill Clandeboye with her giddy friends or Duff's shooting parties for a few weeks, she thought. Quite another to be expected to live there year-round with a child. Now was the time to draw up a pattern, a way of being and behaving, so that later she need simply stick to it and no one could be surprised.

'Mr Henry Channon,' Maureen's butler announced then. Oonagh stirred with irritation. 'Why him?' she muttered, as Chips could be heard bounding up the marble stairs. 'Neither of you trusts or even particularly likes the other.'

'Yes, it's the perfect friendship,' Maureen said loudly. 'He has the hide of an elephant, so never minds what I say, unlike everyone else who is offended the moment I open my mouth.' She rolled her eyes. 'And he's even more of a snob than Mamma, aren't you darling?' she said to Chips, who came in beaming and ignored what she had said. He was like a bottle of champagne shaken hard and opened suddenly, Maureen thought, with a look at Oonagh and a giggle. He bubbled and fizzed over their hands, talking, clasping, even kissing, although Oonagh, she could see, would have liked to twitch hers out of his grasp.

'Why, I was only saying last night to one of my fellow countrymen – Mrs Wallis Simpson, a lady who feels just as I do about this great nation of yours – that one doesn't see half enough of the Glorious Guinness Girls. And here you two are,' Chips said, straightening up and looking around at them. 'And with your most wonderful mamma. Dear lady,' he said, bowing before Cloé with one hand on his heart. His welcome was as broad, Maureen thought, as though it were his house and they the callers. He was all but ready to ring and offer them refreshment.

'Sit down, Chips,' she said. 'What would you like? We are having tea, but I'm sure you'd prefer something stronger.' She hoped he would say yes, and when he did – 'One of those deals your butler whips up,' – she said, 'I'll have one too,' as though being polite.

Chips launched into a description of a recent evening, with all the usual exuberant name-dropping Maureen enjoyed: 'We dined at Fort Belvedere. His Royal Highness is just back from a tour of South America with his brother, the Duke of York. I'm sure you saw the little Princess Elizabeth greeting them at the airport? By golly is he glad to get home! His Royal Highness plans to put in a swimming pool,' and ignored Oonagh when she said tartly, 'Well, aren't you just privy to the most fascinating confidences?'

'And a steam room,' he ploughed on, 'and many more bathrooms. Why, it will be positively American.' And he beamed round at them all.

'So not everything American is inferior?' Oonagh asked. Maureen knew that she hoped to be rude, but Chips was having none of it.

'How clever you are,' he said, sweeping her up in a smile grown ever wider so that Maureen, impressed at the remarkable way he always kept his temper, no matter the provocation, thought they might all drown in his enthusiasm. 'No, indeed. In the matter of sanitation, we are world leaders and proud to be so. For every bedroom a bathroom.'

'And for every bedroom a lovely companion . . . Such is the Prince of Wales's way at the Fort, I hear,' she murmured. It was the kind of thing that, had she said it in front of Ernest, or Duff, would have earned her a stern look. But Cloé, idly turning the pages of a book, could be relied upon to pretend she hadn't heard or understood. And Oonagh, although she looked shocked, made no comment.

Chips, however, roared laughing. 'A tonic,' he said. 'That's what you are. A tonic. And you are correct. Why, I hear that the current *companion*—'

But here he was cut off by the butler announcing, 'Lady Honor Guinness.'

This cousin, a year older than Oonagh, was the second eldest of Uncle Rupert's children, quieter than Maureen, but less shy than Oonagh. Softly spoken, discreet and irritatingly oblivious to the rivalry Maureen had tried to set up: 'They may have the title, but we have the looks,' she liked to say. In Honor came with a parcel of books and said, 'May I sit for just a moment? I have to meet Father at the House.'

Maureen watched as Chips made a great show of seeing that Honor was comfortable, leaping up for extra cushions, exclaiming over her stack of books – an improving lot, from what she could see – and quickly, skilfully, taking her measure. Within a moment he had changed his conversation entirely. Instead of gossip and scandal, he talked of plays and music, asking had she seen *The Good Companions* – 'Gielgud is terrific, I tell you, simply terrific.'

'I enjoyed his *Hamlet* very much, at the Old Vic,' Honor said. 'It is clear that he has studied his craft.' And quickly – so quickly that Maureen was not even sure how it was done – Chips had promised to get tickets and escort Honor and her sisters, Brigid and Patricia, with their mother, to His Majesty's Theatre.

Watching the efforts Chips made, the shamelessness with which he made them and, most of all, that he so clearly thought Honor worth making them for, irritated Maureen. She knew none of it would be lost on Oonagh, who, indeed, was looking from Honor to Maureen and back again with a delighted expression. 'Do carry on with what you were telling us,' she interjected. 'Something about the Prince of Wales and bathrooms and *companions* . . .' She saw Chips flick a sharp look at Honor, and spot the tightening of her mouth, just as Maureen had spotted it, had known to look for it.

Instead of answering, he said smoothly, 'I don't rightly remember, but let me tell you about the book I'm currently writing,' so that Honor drew closer to him, and Maureen sat back in her chair in disgust.

'Mamma, time to go, I think,' Oonagh said, and Maureen knew perfectly well that the minute she exited the front door, even before she was halfway down those seven steep steps, she would burst out into peals of laughter, and that Cloé would pretend not to understand, but even she would give a thin smile.

And so, 'I'm coming with you,' Maureen said on impulse. 'You can give me dinner. Chips, you'll have to go. I simply haven't time for this.'

And even then, he just said mildly, 'Of course. Lady Honor, may I drop you at the House? I have the motor outside,' so that Maureen, furious though she was at the attention he paid Honor, and how quickly he had switched that attention from her, had to admire the adroitness of his manoeuvring. She thought of all the things she could have told Honor that would have caused her to bolt from Chips's company in alarm, and the knowledge of them gave her enough comfort to stay quiet.

Chapter Twenty-Eight

Rutland Gate, London

The morning of Violet's wedding, Oonagh woke feeling so ill she could hardly get out of bed, but when Kathleen said, 'You can't go like that. I'll have Mrs Taylor send up tea and toast,' Oonagh insisted.

'It would seem so odd for me not to go. One doesn't want . . .'

'. . . *to make a fuss*,' Kathleen finished for her.

'Exactly.'

'You're a fool, Oonagh,' Kathleen said bluntly. 'For the sake of not making a fuss, you'll risk much worse. Philip doesn't want to go, you don't want to go. And yet you're both going.'

'I am the one who insisted we come home for this, don't you see?' Oonagh said. 'I can't now leave him to go alone.' And she clung to this, even when she had been sick in a china bowl and a housemaid had carried it downstairs, covered with a linen cloth. 'I wouldn't miss the eleven bridesmaids for the world,' she insisted, trying to make a joke. 'Ring for Burton, will you? I must have my bath.'

'At least promise you'll come back quickly?'

'I will.' And she did, coming home, alone, after just a few hours and allowing herself to be settled in the nursery where Gay was having his tea – a boiled egg and buttered toast cut into soldiers. She was huddled into her coat, which she refused to take off, before a fire that was too hot for the day, with a rug over her knees. And still her teeth chattered with cold.

'The church,' she said, with a shudder. 'So chill, like all churches. And then standing about afterwards while Baby and Zita threw *rice*. As though Violet were a pudding.' She described Violet's dress – 'Ivory silk, fitted to the knee then flaring out into a full skirt, with a long, heavy train. Delicious. But such a last-minute commotion, you'll never guess. Violet is become thinner, and the dress was found no longer to fit and had to be taken in overnight. Essex, Violet's sister – such a name! – told me she found a pin still in it when it came time for Valsie to dress this morning. A pin. I wonder is that luck, or not so much? Luck if one finds a pin, but to have it nearly stuck into one? I must ask Gunnie. It's exactly the sort of thing she knows.' She was babbling, she knew it, and was grateful when Kathleen interrupted.

'Philip?' she asked.

'Gone to his club. He said he had things to see to.' She turned away, looking into the fire. Then her eyes widened in sudden shock. 'Oh, God, Kathleen, quick!'

Kathleen, ever vigilant, grabbed a milk jug and gave

it to her, and under Nanny's appalled gaze Oonagh leaned forward and was sick twice into it. Gay laughed, and clapped his hands. 'Lucky it was the big nursery jug, not the tiny drawing-room one,' Oonagh said weakly. 'I think I'd better go to bed now. I must have caught something.'

But she was sick again the next day, and the next, so Kathleen said, 'I will ring for the doctor.'

'Don't,' Oonagh said. 'Please don't.'

'Whyever not?'

'I don't need a doctor. Not yet anyway,' and when Kathleen looked ready to insist, she said, 'Don't you see? No, I suppose you don't. Well, maybe Le Touquet was a lucky holiday after all . . .' And she began counting backwards on her fingers: 'Twenty, nineteen . . .'

When Kathleen finally understood, she said, 'Surely that is reason more than any to call the doctor. Dr Gilliatt?'

But Oonagh grabbed her hand. 'Don't,' she said, 'please don't. Not yet. A few more days can't make any difference. Just to be sure.' Even though she was sure. Completely sure. And so happy that she didn't, not yet anyway, want to see the worry in anyone else's eyes. She knew the doctor would not approve: he had all but forbidden her to have another child. And because of that Philip would worry, and between them they would rob her of the joy she felt. They would read her dire warnings, or screw up their faces in concern, or begin to monitor her with close anxiety. And she couldn't bear it. Not yet anyway.

And so when she retched in the pale dawn hours and maids scuttled to and fro with foul bowls, when her room smelled of the back-of-throat catching of carbolic soap and there was a shimmer of secrecy to what went on in her bedchamber, she said nothing. She asked that Nancy not be admitted in the mornings, and didn't say why. Trays travelled up and down the stairs with toast and marmalade and pots of weak tea, and still she said nothing.

A full week went by, until finally it was Philip who broke the fragile spell, who stood in the doorway with a tray held away from him, face averted from the smell of burned toast that wafted from it, and asked, 'What exactly is going on, Oonagh? I feel I'm living in a play that has another, entirely different, play happening within it of which I have been told nothing.'

Oonagh scrambled to sit upright in bed, smoothing her hair with one hand and twitching at the creamy satin counterpane with the other. 'Come in and sit down,' she said.

Later, when Kathleen went to collect the tray, Oonagh was up and dressed in an ivory silk chiffon peignoir with skirts that fell heavy to the floor where they trailed in a way that she knew irritated Kathleen, who had asked to take up the hem several times, because it gathered dust.

'Well?' Kathleen asked, staring at the hem of the peignoir.

'He's ringing for Dr Gilliatt straight away.' Oonagh made a face.

'I'm glad.'

'I know you are. Oh, I am too. It's time. I just . . .' She shrugged and picked up one of her silver-backed brushes and began to run it through her hair. 'In any case, it's done now, and they will all be at me so I must make the best of it.'

'But he's happy?'

'Yes, of course. Happy. Worried. You know.' Kathleen waited for her to say something else, but she didn't.

In fact, Philip, although he had said, 'Marvellous news,' had looked shocked. And when Oonagh asked him was he not pleased, he had rushed to say, 'Yes, of course, only I didn't expect . . . so soon . . .' And when she pressed him on that, he insisted only that he was worried for her, after everything Gilliatt had said. Oonagh had to be content with that.

And she tried. But Philip's face – the shock on it, whatever was underneath the shock – stayed with her. And when Aileen, in town for the wedding, called the day before she went home to invite her to 'a cosy family lunch' at the Ritz with Maureen, Duff and Brinny, Oonagh said no, she was still tired, and stayed in bed listening to records on the gramophone and staring out of the window into the garden.

'I don't know why Oonagh is too tired to come,' Aileen said, 'when the wedding is a week ago and, anyway, she left so early.'

'Perhaps that's why she's tired,' Maureen said.

'Meaning?'

'The exhaustion of relief. A campaign fought and won,' – she shrugged – 'the slump that follows . . .'

'Wrestling Philip back from the fair clutching hands of dear little Violet Valerie you mean?'

'Exactly. I never did like that girl,' Maureen mused, 'and I was right.'

'But she and Oonagh are still such pals. Perhaps Oonagh can afford to be magnanimous in victory . . . Now that she's triumphed, Violet is to be allowed to coat-tail a little longer.'

'Oonagh's a fool. No victory is permanent.'

'It's like listening to the strategies of the Duke of Wellington,' Duff said with a laugh. Then, to Brinny, 'Are they always like this?'

'Like what?' Brinny looked nervous, as though he might be expected to say something disloyal about his wife.

'Speaking in code only they understand?'

'Sisters!' Brinny said heartily, relieved that nothing more was required of him.

'Look,' – Maureen nudged Aileen – 'there's that chap who was at Oonagh's party. The funny baron fellow.' They looked over to where the baron sat in the embrace of a window, light falling behind him, with a cup of coffee and a newspaper. He spotted them and gave an urbane wave of the hand, then stood and half bowed in their direction.

'Idiotic fellow,' Maureen said, waving back cheerfully.

'Wonderful dancer, though,' Aileen said, smiling graciously at him.

'What on earth is he eating?' Brinny asked, revolted. 'A cream cake? What kind of chap does that?'

Chapter Twenty-Nine

athleen raced home along Exhibition Road. She had got up early to meet Ned before his shift, and now she was late getting back to Oonagh. She and Ned had walked the banks of the Thames, with Ned pointing out tidal grooves in the mud flats while she told him her news from home: Peggy, who had a new job behind the counter in Dunne's chemist, her da who was thinking of turning the ironmonger's shop over to her sister Mairead's husband, who had worked with the railways.

'Do they not miss you?' he had asked.

'They do, and I them, but it's not for ever. I'll go home to them when it's right.'

'And when will that be? When the Guinnesses let you go?'

'When I decide to go,' she had said firmly. She didn't like that he thought her at the beck and call of the Guinnesses. He must have noticed, because he changed the conversation, describing the ideas in a book he was reading. Because they had talked so much, she had walked further than she'd intended, and by the time she turned to come back, she was late, which made her feel guilty. Oonagh, mindful of Dr Gilliatt, and of Philip, even though very quickly she didn't feel anything like as bad as she had with Gay, had cancelled all her appointments and declined invitations, staying close to home and begging Kathleen to keep her company.

But she must have said the same thing to Diana and Nancy, Kathleen thought ruefully, as she arrived, out of breath, at Rutland Gate, because there they were, sitting in the little drawing room with Oonagh.

'Farve is certain Biddesden is haunted,' Diana was saying to Oonagh, as Kathleen slipped in. 'By the ghost of General Webb who once lived there. He won't set foot in the house but sits outside in his motor. He's told so many people that now the spiritualists want to come down.'

'They do seem to like an especially *firm* haunting, those spiritualists,' Nancy said, tapping her crimson-lacquered nails on the varnished tabletop with a fretful sound. 'The sort of decisive older gentleman you can rely on to show up and really rattle things. The spiritualists themselves are almost always women, you see. The older sort, who wear lace caps and mittens and live in Ealing.' Nancy's use of the word 'rattle' startled Kathleen, because she had been thinking that very thing about Nancy herself. She spoke even quicker than usual, lighting one cigarette after another, and her hand, when she held the slim gold lighter, shook so that she had to click it repeatedly before the flame was steady enough to do its job. 'What are you stitching?' she demanded of Kathleen, then didn't listen when Kathleen said, 'Linen. Left to herself, Oonagh would throw out everything with a tear, so I gather it up and mend it.'

'Delightful,' Nancy said vaguely.

'Does anyone actually live in Ealing?' Diana asked.

Oonagh waved a handkerchief in front of her, to dispel Nancy's smoke. 'Must you?'

'Yes,' Nancy said, blowing two thin streams of smoke from her nostrils, 'I must. I say, can't you ring for a drink? I've had quite enough tea.'

'It's a little early, isn't it?' Diana said censoriously, turning her wrist to examine the delicate gold watch clasped around. She, too, was expecting again and the swell beneath her dress was newly visible.

'Don't be a bore, Honks. What has early to do with anything when one has hardly been to sleep?' Nancy said.

'Good party?' Diana asked with a grin.

'Barking up the wrong tree, darling. No party. But no sleep either. One might as well have been having the *gayest* of times . . . Too sick-making to be listening to the dear little birds from one's bed and not from a taxi cab on the way home, astonished that it's morning already. In any case, it's jolly well time for a drink by my reckoning. And I can't have one at number twenty-six with the Old Pair, who look at one so sideways I worry they will fall over. So go ahead and ring for the tray, Oonagh. If one can't be happy, one might as well be amused, isn't that so?' There was silence then, and Nancy got up and walked to the window. 'Aren't the primroses late?' she said, looking across to the gardens. Oonagh and Diana turned to follow her with their eyes, but neither asked why she was unhappy.

'Aren't you terrified?' Oonagh turned back to Diana. 'Of the ghost of General Webb.'

'I never see him,' Diana said. 'I think he disapproves of me. I imagine he saves his energy for frightening important men.'

'But if one was alone . . .'

'Ah, but one never is. Everywhere one goes, Bryan's chums are hard at it. Augustus John in the morning room, Brian Howard pacing about above one's head, Henry Lamb in the gardens, Lytton Strachey debating Oriental art over breakfast. Everywhere one looks, there they all are, furiously composing and painting and writing.'

'Sounds like the dark satanic mills all over again, only with poetry and watercolour,' Nancy said, coming back to join them. She seemed to have recovered her good humour. 'Bryan and Diana revolutionise the means of creative production. I must say, the two of you really are wallowing in it, aren't you?'

'In what?'

'The Lord and Lady Bountiful bit, generous patrons of the arts. It was a good day for scribblers and daubers when you decided to get married. I see that the purpose of your life is laid out before you.'

'Is it?' Diana sounded wan.

'Well, don't you want it to be? You give a jolly good impression of being made for the part.'

'It was fun, at first,' Diana said. 'Now, though, well,

one rather longs for something more serious . . . You know. Some great purpose.' She looked around, Kathleen thought with a laugh she hid by bending low over her darning, as though she expected a great purpose to make itself known to her then and there.

'Sculpture?' Nancy asked with a grin. She had found a tray of drinks in a corner and was splashing gin into a glass.

'Don't be silly,' Diana said. 'I mean that England is in such a mess, everybody says so, and it feels rather foolish to be hosting painting parties and poetry salons.'

'So that's why you're in town!' Nancy interrupted her gleefully. 'To hear Mosley speak again? Even in your condition?'

'Only partly,' Diana said. 'I had to get my hair done too.'

'Yes, I see you've had your hair done,' Nancy said, adding shrewdly, 'yesterday? Before the meeting?'

'What of it?' Diana was nettled.

'Nothing, nothing,' Nancy said airily. 'And how was the jolly old meeting?'

'You could come with me. Then you'd see for your-self.'

'No more Blackshirts for me,' Nancy said. 'I don't mind the dirty halls so much, it's all the shouting and stamping . . . Simply too exhausting. Why must they insist on so much drama? Like a village-hall theatrical company.'

'But isn't he magnificent?' Diana's eyes shone.

'Mosley?' Nancy asked. 'Well, when you've heard one of his speeches, you've rather heard them all, don't you think? All that guff about Britain needing a new order. And that arm, going up and down, up and down – he looks like a man pumping water at the village pump. A particularly *stubborn* pump, given how hard he works at it.' She giggled.

'I think he looks like a man who's never had to ask for anything twice,' Diana said dreamily.

'Do you?' Nancy looked at her. 'Do you really? Well. Sometimes I quite forget that you are my younger, *married* sister . . .'

Diana coloured red – redder than Kathleen had ever seen her – and made a face, screwing up her eyes and nose and glaring at Nancy. 'Don't be disgusting,' she said. 'Mosley cares for nothing except dragging this country out of the mess that even you must see we're in.'

'Except he can't seem to decide quite how to do it, can he?' Nancy said. 'Or, indeed, decide very much about anything. Conservative, Labour, New Party, British Union of Fascists, goodness knows what next. And he can't make up his mind about his women either. His wife, her sister, their stepmother . . . Best be careful, my sweet. That's a dangerous man. Whether he'll bring glory to Britain I don't know, but he brings trouble to those around him. The women, anyway.'

'Nancy!' Diana leaped to her feet, slamming her teacup and saucer so hard onto the table beside her that they rattled horribly. She glared, her pupils tiny pinpricks in all that angry blue. 'You forget yourself!'

'Oh, very well, I take it all back,' Nancy said with a sly smile. 'I had no idea you would take it so . . . personally.'

Diana looked at her, still standing. Then, 'I must go. Oonagh, please ring for Peters to bring my coat,' she said, in a stiff voice.

'Don't be a goose, Honks. Do stay,' Nancy tried, but Diana wouldn't. After she was gone, there was silence except for whatever sounds came in from outside – a motor-car idling on the kerb, children laughing in the gardens, the sharp clack of heels on the pavement, the squeak of next-door's area railings as someone pushed open the gate.

'Well, I had no idea she was in so deep . . .' Nancy said at last.

So deep in what? Kathleen wondered, but she did not ask because just then Philip came in and immediately, like a whistle that only dogs can hear, one they cannot ignore, Oonagh and Nancy sat up straighter and leaned forward towards him. Only Kathleen stayed exactly as she was, settling into the corner of the sofa with her sewing.

Chapter Thirty

London

For days Kathleen had been puzzling over the drawing-room conversation, trying to make sense of what Nancy and Diana had said to each other, decoding their complicated conversations, fitting together the bits and pieces she knew from Ned, trying them now one way, now the other. But nothing made sense.

'Are your meetings the same as the ones that Mosley holds?' she asked Ned, the next time they met.

'Couldn't be further,' he said cheerfully.

'But he cares a great deal about the state of the country too. I've heard Diana say so.'

'Maybe so, but his solutions are not our solutions. He talks about glory and strength. He's big and grand and wants the rich – your friends,' – he grinned at her – 'to join him and make a new kind of country where they can be even richer.'

'And you?'

'We want to get rid of the rich, take all their money off them and share it out equally.' He laughed, and Kathleen had no idea if he was joking or not. 'Mosley loves the sound of marching men, men with a uniformity of purpose under his command. We let men be themselves, if they will come together to help each other. But don't listen to me. Come with me to hear men who explain it all a deal better than I do. There's a meeting tonight, back of the Queen Adelaide in Bethnal Green.'

'Did you see that chalked on the pavement?'

'I did. Well remembered.' He grinned again, and Kathleen said she would. She wanted to know where he went, what these meetings to which he attached such importance were, and who the Comrades were that he so admired. 'Better not tell Mary,' he said. 'She won't care for you coming at all.'

Mary, Kathleen thought, might tell Diana, who would certainly tell Oonagh . . . 'Not a word,' she promised.

They planned to meet at Cambridge Heath railway station that very evening, and all day Kathleen felt the squirm of excitement. Partly, it was the idea that she was to take a train through London, alone, at night. She was almost never alone, except for early-morning walks. All the rest of her days and evenings were spent with Oonagh, with Oonagh's friends, with Gay, with the household at Rutland Gate or with Ned and Mary. She had discovered that it was only when she was by herself and doing something new – a visit to the National Portrait Gallery, a trip to Harrods' library – that she could fully grasp how much she had changed since leaving Dublin over a year ago. In the rare times that she was alone, she could also see the person she once was, and marvel at the differences. A train at night to a part of London she did not know would surely be such a chance to consider her again – that stilted creature who had come to London filled with apprehensions she didn't understand, which were outweighed only by the certainty that she could not any longer carry on with what she knew, the old familiar Dublin ways that were flat and dulled, like the sound of carriage wheels trundling across sawdust.

And, too, it was a chance to think about what was meant – if anything was meant – by meeting Ned in the evening and not the daytime.

Since the visit to his rooms when he had kissed her, there had been one dance, at Oonagh's party, and since then, Ned had not so much as moved to take her hand. And although she did not expect him to, still she found herself wondering why he had kissed her, and if he would ever do it again. She tried to compare him – her friendship with him – with what she had known with Mr O'Loughlin, but soon stopped because, really, there was nothing similar at all. She had never sought Mr O'Loughlin's company – only agreed to his suggestions that they take a walk – and while she had enjoyed those conversations, she had not much thought about him in between. Partly because he was another woman's husband, but partly, too, because he was not, himself, someone she needed to think about. He had always seemed a little sad, a little lonely – until her anger at his silence when she had needed him to stand up for her had made her indifferent to his sadness.

Maybe Ned was a fellow who kissed girls, she thought now. Maybe by going to his room she had somehow suggested that she wanted him to kiss her. Did the fact that he was younger than her – by two years – mean something for the kiss, or did it not? Kathleen, always so certain in her other roles – knowing where to be, what to do, in Rutland Gate, out with Mary, even in the drawing room with Oonagh's friends, where she knew when to stay quiet and when to speak – had no idea what to do to discover the meaning of Ned's kiss. She wanted to ask him all her questions, but didn't know how. And there was no one to ask in his stead. She couldn't speak of such a thing with Oonagh, and not with Mary either. Above all not to Mary, who had begun to approve a great deal less of Ned. She didn't like the people he went about with, his willingness to say yes to everything – Mary, Kathleen had noticed, prided herself on saying no and had rules for herself that were strict, such as not going to Oonagh's party, not sitting in the drawing room at Rutland Gate, asking Kathleen to come in by the basement steps when she called to Buckingham Street. It was as if, seeing Ned pushing outwards into new places, Mary felt herself obliged to restore balance by pulling back into what she had always known. In any case, Kathleen didn't even know what she would ask either of them, if she had been bold enough to try: *What does it mean when a man kisses you?* She could have asked Ernest, she thought suddenly, except that she needed to know now, and he was away on the *Fantome*. She would find out for herself, she decided.

That evening, she sat on the train to Cambridge Heath with her forehead and nose pressed against the window as though it had behind it a sweet shop. It was that strange part of the day when the sky is still clear but the air is darkening, so that to look up was to be in daylight, but to look down was to see night-time begun. The houses sat in darkness but were still boldly outlined against the pale blue and purple sky, as though someone had sketched them there in charcoal. It was, she knew, the only time to see stars in that city, pale pinpricks in the deepening blue, and then only for a scant few minutes, before the streetlights came on and they were obliterated in a fuzzy orange glow.

The train trundled on, the *clackety-clack* of its wheels reassuringly repetitive when outside everything was changing minute by minute. By the time she descended at Cambridge Heath it was properly dark and she wound her scarf more tightly around her neck, for comfort rather than warmth. But Ned was standing just where he said he would be, and pulled her to him in what was almost an embrace. 'I have followed your recipe for an omelette so well that now I am ready for more,' he said. 'Can you get me a way for making mayonnaise?'

'I'll ask Mrs Taylor. I'll say it's for you, so she might agree.'

'Will she need so much persuading?'

'Of course she will. She's a cook. She parts with recipes only with the utmost reluctance. I have heard Oonagh beg her for the recipe for her apricot preserves, because Diana wanted it – Bryan loves them – only for Mrs Taylor to refuse. "As well ask Mr Ernest to give up the recipe for his stout," she said, which silenced Oonagh.'

The Queen Adelaide stood at the far end of a long dreary street called Hackney Road that, like so many London streets, had a half-finished air, as though the buildings had become tired and given in before they grew to their full heights. The Queen Adelaide reared above its squat neighbours and was proud in comparison, with a broad stone balustrade on the roof. But although once undoubtedly grand, it was by then, like the rest of that patch, tired and faded. The bar was busy – 'Friday night,' Ned reminded her – and a cheerful roar of conversation travelled on thick waves of cigarette smoke spurred on by the clink of glasses. Ned guided her through to the far end, nodding at the barman as they passed behind the bar and up a short flight of steep stairs covered with worn yellow linoleum. A large room, set directly over the bar, was full of people, and the noise was great, as Rutland Gate had been for Oonagh's party, but an entirely different kind. That had been many layers of light chatterings scattered one across the others like hundreds and thousands on a cake, as easy to disperse by a breath. This was the purposeful rumbling of a piece of machinery cranking into gear. It was the sound of Philip's motor-car on a frosty morning when the chauffeur brought it around to the front gate a full twenty minutes before Philip was due to step out the door that the car might build and gather to its full strength.

Fifty or more people were seated on wooden benches and, where the bench space had run out, standing along the sides and at the back of the room. Someone had put together a makeshift stage, nailing planks of wood into a platform that shook rhythmically as people walked across it.

Ned took her hand and pushed through the crowd, pulling her behind him, to the far side and found her space on a bench. The room was not made for so many, she thought; beside her, the windows were closed tight and ran with condensation. She put out a finger to touch one and took it away wet. The walls were clammy too, and there was a smell of beer and breath and the sweat of men. Ned said hello to a few people, smiling at those too far away to speak to. There was so much talk in the room that Kathleen wondered how anyone would be heard. People turned this way and that to confer with those behind or in front of them, while others pushed past the benches with full pint glasses in their hands, sometimes three or four glasses at once so that she wondered they didn't drop them. Then a man stood up on the wooden stage and roared, 'Right, men,' out across the room, and sooner than Kathleen could have believed, there was silence except for the rustlings and breathings and hum of living that cannot be otherwise with so many packed close together.

The talking began. The first man spoke about 'The conditions, as you know well – who better? – that have become intolerable such that it is no longer possible to raise a family on what we earn. The fruits of our labour are no longer sufficient for our decent survival.' He shouted, and the crowd, including Ned, shouted back at him, 'Aye!'

The first man finished speaking and was followed by a second, then a third. Soon Kathleen barely listened, just idly followed the gentle rumbling of the room that told her what the audience thought. She could tell who had their attention and agreement, and who did not, by listening to waves of sighs and mumbles that rose up and died down, like a wind stirring grass, setting it to sway and nod and scrape, then leaving off, letting it fall silent again, only to start up in a new place.

She looked around instead of to the front of the room. Most there were men, of Ned's age, but here and there grizzled, weary faces looked out too. These, she noticed, were silent, less likely than the younger men to explode into cries of assent. There were women too, not many but a handful, and they were generally better dressed, by far, than the men. A couple looked as smart as Oonagh and her friends, in well-cut coats and elegant hats, and had the same air of permanent surprise that Oonagh and her friends wore in public – as if everything, and everyone, were somehow astonishing to them. One had a collar of deep red fur and a matching fur-trimmed hat that she had taken off and laid on the seat beside her, allowing it to take space exactly as though it were human so that she, alone, sat in a small island, while all around her others crammed close. Instinctively, Kathleen sank deeper on her seat in case she was seen, then realised this was the last place anyone would notice her. Here, she thought with a smile, she was as she should be. She looked like the mass of people in the room, blending in easily with them, far more than she looked like anyone in Oonagh's house or at Grosvenor Place.

She was glad she had worn her old coat, tatty and unremarkable, rather than anything Oonagh had given her. It didn't matter how much she tried to make Oonagh's cast-offs plain – even removing trims of beads or lace at times – they were impossible to disguise. Even Mary could tell, at a glance, if Kathleen was wearing what she called with a sniff 'borrowed finery', although Kathleen had explained several times that they were not borrowed but given.

To her surprise, the woman in the red fur collar was the next to get up to speak, moving to stand on the makeshift stage with as much confidence as Oonagh in her own drawing room at Rutland Gate.

'Well,' she said, looking around with an amused expression, 'I've heard a great deal today about the rights of man. Far less about the rights of women.' There was some eye-rolling and coughing at that, and she raised her voice. 'I am talking in particular about the rights of women to be paid the same as men. Because only then can we start to fully deal with poverty.'

'What would the likes of her know about poverty?' muttered a woman in a tight headscarf close to where Kathleen sat. But Kathleen was interested.

'A society in which women are not paid as men is a society that gives itself the right to treat women as inferior to men in all things,' the woman continued. 'In the home, in the workforce, in our colleges. This diminishes all of us.' Kathleen dwelled on that word *diminish*. She thought back to her inadequate degree, the beady-eyed nuns and their mortifying 'letter of recommendation' that was no recommendation at all, even the very opposite. The way she had tried to tell them they were mistaken in what they thought of her, only to be slapped down. The way Mr O'Loughlin had suffered no ill effects, or not as Kathleen had. And she realised that *diminished* was what she felt, then and now, by it all.

The woman's speech, with its emphasis on the work women did and the pay they were entitled to, was clearly unpopular. The shiftings and mutterings around Kathleen told her that. And when she finished speaking and sat down, the response was muted. But Kathleen clapped, hard.

Ned nudged her then. When she looked at him, he nodded towards the man now taking the stage. 'Tom Wintringham,' he said. This man was different from those before him, Kathleen soon saw. His voice was lower: instead of shouting, he talked, so that they all, even Kathleen, leaned forward a little to hear him better. He sounded, she thought, like Duff – like someone who does not wish to speak but feels he must. As though the sound of his own voice in his ears was not the reward he sought.

'You deserve what all men deserve. A right to work. A right to be paid. The labourer is worthy of his hire.'

Kathleen thought then of Ernest, who had used exactly the same words to her when she had tried to ask him about the packet of wages that appeared each week in her room.

She was not surprised when Wintringham got the biggest cheer of the night. Perhaps, too, she thought, it was because he was the last and they were finally able, after more than two hours, to stand and move about. Whatever it was, those who were seated rushed to their feet when he was done, and those who were standing pressed forward, all cheering mightily, Kathleen with them. After that, the room emptied quickly, people streaming to the bar downstairs. Kathleen tried to get close to the woman in the fur collar, but she, unlike the others, didn't linger, gathering her hat from the seat beside her and leaving promptly.

'What did you think?' Ned asked, as they walked out.

'Very interesting,' she said. 'Especially that lady. Is she a Comrade?'

'Not exactly,' Ned said. 'She's from the Women's Freedom League.' Kathleen felt a surge of energy that such an organisation should exist. But Ned was less interested. 'Come and meet Tom,' he said. 'Wasn't he mighty?'

Close to, the man, Tom, was thin, and bent forward at the shoulders in the way tall men do. A lean face made long by the hair retreating from it was bisected by a thick clipped moustache. He had taken off his spectacles and his eyes were shrewd, but laughing too. Kathleen saw all this close up because they were squashed into a narrow space between the bottom of the stairs and the entrance to the bar. 'The fifth columnist,' he said with a smile, holding out his hand to her.

'The what?'

'It's a joke,' Ned explained. 'I've told him about you.

How you live with the Guinnesses but are like us at heart. He knows your Mr Ernest.'

Kathleen smiled back and did not say the first thing that came to her mind – *Am I like you? I have not yet decided any of that.* 'But surely the Guinnesses are not your enemies?' she said.

'Not individually,' Tom said. 'In fact, they are among the very few honourable employers. Ernest himself is a good chap. But as for what they represent . . .' He lifted his shoulders in a shrug. 'Come for a drink?'

'Kathleen?' Ned looked at her, but she felt it wrong to say yes. Attending a meeting was one thing. Sitting for a drink, in a pub, with one of the speakers . . .

'I can't, I must get the train.'

'I'll walk you to the station, then come back. Tom, I'll meet you in half an hour,' Ned said. All the way, he talked about Tom – what he had done, what he had said, what plans he had, so that when they reached the station and he said goodbye, Kathleen wasn't surprised that he didn't kiss her, just shook her hand and turned back towards the Queen Adelaide. But all the time he had talked about Wintringham, she had been thinking about the lady with the red fur collar, and how her use of the word *diminish* had made Kathleen feel as though, for the first time ever, someone knew how she had felt when the Sisters had mortified her; and that if someone knew, then maybe it wasn't just she, Kathleen, who had been made to feel like that, but other women too. The idea gave her a kind of wild energy – of relief mostly, but something else too – as though she heard a chorus of voices all calling, 'Unfair!' along with her.

And that energy must have been why she called after Ned as he went to walk away and why, when he turned around, she quickly caught his face in her two gloved hands and kissed him.

Chapter Thirty-One

Rutland Gate, London, Summer 1931

As Oonagh became stronger in the middle months of her pregnancy, Philip, at first careful and attentive, became distant once again. He was gone from the house more often – at his office, and then his club. Sometimes Oonagh fancied that the crack that had appeared in Le Touquet, when she had said no to staying longer, was still there, had widened. And then he would come in and sit with her and tease her and make her laugh, and she would tell herself she was mistaken.

'It's what men do,' Maureen – back in London now that her date was approaching – told her when she complained. 'It's a private world they have that has only other men in it.'

'As long as there are indeed only other men in it,' Oonagh said.

'What do you mean?' Maureen, sharp as always, demanded. 'Is it because Violet is back from honeymoon in two weeks?' She took the cup of tea Oonagh handed her and settled back against the many cushions she had placed behind her. Oonagh saw that she had draped a shawl over her middle; she liked to disguise the extent of her bump whenever possible.

'No, of course not. Anyway, she's back next week. She wrote to say they were coming home early.'

'I see.'

'There is nothing to see,' Oonagh said. 'But I think I'll convince Philip to take a house in the country for the summer, somewhere close enough that we can motor down. I know he'll say no at first, but I think I can persuade him.'

'What about Plaw Hatch Hall? Won't you go there?'

'Not if I can help it. I cannot spend any more evenings with Robert and Gladys. "Will you ride out?" asked every morning, even though my answer is always no, so that every day starts by disappointing them, reminding them yet again that I am not the sort of person they are. Then, in the afternoons, over tea, "Is that another new dress, Oonagh? What can you want with so many?" and always with that little laugh that isn't real. No, I must persuade him to take a house of our own. Myself, I'd go to Ireland, to Luggala.' She sighed. 'How I long for the smell of that water blackened by peat, and the mist that rolls down along the mountains, collecting through the night in our little hollow, then vanishing with the early-morning sun, taking all the staleness of the night with it. But Philip will never say yes to that.'

'But couldn't you just go? To Ireland?'

'I couldn't leave him alone. He wouldn't like it at all.'

'As though he were a house untended that might be broken into,' Maureen said. 'Well, then, take a place yourself. Why must you have Philip's agreement? You have money.' Oonagh flinched at the word. 'There!' Maureen said, 'I knew you'd do that! It's why I said it. You're like a tall girl stooping and bending at the knees to seem tiny, buying yourself only trifles and trinkets. Always waiting for Philip to give you presents you could easily buy yourself.'

'But I want Philip to do it,' Oonagh said. 'It's no good for him, for us, if I take my own lead on this. He is a man, and that is what men are like – providers. Papa warned me that it would be so . . . Surely Duff is the same.'

'Not a bit of it. I do what I want with my money, and he doesn't care.'

'You pour it all into that coal-hole that is Clandeboye.'

'Not all of it,' Maureen said. 'And, anyway, I choose to, because it makes Duff happy.' They didn't mention Duff's gambling, but Oonagh could see the knowledge of it in Maureen's evasion.

'Well, if I can suggest this country house to Philip, in such a way that he believes it to be his idea, then I will get what I want and we will all be happy.'

'You say it like you're putting on a play,' Maureen said, 'with lines to deliver and a stage to dress and actors to move carefully around. Surely so much easier just to do as you wish.'

'Easier, but not so pleasant. Philip gets cross if he's reminded that in the seesaw of money mine weighs more heavily than his.'

'People are such a bore about money, aren't they?' Maureen said. 'But I jolly well hope you do persuade him. We can't be going back and forth to Clandeboye, not now with the baby so close, but we will need somewhere to escape London.'

'I thought, if I find somewhere, Aileen might come too, and bring Neelia.'

'You'll fill the place with children,' Maureen said, rolling her eyes. 'I know you will.'

'Well, I'm determined to find the perfect place for us all,' Oonagh said. 'And I'll make Philip think it's his idea too! We can both get larger there together . . .'

'I'm not sure it's possible,' Maureen said, looking ruefully down at the shawl covering her.

'. . . and plan what to call our babies. It will be a perfect summer.'

In fact, it was Diana who found the 'perfect place', a house in Surrey called Great Tangley Manor, so old that it appeared in the Domesday Book – 'as a royal hunting lodge,' Oonagh told Philip when she cajoled him into agreeing, with much talk of how a 'man in his position' needed a summer place of his own – and with the initials of King George V and Queen Mary scratched with a diamond on the glass of the dining-room window. 'Probably trying to signal they needed an escape, poor things,' Diana said. 'But it will do for your lot.'

Violet, Oonagh thought, must have rung her up the very second she arrived in London. 'I'm back!' she announced. 'And I need you to tell me everything. I'm rushing right round in a taxi.' And she did just that, arriving on the doorstep with some rather faded-looking *macarons* – 'From Ladurée. We picked them up in Paris. I know how you love them' – and kissing Oonagh extravagantly on both cheeks. 'See how French I am, darling,' so that Oonagh remembered all over again that Violet, when not being cross and demanding, was funny and charming.

'You look well,' she said, admiring Violet's beautifully coiffed hair. 'Antoine?'

'Yes.' She shook the blonde curls. 'He only charged me half, because he said I would be an advertisement for him. Now, do tell.'

'Tell what?' Oonagh was amused at her eagerness.

'Everything. Isn't it the very worst, having to leave one's own wedding and go on honeymoon, when all one really wants to do is stay behind and find out what happens next? Didn't you feel that?'

'Well, not really,' Oonagh said. 'I was happy to go . . . But how was the honeymoon?'

'Delightful.'

'Shorter than expected?'

'Well, you know . . . France . . . It does all get rather tedious.'

'And how is married life?'

'Surely you know the answer to that. You've been married two years now.'

'I meant *your* married life, silly.' Easier for both if they pretended Violet had been joking.

'Delightful.'

'Like the honeymoon?' Oonagh couldn't resist. *Shorter than expected* hovered in the air between them.

'I see you've been busy,' Violet said then, looking Oonagh up and down in a way that was almost, Oonagh thought, rude.

'Yes.' Oonagh sat up a little straighter, allowing her small bump to appear larger. 'I'm due in January. A little sister for Gay, I think.' And then, when she saw Violet's face, she felt suddenly mean and said, 'I'm sure you will have a little one very soon.'

'Hmm.' Violet looked vague. 'What shall you do for the rest of the summer?'

'We have taken a house, in Surrey. You must come and stay.' Even as she said it, Oonagh wondered what she was about, and hoped Violet – after all, now married and surely with other things to do – would refuse.

'Yes, please,' Violet cheered up. 'Brougham Hall is in Cumberland, too far for short visits.'

'You and Victor,' Oonagh said firmly.

Chapter Thirty-Two

Great Tangley Manor, Surrey

Great Tangley Manor had been built for comfort not beauty – an Elizabethan manor house set inside its very own moat, now overgrown with an abundance of flowering shrubs so that, from a distance, the house seemed to float in a sea of pink and yellow and white blooms.

These were happy days. Mostly it was Oonagh's friends with children who came, so that Gay, now old enough to toddle about, had company Nanny approved of, and Nanny had company too, other nannies to sit and knit with her and compare notes on the brilliance of their charges.

The time was spent pleasantly, most often out of doors. English summers, Oonagh thought, were kinder by far than Irish ones. The long days were strangely content, like people in middle age, at ease with sameness: sunshine, gentle winds, drawn-out dusks that grew in glory as flowers poured out their scent in a last hurry before shutting tight for the night. So unlike the Irish summers of her childhood that were petulant, over-eager, forever changing, equipped with sharp elbows lest anyone became too comfortable.

At Great Tangley, theirs was not the furious, energetic kind of outdoors, riding and shooting, like it had been at Plaw Hatch Hall, but the kinds of gentler pursuits that Oonagh, especially now in the middle months of her pregnancy, enjoyed. Picnics were ordered, trips to a nearby wood to see campion in bloom, fishing in the river by the back of the house. Games of badminton were set up on the lawn, tennis – the house had its own grass court – and croquet. The children were encouraged to join all of these activities so that days were spent in family groups, and it was only once evening fell and the children were taken to the nursery for their supper that the cocktail trays came out. Then, records were put on the gramophone and there was music, even sometimes dancing, before dinner, and more again afterwards. But just as often there was bridge or whist, in front of a fireplace large enough to stand up in, where a fire was lit every afternoon, even though the weather was so warm that often they had the French windows open onto the garden, so that the room smelled of wood smoke at one end, and jasmine the other.

She marvelled at her own happiness. She was happy to be out of the city, away from the buses and motorcars and too-crowded streets. The invitations and expectations of London social life. Happy to pull on a pair of white trousers and a short-sleeved shirt in the morning, or a simple smock, and change only when the dinner bell was rung in the evening. Gay was happy. Even the dogs were different, she thought, her pugs, Diana's little dachshund Jacob, the other house dogs, all tumbling about in a friendly pack just as the children did.

Her friends were different here too, Oonagh had found. Not the same as the discontented ladies of London – always late, always running to something, with time only ever to swap bits of news and ask cross questions – 'Where did you get that?'; 'Where are you going?'; 'Have you heard . . . ?' Here, they sat and chattered, their voices softened, matching the gentler sounds – wood pigeons, the hum of insects – rather than the angry ones of horns and brakes and cars backfiring. On wet days, they gathered in an upstairs sitting room and shut the door, leaving the menfolk to their newspapers and billiards. They talked of fashions and hats, books and paintings, of who had been seen where and what the papers said about a show. They talked like others work – with energy and conscience. And here, they were kind to each other more than not. The edge of competition had been dulled, it seemed, because they were no longer in the arena of their London social lives.

Midway through the summer, Violet began to come too, without Victor. 'He is busy in the House,' she said, when Oonagh asked why he didn't accompany her, but that wasn't what was whispered about her. For some reason, Oonagh found, Violet was the exception to the new rule of kindness. To her, they were their same spiky city selves.

'Busy in the House? Busy gambling, is what I hear,'

Baby said one afternoon, when Violet – newly arrived from London – had gone to wash after her journey. 'They say he can't burn through it fast enough.'

'I have heard he is planning an auction of objects from Brougham Hall, to pay his debts.' That was Zita.

'I hear the hall is to be let, and that's why they don't go there.'

But Violet, when she came back, hair neatly set, fresh lipstick applied, gave no sign she was aware of the whispers, or of the instinct to goad her that lay behind them. She answered their questions coldly, and soon she excused herself, saying she wanted a long walk. From the window, Oonagh watched her setting off with Philip across the lawns, the game dogs, released from the stables, turning and churning madly at their feet.

'I don't see that marriage lasting,' Zita said complacently, after Violet had gone. Zita herself was soon to be divorced, saying only, 'Marriage, so much less fun than one thought,' when Oonagh asked her why – and there were bets laid as to how much longer Elizabeth Ponsonby and the elusive Denis Pelly would stay together.

'You think them shocking, don't you?' Oonagh said to Kathleen later, when they were alone in her room as she dressed for dinner. She sat with feet tucked up beneath her on the window seat, watching the gentle downwards drift of the sun behind the line of poplar trees that marked the furthest edge of the garden. Violet and Philip were still not back.

'Surprising,' Kathleen said cautiously, 'more than shocking.'

'No, they are shocking.' She dabbed scent from a large bottle behind her ears so the smell of Bois des Îles filled the room. 'They see marriage so differently. As a temporary arrangement. I think because of growing up in Ireland, I'm not the same as them. I see it as something that must be made to last.'

'Like the ha'pennyworth of sweets we were given after mass on a Sunday,' said Kathleen with a grin.

'Precisely. It's why I try so hard with Philip,' Oonagh continued. 'Because he was brought up here, he does not see matters as I do. And I must make him – I'm sure I can make him.' As she said it, she strained her eyes across the yellow fields to catch sight of Philip and Violet, but there was nothing. Why had she let them go off together? But how could she have stopped them? What could she have said? And, anyway, she could hardly blame Violet for wanting to be gone, she thought, when Baby and the others were so mean. She saw them then, coming out from a copse of scrubby trees, heading towards the house. They walked slowly, companionably, side by side. 'What does Ned think of marriage?' she asked.

'I'm not sure he thinks of it at all,' Kathleen said. 'He is busy with politics and change, not home and hearth.'

'Well, what do you think of marriage to Ned?'

'That to be the wife of a man whose interest is always elsewhere would be hard,' Kathleen said tartly. 'And that I'd do better to have prospects of my own.'

'That sounds a bit gloomy,' Oonagh said.

'I don't mean it to. It's just that . . . Well, I like him

very much. But I don't think that is enough. Not for him. I even feel a fool, saying that. At my age.'

'What has age to do with it?' Oonagh asked reasonably.

'I'm old enough to know better, that's what. Anyway, we've never spoken of such a thing, not ever.'

Philip and Violet had reached the house. Oonagh got up. 'Perhaps you must force that conversation,' she said. 'Sometimes it's the only way. There's the gong. I must go down. Will you?' She held out her wrist, underside up so that it showed silver-white like the belly of a fish, for Kathleen to close the clasp of her diamond bracelet.

After dinner, over cards, they made plans for the next day. 'There is a fête at the local village,' Oonagh suggested. 'Country dances, white elephant stalls, coconut shies. Rather jolly, I should think.'

'Must we?' asked Baby wearily. 'I can imagine – Guess the Weight games involving some frightful giant marrow, and ghastly jam made out of too-ripe fruit. Couldn't we just stay here?'

'I don't know how you can all bear it, sitting around all day so idly,' Violet said. 'Philip and I walked for simply miles today.' She wore a sleeveless black dress, the sharp lines emphasising how thin she was, and reclined lazily in her chair, stretching her arms high above her head.

'We can't all have your sense of purpose, I suppose,' Baby said. 'Not that I know exactly what that purpose is . . . Perhaps you'd like to tell us.'

There was a pause then, the kind that comes after

something has been dropped and broken, and before this thing that wasn't anything could take substance, Oonagh lifted her cards and said loudly, 'Mine to bid.'

It was the last time Violet visited that summer. Soon, Oonagh heard she had gone to Cumberland, to stay a while, and then Philip stopped coming down too. First, he was busy at the office. Then he was invited shooting elsewhere, then he must see his parents in Sussex. And, gradually, Oonagh lost her love for Great Tangley.

'I will go up to town this week,' she said to Kathleen towards the end of July. 'And I think I will stay. Now that I am halfway through this pregnancy, I prefer to be closer to Dr Gilliatt. And Maureen has baby Caroline and would like company before they go to Clandeboye. She is simply sick that Caroline is a girl because she counted on a boy. Silly Maureen . . . There is even a fancy-dress party that sounds rather fun. The Famous Beauties Ball.'

'Who will you go as?' Kathleen asked. They were alone, for the first time in weeks. All Oonagh's friends, with their polite, silent husbands and children, had left that morning, and there were no new guests arriving.

'Madame Récamier. She had a salon in Paris and was considered so irresistible that she was once asked by a hostess to make herself less charming. Everyone was in love with her but she was already married. To a banker. When she was fifteen.'

'I see. Just like you who married a banker at nineteen. Were they happy?'

'I don't know. He said he didn't love her, but felt a genuine attachment to her.'

'So everyone was in love with her except her husband?'

'Yes.'

'Did he grow to love her?'

'No. But many others did. And she was painted by all the great portraitists of the age.'

'And was that enough for her?'

'I don't know.' The dullness of the day had closed almost to darkness now, like a cloth wrung tight. A fat drop of rain landed on the back of Oonagh's hand. She watched it trickle across her pale skin and get caught in the diamond bracelet. 'We'd better go in,' she said.

Chapter Thirty-Three

Clandeboye, Co. Down, Autumn 1931

Summer ended, and more and more Kathleen felt it time to leave London. But always, something stopped her – Gay, Oonagh, her troubles with Philip, the second pregnancy. But the truth was, it was Ned – thoughts of Ned – that stopped her most. She couldn't imagine leaving him, and knew he would not come with her. What could she say to him? 'Come back to Dublin with me. I will teach and you can . . .' Can what? Work unloading ships as he did in London, but back in a place he believed to be small and mean, which he had no interest in and had longed to be out of?

Her sisters wrote less often, but asked for her return more. 'Da,' Peggy wrote, 'is getting older and asks for you. A year and a half and not a visit. He wants to see you settled in Dublin.' Kathleen tried to imagine being 'settled' in Dublin. The words of the lady from the Women's Freedom League were still in her ears – 'A society in which women are not paid as men . . . diminishes all of us.' Would she now, Kathleen wondered, be able to find herself a place that felt fair? She thought she could. But what of Ned? What even would he do, if he did come with her? And, again, she found she had talked herself around in a circle.

And then Oonagh offered the perfect halfway house: some months at Clandeboye. 'Baby Caroline is sickly,' she said, one grey autumn morning. 'I imagine it's the damp of that house. Maureen is not well either although she won't admit it, only says that she would welcome your company. It wouldn't be for long. A few months.'

'Very well,' Kathleen said. 'I'll go.' It would be, she thought, a way to 'force the conversation' with Ned, as Oonagh had suggested.

When it came the day for her to leave, it was Ernest who arrived at Rutland Gate in a long, low cream-and-burgundy motor and insisted on waving Kathleen off from Victoria station, even though she tried to say she would do perfectly well by herself. As they drove the short distance, he quizzed her first about Oonagh – although she had nothing to tell him he didn't already know – and then about Ned, whom he had met the night of Oonagh's party, and what she thought of Ned's ideas.

'I don't know,' Kathleen said truthfully. 'When he talks about the conditions of the families who live close to him, I cannot help but be compelled . . . But when he talks of the ideas of those Comrades, they seem fanciful. What do you think?'

'Ned says plenty that is true, and plenty that is sensible. But I worry about the company he keeps and where it will all lead. There is a rising feeling of discontent in the country that is setting even those who have similar aims against each other. My fear is that the din coming from either end will drown out the sensible voices in the middle. Ned's lot and Mosley's lot are ready to do battle, and the prize they fight for is allegiance – the allegiance of all those men who are desperate and look for change, and care little where they find it, as long as it is profound and far-reaching. Mosley, Ned too, will not be satisfied until they have overturned the order that now exists. Whoever wins the greatest part of the allegiances has won the battle.'

'Will it really be a battle?'

'I suspect it will.'

'Or maybe they'll cancel one another out and neither will win,' Kathleen said, thinking of the way Aileen and Maureen – 'either end' – used to argue, and how they could neither win nor lose but simply kept arguing.

'Someone always wins,' Ernest said. Then, 'Is Ned not coming to see you off?'

'No. I asked him not to.' That much was true, but she didn't give the reason why she had asked him not to, did not describe the sudden flash of fury that had caused her to say, 'No, thank you,' coldly, when he suggested it.

She had scanned his face so carefully when she told him she was going away, looking to see the effect her news had. Would he ask her not to? she had wondered. Or question her about her reasons, about the date of her return? Instead he had said only, 'Swapping Oonagh for Maureen, eh?' and then, 'Frying pan to fire, I would have thought,' with a laugh. When she said nothing, he asked, 'You will be back, though?' and when she said she would, he just nodded. That was when the flash of fury arrived that made her say, 'No, thank you,' when he offered to accompany her to the train.

She had forced the conversation – tried to – but Ned had evaded without even seeming to know that he did so.

In fact, Mary was more put out. 'I wish you weren't going,' she said. 'Here I am with Jonathan and now little Desmond.' Diana had given birth to another boy just days before, so Mary's duties would soon be doubled. 'I will miss your company, Kathleen. And your way with babies.'

At Victoria, Ernest insisted on coming right into the station with her, buying magazines and chocolate, and pressing her hand in his gloved one warmly on the platform as he said goodbye. 'Hurry back,' were his last words.

Kathleen arrived at Helen's Bay station and was found, standing with suitcase in hand, by Tommy with his pony and trap. 'For the house?'

'Yes.' She asked him questions on the short trip along the private carriageway, sitting up front beside him as the carriage moved through tall weeds that almost met overhead, but his answers were short and dull so she gave up. She had hoped to understand something of Clandeboye before arriving there – the sorts of things that Oonagh could not tell, servant things, such as who ruled below stairs, and were they fair, or not, where the power in the house really lay, and how careful she would have to be. Belonging nowhere meant she needed to know those things.

In the entrance hallway that was full of madness – dead animals, savage weaponry, dust and the kind of weary light that seemed to have been trapped there for too long – Maureen came to say hello, then immediately, 'I can't talk to you now. I must do something. Manning will show you to the drawing room for tea.' But Manning disappeared, vanishing behind a tarnished suit of armour, so Kathleen put down her case and walked through the house by herself, watching it switch and rearrange itself around her so that grotesque grandeur gave way to a more staid and recognisable shabby country house. She settled in the most lived-in of the drawing rooms – it had at least a fire, and the surfaces were largely free of dust – and began to read a copy of *The Times* from several days before that someone had left lying around. The headline told her that the British Labour Party had banned all supporters of Sir Oswald Mosley from its ranks. *Will it really be a battle?* she remembered asking Ernest just the day before, which already seemed an age ago, and his answer: *I suspect it will.*

After a while, a woman came in, humming to herself. She wore a dress of dirty-looking white lace with a hem that dragged so that Kathleen itched to take a needle and thread to it. She looked at Kathleen without surprise, came towards her and put out a hand to touch her cheek. She wore white elbow gloves even dirtier than the lace dress and her feet, when Kathleen looked down, were bare of shoes.

'You're welcome, child,' the woman said, and carried on walking, through the room, and out through one of the French windows, which she left swinging open behind her so that Kathleen had to go and close it, or suffer a brisk draught that tore through the room and set the fire smoking. She had just sat down again when Maureen joined her.

'I think I just met Lady Brenda,' Kathleen said.

'Hard to mistake her,' Maureen agreed. 'Where is she now?'

'She went out that way.' Kathleen pointed.

'Good.' Maureen went to the door and drew a faded silk curtain across it.

'You won't see if she taps to come back in,' Kathleen said. 'And you'll never hear her, not with everything banging the way it does.' She meant the way the windows rattled in their frames, the wind pushing its way around the house, trying to get at them. Somewhere deeper in the house a door slammed.

'Good,' Maureen said again, sitting into an armchair closest to the fire and picking up one of the dogs that followed her about.

'Shall we go up to the nursery?' Kathleen asked then. After all, baby Caroline was why she was there.

'No need. Nanny will bring Caroline down in a bit. So tell me how everyone is.' Kathleen tried, but Maureen asked questions she couldn't answer – 'Do Bryan and Diana seem happier?'; 'What does Philip think of Oonagh's pregnancy?' – so it was a relief when Nanny, a stout lady with flushed red cheeks, arrived with Caroline, who had eyes the size of her father's and the colour of her mother's: the ferocity of her unblinking blue gaze was something Kathleen had never seen before in an infant of that age. She stretched out her arms to Maureen, who clutched the dog tighter to herself, patted one of the child's hands and said, 'Put her on a blanket,' to Nanny. She watched the baby, lying on her back in a white knitted romper suit for a while as she kicked and squirmed, then rose, dog still in her arms, saying, 'I must dress. There are some people arriving later and I'm determined to make apple-pie beds for them all.'

'Which bedroom am I to have?' Kathleen asked, before she could leave.

'Take your pick,' Maureen said airily. 'They're all made up, for the people coming later. I suppose I can trust you not to be too greedy.' Once Maureen was gone, Nanny gathered little Caroline to herself as though offended, and left too, without a word. So Kathleen went up the stairs that curved beneath the window of coloured glass. On the first floor she came to, a broad landing had doors on either side, many of them open. She looked at each of these rooms – they were indeed made up, with fresh sheets and fires and posies of wild flowers in pretty vases, although, she saw, the windows rattled here too and the ceilings were grimy – but they were all too grand and she did not feel she could sleep in any of them. She was standing with her suitcase in hand, dithering, when a door slammed behind her. She jumped and turned around. It was Duff, coming towards her with a cigarette in his hand. The landing was so gloomy that at first she could only guess it was him, based on his height and the shape of his large head. Closer to, he took a drag on his cigarette and the deepening red glow of the tip revealed the heavy eyes and mobile mouth so she knew it was indeed him.

'Hello,' she said. 'It's Kathleen.' In case he didn't recognise her.

'Yes,' he said patiently. 'I know who you are. What are you doing?'

'Maureen told me I might choose a room,' she blurted, awkward as she so often was in his presence.

'And have you chosen?' As usual, there was, she thought, a hint of laughter in his voice. Was it her he laughed at, or everyone?

'No. They all seem . . . Well, are there any other rooms? Smaller rooms?'

'Do you like small rooms?' Again that hint of laughter.

'Yes,' she said defiantly. 'I do.'

'Well, then. There are smaller rooms upstairs, near the nurseries. The ones at the back of the house are in better nick. Find yourself one you like and I'll have someone prepare it for you. Ellen!' he shouted.

'Yes, sir.' An elderly housemaid emerged from the shadows and Kathleen wondered how long she had been there.

'Ellen, take Miss Kathleen upstairs, show her about, and when she has chosen a bedchamber, see that it is properly prepared.'

'Yes, sir.' The housemaid curtseyed, and Kathleen thought she had not seen that done in many years. No servants, now, curtseyed in London.

Dinner was a confusion of people, one or two Kathleen knew from London, most she didn't, in a vast dark dining room where the only spots of light were from the branched candlesticks set at intervals illuminating those closest to them unevenly – a nose, the angle of a brow or cheekbone – and leaving everyone else in flickering shadow. From the end of the long mahogany table Kathleen watched and said little, and excused herself early to go to bed. Only Duff noticed her leave.

'It's a long journey,' he said with a smile, but Kathleen thought from his face that he knew well that it wasn't the journey so much as the switch from the pleasant orderliness of Oonagh's London to this more brutal and confusing place, where guests shouted across the table at each other – one even threw a bread roll at the lady opposite him to get her attention – that tired her.

That night, Caroline cried and cried. So hard that Kathleen assumed the nanny must not have heard her, and despite her weariness got up to go to her – exactly as she would have done with Gay. She followed the sound of the cries and found herself in the night nursery, a place more fearsome even than the entrance hall, because where that was mad and frenzied and filled with drama, this was bleak and empty, and so cold that by the time she reached Caroline's cradle, her feet in their thin London slippers were half frozen. She picked the child up and rocked her and sang what she could remember of Mary's song, the one about the bumblebee: '*Sleep, O babe, for the red bee hums / The silent twilight's fall*'.

After the carousel of noise that was London, day sounds giving way to night sounds but never to silence, Kathleen found herself spooked by the dark of

Clandeboye – so thick it was as if someone had thrown a cloak over the room – and the quiet outside. There was no noise at all, until a short, high-pitched yowl, a vixen perhaps. And that only emphasised the return to silence when it was bitten off abruptly.

Caroline was starting to soothe, to let her small rigid body slump more comfortably against Kathleen's chest. Kathleen was crooning into her warm neck when Nanny came in, shuffling in an outsize pair of men's slippers. 'What are you doing?' she demanded, in an angry hiss.

'She was crying.'

'Babies cry. Lady Caroline is not to be picked up. You will only encourage bad habits in her.' She came alongside Kathleen and reached for the child. Kathleen smelled a whiff of something sour – whiskey – from her breath and instinct made her turn protectively, to put her own shoulder between that foulness and the baby, but Nanny leaned in and grabbed at the child so that Kathleen must either squeeze too tightly to keep her, or let her go.

Nanny put Caroline back into her cradle and tucked the sheet and blanket firmly around her. Caroline started to cry again.

'The sheets are damp,' Kathleen said. 'I will change them if you wish.'

'You may go,' Nanny said, crossing her arms over her bosom. 'I will see to it.' See to what? Kathleen wondered. She showed no sign of changing sheets. The room itself was so damp, perhaps there wasn't any point. Kathleen left. What else could she do? She could not have a midnight fight over a child's cradle with a woman she had barely met. But she vowed to talk to Maureen the next day.

In the morning she found her alone in one of the front rooms before her guests were down, sipping coffee and flicking through a magazine in a gorgeously embroidered dressing-gown. From India, Kathleen thought, looking at the deep blues and oranges that chased each other across the silk. On her lap two pugs were curled sleepily against one another. Kathleen stumbled through her story of the night before. When she was done, Maureen said, eyes still on the magazine in front of her, 'Whatever Nanny thinks. It's her concern, not mine.'

'But she was crying,' Kathleen said, certain she could not have understood.

'Babies cry. Certainly this one does.' Maureen made a face. 'I wonder does she do anything but cry . . . I say, you haven't taken on all that rot of Oonagh's, have you?' she asked then, narrowing her eyes suspiciously. 'In any case we're going to have to lock the nursery door at night.'

'Why?'

'Lady Brenda. It seems the Little People have been whispering that Caroline is a changeling.'

'But what can that matter?'

'Well, it might . . .'

'How?'

'We don't know. Better not find out. There was a puppy, the Little People told Brenda it was a Puca, or possessed by a Puca or some such . . .'

'And?'

'She drowned it in a rain barrel.'

Chapter Thirty-Four

Before Caroline's birth, Maureen had believed that the restlessness she had felt all her life would go once she became a mother. As much as she had mocked Oonagh and her devotion to Gay, even Aileen and the distant pride she took in little Neelia, she had looked forward too, thinking that soon she would join them, and that to have a child would be to answer, at last, the question she couldn't stop asking, even though she had never had words for it – only an itch under her skin that kept her moving, searching, uncomfortably pushing forward. But it hadn't.

Caroline's birth had been easy and quick, and within days Maureen was up and about almost as normal, pretending to be as ever. But, secretly, she had been first disturbed then disappointed by the lack of change within.

It's because she is a girl, another girl, she told herself. A boy would have been different – a break with the chain that linked her to Cloé, tied her in so tightly that even now, a married woman, it was still Cloé's voice she heard in times of doubt, the look on Cloé's face that was conjured up when she felt uneasy.

From the start, Caroline cried, in a way Maureen didn't understand, and that frightened her, although she would never have said so. Duff seemed to understand these cries – 'She's just hungry,' he would say, or 'She's tired but doesn't know how to drop off, poor mite.' He didn't take the cries personally, the way Maureen did, so that she couldn't tell him how they made her feel: hot, prickly, urgent, as though she must be doing something but didn't know what. For Maureen, the cries were accusations; stones thrown perhaps indiscriminately that yet landed with precision. And when she found she couldn't soothe Caroline, she found she could not happily be near her.

'Better if Nanny does it,' she said, just a few days after Caroline's birth, unable to face the squirming bundle that was her baby, the way she felt stiff and unnatural in Maureen's arms, seeming always to want to be elsewhere. They were alien to one another, Maureen thought, not mother and daughter but two strangers locked unexpectedly together. And when Nanny plunged a bottle into Caroline's open, howling mouth so that she fell silent, looking warily out over the thick rubber teat, Maureen said, 'Nanny knows best, isn't that so?' with an ironic twist of her mouth.

Once it became the custom for Nanny to have to do with Caroline, not her, Maureen found that within a few weeks, she hardly recognised the child. Caroline would be brought to her every day, just as she had been brought to her own mother, on a kind of formal visit, and Maureen would look at her and wonder, with a chilly prickle along her spine, *Who are you*? As if Caroline was indeed, exactly as Lady Brenda's fevered mind would have it, a changeling. She looked at Caroline, and saw nothing in her that she recognised, except those huge grey-blue eyes that were Duff's when she knew him first, before he fell in love with her – indifferent, only mildly curious about her. Soon Maureen scarcely looked at Caroline, finding it easier to avoid her. That was when she sent for Kathleen.

The place she had expected Caroline to occupy in her heart still only had Duff in it. He was everything to her, as he had been since they first met. And to her own secret astonishment, she was jealous of the gentle way he held Caroline, how absorbed he became in staring at her and playing with her tiny hands.

'Give her to Nanny,' she said, watching Duff take Caroline onto his knee one day when the child was three months old. 'It isn't good for her to be fussed over so much.' And Nanny – as Maureen had known she would – stepped immediately forward, jealous for her charge, saying, 'Lady Dufferin is right. It does a baby no good to be spoiled.' She was minded, just as Maureen was, to keep Caroline tucked far away in the nursery and not be bringing her to the drawing room or looking to involve parents in her upbringing.

'Now, come and talk to me,' Maureen said, holding out a hand to Duff. 'Tell me if you think I'm looking more like myself again.'

That night, Duff asked if Maureen was entirely sure

the nanny was the right choice – 'I have seen that she can be a bit rough' – and Maureen defended her.

'That's just her way. She came highly recommended and can be trusted to know what she's doing. And how easy do you think it is to get trained staff to a place like this?'

At that he fell quiet, as Maureen had known he would, eventually saying, 'Well, you must know best.'

'She knows more than I do,' Maureen said, after a moment. 'By which I mean I have to trust her . . . Trust that she knows more . . .' How to say that she did not trust herself? And that if she chose not to believe that Caroline was better in the nanny's care, she would have to find a way to care for the child herself, or find someone else to do it, and that she didn't know how to do either of those things. *How to say my child scares me and I am happier when I am not with her and reminded of that?* 'For all that to be a mother is the most natural thing,' she began in a low voice, 'it doesn't quite feel like that . . .'

But Duff seemed to think she was warning him off meddling. 'You must know best,' he said again, but stiffly this time.

In that house, Kathleen quickly learned that she would have to find a new rhythm for herself. That the habits she had fallen into with Oonagh would not do for Maureen. A few days after her arrival, she knocked on Maureen's door, as she always did with Oonagh, to see did she want anything, or simply company with her morning tea.

'What is it?' Maureen's voice was sharp through the heavy door.

'It's Kathleen. Shall I come in?'

'Goodness, no!' she snapped, and then Kathleen heard Duff's voice too, a low amused rumble, like a train trundling along a siding, followed by Maureen's laugh. She was mortified. It had never occurred to her that he would be with her, and not in his own bedroom, which was on the other side of the dressing room that stood between their chambers. At Rutland Gate, Philip kept to his own rooms, and knocked on Oonagh's door just as everyone else did. Whatever may have been their private communications, there was a politeness, almost a formality, between them in public that meant they never intruded the intimacy of their marriage upon others.

Maureen and Duff, she found, were nothing like Oonagh and Philip. They had a closeness so obvious that Kathleen didn't always know where to look. Maureen would sit beside him on the sofa, and he would put his arm around her, and they whispered together, Maureen's infectious giggle laid over his rumble of a laugh. Or he would put a hand on her shoulder as she sat, and sometimes the shoulder would be bare, if she was in evening dress, and even from the other side of the room it seemed to Kathleen that she could see the heat rising at the point of contact, growing warmer and warmer so that she could almost feel it. And Maureen would turn her head and look up at him as he looked down on her, and even if they said nothing, there would be something rapt in the glance that made Kathleen, bent over her stitching or reading, awkward.

They walked about the grounds together hand in hand, and disappeared at odd hours, without a word to anyone, even when they had guests.

'I say, where *is* Maureen?' Baby demanded, one afternoon, shortly after she had arrived for a visit from London. It was a day full of rain, when the hours after lunch and before it was time to dress for dinner were hard to fill. In the few weeks since she had been at Clandeboye, Kathleen had learned to dread those afternoons. Drops slid morosely down the windows so that even with the curtains drawn and the fire lit, they could still be heard, plaintively reminding of their presence as though they did not like being shut out.

'Busy,' Stephen said, with a smirk. He was bent over a piece of embroidery, and Kathleen was secretly shocked that a man should spend his time with a needle and threads. 'Upstairs, I believe.'

'Oh.' Baby pulled a face. 'What a bore they are, sneaking off. I was going to propose a game of charades.' And then, with a sly wink at Stephen, 'I say, Kathleen, do go and find her. She'll be so sorry to miss this. This morning she particularly said she wanted to play. Run up and get her, there's a dear. I'm sure she must be in her bedroom.' She smiled at Kathleen, head tilted to one side. So Kathleen stood and was about to do as she asked, when she caught sight of Stephen, shaking his head vigorously at her from the other side, shoulders heaving with silent mirth. She blushed and sat down again.

And yet they fought too, Maureen and Duff. How they fought. Like large angry dogs, with teeth bared and hackles raised. Kathleen heard them sometimes from her room at night, loud voices rising through the cracks between the floorboards and sliding in through the ill-fitting edges of the windows. There might be the crash of something dropped or thrown, and once they must have pulled the curtains right down because the next morning, as she passed Maureen's room, she saw the young housemaid, Helen, directing a man on a ladder to rehang them. Often, these rows happened when Duff had come home from London to find the house full of people visiting, with more yet to arrive, one group giving way to the next so that it seemed Tommy, with his pony and trap, was up and down to Helen's Bay to meet every train, dropping and collecting, and the hall was permanently full of trunks.

Sometimes, to Kathleen's confusion, Maureen would look especially pleased with herself after such a row. Tired – the blue circles under her eyes pronounced as bruises – but humming happily the next morning.

Chapter Thirty-Five

Maureen was right about Caroline crying, Kathleen soon discovered. She did indeed cry, and cry. Gay had never cried, or never for long, because he was not left. Always, someone went to him, rocked him, sang to him, played with him, because Oonagh insisted, so that very soon he did not cry at all, simply called, secure in the knowledge that someone would come. There, early mornings and most nights in Kathleen's bedroom were punctuated by the sound of Caroline wailing, with no one going near her. There was something so terrible about listening to her cries, hour after hour – they sounded so lonely, as though she cried because she believed herself to be the last person left alive. Oonagh was right, Kathleen thought then. No baby should cry like that. All babies should be loved as Gay was.

She offered to do some of Nanny's work for her – mind Caroline in the afternoons, sit with her in the nursery after tea – but Nanny refused. It was as if she guarded her rights over the child – her right to be stern, even cruel, to neglect her distress.

The other servants were uneasy with Caroline. Kathleen knew that thanks to the housemaid, Helen, who quickly became useful to her because she spoke, it seemed, both languages – that of the upstairs, and that of the kitchens – and liked a gossip well enough that she could be asked all sorts of questions.

'They think Lady Brenda might be right,' Helen said, 'that she is indeed a changeling, so they avoid Caroline. They don't like the way she stares, with those eyes . . .'

Without the usual duties that Oonagh might have expected of her, and hard put to spend her time with Caroline in the face of Nanny's hostility, Kathleen found herself with much stranger requests, many of them impossible.

'Is there ever any hot water?' Evelyn Waugh asked plaintively one day, when Kathleen came upon him in a large patterned dressing-gown, returning from the vast bathroom at the end of the passage. It contained a claw-footed bath that could easily have fitted three but could not possibly be filled with anything but tepid water. The answer, Kathleen knew, was yes, but not much, and its arrival was unpredictable. Plus Maureen was cunning at gauging its coming by the clanking of certain pipes, and had no qualms at all about skipping off to her own bathroom and running what water there was into a deep bath for herself.

She liked company while she bathed and, if Duff wasn't around, would often call for Kathleen to sit on the armchair in her room with the door open between them, while she chatted. From where Kathleen sat, she could see the back of Maureen – golden hair piled high on her head, and the cigarette between her fingers that dropped ash onto the black-and-white tiled floor.

'You think the house is bad now,' she said one evening, smoke curling up to mingle with the steam from the hot water, the smell of tobacco battling the Rose Otto that she poured in great drops from a glass-stoppered bottle. 'You should have seen it when I first came. Nothing Duff told me prepared me. I thought I'd stepped into a novel by Mrs Gaskell. And it simply eats money,' she said. 'Calmly, like a cow eating grass – getting through great quantities, almost without noticing. I said we'd be better off pulling it all down and starting again but, well, Duff loves the place. And so . . .' She shrugged.

When not talking improvements, she used her bath time to plan for new arrivals. And while some of the planning was for charming entertainments, more was for her practical jokes.

'Be a dear and see if you can persuade Cook to get me some really *lumpy* porridge,' she asked one evening. 'I need something that looks like sick. I'm determined to put bowls of it by everyone's beds tonight. Perhaps she could put something into the porridge – you'll know the type of thing – that will make it look real?'

'Wouldn't it be better if you asked?' Kathleen said. 'I'm not sure she'll do it for me.'

'I've never been to the kitchens, and I don't intend to start now,' Maureen said.

'Well, I'll try,' Kathleen said, 'but I'm not sure how successful I'll be. Mrs Samuels doesn't like me.'

'She doesn't like anyone.' Maureen gave a gurgle and flicked ash into a soap dish. 'Duff says he's simply waiting for her to do away with all of us some evening. Arsenic in the soup or some such, like that woman in America who poisoned thirty people. Half of them died and the others were in agony,' she finished with relish. Kathleen was about to ask could she have the bath water after – there wouldn't be any more hot water that day, for sure – when Maureen dropped the end of her cigarette into it, pulled out the plug and stood, naked, water streaming down her marble-white body. 'Pass me a towel, there's a dear.'

She heard little from Oonagh, who had sworn she would write and didn't. Ned and Mary both did; Ned's letters were short and infrequent, and told her that meetings had turned into marching: *There is a new organisation now, the National Unemployed Workers Movement, with clear demands. A few days ago there was a march to Hyde Park, over one hundred thousand of us, to deliver a petition to Mr MacDonald's govern-ment. Police on horseback attacked the crowd and there was fighting all around Marble Arch, into Oxford Street and up the Edgware Road.* Through the thin paper she could feel him all but clapping his hands in excitement. *Seventy-five of our men were badly injured. They will never say how many of the police were hurt because they don't want us to know, but I reckon we gave as good as – better than – we got.* He wrote nothing that was personal and asked few questions about her, but she was glad to hear news of him, and glad that the bitter mood in which she had left him seemed to have been forgotten, or possibly, by him, remained unnoticed.

Mary's letters were longer and fuller, and from her Kathleen learned that Ned had not been well. That he had a cough that would not go away. *I wish he would move away from that place where he lives. It is damp and cold and cannot be doing him any good and I know he could afford to now, but he says the room is grand and he likes where he is.* She learned, too, of a girl called Miriam. *The daughter of one of his neighbours. Jewish.* She could hear the sniff in Mary's voice coming up from the page. *He goes about with her sometimes now. I wish you would come back, Kathleen.*

Kathleen read and re-read, surprised at the pain she felt. Why would Mary write such a thing to her? What did 'goes about with' mean? Perhaps, she thought, she had forced a conversation after all – a conversation to which Miriam was now the answer, not her. Would Ned be making friends with this Miriam if Kathleen was still in London? And, more importantly, did Miriam have any more reality for him than Kathleen had? With no possibility of an answer – she wouldn't ask Mary more, and she couldn't ask Ned – the questions turned and turned inside her, rising and falling with the rhythm of the days – worse at night when she was alone, better by day when she was busy, punctuated by Caroline's cries and Maureen's shrieks.

After a couple of weeks Kathleen realised that Nanny was a heavy sleeper, both for her afternoon nap, and at night, so she took to creeping in to soothe Caroline when she knew Nanny would not hear her. The door to the night nursery was rarely locked, for all that Maureen said it would be, either because Nanny forgot or because she didn't think the threat to Caroline was real, so Kathleen went in and out to the child, quietly but often, hoping that she could show her there was, after all, someone to care for her distress. *When she is older, Maureen will have more time for her*, she thought, remembering the hours in which Oonagh played with Gay, and how much he made her laugh.

But, so far, it was Duff Maureen asked for, always and only. 'Where's Duff?' she asked Kathleen one evening, as she prepared to go up. Stephen and Baby were playing gin rummy, with Duke Ellington's 'Mood Indigo' so loud on the gramophone that the scratches on the record echoed up the main staircase along with the notes.

'If I see him, I'll tell him you're looking,' Kathleen said, as she always did. Upstairs, she went to look in on Caroline, quiet for once, before she retired. She turned the door handle silently and stepped into the gloomy night nursery. By the moonlight that came through badly drawn curtains, she could see someone beside the cradle. It must be Nanny. She was about to withdraw, just as silently, and hope she hadn't been seen, when a whisper came.

'Kathleen?' It was Duff.

'I was just going to check she's warm enough,' Kathleen whispered back, guilty that he should find her creeping about his house.

'It's all right,' he said. 'You can come in.' Kathleen

walked further in and saw that he was holding Caroline in his arms, her head high up on his shoulder. She was awake and looking around her with those enormous eyes. The moonlight from outside didn't reach so far in, but there was enough to reflect off the shiny blackness of them so that she looked, with her small neat head, like a seal that had popped up before diving deep again.

'I was passing by,' he said, almost as though explaining himself. 'She was crying.'

'Nanny must not have heard,' Kathleen agreed, noting that, for all they were pretending that their presence there was normal, a simple consequence of passing by, they did not speak above whispers or turn on any lights.

'Does Gay cry like that?' he asked, after a few moments, and Kathleen said no.

'But some babies have the colic,' she said. 'And then they cry more.' She had a sudden memory of Oonagh sitting up one night with Gay, just a few weeks old, feeding him warm water with a bit of sugar from a teaspoon, because he had the colic and howled in agony. If Nanny hadn't stopped her, she would have had the doctor out, and even when persuaded that he wasn't in danger, still Kathleen had seen tears run down Oonagh's cheeks in time with the child's, until at last the sugar-water did its work, and he fell silent and slept.

'I see,' Duff said. 'Perhaps that's it, so. Perhaps she has the colic.' He stood there and patted Caroline gently, rhythmically, until her eyelids began to droop, pale shades descending over those wide eyes straining in the dark, and Kathleen stayed silently beside them. There was something about being in that obscure room with him, both of them silent, concentrated upon the same task, that made her feel she knew him in a new way, and that she would never again be made awkward by him.

Caroline's eyes were closed and her breathing the steady, rasping sound of any sleeping baby, as soporific as a tractor engine. 'Shall I take her?' asked Kathleen. 'I have learned how to put her down so gently that she doesn't wake.' Only when the words were out did she realise she had betrayed herself, given away that this was not her first or even second time to the night nursery. But he only said, 'Very well,' and held her out carefully so that Kathleen might take her from his arms.

She stooped low to the cradle, first checking the sheet with the back of her hand to make sure it wasn't damp, Caroline held close to her chest, then slowly, gradually, laid her down. She stirred and Kathleen held her breath in case she cried again, but she didn't.

'You're good at that,' Duff said, once they were safe outside and the door closed behind them.

'I learned with Gay,' Kathleen said. 'Oonagh could never bear to hear him cry, so we all got good at such tricks.' Again she thought she had said the wrong thing – would he think she was criticising the way Maureen chose to be with her child? – but he said nothing. 'Maureen is looking for you,' she said awkwardly.

'Very well,' he said. And if his voice was weary, Kathleen thought, was it any wonder when the hour was so late?

Chapter Thirty-Six

Soon Maureen began to feel, with a sickening fear, that her husband was slipping from her. That his friends, his work, now that he had made his maiden speech in the Lords, politics and the affairs of the world were almost as important to him as she was. She could feel it, but she didn't know what to do about it, beyond what she had always done. And so, within months of Caroline's birth, she was as busy as ever, only the extra inch and a half around her waist a reminder that there was now a child upstairs.

She filled the house with guests, threw parties and entertainments and days out, even though she knew he longed 'just sometimes', he said, to come back from London to a house empty of all but her and his daughter.

'I do it for you,' she said, 'for your career.' He laughed at that.

'I don't see how Baby Jungman and Stephen Tennant can be of much help to my career,' he said. 'Unless I decide to go on the stage. Please, when I come back from London next, let there be no one here, only us.'

'But don't you see? You go to London and are busy, at the House, and in your gambling dens – don't bother with that face, I know jolly well what you do,' and she pouted, but good-humouredly at him. Gambling, she understood. It was when he preferred the company of other people to her that she felt unhappy. 'And then you come here, to Clandeboye, and you wish to rest. Whereas I have been here all alone and am in need of company.'

'But you'll try?' he said, and she said she would.

She did try, telephoning to invite Aileen and her two little girls, Neelia and baby Doon, who looked oddly like Caroline, for a few quiet days. But when Aileen had left, and Duff telephoned to say he would be delayed by more than a week, that there were things in London he must attend to, Maureen was furious and responded by inviting Baby, Zita, Stephen, anyone else who would come at short notice.

'I see we have a full house,' Duff said wearily, when he arrived, late, from the train. He looked with disapproval around him – the gramophone played loudly, a couple danced in front of the double doors that were open to the autumn evening, while a girl with short black hair wound a string of pearls around the rumpled neck of Maureen's pug.

Maureen, playing bridge with her usual intense focus, barely looked up from her cards. 'Well, you didn't expect me to sit here all alone, waiting?'

'I expect nothing,' he said tightly.

'Come and have a drink, old chap,' Stephen called, from the other side of the room.

'No, thank you,' Duff said. 'I won't.' But he did have a drink, only not with them, and Maureen, on her way to bed, found him asleep in the library, stretched out on the green leather sofa with the decanter beside him. When she couldn't wake him, she pulled a rug over him and went upstairs, alone.

The next day, as she was about to tell him that she would happily send her friends away, he announced that some of his Oxford lot would be arriving, to shoot.

'Fine, but I'll be too busy to entertain them,' she snapped.

'We don't wish to be entertained, only left alone.' It was the 'we' – the way he lumped himself in with his old friends, against her – that did it.

'Well, you'd damned well better not come to me with more of your London gambling debts.' She picked up a bottle of Bronnley's face lotion from her dressing-table and threw it to the floor so that it smashed. 'It's one thing pouring money into this bottomless pit of a house, but I'll be damned if I'll pay them too,' and she cast around for something else to throw. Duff came close to her then and grabbed her wrists with his hands, hard, and said, 'For God's sake, Maureen, stop it,' in a low voice that was no less angry than her shouting. And Maureen, seeing how intently he looked at her, pulled one hand free and took up another bottle, this one with a chunky cut-glass stopper, and dropped it insolently at his feet where it, too, smashed, splattering rose water everywhere.

With a shiver of excitement that was close to revulsion, she found she knew, as though following a recipe, exactly the amount and type of violent disorder to enact. And, sure enough, Duff, his shoes covered with rose water and bits of broken glass, closed his hands more tightly around her wrists until Maureen, ecstatic, said, 'You're hurting me.' Even as she spoke, she was astonished at the accuracy of the instinct that drove her to goad and challenge him. Somewhere she was sickened too, but she didn't allow herself to think about that because he gripped her wrists more tightly and crushed his mouth against hers.

'I'm surprised you're up,' Kathleen said to her a few days later, coming upon Maureen early. 'I heard you all going to bed so late I wondered why you bothered. Why not simply stay up another hour or so and let the sun find you?'

'Duff woke me when he left,' Maureen said. 'He's gone shooting with those fellows who arrived yesterday. His Oxford chums.' She knew she sounded bitter, but it was Kathleen, so she didn't bother to disguise it. 'Come for a walk? No one else will be up for hours and I'm bored.' She fidgeted with the belt of her coat, to hide the fact that she was not so much bored as aimless.

'I'll come if you walk properly,' Kathleen said. 'And not potter about the lawns close to the house.'

'Fine,' Maureen said, linking her arm through Kathleen's. 'But aren't you bossy? I suppose you've got used to that, with Oonagh.'

Outside it was a bright, cold morning, with mist still rising off the wet ground so that the trees seemed to float before them. The air smelled of sharp edges and wet earth. 'It's better in the summer,' she said, once they were away from the house. 'Then Duff's chums don't visit as much.'

'Do you really mind them?'

'When they're here, he has thought only for them, the next day's sport, and the evening's play. I prefer he gamble in London, if gamble he must.'

'And must he gamble?'

She shrugged, pretending to be indifferent, even though she had a good idea that Kathleen, whose room was above hers, had heard the row of a few days before.

She and Kathleen walked, each blade of grass iced with frost crunching under their feet, and Maureen talked about the modernisations Duff had proposed to the estate – including a scheme for electricity 'that will cost me money and benefit only the workers,' she said glumly. 'He tries to halt spending on the house – he cannot see why we need to do more than will make it adequate, and despises anything he calls "luxury" – as though there is something heroic about living in a place so cold and damp that there are whole parts we never go into, and there is never not the sound of coughing. If it's not Caroline, it's one of the servants. Cough, cough, cough endlessly.' Maureen herself was never ill, nor Duff, and her voice was impatient.

They came to a stop at the top of a small hill. From where they stood, they looked down across the woodland, towards the place where Duff and his friends had taken up position with their guns. As they watched, a scattering of pheasant erupted noisily from the trees, confused and frantic, wings flailing. Guns were fired, and the dogs hurled themselves forward violently, as though their bodies would tip over their own heads, such was the maddening effect of the dead birds falling from the sky and landing all about them. They were propelled back and forth, questing urgently, driven by the hail of feathered bodies that landed with soft thumps. Maureen disliked the way they rushed about, and how different they were out here, in action, from the sleepy creatures she saw when they were about the house. Now their purpose was death or, rather, the retrieving of death, and they were so very eager about it. She had discovered that she found it hard to forget these moments at other times when the dogs were drowsily affectionate in the late afternoons, lying before the fire or coming to put a heavy head on her lap that she might stroke them. There was something about the way they were that reminded her of Duff and his friends. Of how they – he – could go from a sedate drawing-room demeanour to the energy of hunting and killing, and then so swiftly back again.

'I'd better go and see who's awake,' she said. 'We're due to start for the races shortly. Will you tell Cook we'll lunch from home?'

They left late, Stephen complaining that it was 'too early' to go out, Baby demanding why they must 'keep such country hours'. By the time they returned, it was almost dark.

'Manning, bring cocktails to the drawing room,'

Maureen called. She pronounced her words carefully, lest it be obvious how much she had been drinking. Instead of going to change, as she usually would, she went straight to the drawing room, heels tapping on the wooden floors, muted every now and again by a rug, so that her progress felt weirdly disjointed: *tap, tap*, silence, *tap*, silence, *tap, tap*. Behind her, she heard snatches of conversation from the others ' . . . a sure winner', ' . . . that extraordinary little man, almost as teensy as a jockey himself . . .'

In the drawing room, Duff and his friends, the day's shooting done, sat in deep shadow. They had neglected to turn on the lamps or draw the curtains and were lit only by the fire on one side and the last grey light of afternoon that struggled through the window on the other. In the furthest corner, Kathleen sat reading by the same bad light. The men were talking in low voices, a decanter set on a small table by Duff's elbow, and they fell silent as Maureen stepped briskly in.

'Darling, there you are,' she said loudly. 'I need you to adjudicate.' She launched into a complicated story, told with extravagant gestures, about a betting syndicate they had made up, with various wins and losses, appealing to him to say where the money should now be disposed.

'I cannot make head or tail of it,' Duff said.

'Then, Kathleen,' Maureen demanded peremptorily, 'you must decide.'

'I was about to give Caroline her bath,' Kathleen said evasively, standing up and moving towards the door. 'I'll come back.'

'Don't be silly. That's what Nanny's for. I do wish you'd stop hanging about the nursery. She's not your child, or have you forgotten?' There was one of those sharp little silences then, the kind that maybe fell by accident, because everyone somehow stopped talking at once, but then remained a fraction too long, because no one knew what to say to follow such a strange remark. It was the kind of silence, Maureen knew, that often followed her these days – sharp pauses that were filled with all the things others didn't dare say to her.

'She's not Nanny's child either,' Duff said, his words steady and distinct from the other side of the room. 'Although anyone would be forgiven for thinking differently.'

'I'll see her later,' Maureen said, deciding to placate, 'when Nanny brings her down.' But something about Duff's silence then made her irritable, so she put a record on the gramophone. When Duff and his friends drew their chairs closer together, to continue talking, she turned the sound up higher and began to sway to the music, grabbing a cocktail glass from the tray that Manning produced. From it protruded an olive on a stick that was like a miniature exclamation mark to her every move.

'Good God, must we have "Little White Lies" at that volume?' Duff called.

'Some of us like a spot of fun. Not your lot, of course, but the rest of us.'

The way she said 'your lot' was as insolent as she could make it and Duff, nettled, responded, 'Turn it down, Maureen. Infernal racket!'

'Oh, don't be such a stick.' She changed tack suddenly. 'You must have all bored each other quite enough by now with the India Question and those ridiculous unemployment figures.' As always, she was secretly surprised at her own infallible instinct for the most violent blow.

'Nothing ridiculous about three million men without jobs,' Duff said. 'Especially when they take to the streets to demand help to feed their families. These are men who came back from France, from Flanders, who left their comrades dead in the mud, and found the country they fought for couldn't even give them a living wage. Street violence isn't the answer, but one can hardly wonder they're angry.'

'That damned war. I wish it had been the War To End All Talking About Wars . . .' Maureen drawled, scratching the needle violently across 'Little White Lies' and putting on something louder and faster.

'How much you dislike discussing anything you find unpleasant,' Duff said, almost in wonderment.

'Doesn't everyone?' she asked in honest surprise. 'Anyway, why don't they get jobs if they're so keen? It can't be all that difficult. Even you have one.' Again that sharp, uncomfortable silence. From the corner of her eye, Maureen saw Stephen edge out of the door. The girl with the shiny black bob slid down into a pile of cushions on the sofa as though she wanted to hide.

'Come and dance!' she demanded. 'Baby, you'll dance?' Baby shook her head mutely and turned back to the game of patience she was dealing. Unlike Stephen, she was too indifferent to leave, Maureen knew, but neither had she any intention of being drawn into the row.

'No one wants to dance, Maureen. Now turn it down.' Duff was angrier, his voice deepening.

'Andrew wants to dance with me, don't you, darling?' Andrew, a friend of Baby's, barely more than a boy, was on a visit for the first time. Maureen had already decided he was idiotic and tedious, but now he would do.

'Of course,' Andrew said, although she saw him cast a wary look at Duff. He caught up her hand and began to twirl her about energetically. A couple of the others joined them, though without much enthusiasm. The record ended and Maureen put on another, catching Andrew's hand again and drawing him closer to her. The music was slower now, and she danced pressed against the boy, but keeping her head turned so she could see Duff from the corner of her eye. When Duff did nothing, she put her arms around Andrew's neck and drew him closer still to her, slowing her movements even more so they barely swayed together. Duff watched them for a moment, then rose from his chair and began to walk from the room. His friends, almost as if they had predicted his move, rose with him and placed themselves around him as though a bodyguard. Seeing them go, Maureen smiled up at Andrew and placed his arm more tightly around her waist.

'How like you to invite only people who are as foolish as you are,' Duff said, as he reached the door.

'As long as it's my money that keeps this place going,

I'll invite who I want,' Maureen called after him, her words like scissors through silk.

And then he was gone.

Andrew tried to keep dancing but Maureen pushed him away from her and removed the needle from the record. 'It's time to dress anyway,' she said. 'Kathleen, draw me a bath.' She saw Baby twitch irritably, knowing that would be the end of the hot water, but she didn't care.

As she bathed, she listened for sounds that would tell her Duff had come up. Perhaps he would come to her room and she could tell him she hadn't meant it, describe something from her day that would make him laugh, and then they would go down together, hand in hand, and everyone would see that they were all right.

But Duff didn't come. She heard him in his room, opening drawers, the wardrobe door that needed a good tug, but he didn't come near her. And even when she dressed in a hurry, in a dress of pale green silk that she knew he liked, and was ready to go down when she heard his door open, so that she opened her door as though by chance at the very same moment, he simply looked at her, nodded curtly, said, 'Maureen,' and stood back to allow her to pass as though repelled by the idea of walking beside her. There was nothing she could do except put her head high in the air and walk past him.

Dinner was uneasy – too many people chattering brightly and watching each other warily – and afterwards Maureen demanded everyone play charades, thinking that might force a merging of the two groups. But Duff refused. 'I'm in no mood for play-acting.'

'I suppose you do enough of that in the House,' Maureen said with a stinging pretence at sweetness in her voice.

Duff ignored her. 'Gentlemen, billiards?' he asked. His friends stood up to follow him, and so too did Andrew, leaping eagerly to his feet. Duff looked at him. 'I said, "gentlemen". Not "puppies".'

'One wonders why Betjeman is included, then,' Maureen drawled. Even for her, it was too much, she knew. Everyone began to talk at once, of anything at all, trying to cover her words with their more innocuous ones. But Duff said nothing, just left, and soon Maureen heard their voices, low and serious, and the click of billiard balls.

'We can still play charades,' Stephen said, which she supposed was kind, but she found she had no heart for it, and after the first round said, 'I'm going to bed. You can all play if you like.' It was, she reflected as she went up the stairs, the hem of her pale-green gown held up like a handful of spring shoots, the earliest she had been to bed in a long time. In her room, she changed into a dressing-gown, dismissed her maid, and sat down to wait. It didn't take long. Exactly as she had expected, Duff came up early too, drawn, like someone in an enchantment, to continue the argument. And when he had shut the door behind him, Maureen felt, with a sickening lurch of excitement, that he was already angry enough, jealous enough, that it would take very little from her to burst it all into flames.

And even though somewhere she understood that she couldn't keep doing this, that a piece of metal made molten again and again will finally change its nature until it can no longer be used for its original purpose, she couldn't stop, so she began to insult him, heaping vicious words one upon another until, with a flicker of sick triumph, she saw him cross the room towards her, into her arms.

Chapter Thirty-Seven

That night, the sound of Maureen and Duff rowing worse than ever meant that even when they finally fell silent, Kathleen could not sleep. As if agitated by the undercurrents of anger through the house, Lady Brenda was restless. Kathleen heard her padding softly about, singing under her breath, back and forth along the landing. It was when she went quiet that Kathleen worried. She got up to go to her. The landing was bitterly cold and a foul breath came down from the attics, carrying a whiff of whatever it was that had got lost and died in those damp corners. Ahead of her, she saw Lady Brenda, muttering something rapid and repetitive. She seemed to be in one of her fantastical arguments against an unseen opponent, and Kathleen had decided to leave her be, when she heard a low cry cut through Lady Brenda's muttered recriminations. She speeded up and, after a moment, heard her singing to herself in a high cracked voice. Close to, she could make out the words:

'Hush-a-by baby, babe not mine,
You're not my own sweet baby O!'

The song gave her a chill. She could see then that Lady Brenda carried something in her arms, a bundle of clothes. Or a very small child. She carried it – whatever it was – pressed tightly against her, shoulders hunched protectively over it, and swayed as she walked, as though whatever she carried must be lulled by the motion of her arms and body. Kathleen heard again the muffled sound from the bundle but dared not get too close or startle her because she walked along the gallery above the main staircase. On one side of her was the polished wooden balcony railing, and below that a plunge into darkness that ended in the flagged marble floor of the main hall.

On the other side, large portraits of Blackwood ancestors stared down in disapproval.

'Hush-a-by baby, babe not mine,
You're not my own sweet baby O!'

Lady Brenda sang again, rocking her arms more violently now. Whatever was in the bundle made a choking sound and Kathleen was about to rush forward, too desperate to hang back any longer, when Duff appeared behind her and then passed her, in a crimson dressing-gown. In three strides he reached his mother and put out a hand to stop her.

She turned and stared up at him with a pleased smile, for all the world as though she had been introduced to someone interesting at a party. 'What has you here, Basil?' she said. 'I thought you were at school.'

'I'm back,' he said.

'We must tell your father. He will be pleased. He's out with the gamekeeper.' She looked doubtful suddenly and turned to peer through the large window behind them where deep black pressed against the dusty glass panes, which seemed to shrink away from it. 'He'll be back,' she said more confidently.

'What have you got there?' Duff asked, and reached forward to take the bundle from her arms but he did it reluctantly – Kathleen could see he was loath to touch her – and Lady Brenda stepped back and clutched it more tightly. 'Mother, what is it you have there?' Duff stepped around behind her, to put himself between her and the balcony railings, because she had moved closer to them. Kathleen could hear the exasperation in his voice, but also the impotence. He didn't know what to do with her, whether to use his strength to wrest the bundle from her, or try to coax her to hand it over. And he was restrained too, she saw, because he could not bear to touch her. Could not bear that any part of him should have contact with any part of her, as though he feared the coldness of her flesh.

Lady Brenda looked up at him with a bright smile on her face, as though they were together in some delightful exchange, and said, 'There now, we'll have tea shortly, when your father is in,' but Kathleen saw the shifting doubt in her eyes.

There was another choked cry from within what Kathleen could see was a lace shawl or veil, something cobwebby and white, wound round and round so that nothing of what was inside showed – but the cry was fainter.

'Let me help you,' she said, moving quickly forward so that she and Duff stood one behind and one in front of Lady Brenda, whose feet, bare in thin slippers, were bluish in the poor light that came from the lamp she held. 'I'm sure that must be heavy.' Lady Brenda stayed still, meek as a child, as Kathleen gently lifted the cobwebby parcel from her arms.

'It's the wrong one,' she said, as she let go. 'It's not my babe.'

'Let me mind it for you, so,' Kathleen said. Already she could tell that whatever was inside the bundle, although it was warm and wriggled, was the wrong size – too small – and could not be Caroline. Sure enough, when she unwrapped what was there, it was the face of one of Maureen's pugs that emerged, the wrinkled black snout and damp black eyes devilish in the half-light. Suddenly heavy with relief, she handed the dog and shawl to Duff, who put the animal down, whereupon it raced off, to scratch at Maureen's door, no doubt.

'Shall I help you to your room?' she asked Lady Brenda.

'You're a sweet child,' she said, 'but why would I go to my room now when there is so much to be done?' She turned and patted Duff gently on the cheek. Kathleen saw him flinch at her touch. 'My bright-eyed boy,' she said. 'You were my babe.' He didn't respond although Kathleen could see both horror and pity in his face, and his teeth clenched tightly. Lady Brenda gathered her own shawl, which had drooped to the small of her back, more securely around her, and set off again, slippers scuffing against the worn wood of the floor, singing the same song

> *'Hush-a-by baby, babe not mine,*
> *You're not my own sweet baby O!'*

'I'm sorry you had such trouble,' Duff said, as they watched her drift along the gallery.

'I don't mind,' Kathleen said. 'I'm happy to help. It's not the first time I've come out at night when I've heard her.'

'I have tried to persuade her to keep to her own wing,' he said, and she heard the helplessness in his voice. 'Even, for a time, I took to having the doors between there and the main part of the house locked. But there are so many passageways, so many ways through, and she knows them far better than I. And when she couldn't find a way, she would set up a terrible wail that was almost worse than the nightly wanderings.'

'For myself I don't mind at all,' Kathleen said, 'but perhaps for Caroline . . .'

'My mother would never harm her,' he said stiffly.

'I know she would never mean to, but she might . . .' She didn't finish what she was about to say. She knew very well that he had thought, just as she had, that it was the baby trussed up in that shawl.

'She is not herself recently.'

'No, but perhaps while she is not herself . . .' She

didn't know what she was asking – for Lady Brenda to be locked in her room? For Caroline to be locked in hers?

'Caroline must be Maureen's concern,' he said, helpless or angry, she wasn't sure.

And then, in a rush before her nerve failed her, because she couldn't forget the ferocity of what she had half heard earlier that night, Kathleen said, 'You know, if you give Maureen what she wants, she is much easier to manage.'

'Meaning?' he said.

'Well, just that. Why not just give her what she wants? That's what we had the habit of doing at home in Glenmaroon. It makes for a quieter life.'

'Except she doesn't want a quiet life,' he said gloomily. 'Not with me anyway. She doesn't want what's given, only what she takes by force. And if I start to give too easily, she won't want me. I must fight her for every small thing. And I must resist her too.'

He looked so tired that Kathleen thought of asking him to sit down. 'Do you not worry,' she said, 'what this does to her character?'

'How do you mean?'

'Well . . .' she paused, and tried to put words to the thoughts she had about Maureen and her cruel wit, the barbed words she said but didn't always mean, and how she used them more now than she did before. About her temper, which was maybe tested too often, and how she no longer seemed willing to distinguish between those who were able for her – Duff, Chips, her sisters – and those who were not, turning the vicious side of her wit without first checking the robustness of the recipient. And how she worried that soon the cutting side of Maureen would entirely dominate the kinder. Mostly, how she worried at the gap between Maureen and her baby that she no longer tried to bridge.

'Sometimes,' she said cautiously, 'it seems to me that Maureen is always, now, ready for battle. And perhaps that makes her unkind.'

'I see.' And, after a moment, 'I do see. You worry that Maureen constantly primed for combat is somehow losing sight of her gentler self?'

'Yes, that's it.'

'I'll think about what you've said.' Outside, a thin streak of grey said there wasn't much night left. 'Get some sleep,' Duff said.

When it was morning proper, Kathleen, eyes gritty with tiredness, went to Maureen's bedroom. She was up but not dressed, standing at the window. Kathleen rushed into her tale of the night before – leaving out the detail that she had been awake because the sound of Maureen and Duff quarrelling had made sure of it – but dwelling on the ambiguous bundle in Lady Brenda's arms, and the ease with which she carried it about with her.

'I will speak to Nanny again,' Maureen said, when she was finished. 'She really must remember to lock that door. Poor Brenda isn't responsible in such a mood.'

'Poor Brenda? Yes, I see that behind the attempt at gaiety she is a sad figure. But what of Caroline? And the possibility of the tragedy Lady Brenda may bring her?'

'Caroline must be Nanny's concern. I haven't time. Now, I'll need a trip to London. I must order all new clothes.'

'All new?' Normally, like Oonagh, she ordered by the season.

'Yes, all,' she said happily. 'Go and see.' She gestured towards the dressing room and Kathleen went to look. Inside, it was as though some painter had squeezed out colour from every tube into a heap on the floor. There were pinks, scarlets, golds, creams, greys, blacks, the particular shade of deep blue that Maureen loved, all heaped into a shining mass together. They looked beautiful and Kathleen almost wanted to throw herself down and lie among them. She bent to look closer and picked up the pale green dress Maureen had worn for dinner the night before. She held it up, and saw that it was no longer a dress. It had been slashed at the waist, cut right away, so that it was barely now a top. She dropped it and picked up another, rose pink silk, and it, too, was cut, across the bodice. Then she took up a handful to examine: all cut. Some were cut crossways, some straight, others halfway, and the rest torn savagely. Sometimes it was a hole that was cut, a jagged absence in the heart of a dress or blouse. Nothing was whole. Shreds of glory falling into disordered puddles.

'Duff did it last night. With scissors. Everything is in tatters.' She spoke with a strange kind of satisfaction.

'He must have been very angry,' Kathleen said slowly. Angry enough to stalk out and wander the dark hallways.

'Oh, simply furious,' Maureen agreed. And she was

delighted. Kathleen could see it in her eyes even though she held her face steady. Delighted, Kathleen supposed, at the intense focus of Duff's attention trained upon her, even in all its savage destruction. Delighted that she, not his friends from Oxford, was what he thought of, was driven mad by, made passionate by. No wonder she didn't have time for Caroline. No wonder Duff looked so weary. To sustain her interest, when this was what it took? They had been married barely a year and a half.

She had no idea what to say. And so she said what she thought, said it coldly: 'You have plenty more.' And it was true – for all that there was a heap on the floor of destroyed finery, all around hung more gowns, suits, blouses, with shoes lined up in rows and an entire cupboard devoted to her furs.

'I will be leaving for London soon,' Kathleen said, that moment decided. 'It's time I went back.'

'We can go together,' Maureen said.

Part Three

1932

Chapter Thirty-Eight

Rutland Gate, London

It had been a cold, damp spring, so that the first warm days of summer came, Oonagh thought, like delicately wrapped gifts, the kind that are almost too pretty to undo. She felt herself stretch out, content, like one of the dogs that had been well fed and petted.

'Isn't she a wonder?' she said to Aileen, watching as Tessa, now four months, tried to push herself towards a silver rattle that lay at the edge of the rug on which Oonagh had placed her.

'She seems a capable child,' Aileen said. 'More active than my little Doon, even though Doon is older by nearly four months. Certainly more active than Caroline at that age. The last time I saw Caroline, she did almost nothing except sit and stare with those great big eyes. She and Doon look alike, but in temperament, well, I hope they are not. I think Maureen is rather frightened of her daughter.'

'Imagine Maureen frightened.' Oonagh sounded almost frightened herself at such an idea.

'Indeed. Very disconcerting. And it makes her more demanding of Duff than ever before. She hates to let him out of her sight. I feel quite sorry for the poor fellow.'

'I've always found him rather alarming,' Oonagh confessed. 'Those heavy-lidded eyes and the way he stares at one, as if he's certain one is about to say something perfectly idiotic. And then of course, because of that, one does.'

'Well, you'd feel for him now, being pursued around his own house by Maureen – "Where's Duff? Where's Duff?" all day. Still, she's happy, I suppose.' She sounded more curious than certain. 'And you, are you happy?' she asked, in a way that tried to be idle.

'I could not be more in love,' Oonagh said. 'Tessa is such a darling.' She looked fondly at the baby, who now had the rattle in her hand and was shaking it vigorously. 'Even Gay didn't prepare me for this.'

'We know you're happy with your children, Oonagh. Impossible *not* to know. But Philip?'

'Philip and I do very well,' Oonagh said, wondering, even as she spoke, what on earth she meant. They *do very well*? She supposed she meant that he worked and went to his club, and she played with the children and lunched, and together they went to parties at which he was polite and solicitous, and everyone who saw them said what a handsome couple they made. And if they were both lonely, so that even Violet's company would have been something, only she was pregnant and still in Cumberland because London was 'too expensive' – said with a sidelong look under her lashes – then no one would have known it. And why should that not be *very well*? she thought. It was a marriage like most marriages, and perhaps they might still learn to find company in one another. 'With Tessa,' – she changed the subject – 'I feel I can do everything right that with me was done wrong.'

'Meaning?'

'I shall be kind and loving to her always and never make her feel that sickening dizziness I felt when Mamma would look at me, eyes sweeping from my head to my feet and all the disappointment she felt in me gathering in her face.' Aileen wrinkled her nose in sympathy. 'I'm determined Tessa will never know that. She will be educated and strong and wise. Having a daughter is to have a chance to set right everything I learned that was wrong!'

'How excessive you are,' Aileen said disapprovingly. 'Shall you have more?'

'Dr Gilliatt is determined that I should not, even though the birth was easier than with Gay. Philip too. He says he is happy with a brace, a boy and a girl, and what need could there be for more?' She giggled. 'I think he sees children like motor-cars: you can only drive one at a time.'

'What other news?' Aileen asked. 'Diana and Bryan?'

'She is planning a magnificent party for Unity's coming-out.'

'And how are they? One hears rumours . . .'

'Even the ghost bores her now.'

'And the baby, little Desmond?'

'That too, from what I can see.'

'And is Diana . . . ?'

'Still yearning? Oh, yes. Or maybe rather more than yearning now . . .' Oonagh paused delicately, as a cat will pause halfway through washing a paw. 'She is far less amusing than she used to be. Always talking about politics and Mosley and Britain First. And she's having two portraits done, you know. Bryan has commissioned Augustus John and John Banting.'

'One more than you? Well. What is it about husbands that they think a portrait will fix everything?'

'Oh, but a portrait does fix everything,' Oonagh said, mock serious, turning towards the de László that seemed to float above them. 'Now that Philip has demonstrated his regard for me in oil and canvas and a great deal of money, no one may ever question it.'

Tea arrived and they sat, one at either end of the sofa, balancing teacups on saucers and resting heads against cushions. Aileen unbuttoned the jacket of her navy suit, revealing a cream silk blouse that caused Oonagh to say, 'Paris?', lit a cigarette and started to describe a party at Luttrellstown.

She talked about the party, then another party, her guests, a racehorse called Millennium that had won some important race, trips to Paris and London to buy clothes, and almost nothing about her husband, so that Oonagh eventually asked, 'And Brinny, in all this whirl of activity?'

'Fine,' Aileen said.

'And does he enjoy the parties and the film stars as much as you do?'

'Stop fishing, Oonagh. He's perfectly all right,' Aileen said.

'But not in London with you?'

'He'll be here later, for Diana's party. He didn't want to come quite yet. And I didn't want him to either. Nothing is so awful as the company of someone who'd rather be elsewhere.'

She didn't meet Oonagh's eyes, fussing with the clasp of her purse. And because of that Oonagh, although she wanted to ask, 'Why would he rather be elsewhere?' said nothing.

It wasn't true, Aileen reflected an hour later as she motored back to the Ritz, looking out at the hot and lazy city streets. Or, at least, not true in the way she had said it. Brinny had been angry with her when she refused to wait for him. Angrier than she had yet seen him.

She had dressed early and walked down to the Luttrellstown stables, planning to catch him after his morning ride, when he would be in a good humour, and have the matter agreed before they got back to the house for breakfast. Perhaps she should be up at this hour every morning, she had thought, taking in the jubilant birdsong all around and the pale eagerness of the sunlight. Above her, a fat wood pigeon crashed into the branches of a tree and clung to a shaking branch half covered with early summer leaves.

Brinny was dismounting from a sweating chestnut hunter as she had arrived at the stable yard. 'Hello,' he called to her. 'Are you riding out?'

'I came to meet you,' she had said, and watched his face break into a broad smile. 'I thought we could walk up to breakfast together.'

'Capital!' He gave her his arm, and as they walked briskly back, Aileen put forward her plan.

'Let's go to London sooner than we said. I'm so bored here.'

'I can't,' he had said firmly. 'I have things to do. We will go in time for Diana's party.'

'Unity's party,' Aileen corrected mechanically, thinking how she might change his mind.

'Unity's party hosted by Diana,' he agreed pedantically. 'I still can't.'

'Then perhaps I might go without you?'

'I don't want you racketing around London on your own, with people talking and saying what they please.'

'What would anyone say? London is full of women whose husbands are safely at home in the country and no one says a thing.'

'I don't want you to be one of them.'

'Well, come with me, then.'

'I can't and you know it. Would you not wait?'

'No, because I cannot stand another minute of being here.' It wasn't exactly what she had meant to say, and she saw how it wounded him, but she didn't take it back. Instead she let it stand there between them. 'Do you forbid me?' she asked, when Brinny said nothing. Brinny never forbade her anything.

'No,' he said stiffly, 'but I ask you not to.' Brinny almost never asked anything of her either, and Aileen had contemplated giving in. But, no, she was so sick of Ireland, Dublin, Jammet's, poky nightclubs, last season's dresses everywhere she looked.

'Don't be silly, darling,' she had said, 'there is no need

for me to be here. I will go ahead and you will join me.'

'The girls?'

'The girls don't need me.' He had said nothing more, but she could see how angry he was, so she had brought her departure forward, ordering her maid to pack in a hurry and leaving the very next morning, before his bad mood could change her mind. 'I'll see you in London,' she had said, as he watched her go.

The taxi stopped outside the Ritz then and the liveried doorman, catching sight of her, sprang forward to open the doors. Aileen, comforted by the alacrity of his movements, walked towards him smiling.

'Madame Plunkett.' A dark-haired man moved smoothly into her path, holding out a gloved hand. It was the baron from Oonagh's party.

'What are you doing here?'

'Why, I am in town for a little while and staying here. You?'

'I'm staying here too.'

'Well, isn't that jolly?' he said in his faultless English.

Chapter Thirty-Nine

After the savage seasons of Clandeboye, the return to London had felt to Kathleen like a homecoming. Travelling in by train, she had watched as banks of squat houses in serrated rows rushed closer and closer together, then yielded to larger buildings, warehouses, blocks of offices rising grandly over the houses and looking down upon them, held apart by wide streets and chequered here and there by neat parks picked out with slender iron railings. Newer buildings crowded in above and around older ones, like a half-unravelled tapestry restitched in a different, brasher palette. She had her nose and forehead pressed hard against the window of the third-class train carriage – Maureen, up ahead, was in first class; Kathleen had refused to allow her to buy a new ticket so they could travel together – so she could see what was coming, marvelling at the blur of bricks and pavement that came into focus for a moment as they passed it, then blurred again as it went by, all surrendering to the rolling noise and activity that was Paddington station.

At first the noise – the loud and varied nature of it – confused her after so many months away: it had been autumn when she left and now it was summer. Until she recalled with a wonderful sense of freedom that this noise was not personal. The shouts and calls were nothing to do with her. The sounds of trains arriving and departing were independent of anything she had done or needed to do. None of this was her care, and therefore she could ignore it. Unlike at Clandeboye, where every noise might be the beginning of an argument, the start of Caroline crying, trouble of some kind brewing. The realisation gave her a giddy sense of freedom.

London was hot that summer, with a sodden heat. The kind that gets trapped for days at a time, stuffed down among all the people and houses where the cooler night air cannot find and dilute it, so that it was stale and smelled of rubbish, yet comforting too, tangible as a blanket.

The quiet, rather spare elegance of Rutland Gate was such a contrast with the clamour of Clandeboye: the gentle stirring of a curtain in the evening breeze, the throaty call of a wood pigeon from the gardens, the discreet progress of Peters about the place, all these sounds numbered and contained. There was no crying child, no unexpected shrieks, no shouts, no gramophone, no clatter of heels up and down stairs and, most of all, no near-silent scuffing sound of Lady Brenda's slippers.

But Oonagh – who was gay when she first arrived,

and happy to see Kathleen, eager to show her Tessa and all she could do, Gay and how much he had changed – seemed very soon to slump, like someone winded.

She was far more often at home than previously, Kathleen found. The lunches, dinners, parties of before were fewer, or she didn't attend them as she used to – and spent her time in the nursery with Tessa and Gay unless she had callers. Philip was hardly in the house at all, and when he was they didn't speak, except to convey information: 'The motor-car will come for you at eight o'clock.' It might have been a silent quarrel, except that it was sadder than that. It was as though they had nothing to say to one another, not even in anger. Oonagh drooped, for all that she tried not to let that be seen, and often said she was 'too tired' for whatever entertainment was suggested.

Ernest was more often at Rutland Gate – both to cheer Oonagh and also, she hinted, because Cloé was now so reclusive, and Gunnie so full of her usual recriminations, that Grosvenor Place was hardly pleasant for him. Instead, he looked for refuge with his daughters – who were all then in London. Maureen, arrived with Kathleen, was at Hans Crescent with Duff, and Aileen was at the Ritz, without Brinny, so the sisters were frequently together, bickering as they ever did, although Kathleen wondered did she not now detect a spine of something more serious in them: the squabbles were harsher, and not put aside so lightly. Each argument dragged with it the unvoiced memory of all the others, the way a cat will drag a tin can tied to its tail. And all three carried discontent with them, like a weight.

Once Kathleen had understood her duties at Rutland Gate with two children, she went to see Mary, in the new house at Cheyne Walk where Bryan and Diana had moved. 'They think they will be happier here,' Mary said, as they sat in the large, warm nursery. She cast a wary look at Jonathan, who was now two and almost old enough to understand what they said. 'He called it a fresh start, but I can't say I see any great difference. She is always out, and he is always in his chambers or shut up in his study.' Mary looked tired, Kathleen thought. Desmond, she said, was not an easy baby, and Diana found much fault with her because of his crying. Kathleen told her about Caroline then, about how terrible she had felt leaving her, and how still sometimes she would start awake at night, thinking she could hear the child cry, and that knowing she didn't was no comfort, because of how sure she was that Caroline was indeed crying, all those miles away, without anyone to go to her.

Maureen, she said, no longer pretended to any interest in her daughter. Instead, she spoke ruefully of having 'to go again, because Duff will want a boy, or at least a spare, but, goodness, how I dread . . .' Duff, Kathleen said, did his best but was often away so the nanny had full dominion. 'And she is a rough and harsh person who should have the care of sheep or goats, not babies.'

Kathleen talked and Mary listened. 'You were gone a long time,' she said. 'Longer than you expected.'

'I was,' Kathleen agreed. 'It was hard to leave at all, because of Caroline. Even at the end, when I knew I must go, I wanted to stay with her.'

'They're not our babies,' Mary said wisely. 'No matter how much we love them, they aren't ours, and we would do well to remember that. Although it's hard,' she added, as Jonathan came to where they sat and raised his arms for her to lift him, then put his head against her shoulder and turned it into her neck, from where he watched Kathleen out of the corner of his startling blue eyes. 'Ned is furious with me because he says I do the job of Nanny, but am paid as a nurserymaid. But in truth, if he knew, it's the job of a mother I do.'

'What of Ned?' Kathleen asked then, looking carefully at her hands. The letters had continued during her long months at Clandeboye as they had begun: few, short, always accounts of the Comrades, their plans, his doings, nothing more.

'He's the same,' Mary said. 'Determined to change the world because he thinks he knows a better way.' She smiled. 'And still coughing,' she looked worried, 'but he won't hear of me being concerned.' Of Miriam, she said nothing, and Kathleen didn't ask. Because maybe there was nothing to say and Miriam had already vanished, like vapour on the summer air.

Having turned over in her mind all the ways she could let Ned know she was back – write to him, wait till Mary told him, leave a message in chalk on the pavement – Kathleen decided simply to visit him unannounced. Go to his room in Berwick Street and call up from the street that he must come and let her in. As she approached the front door of the rickety building, she realised that if his window was closed she had no idea how to let him know she was there. But it wasn't, and she stood below and called his name, hearing her voice bounced off the houses opposite and flung into his open window, like a stone.

'I thought that sounded like you,' he called to her enthusiastically. 'Wait and I will come down.' He must have run because he was a little out of breath by the time he got to her. He put out his arms and hugged her close. Breathing in the familiar smell of him – coal dust, clean earth, warm bread – any resentment left over from the time of their parting was gone. Ned, Kathleen realised, was someone who lived the very moment before him. He didn't dwell on the past, or think about the future, or not his own future anyway, only the future of his cause.

'You stayed away a very long time,' he said, when they were upstairs.

He said it, she noticed, as a simple fact, little curiosity, no resentment, so she responded in kind. 'I did.'

Ned's room was a more pleasant place in the summer. The large windows, instead of closed and stuffed with rags to keep out clammy air and deaden the rattling of the rotted wooden frames whenever a car or cart passed underneath, were wide open to the sounds of the street below. The cries of the stall-holders and chatter of women with their baskets was cheery; the giant birds seemed benign rather than beady-eyed; and even the children who played there seemed almost merry, unlike the miserable crew of her first visit. They ran about with loud cries and wild laughter in the slow-moving late-afternoon air. She looked out at the houses opposite. All had their windows open and most had washing lines tied across them, with sheets pegged so that they flapped wildly, like tongues in open mouths.

The room was cleaner too, the corners swept and Ned's few things arranged on the table and washbasin. Someone had put a posy of flowers in a jam-jar on the small table. They were city flowers, found in cracks in pavements and growing wild in abandoned spaces – weeds, really, dandelions, dog daisies – but they were jolly in their yellow, white and purple. Because the daisies were still alive, Kathleen knew they couldn't have been there longer than a day, maybe just a few hours, and she could not imagine Ned gathering them himself.

Perhaps the neighbour's daughter, Miriam, had done all this. She had thought so much about her, and wondered if she would mention her, but now that she was here, with Ned, she found she could not. Not unless he mentioned her first. After all, what would she say? Miriam had no reality – was just a name, in a letter, from Mary, who so clearly disapproved because she was not Irish or even English. And if Ned was more comfortable, maybe that was good, and not something to be questioned.

'I saw Mary,' she said then. 'She is very busy with those two little boys.'

'Mary does too much. Though I don't care about that. I do care, though, that she has fallen into the trap those people set. The great trick of the ruling class.' He laced his hands behind his head and stretched out his elbows. Ned, Kathleen thought, with a smile, always took up an awful lot of space.

'Which is?'

'They have made her believe she is part of the family so they command her heart and her loyalty, when all she is is a servant, whose labour must be properly paid for, and whose loyalty should never be directed anywhere except towards her fellow workers. But she has chosen to wear the disguise they offer and to believe herself needed by them. She loves those little boys like they are her own, but they aren't, and for all her kindness to them, they will grow up to dominate her and all of us.'

'Is it the same for me?' Kathleen asked. She thought it must be, but Ned said no.

'If anything, I think those Guinness girls are a little afraid of you,' he said with a laugh, 'as we all are.'

'What do you mean? That's nonsense.'

'You don't know how intimidating you are, do you?'

'Me?'

'Yes.'

'The idea! I'm nothing of the sort.' She was shocked he would say such a thing.

'But you are. You know what to say, you speak as well as any of them, better even, and are so clear in your thoughts and arguments. And then there is something *sturdy* about you.' He laughed.

'Sturdy?'

'Yes, sturdy,' and he took her hand and squeezed it so she knew he was teasing her.

He talked fast and was so full of news and plans and questions that when he paused for breath, Kathleen said, 'I think you're the first person I've seen since I've been back who is not unhappy. Why do you think that is?'

'These are unhappy times,' he said, looking cheerful. 'Though I'm surprised to hear that your friends feel it too. I thought it was only us workers.'

'Well, I'm not sure if everyone is unhappy for the same reasons,' she said cautiously – Oonagh, Aileen and Maureen were unhappy only for their own selfish reasons – 'but certainly there is a lot of it about.'

Indeed he still had the cough, Kathleen noticed, just as Mary had said. A bad one. Every few minutes he got up and walked to the other side of the room and coughed there, so that it was clear he didn't want her to mention it. But she couldn't help herself, and asked how long he had had it, and had he seen a doctor. 'It'll soon be gone,' he said. 'Now that summer is here. Already it's much better.'

He had brought up a jug of buttermilk that he poured into two tin mugs for them, and a plate of some kind of bread baked with cheese that was very good, and peaches that were juicy and delicious. 'So tell me about Clandeboye,' he said, settling back against the wall with a peach.

She talked and Ned, seated on the bed as before, listened intently, asking questions – how many servants? Their duties? How many men working on the estate? Of Caroline's plight he said only, 'They raise them tough. They have to. An oppressive class doesn't tolerate weakness, even in its own,' until eventually Kathleen asked him if he was interested in her stay, or if he was gathering information for the cause.

'Would "both" be wrong?' he asked.

She didn't say yes, although she thought it. 'So, these are unhappy times?' she said. 'But you seem unaffected.'

'I like to be doing. And there is much to be done. Now that Mosley has set up his new party, our enemies are out in the open, above ground, and conveniently uniformed in black shirts so that we see them, know who they are, and can deal with them.'

'Why are they so bad, these Fascists?'

'They hate everything that's good about this city. If they had their way, they'd turn it into a place where everyone gets to be poor and die in the place they were born, surrounded by the same old faces, as pinched as theirs. Never any new ideas, new blood. They don't want things to be different, they want them to be the same, the way they used to be. Or the way they imagine they used to be. They try to destroy businesses belonging to Jewish friends, and so we go against them. We Communists want change, difference. We are the future, they are the past. And when it comes to a fight, we will win.'

'Will it come to a fight?'

'Oh, yes. And soon.' He sounded like he couldn't wait. 'Already we have had a few rucks in the street, nothing major, but more will come.'

'Will Tom Wintringham fight?'

'He does already. He may even organise some of the fighting. He's clever at finding out what the Blackshirts have planned, so that we can fix our plans too. They march; we march against them.'

'So there is trouble coming?'

'Can't you feel it?'

'I suppose I can.' She watched the easy way he moved his shoulders into the wall to find a more comfortable spot, the ready grin with which he greeted her gaze. She had forgotten, those long months in Ireland, how much he made her laugh; how, when she was with him, she didn't feel careworn or perplexed or anxious for a future she couldn't see clearly. She felt intoxicated by the vigour he brought to everything. 'Usually one looks for trouble to avoid it,' she said, 'but you look for it to dive right in.' He laughed, as she meant him to, and then he kissed her, and she meant him to do that too. And this time, when he drew back, it was she who leaned forward, sinking down beside him onto the hopelessly sagging bed. And she stayed there, with his arms around her, his mouth on hers, and then his hands under her shirt, warm against the skin of her back. She felt dizzy, reckless.

As she listened to the warm breeze of the afternoon, the cries of the traders on the street below – all the strange foods they offered, in their wild blur of unfamiliar accents – it seemed to her for a moment that they were not in London at all but in the kind of place Ned talked of when he described the future he wanted. The energy and possibility of all these other people with their strange languages, countries and customs coming together and being, in their mass, more than any of them could have been while separate. And in that moment, Kathleen saw the future as he did – a place filled with the new and wonderful, where what looked like rules would become no more binding than the old folk at home in Dublin, who stared to see her out without a hat or headscarf. And she marvelled at the brightness of it.

And because of that – the beauty and strangeness of what she heard in the afternoon air, and because he was serious for once and not laughing – when he asked again, 'Will you stay?' his hand hot on her back, Kathleen sat up, put a hand to his face and pushed back his fringe so she could see a paler patch across half his forehead where his hair hid it from the sun.

'For a little,' she said, smiling at the half brown, half white of his forehead.

Chapter Forty

The difference Kathleen had noticed in Ned, the lazy way he used to move from one thing to another, certain that all of them would amuse him, or that he could abandon whatever turned out to be a disappointment, was gone. Now, he was almost harried, constantly on the run from one task to another. He still worked at the docks, unloading the ships that sailed up and into the very heart of London, organising meetings and demonstrations, but now he wrote, often, for the *Daily Worker* and increasingly for *The Times*.

But still they managed to find time alone together, in his room, where Kathleen, lying in his bed, which was like a warm hammock, discovered that although his hands were rough and calloused, sunburnt like his face, his chest and back had an astonishing milk-white smoothness. 'You're like a girl,' she said, drawing a finger softly along his bare shoulder and down his arm.

'I am not. But you are, and a most beautiful girl. A *cailín deas*.'

'Don't call me that.' She wriggled away. Hearing him say *cailín* – 'girl' in Irish – reminded her too much of what her people at home would say to see them or hear of them. It brought her back to the narrowed eyes and strict expectations of her city, and the person she had been there – a person who would never have done what she did with Ned. 'Don't call me that,' she said again.

'Then I'll call you "darling love". How's that?'

'That will do,' she said and kissed him. Then, curious, 'How is it that you write for *The Times*?'

'It's thanks to Duff.'

'Maureen's Duff?'

'Yes.' She wasn't sure how much she liked this running together of the two parts of her life. 'I remember you met on the night of Oonagh's party, but I didn't know you had stayed in touch.'

'I didn't expect that we would, but he found me through Ernest, as it happens.' Of course, Kathleen thought, Ernest would know how to find Ned. 'And he was true to his word – he put me in touch with someone he knows on *The Times*.'

'Does Duff know what sort of things you write about?' She was truly curious.

'He does.'

'And what does he think?'

'I don't know. And neither, I'm afraid, do I care.' He stroked her hair. 'He was decent to put in a word for me, but he's not my friend and I don't need his good opinion. We have fundamentally different objectives.' That was how Ned talked these days: objectives, labour, capitalism, means of production. 'If you care so much, ask him,' and he kissed her.

'I? Why should I care?' she joked. But she did wonder.

Because of that, some days later she found herself listening more than usual to the conversation between Duff and Ernest, as they all sat in the drawing room at Rutland Gate.

Ernest was telling Duff his worries about the brewery in Dublin. 'This trade war will do no good for any of us,' he said. 'If things carry on this way, we'll move the brewery to London. We have a site already. I will not be held hostage by the Free State government.' He sounded, Kathleen thought, as though he would like to thump his fist upon the tabletop, but of course he did not. Duff listened, and asked questions, and made comparisons with the India Question that Ernest clearly found interesting. And Maureen, she saw, listened as keenly as Duff, and asked her own questions, which were taken seriously by both men and answered in detail. Aileen hovered on the edges of the conversation for a while, interjecting every now and then with comments such as 'I wouldn't stand for that,' that were mostly ignored. Then she said with a yawn, 'De Valera is clearly a most frightful bore.'

'I don't know about that,' Ernest said. 'He is certainly a shrewd negotiator. Kathleen,' – Kathleen jumped: she hadn't expected to be included – 'wasn't he professor of mathematics at your teacher-training college?'

'He was,' Kathleen said, 'but before my time. Although he was still talked about in my day. They say he would not answer questions, and set up the mathematical problems he gave out based on weapons and ammunition, even the principle of the torpedo.' She laughed. 'They wondered was he training an army, or a group of girls who wished to be teachers.'

'Perhaps an army is exactly what he had in mind,' Ernest said thoughtfully. 'That man is certainly cunning enough.'

'Machiavellian,' Duff agreed.

'An army of teachers,' Maureen mused. 'Rather clever, don't you think? Each one of them, properly trained, could then train so many more, and soon the whole country would be ready for recruitment.'

Kathleen waited for the slight squinting of the eyes that showed Maureen was joking. But it didn't come, and no one laughed. She wanted to tell them how ridiculous the idea was – but didn't know where to begin. She remembered Ned: *We have fundamentally different objectives*. Maybe Ned was right – maybe there were more differences even than the obvious ones.

They fell silent, Oonagh humming a song to herself, Aileen leafing through a book of dress patterns. The house was unusually still.

'Duff, I must go home and dress,' Maureen said eventually, putting her hands above her head and stretching like a cat. 'Aileen, come with us and we can drop you on the way.'

'I'm going up to see Gay and Tessa,' Oonagh said, as soon as she had seen the others off.

'I'm glad you're back in London,' Ernest said to

Kathleen, when everyone had left. 'Tell me, how did you find Maureen during your time at Clandeboye?'

She had known he would ask her. It was the first time they had been alone together since her return to London, and Ernest, she well knew, was as busy for his daughter's comfort as he was for his business. 'Her spirits were generally better than I expected to find them.' Kathleen said cautiously.

'You think she's happy?'

'She's certainly animated.'

'How does motherhood suit her?'

How to answer that? 'She is not a mother the way Oonagh is,' Kathleen said thoughtfully. She remembered Bryan, talking about Diana, at Oonagh's party, what felt like a century ago. *Some women find fulfilment in motherhood* . . . No one could say that of Maureen. She weighed up what to tell him. She didn't know where to begin. 'I think the nanny is an unpleasant person who does not discharge her duties,' she said at last, keeping her eyes on the vague shape of the ground ahead of them, lost now in rising obscurity. He looked at her for a while then, silent, almost abstracted, weighing up what to ask, and not to ask.

'I will see she is replaced,' he said. And changed the subject so that Kathleen marvelled at how little anyone minded that Maureen wouldn't care for her own daughter. 'There are constant improvements to the house?'

'Rarely a moment when there are not men with ladders.'

'It's a bad investment, a house like that,' he said

irritably. Ernest disliked bad investments above all things. 'They eat money and give little or nothing back.'

'I think her marriage may be the investment.'

'Well, perhaps you're correct. It seems that none of my daughters has made an entirely happy choice.'

'I think Maureen is happy,' Kathleen said, 'but maybe not very tranquil.' What she didn't say was that, more and more, Maureen reminded her of the beaters she saw going out before Duff and his friends went to shoot – stirring up the undergrowth, whacking at bushes and the low-hanging branches of trees with their sticks, poking and swinging, desperate to stir up some kind of activity, some bird that could be sent up into the air for the men with guns to aim at. Like them, Maureen was frantic, in action, flailing about, not caring what she sent up in her desperation.

Chapter Forty-One

'Papa says we must be careful,' Oonagh said, stirring sugar into her tea. She stirred so long that Aileen resisted the urge to reach out a hand and slap hers still. She kicked one of the many shopping bags that lay at her feet instead, and looked around at the other thin, rich women, with small dogs and large handbags, who occupied every table of the Ritz drawing room. The clatter of their conversation rose into the air like, she thought, steam from a manure heap. Foul, but necessary. Inevitable.

'Why?' she demanded.

'He says it's not a good time for Bryan and Diana to be having such a party.'

'But it's Unity's coming-out.'

'Yes, and Papa says that shouldn't matter at a time like this, and that what looks like a lantern can be a match.'

'Do you even know what he means by that?' Aileen asked, nettled at the way Oonagh seemed to assume such intimacy with what Ernest felt and thought. *Papa says . . . Papa says . . .* Like his thoughts were hers to interpret.

'I know he doesn't much want us to go,' Oonagh said.

'Well, you may do as you wish, but I don't plan to stay away,' Aileen said.

'I hear you have that girl Annie, Mildred's niece, with you?'

To Aileen's fury, Annie had arrived the day before, dispatched by Brinny, after a stiff telephone call in which he said, 'Mildred has sent that girl again. I can't have her here so I'm sending her to you. She will be with you in the morning. I've engaged a room for her beside yours. You'll share a connecting salon.' Aileen had instantly rung up Mildred, who laughed heartily and said, 'You can't send her back to me. I'm going to America. And you'll be glad of her in the end. She's a useful little thing.'

Annie had arrived at the Ritz clutching a scuffed brown leather case and been enough overwhelmed by the place that Aileen had begun to feel better about her. After all, it was nice to have someone to admire one, she thought, laying out the clothes she might wear that evening on the bed and seeing Annie's eyes widen as the maid brought in jewels to go with them.

'This?' Aileen said, holding up a long gown of midnight silk, then laying a thick collar of diamonds and pearls against it.

'Wouldn't it be very heavy?' Annie asked.

'What has that to do with anything?'

'Uncomfortable, I mean.'

'One doesn't look for comfort,' Aileen said grandly, liking the way it made her sound – as though she had great and terrible duties. Then, 'I don't know what you will do while in London. I shall be busy and mostly I shan't want you with me.'

'That's all right,' Annie said. 'I have plenty I'd like to do.'

'Such as?' Aileen was nettled by the ready response.

'There are a great many papers I wish to read at the British Library. Any time I have, I will go there.'

'Well, remember that I will sometimes have need of you, and I don't expect to share you with the British Library.' The fact that Annie had already made a plan, one that didn't include waiting on Aileen's wishes, annoyed her. 'This isn't a holiday, you know.'

'I know,' Annie said, but not as humbly as Aileen would have expected.

'I didn't bring her,' Aileen said now, 'Brinny sent her.'

'Like a parcel,' Oonagh said admiringly.

'I'm jolly well going to get rid of her. If Mildred wasn't leaving for America, I'd have done so already. She's better company than I first thought, but she interferes with my plans.' She didn't say that Brinny, in the same stiff telephone call, had said he wouldn't be coming to London for Unity's party after all, and that he hoped to see her at home very soon.

'What plans?' Oonagh asked sharply.

'In a moment. Where is Maureen?'

'There.' Oonagh nodded towards the doorway, and

they watched as Maureen made her way slowly towards them, stopping to say hello here and there, determined not to hurry simply because she was late.

'The Royal Progress,' Aileen said, when Maureen finally reached their table and sat down. 'And now here's Annie too.' The girl had glided silently to the table unnoticed in Maureen's wake and stood, waiting. There were four chairs, but the fourth had more of Aileen's shopping bags on it. She didn't move them. 'This is Annie,' Aileen said. 'Annie, my sisters – Lady Dufferin and Mrs Kindersley.'

'How do you do?' Oonagh said.

'I've been rather tired, but generally well, thank you,' Annie said.

'It's not a *question*,' Aileen said. 'I've told you that before. No one really wants to know how you do. You may say, "How d'you do?" back, and that will suffice.'

'How d'you do?' Annie said.

'She speaks German,' Aileen said then. Maureen and Oonagh looked at her in surprise, as if Aileen had given them something unwieldy and asked them to hold it. 'Annie, go upstairs and wait for me there.'

When the girl had gone, picking her way silently through the room, Maureen, looking after her, said, 'So that's Mildred's protégée?'

'Rather Aileen's protégée now, I would have thought,' Oonagh said. 'Is that one of your old suits she's wearing?'

'Yes.'

'Not one of the ones that would actually have suited her, I see.'

'She looks like a puddle of orange squash,' Maureen said.

'Enough about Annie. Now that you're here, I need you to give me your opinion on this.' Aileen pulled a black straw hat with a large brim from a box by her feet, and put it on at the same moment that a waitress passed by with a tea tray. Such was the size of the hat, and the angle of Aileen's elbows as she adjusted it on her head, that the waitress had to swerve suddenly. As she did so the tray tilted and a teacup and saucer slid to the end of it. The saucer was halted by the edge of the tray, but the cup carried on forward over the edge and smashed on the floor behind Aileen, who whipped around.

'Do watch out!' she snapped.

'I'm sorry, madam,' the waitress said, casting a morose glance at the smashed teacup, which would come out of her wages.

'Now, the hat?' Aileen demanded, looking around at her sisters. The straw of the hat was loose-woven in such a way that her face through it was almost as through a veil. The effect, she knew, was very dashing, but she wanted to hear them say so.

'Are you auditioning for the part of a milkmaid in something?' asked Maureen. 'Or is it just the Tyrolean-peasant look you're going for?'

'What do you mean by that?' Aileen demanded.

'I think you know jolly well,' Maureen said slyly.

'What?' Oonagh looked from one to the other. 'What are you talking about? Do tell.'

'Well, I suppose I may as well, because you're sure to hear it soon enough.' Aileen straightened the hem of her pale blue summer dress. 'And apparently Maureen has heard it already. I have a new friend.'

'What kind of friend?' Oonagh demanded.

'I'm not exactly sure yet.'

Behind them, a pianist was playing 'All of You'. Aileen thought how sad all the songs were that year. But she kept the smile on her face. So successfully that Oonagh said, 'If you mean what I think you mean, then it's no reason at all to sit there smirking like that. What about poor dear Brinny?'

'I have no idea what you think,' Aileen said. 'And as for Brinny, why should he know anything about my friends?'

'That's not what I'm asking and you know it,' Oonagh said. 'Will you get divorced?'

'How you do jump the gun, Oonagh. We're friends, that's all.'

'What kind of a baron is he, anyway?' Maureen asked.

'The Austrian kind,' Aileen said.

'How frightful.'

'A baron,' Aileen emphasised. 'And so clever about all the things one cares about. Notices when one has had one's hair styled, knows where to have a dress altered and the tiny changes that will make it fit perfectly.'

'Still frightful. And probably a liar. Certainly a bounder. European royalty is always so shabby.' Maureen considered herself a great expert on royalty. 'I suppose he has a crumbling castle somewhere he wants you to sink all your money into? As an *investment*?'

'There is a castle. Half an hour from Vienna,' Aileen said cautiously. 'But I don't know if it's crumbling.'

'You can be sure it is. And I suppose he's a great friend of those goose-stepping National Socialists?'

'Hates them,' Aileen said. 'Not his type at all. So very serious, and the baron is always up for larks.'

'They are dreary all right, those old Nazis,' Maureen agreed. 'I do wonder why Diana is such a fan.'

But Oonagh was not to be distracted from her questions. 'Does this mean your marriage to Brinny is over?'

'Why would you think such a thing?' Aileen asked. 'But . . .'

'Oh, Oonagh, don't be a child,' Aileen snapped. 'It means nothing of the sort. In any case, do you really think people should stay married when they aren't happy?' She fitted a cigarette – slim and black with a gold tip, the type the baron smoked – into a long holder and lit it with a snap of a gold lighter, blowing twin plumes of smoke through her nostrils. 'I mean to say, I know you and Philip have . . .'

'We are happy,' Oonagh said mechanically, 'and we're talking about you. What has Brinny done wrong?'

'He hasn't done anything wrong. But one does get tired of only ever hearing about motor-cars and race-horses. The odd round of golf.'

'Well, surely if he has done nothing wrong, there is no reason for this.'

'For what? A new friendship?' Aileen made great play of looking confused, so that Maureen, in admiration, said, 'You are maddening, Aileen.'

'I find we have, after all, little in common, Brinny

and I,' Aileen announced, as though the failure for that was all Brinny's. As though all of her discontent and unhappy irritability could be explained by having little in common; as though having more in common could have rescued her from her sense of life flowing fast and urgent somewhere beyond her reach.

'But Mamma and Papa don't have things in common,' says Oonagh, 'and they are still married.'

'And you really think that's a good thing? When Mamma barely leaves her room, and Papa, when he's not in his office, is for ever off on the *Fantome*, or that speedboat. Or his plane. I don't intend to go that way, I can assure you,' Aileen said. 'All his favourite companions are mechanical. Apart from us.'

'But . . .' Oonagh looked at a loss, and Aileen thought of trying to tell her how she felt about what her life had become, the loneliness of endless irritation and the effort to bite back words of contradiction every time her husband spoke, but before she could, Maureen interrupted.

'Does the baron know your views on marriage and friendship and amusement?' she wanted to know.

'Ask him yourself,' Aileen said. 'Here he is.' The baron had already spotted their table and made his way towards them, weaving through and past people, chairs, tables, as though performing his part in a complicated dance. Aileen introduced her sisters, and he bent low over all their hands, affecting to kiss them, then stood straight and bowed sharply at the waist. Maureen didn't even try to disguise her hilarity, laughing loud, head thrown back. But instead of being offended, the baron laughed merrily with her.

'My manners seem ridiculous, I suppose,' he said, in crisp and flawless English. 'I was brought up in the old school. Rather an absurdity now, but what can one do?' And he twinkled at them all, so supremely confident in himself that Maureen and even Oonagh smiled back. 'I will wait for you in the car, my darling,' he said to Aileen. 'But first I will send someone in for your parcels. Please,' he waved a hand, 'do not hurry. Take your time to say your farewells to your exquisite sisters. Ladies,' and he bowed low again.

'I say, don't overdo it, Baron. She's only going off for an hour or so,' Maureen said, but without the sting Aileen knew she was capable of.

'Isn't he divine?' Aileen said, after the baron had left, stubbing out her cigarette in a plate of iced cakes and starting to gather her bag and gloves.

'Certainly very polished,' said Oonagh. 'But, oh, poor Brinny. How can he possibly compete with *that*?'

'Who says it's a competition?' Aileen asked.

'Honestly, Aileen, I don't understand you at all.' Oonagh looked close to tears. 'And what about the girls? Poor little Neelia and Doon?'

'What *about* the girls?' Aileen demanded, exasperated. 'What have they to do with anything? Honestly, Oonagh, your mania for children is becoming impossible. I'll see you at Diana's.'

'What about Annie?'

'She can wait.' She strode out, wishing she had the nerve to kick something, as Maureen surely would have done. For all her attempts at indifference, Oonagh's questions had annoyed her. Because they were much too close to the questions Aileen asked herself in those few moments when she stopped being very careful not to ask them. They were easily banished, these things she asked herself, but always tiresomely ready to return.

Chapter Forty-Two

Cheyne Walk, London

Diana's party – or Unity's party, Oonagh reminded herself – started badly. There had been another hunger march, and although it had finished hours before they set off for number ninety-six Cheyne Walk, there were still men in the streets, wandering in groups, mostly drunk, singing snatches of *'The people's flag is deepest red / It shrouded oft our martyred dead.'* Some of them jeered the motor-car as it went past with all the windows up, although it was a warm night, and Oonagh shrank into her corner in fright as one man made a lewd hand gesture. Philip did nothing to comfort her beyond saying, 'I'm sure he means nothing by it.'

'I'm sure he does,' she said gloomily.

'Bloody Communists!' Philip said. in a loud voice that made her flinch again. But she noticed that he made sure the car window was rolled tightly up before he said it.

Number ninety-six Cheyne Walk was actually two

houses, ninety-five and ninety-six, and had once belonged to the American painter Whistler, Diana had told Oonagh, indifferent to the fact that Oonagh barely knew who Whistler was. On the pavement outside the railings, a small crowd had gathered. This often happened – they came to look at the men and women, mostly the women, alighting from cars and walking up the steps, that they might *ooh* and *aah* at their jewels and dresses. Usually they called out compliments and admiring comments – 'Isn't she lovely?' that kind of thing – and Oonagh, familiar with the proceedings, readied herself to smile and be gracious. Except that when they stepped down from the motor-car there was a curious sullen silence. A sort of appraising once-over, rather than the cheers she was used to. She went to take hold of Philip's arm, but he had moved ahead of her and was already halfway up the front steps. The door at the top was open, and as Oonagh reached the bottom of the steps, a man was half carried through it by two footmen, who supported him down the steps. It was Augustus John, the painter. As he was helped through the crowd, a man called, 'Look at him, dead drunk,' and another shouted, 'Degenerate!' whereupon the whole crowd fell to booing loudly.

'Come along.' It was Philip, back for her. He took Oonagh's arm and almost pulled her along in his determination to make her hurry.

'What was that?' she said, as they hurried up the steps.

'A mutiny.'

Inside, the house was painted in carefully subdued blues and greys, like reflections in water of an endlessly mutable sky, and every painting, object and piece of furniture Oonagh saw was so perfectly right that she couldn't help saying in surprise, 'Why, Diana has the eye of an artist.' Upstairs in the ballroom, Diana stood ready to greet her guests. She was wearing a dress of many layers of pale grey chiffon and tulle, and 'All the diamonds she could lay her hands on,' Oonagh hissed to Philip. She was radiant, her beauty, so often cold and rather repellent, conjured into a living, breathing thing. Oonagh thought she would not like to be Unity, whose party it was, and who was not at all beautiful – her hair had been coaxed into waves that became her far less than when it fell unstyled about her face, and her dress was the wrong length for her height. However, she was in high good humour, romping with a group of fellow debs – she stood head and shoulders above any of them so that she was like a grown-up at a gathering of children – and saying, 'What marvellous fun it all is.'

'Of course, it's totally different for her,' Nancy said, coming to meet them and beckoning a waiter with a tray of drinks. She took two, downed one quickly, then put the empty glass back on the tray. 'By the time Unity was presented, she already knew half of London. Not like my coming-out, hiding in powder rooms and absolutely everything simply too shy-making. Remember that, Maureen?' Maureen smiled vaguely. There was, Oonagh thought, no way she was going to admit that she, too, had once hidden in powder rooms. 'Plus,' Nancy continued, 'the poor old Subhuman has been through it all enough now that he can be trusted not to explode, so you see there's that too. So much more relaxing for Unity than it ever was for us, when being asked to lunch by a young man was treated by Farve as though he had offered to put one up in a little flat in Bloomsbury . . .' The poor old Subhuman, as she called her father, stood at the edge of the ballroom, glaring around him at the revellers. 'I think he rather enjoys it all now,' Nancy said fondly.

She was, Oonagh thought, thinner, and drawn about the mouth, with dark shadows under her eyes, and darted rapid glances around, as though looking for someone she did not expect would come to find her. She was still unhappily in love with St Clair-Erskine, so much so that Oonagh had heard it said Nancy had put her head in a gas oven not long ago. When she asked, though, Nancy just laughed and said, 'It's a lovely sensation, just like taking anaesthetic, so I shan't be sorry any more for schoolmistresses who are found dead in that way,' so Oonagh had no idea if she was serious, or making fun. Looking at her now, the nervous turn of her head, the rattle of conversation, Oonagh rather thought it might be true.

The ballroom was so full it was impossible to do more than pick out a face or form here and there from the mass of tossing heads, hands waving cigarettes and throwing down drinks. A woman in a Venetian Carnevale mask went past. 'Why is she in fancy dress?' Maureen asked. Then, 'Never mind, who cares?'

They walked to another part of the room where it was more sedate, with older people seated, and conversation rather than shrieks and exclamations. Chips was standing talking to an elderly woman who was seated so that he had to bend low to hear what she said. He had recently announced his engagement to the girls' cousin, Lady Honor, and waved when he caught sight of them, making his way over to tell Maureen. 'That was a good turn you did me there.'

'I didn't mean to,' she said.

'No, I know you didn't. I can see that,' he chuckled, 'but all the same you did. Now what is it you English say? "It's an ill wind that does no one any good"? I never did understand that expression until now.'

'It's not like you need the money.' Maureen was determined to believe that to be the only reason he would marry Honor. 'Or is the Channon family shipping fortune a bit of an embellishment too?'

'No, that's real enough,' he said comfortably, 'but the heart of the British establishment? Well, that wasn't open to me until now. Oh, I know you're all very polite,' – he winked at Oonagh – 'and good at pretending someone is let in, as long as they're useful, but for all you think me crass and not so bright, I'm smart enough to know where I can't go, and until now, there were plenty of places I couldn't go. Not any more, though. Not now. With my marriage, and now with Mrs Wallis Simpson so much at the heart – or should I say *in* the heart?' – he twinkled significantly at them – 'of His Royal Highness, well, there is nowhere my countrymen and I cannot go.'

'That's all nonsense with Mrs Simpson,' Maureen said. 'Papa says he'll tire of her any day now, just as he did of Lady Furness.'

'Does he indeed?' Chips smiled broadly. 'Well, I wonder . . . I'd stay and ask him myself,' – he nodded towards Ernest, walking towards them – 'but I must go in search of my dear one.'

Ernest's appearance was cue for the girls to begin to fuss, offering drinks, ashtrays, asking would he prefer to move closer to a window, but he waved a hand at them to be quiet. 'Not now,' he said, inclining his head towards Diana, who was making her way to them, cutting smoothly and gracefully through the waves of her excitable guests as though they were minor disturbances below the surface on which she glided. Oonagh thought of one of the mechanical toys Ernest had brought Tessa – a doll-like figure set on wheels that could be wound up and would move forward, inexorably, until the mechanism ran down, propelling everything in its path out of the way. Diana moved in the same smooth, dauntless fashion. She came to a stop in front of the little group but said nothing at first, simply surveying them all with her top lip curling upwards in the way that was almost, but not quite, a smile.

With her was a man Oonagh recognised from his newspaper photographs: Mosley. In person he was slender, with a luxuriant black moustache that almost hid a thin red mouth, and liquid black eyes, like the tar on the roads that turned hot and sticky in the summer.

'Ernest.' He nodded. Diana introduced him to the girls. Oonagh noticed that she called him 'Kit'. He smiled politely at each of them and said, 'How do you do?'

Everything in his face, Oonagh saw, came forward to a point at the centre of his top lip. Exactly like a fox. Even his sharp white front teeth were thrust forward, so that he looked as if he would bite off the world, piece by piece, and consume it. Without the moustache, those teeth would, she was certain, give him a look too animalistic, and she felt sure he knew it.

'Oh, we've met,' Maureen said, giving him a considering sort of look. 'I remember it so well.'

There was a faint, awkward pause, then Ernest said, 'Mosley,' and nodded. As he did so, someone passing behind them bumped him so that he was pushed slightly forward, closer to the man before him. Oonagh saw that he stepped back immediately, as though he had encountered something unpleasant – an odour, excessive heat, something that repelled him – then said, 'How's the polo?'

They talked idly about sport and Oonagh asked Diana about her dress, but Diana ignored her because Mosley was saying to Ernest, 'You will have seen that Hitler's Schutzstaffel, the SS, are no longer banned in Germany, from today? Nor the SA. So, you see, more and more, the people are seeing where the future lies, and with whom.'

'Thugs and paramilitaries,' Ernest said loudly. 'No respectable man would engage with them, and certainly not if he hopes to become a democratically elected leader, as I understand this Hitler does.'

'The Reichspresident,' Diana said. She pronounced the word correctly, respectfully – and Oonagh recalled once hearing her scream with laughter at a friend of

Nancy's who spoke
it 'too bogus'.

'Not thugs,' Mosley cou
And providing required prote
starting my own version, a Defence
to deal with the rabble who try to dis
For all that we are a modern movement, th
disagreeing with us in the most old-fashioned w
bricks and bats.'

'I hear your lot can be old-fashioned too in that regard,' Ernest said drily.

Mosley began to talk at length then, with phrases such as 'The necessity for a fundamental change . . . a high conception of citizenship . . .' easing forward gently so that Ernest took another small step back – yet he was neither boring nor pompous. He leaned forward on the balls of his small feet as though he might strike, like a snake does, in one quick, fluid movement, and there wasn't any of the touch of absurdity that pomposity usually brings. Instead, there was something menacing about his conviction, about the alertness in every line of his frame and the wet black eyes that held Ernest's so steadily. 'You cannot deny we are in crisis?' he asked at last. And when Ernest agreed, but objected that Fascism was unBritish, Mosley seemed to welcome the clarity of the objection.

'If our crisis had come first among the nations, instead of last, Fascism would have been a British invention,' he insisted. 'Each of the great political faiths has been a universal movement, whether that is conservatism, liberalism or socialism. As it is, our task isn't to sm. It is to find, here in Britain, its highest ression. We can do so much more here, with our British nation, than Mussolini can with Italy, or Hitler with Germany.'

Maureen and Aileen had drawn back and away, ducking out of a conversation they found dull and were looking around, greeting friends, but Diana, Oonagh saw, stayed close beside Mosley, so Oonagh stayed too. She wanted to hear what they said. And how they said it. Ernest, she could tell, was exasperated, and tried to out-argue Mosley, putting forward objections and disagreements. And Mosley, bouncing gently back and forth on the balls of his feet, in command of his body as he was of his arguments, took great satisfaction in demolishing everything Ernest said, like a child knocking down a line of dominoes. He paused deliberately at strategic moments, waiting a beat, as though to give Ernest time to catch up with him. His pride, Oonagh thought, was immense, like a strutting cockerel that he brought around with him on a string. Diana, in her cloud of pale grey, leaned close, almost to touch her arm to his – almost, but not quite. She remained at a fractional distance, and there, she almost vibrated with his nearness.

His arrogance, Oonagh realised, was physical as much as it was intellectual. And Diana seemed utterly in thrall to it. She had a dazed look on her face, such that when he appealed to her to agree with him, she almost didn't know what she was being asked, just nodded. Her pupils – always small – had almost disappeared entirely so that her eyes were a disconcertingly rudderless sea of blue, unclouded by whatever thoughts had brought a pink glow to her normally pale cheeks.

'Where's Bryan?' Oonagh asked, and enjoyed the start Diana gave, the way something practical flooded the rapt emptiness of her face and her pinprick pupils flared momentarily.

It acted as a signal, with Diana saying, 'We must get on,' and the two of them left.

'Vile fellow!' Ernest said, when they were gone.

'He made a most frightful pass at me once,' Maureen said, moving closer now that Diana and Mosley were gone. 'I blacked his eye for him. Do you think Diana understood that's what I meant?' Ernest's moustache twitched but he said nothing.

'I'm sure she didn't miss it,' Aileen said.

'What do you think of his politics?' Oonagh asked Ernest.

'I think Fascism is an unpleasant foreign import, and Mosley an unpleasant and dangerous fellow. But we may need them to counter-balance the Communists.'

'Diana may say the party is a debut for Unity,' Aileen said then, 'but if you ask me, it's more like a political statement. Look at the guests.' They glanced around. The party had swollen again, like a river after rain, and many of the newcomers were dour-looking older men.

'Viscount Rothermere, John Beckett, St John Philby. Indeed, Mosley's crew,' said Ernest.

'Not at all the writers and artists who used to be Diana's friends,' Aileen agreed.

'Men of action,' Maureen said wryly.

'Perhaps. Not composing odes and sonnets, that's for

sure. So, a coming-of-age, and perhaps rather a farewell, too,' Aileen mused.

'Whatever do you mean?' Oonagh asked.

'What I say.'

'And how would you know that?'

'Call it instinct.'

'The instinct of one Bolter for another?' Maureen asked, at which Aileen turned on her heel and walked away, and Ernest looked pained. Within the family, the fact that Brinny was not with Aileen was not alluded to, and if it was, he was said to be 'busy'. Oonagh knew Ernest hoped that, if nothing was said, Aileen might simply tire of London and go home.

Chapter Forty-Three

Rutland Gate, London

It was after Unity's party that Diana left Bryan, declaring herself 'never more sure of anything in my life', when she was asked by everyone who knew her, had she really considered what she was doing, and could she not just . . . 'Just what?' she demanded loftily. 'Sneak around like everyone else does? No.'

The press, salivating for news – any news – of her took up residence at Rutland Gate, attention trained on number twenty-six, Lord and Lady Redesdale's house, but happy to roar at anyone who went past.

'How do you stand it?' Aileen asked, coming into the drawing room with Annie. 'The minute they saw me,' she continued, voice shaking slightly, 'they surged forward in a mass, and only for one of them shouting, "It's not her, lads," I think they would have knocked me over. I know you said to wear a scarf, Oonagh, so they would recognise and not pester me, but, honestly, I think one would be better to arrive with a large sign saying *Not Diana*.' She unwound a silk scarf from around her neck and gave it to Annie, saying, 'Fold that carefully. Annie was terrified,' she continued. 'Convinced our every move will be dogged by that terrible lot.'

'Not terrified,' Annie said then. 'But I wouldn't like them to take my picture.'

'They won't be taking *your* picture, Annie, I can assure you of that,' Aileen said.

'My taxi driver wouldn't bring me to the door,' said Maureen, from the far edge of the room. 'He insisted on dropping me around the corner because he says they think nothing of putting their cameras right up to the window of the cab, and he knows a fellow whose door they scratched. And you know how cabbies hate that. But why are they all here?'

'They haven't found out about the new house yet, so they camp out here instead, taking pictures of poor Lord and Lady Redesdale and hoping Diana will show up,' said Oonagh.

'So it's true?' Aileen asked. 'She has really left him, even though Mosley's wife, Cynthia, will never give him a divorce?'

'Diana says she doesn't care,' Maureen said, wondering. 'She's leaving everything. All that money, even her clothes. She says she will take almost nothing with her, except the boys. She has moved to Eaton Square, which she calls the Eatonry, where Mosley can come and go as he pleases, like the shabbiest sort of affair.'

'I suppose he skulks in and out at night,' Aileen said.

'Not a bit,' Maureen said. 'Bold as brass in daylight and at all hours, I hear. One almost has to admire her.'

'One does not. It's horrible,' Oonagh said indignantly, with a flick of a sideways glance at Aileen, 'and Diana is horrible to do it. Poor Bryan. How is he?'

'Terribly upset but trying to hide it,' said Maureen. 'You know Bryan. Being reasonable and modern and brave, and simply dying inside. Waugh said he looked like a shattered white rabbit, and that Mosley is revoltingly triumphant.' They sat, Aileen noticed, rather closer together than normal and at the far end of the drawing room, away from the windows, almost as though huddled protectively against the noise from outside.

'It's like a clear morning with the Duke of Beaufort's hunt out there,' she said, trying to be funny about the loud rumble from outside.

'Makes one feel sorry for the fox,' Oonagh said, with a shudder. 'I wish they would go away. It's terrible to feel so besieged in one's home, even though it isn't one they're after.'

'They have the scent of blood in their nostrils,' Annie said suddenly. They all turned to look at her, whereupon she blushed a hot red.

'Well, aren't you wise all of a sudden?' Aileen said.

There was a silence then, and Oonagh looked at Aileen and made a face. 'Must you?' she whispered, as Annie got up and went to look out of the window, standing well to the side that she not be seen from the street.

'Must I what?' Aileen hissed back.

'Be so mean?' Annie came back then, pulling at the sleeves of her cardigan, which were slightly too short, so Oonagh contented herself with frowning silently at Aileen.

'How are the Old Pair managing?' asked Maureen, falling into Nancy's nickname for her parents.

'Lady Redesdale has taken to carrying an umbrella to put up over her face, and comes and goes from the tradesmen's entrance at the back,' said Oonagh. 'The only one who seems to enjoy it is Unity, who likes to come out onto the steps and pretend she'll tell them what is going on. Then, when they all surge forward, pens and notebooks at the ready, she gives that Nazi salute she's so fond of, clicks her heels sharply and disappears back into the house.'

'There is something really rather gruesome about that child,' Aileen said.

'And Nancy has moved in with Diana?' Maureen said.

'To the Eatonry? Yes. And she says there's no point looking boot-faced at her, that even though she disapproves terribly and feels unbearably sorry for "poor sweet Bryan", the chance of getting away from the Old Pair at last is too good to resist.'

'Typical Nancy.'

'She also says Diana is not quite as bloodless as she seems, and is rather upset at all the fuss, actually.'

'Well, I don't believe it,' Oonagh said. 'She's exactly as bloodless as she seems.' Then, 'Kathleen, remind me, your friend Ned – his lot are against Mosley's, isn't that so?'

'They are,' Kathleen said, from her seat by the window, where she watched the comings and goings of the press with frank interest. 'Ned says that his people, the Communists, are modern, the future, and Mosley's Fascists are the past.'

'In that case,' Oonagh said, 'now that wretched Mosley has infected Diana so that she can't think straight, well, I'm on their side.'

'Me too,' Maureen said. 'I'm positively a Communist, these days.' And she said the same thing, proudly, when Ernest joined them half an hour later, come to say goodbye before a sailing trip on the *Fantome*.

He laughed at Maureen and said, 'And thus are the weighty matters of history and allegiance decided; reduced to a popularity contest,' but then he grew serious. 'It's hardly a joking matter. But on balance, though both are bad, I find myself more disgusted with Mosley's Blackshirts. And those Biff Boys of his . . .'

'What are Biff Boys?' Annie asked. Again, everyone turned to her. Quiet as she was around the sisters, she almost never spoke in Ernest's presence.

'Mosley's bodyguard. A bunch of bullies who guard the man and his meetings and ensure no one interrupts.'

'But surely that is not allowed? By law?' Annie asked, her voice stronger, almost indignant. 'That is the job of the police after all.'

'How very well informed you are, Annie . . .' Aileen said.

'Annie is correct,' Ernest said. 'He calls them stewards but they are street thugs.'

'They should be forced to disband,' Annie said.

'Such fighting talk,' Aileen said lightly, but with a quelling look at Annie.

'Honestly, I don't understand Diana at all,' Oonagh said then. 'What does she see in him?'

'Oh, I think I understand that,' Maureen said with a smirk.

'But I thought you hated him?'

'I do. Horrid creature.'

'So, what is it you understand?'

'Well, he clearly has sex appeal . . .'

'Maureen . . .' Ernest said warningly.

'For Diana,' Maureen added hastily, 'not me. But for her, heaps. She's drunk with it. Can't see straight.'

'But what does that mean?' Oonagh asked, petulant as she used to be when she was a child and Aileen and Maureen talked – deliberately – about things she didn't understand.

'I think I see it,' Aileen said. 'He is the match of Diana. If she is the huntress, he is the hunter.'

'Exactly,' Maureen said. 'She'd follow him anywhere, do anything at all he asked of her.'

'Did she tell you that?' Oonagh demanded.

'No, but I recognise the look . . .' she said a little dreamily, at which Oonagh snapped, 'Oh, for goodness' sake, Maureen!'

'That's quite enough,' Ernest said, rustling his paper angrily. Outside, the rumbling erupted into a sudden roar, in which Aileen could distinguish the frantic exploding of flashbulbs and voices shouting, 'Over here! Look this way!'

'Someone must have opened the door of number twenty-six, or appeared at a window,' Oonagh said. 'Let's go and sit in the library. It faces the back and is more protected.'

Chapter Forty-Four

London

The baron tried to persuade Aileen to go to Paris with him – 'We can take in the ballet, the opera, there are showings at Chanel,' and although she planned to say yes, somehow she couldn't quite bring herself to do so. To be alone in London was one thing, and if the baron happened to be staying in the same hotel, why, what business was that of anyone's? But to take off for Paris with him, that was another thing entirely. What would she say to her sisters? To Ernest? To Brinny? When she thought of her husband, it was with a kind of heavy, mournful guilt that followed her around like an old dog. He still telephoned most days, asking when she would be back, and pretended to believe her when she gave reasons why she couldn't yet. Perhaps she should just go to Paris, she thought. Be done hedging and hesitating, show her hand with a flourish. But she couldn't decide . . . the baron's fluid charm set against Brinny's solid devotion – she played first one then the other through her mind, like someone admiring a painting, viewing it now from one side, then the other. And could not choose. And so 'Paris at this time of year?' she said instead.

'It is exactly perfect,' he insisted. 'Not too hot, and the chestnut trees on the Champs-Élysées are in full bloom. They are like magnificent ballrooms of old lit up with a thousand tall white candles . . .'

'You make it sound exquisite.'

'It will be, if you are there.'

'But the tedium of packing . . .'

'The maid will do it.'

'Besides, what will I do with Annie?' she said. 'It's one thing to send her to the British Library during the days when I have no need of her, or leave her alone with supper on a tray in the evenings. But to go to Paris?'

'Bring her, leave her, whatever you like.' He shrugged.

'I can't leave her, what would she do? And I can't bring her . . .' And so she procrastinated a while longer, and tried out the idea in conversation before she made a move. With Annie, on a rare evening in, she said, 'I am thinking of going to Paris.'

'I see,' the girl said.

'I have not yet decided. But you wouldn't be coming with me.'

'No, I suppose I wouldn't,' the girl agreed meekly. Then, 'Will it be in all the papers, if you do? And will you like that? I suppose you will.'

'What on earth do you mean?'

'Well, it won't just be Viscount Castlerosse's column

but all the papers. And if you liked appearing in his column, I thought . . .'

'Do you not see what a difference there is?' Aileen asked. She wanted to slap the girl for her idiocy, but something in Annie's face, something so much less timid than her usual expression, stopped her. Almost, she thought, as though Annie hadn't so much put her foot in it as stepped carefully . . . deliberately.

'Being written about is sometimes a necessity,' she said tightly. 'Such pinpricks are a consequence of one's position.' For some reason this made her think of Gunnie and her story of the pin. She began to tell the story, but broke off when she saw the expression on Annie's face. 'Never mind that,' she said. 'I don't suppose you would understand.'

'But I do understand,' Annie said. 'My mother used to tell a story just like it. Only hers was a sharp stone in a girl's shoe that caused her pain but she wouldn't complain because it was a walk to church and only when she fainted was it discovered. She told it in a hushed voice, as though the girl were someone I should admire, but I always thought that girl silly as anything not to just take the stone out.' They both began to laugh at that.

'Why do they love those stories so much?' Aileen asked.

'I know,' Annie agreed. 'Sacrifice and pain and bleeding. And always girls, in the stories. As though one's highest duty is to suffer silently. I would complain like anything.'

'I hope I would too,' Aileen said, recalling the way

Gunnie's story had once made her feel – as though she understood why the girl said nothing about the pin: because she liked knowing she had something that was different, and that caused pain that was easily understood. That didn't seem so appealing any more. 'I'm sure I would.'

'If you go to Paris, will you come back?' Annie asked then. 'Or will you be one of those people who live abroad? I suppose if you are, the press will leave you alone. No one much seems to care what happens to the people who live abroad.' Aileen looked at her closely, but Annie's face was clear and guileless.

'I haven't decided anything yet,' Aileen said.

After that, Aileen told the baron firmly that she couldn't possibly go to Paris, and that she had decided to move in with Oonagh, at Rutland Gate. 'She needs me,' she said, to which the baron instantly said politely, 'But of course. Let me know if I can be of assistance.'

Oonagh was delighted at the move – 'How cosy,' she said. Maureen told Aileen she was mad, and to stay at Hans Crescent instead: 'You'll be driven out of your mind. Impossible to forget that silly scandal when it's playing out under your very nose.' But Aileen found she couldn't forget the scandal, became in fact consumed by it, reading everything she came across, in a kind of frenzy of horror.

The newspapers continued to print every photo of Diana they could get their hands on. They lurked outside her favourite haunts, disguised themselves and attended BUF rallies in the hope of catching a glimpse of her alongside the man they dubbed 'The Fencing Fascist'.

All her life, Diana had been written about in glowing terms – called 'beautiful', 'radiant', 'exquisite', just as the Guinness girls had – so the tone of the new stories took Aileen by surprise, because they were not at all adoring.

There was a chill over the pens that had formerly spluttered with praise for Diana. Clinical accounts of her comings and goings without the usual flattery. And, as a kind of sideswipe, they often, now, carried gushing praise for Lady Cynthia, Mosley's wife.

'Listen to this,' Aileen said to Oonagh, one morning over breakfast. 'From the *Bystander*: "I wonder if all of us admire Lady Cynthia Mosley sufficiently. She is so good-looking, so intelligent, a faithful friend, whose loyalty, once given, can never be taken away . . ."' The piece was written below a photo of Lady Cynthia looking, if not beautiful, then certainly elegant and distinguished, and close by, a small photo of a coldly glamorous Diana who was referred to as 'Mrs Diana Guinness' without any of the usual adoring preamble.

'Poor Diana, you'd almost feel sorry for her,' Oonagh said with satisfaction, peering over Aileen's shoulder at the small print in which Diana's humiliation was recorded. 'The only good thing is that, for all Bryan will do the decent thing and allow her to divorce him without contest, although I don't believe he should, Mosley will never be free to marry her so she will be a divorced single lady. And say what you like, that's still very *infra dig*.'

But it wasn't speculation around when and if Diana and Mosley might marry that obsessed Aileen, it was the savagery of the newspapers. She read everything, denouncing the papers as 'So disgustingly fickle, how can they?' and vowing that she would stop following the story, yet buying everything she came across in which Diana was mentioned. She read again and again the hostile headlines, squinted at the snide photograph captions and asked repeatedly, 'How can they?'

Even though by now the newsmen had realised that she was a regular figure on the street and had come to leave her alone, Aileen still felt a surge of fear whenever she approached the steps of Rutland Gate, either from within the house or outside. For that moment, that stilled second when heads turned her way and she was seen and scanned, before being registered and discarded, her heart would thump sickeningly and she would think, *What if? What if they all run towards me shouting and jostling and demanding? What if they pursue me as they pursue Diana? Where would I go?* 'How can they?' she asked again. 'How can she?'

She was so shaken by the madness surrounding Diana and Mosley that she didn't believe Oonagh when Oonagh said, 'She's happy. You'll see. Don't ask me why, or how, but she is.' And then, very early one Sunday morning, when Aileen had slipped out for a quick walk around the gardens, she did see.

'Darling!' Diana greeted her effusively, with kisses on both cheeks. 'How divine.'

'How brave,' Aileen said, pretending to irony.

'Oh, if I go early enough, the newsmen don't see me.' Diana sounded unconcerned. She looked around boldly, and walked, Aileen saw, without disguise. 'Not that I care for them really! But Farve still won't unbend, and has forbidden me the house. So I come early, while he's out for his morning walk, and go up the back stairs so the little ones don't see me because they'd blurt it out, and Muv lets me sit with her while she has her morning tea.'

It seemed to Aileen a sorry thing, to be sneaking around her parents' house at daybreak, but Diana didn't seem to mind that either. She was as unvaryingly beautiful as ever, in a blond fur coat, her little dachshund tucked into the crook of her arm. But, Aileen thought, she was different, too: engaged and purposeful. As though someone had taken the vague, charming frame that was Diana and firmed it up, given it edge and heft and density.

When Aileen asked her how she was, she smiled and said, 'I couldn't be happier,' and there wasn't a trace of defiance in the way she said it. 'Of course I'm sorry for Bryan's sake, and it's rather a shame for the boys,' she went on, 'and Muv tells me I've given up everything, but, oh, the joy . . . Every bit as wonderful as I hoped.' And she gave a sleepy smile and dropped a kiss on the head of her little dog. 'Even Dixie is happy, aren't you, poppet?' she crooned to it.

'I thought his name was Jacob,' Aileen said.

'Well, it's Dixie now. Kit didn't like "Jacob". Too Jewish.' She laughed, and walked away, her fur coat swinging around her like a hunting trophy.

'Diana says she's given up everything,' Aileen said to Oonagh when she got back. 'And that it's every bit as wonderful as she'd hoped.'

'I suppose it would want to be,' Oonagh said. 'At that price. "Everything" is rather a lot.'

'An awful lot,' Aileen agreed sombrely. Outside, there was a bestial roar as the newsmen caught sight of Diana leaving number twenty-six and the sound of breaking glass as they surged forward. Aileen shuddered.

And when Brinny arrived, unexpectedly, at Rutland Gate the very next day and said, 'See here, we need to talk,' she listened meekly enough, and allowed him to order the packing of her trunks, saying to Oonagh, 'It's time I went home.'

And when Oonagh asked mischievously, 'And the baron?' Aileen ignored her. 'What about Annie?' Oonagh asked then.

'She's coming with me. I've decided I rather like her. She's tactless and awkward, and absolutely no style and very little subtlety. But when everyone else is so very subtle that one never knows what on earth they mean – sometimes I doubt they know themselves, like Nancy, so busy being clever that her cleverness is as good as nonsense – bluntness can be useful. I have found a teacher in Dublin so she can continue to study German. It's what interests her.'

'So she's staying with you?'

'For now. Mildred was right.'

'Right how?'

'She did come in handy.'

Chapter Forty-Five

Rutland Gate, London, Autumn 1932

The Diana scandal began to die down, drifting to the corners of the newspapers every few days rather than bold headlines every morning – just, Oonagh thought, as piles of leaves in autumn will dry out and drift into obscure corners. And as the frenzy died down, so her mood sank too. There was nothing to do any longer in London that she hadn't done a thousand times before. The city felt thinned out, like a forest, and what was gone were all the things that had made it exciting and vital. Even the air felt tired and bleached of colour. Autumn was wet and cold so that winter seemed to hurry forward, and an especially large hunger march gathered in Glasgow, intent on marching the four hundred miles to London. 'They will be in their tens of thousands, Ned says,' said Kathleen. 'He is to meet them halfway and walk the rest with them. By the time they get to London they will be sore tired.'

'And even more hungry than when they set out,' Oonagh said wryly. 'How will they be fed?'

'Ned and his Comrades are organising canteens along the way. I will help where I can.'

'For the men's sake, or for Ned's?' Oonagh asked.

'Both.'

'What exactly is happening with you and Ned? I feel I should ask.'

'Nothing much,' Kathleen admitted sadly. 'He's delighted for my help, delighted at what he thinks is my new understanding. And for my company too, but last of those, I think.' She blushed a little at that.

'And is your new understanding a comfort to you – all that talk about the rights of working men?'

'Actually, it's the talk about the rights of working women that really interests me, although I don't know what to make of it all just yet.'

'Ned may find you learn more than he bargained for,' Oonagh said with a grin. 'Now, put me down for a contribution to the canteens.'

But not everyone was as tolerant of the marchers, and many of Oonagh's friends went away. 'Not such a fun time to be here,' said Baby, pulling a face, when she came to say goodbye. 'Much better to disappear for a few weeks.'

Oonagh telephoned to Bryan, in an effort to help and be of comfort to him, suggesting he bring the boys around, and himself take tea with her, but he politely turned her down. 'Thank you, but I don't feel I wish to talk about it all, and I know you will want me to.'

'We can talk about anything you like,' Oonagh said. But it wasn't enough.

'Thank you, but no. We would only find our way to it sooner or later, and really, Oonagh, I cannot. It is far too painful still to put into words.' He spoke briskly, more briskly than usual, so that it seemed to Oonagh he rushed to finish his sentences as she had once rushed to finish rice pudding in the nursery at Glenmaroon, before she had had time to see the skin that lay across the top and find herself sickened.

'Well, perhaps we can go out for an evening instead? I could introduce you to some jolly people.'

'I thought that's what you might say. No.'

When she told Kathleen that Bryan wouldn't allow himself to be helped, Kathleen said gently, 'It isn't a broken toy, Oonagh, that can be replaced with something shiny and new.'

Oonagh felt her spirits slump completely. Almost, she felt, as though she had disappeared from her own life. All the scaffolding of that life remained – dress appointments, Monsieur Fabrice came to the house to do her hair, the motor-car was brought around and she got into it, draped in furs, heels clacking on steps and pavement. The telephone rang, flowers arrived in great armfuls and she put them into vases. Occasionally she still asked Kathleen to pack up and they travelled down to Surrey, to Great Tangley Manor, although Kathleen, now, was busy with the canteens and Ned – but it was as if she herself was absent from all of that. She felt mechanical in her movements and responses: mouth moving into a smile, voice shaping and saying words, arms and legs moving obediently, but nowhere did she feel as if those things belonged to her.

Only with her children did she feel anything like she used to. Gay could always make her laugh, and now Tessa, eight months old, did too. Confiding and outgoing, she laughed easily, rarely made strange, and was already crawling, earlier than Gay by several months. She was fearless, following her brother around as fast as her chubby legs, and Nanny, would allow. And Oonagh watched over her with pride.

'I will never let her feel that it is only her looks that matter. I want her to grow into a woman who knows her own worth, and understands that it lies within her and not on the surface,' she said to Kathleen, gently brushing the child's wispy hair. 'I want her to grow up strong and certain of herself.'

'And she will,' Kathleen said. 'I'm sure of it. She's the very opposite of Caroline, that's for sure, so merry and friendly, where poor little Caroline is still like a half-tamed thing that views all the world with suspicion. Helen tells me so in her letters from Clandeboye. I think you must be right,' she said then, 'in your way of raising babies, when I see Tessa with her cousins.' And to Oonagh, whom everyone had dismissed as 'tiresome' and 'absurd', it was as if she had received a gift.

When Violet came back to London from Cumberland, heavily pregnant and soon to give birth, Oonagh was delighted. Here was company. Even, she welcomed Violet's company for Philip. After all, with Violet so soon to have a baby, it couldn't be the way it used to be between them. She looked forward to the house being cheerful again – the three of them could surely be friends as they had been, with all the unpleasantness forgotten.

And, at first, it seemed she was right. Violet called at Rutland Gate, looking swollen but pretty, and when she had settled herself in a chair said, 'Now you go away, Philip, so Oonagh and I can talk, and later you can come back and we'll take tea together.' Philip, clearly enjoying Violet's peremptory charm, looked brighter than he had in a long while, and said he would do exactly as he was told.

But once Philip was gone, Violet began to talk of how unhappy she was in her marriage, complaining greatly of her husband and his gambling debts: 'Not just cards and roulette, Oonagh, he gambles on the stock market, on the home farm. He has a hefty bet placed on whether this,' – she patted her stomach – 'will be a girl or a boy. And he loses. Every time. He has placed money that I'm carrying a girl. That's how I know for certain it will be a boy.' She laughed bitterly. 'You cannot imagine what it's like to feel that everything you have may be snatched up and taken away at a moment's notice, even the chair you sit on.' She looked around at the solid, unvarying comfort of Rutland Gate. 'Already Victor has auctioned the contents of the house, so that to be at Brougham Hall is to rattle around in a place that is half furnished. Only the bits that didn't sell are left.'

'I'm sorry to hear it,' Oonagh said gently. She could see Violet, for all the slowness of her bulk, was agitated, picking at her nails and fidgeting with her hair as though she would have torn herself into tiny fretful pieces if she could have mustered the energy.

'Partly I blame you, you know. You told me to marry him.'

'I?' Oonagh was astonished.

'Yes. You told me "All men do something terrible—"'

'I'm sure I never said that!'

'You said as well marry him as another. And so I did. And now look at the mess I'm in.' She glared at Oonagh, who found herself considering the childish logic by which Violet might blame her for her own unfortunate marriage, and what that blame might allow her to do.

'I'm sure I never said such a thing. And if you're so unhappy, why not divorce? People do, you know. Look at Diana.'

'Easy for you,' she said bitterly. 'Easy for Diana too, with more Guinness money to smooth her way. The expense. You cannot imagine. You may be able to walk clean away from your mistakes, but not everyone is so lucky.'

'Always money, with you,' Oonagh blurted out.

'That's the way it is when you don't have any.' Violet shrugged, her bump moving up and down beneath her dress with the rhythm of her shoulders.

'Well, you cannot let that stop you, if you're unhappy.'

'Only those with money ever say you cannot let the lack of it stop you. But it may be that I haven't any choice. He is ruined. I cannot stay with him or I will be ruined too.' She was silent then, picking so hard at her nails that Oonagh saw a spot of blood appear, before she wiped it on her dress. 'You know, I don't think having everything you want is very good for you, Oonagh. You are become vilely smug.'

'I don't have everything I want,' Oonagh said quietly. 'You know that very well.'

It was as close as they had ever come to openly acknowledging the truth: that Violet had had something Oonagh wanted. Maybe still did.

Within a week of Violet's return to London, Philip was at home even less. 'He is busy,' Oonagh said to Kathleen. 'He is needed in the office.' Kathleen said nothing, didn't even look a question. And Oonagh, in the hours that she was at home and alone, thought how perhaps Philip had never really been hers because he had been Violet's first. Did that make it easier? she wondered. The Wronged Wife. The Wrong Wife. She pushed away the thought. He was her husband, whatever might once have been between him and Violet. He was her husband, and she would assert that. Somehow she would.

Chapter Forty-Six

Clandeboye, Co. Down

'Have you seen Lord Dufferin?'

'Not lately, m'lady,' Manning said. He paused and hovered as though waiting for her to say something else, then resumed walking, gliding noiselessly across the black-and-white marble of the hallway. Around her, weapons bristled on the walls, light catching on curved blades and sharp points. Maureen continued to the library in case Duff was there. Through the large, many-paned windows she saw the new nanny setting off with Caroline in the giant pram. The child was strapped tightly into a seated position, looking around with her usual solemn gaze. The nanny, Maureen knew, would park the pram in a patch of sunlight at the bottom of the formal gardens, and leave it for two hours, and Caroline would howl for much of that time. Sometimes, she heard Caroline's cries drift towards the house, but only if the wind was in the wrong direction.

'Fresh air is what she needs,' the nanny had said when Maureen had raised the cries, adding, 'It's good for her.' For all this was a new nanny – Ernest had insisted the other be sent away – she didn't, Maureen thought, seem very different, laying down the same rules about fresh air and bedtime.

'Sometimes I wonder how any of us survive our childhoods,' Maureen said to Duff that night. 'They seem rather savage when one looks at them as an adult.'

'They seemed rather savage at the time, too,' he said.

'Well, we all survived, and Caroline will have to.'

'I see Oonagh has different ways.'

'Oonagh's children are spoiled.'

'Nonsense. Gay is a delightful fellow, and Tessa seems a charming little thing. They are happy, friendly children. No one could say that about Caroline.'

'Caroline is fine,' Maureen had said, adding bitterly, 'but she's certainly learned how to make you dance on the end of a string.' Duff was the only person Caroline smiled at. Not often, mind, but what few smiles she gave were for him. At a year, she was as watchful and silent as she had been as a tiny baby. Maureen had a feeling – one that prickled uncomfortably at her – that it had been her job to tame her, and she had failed. She did what Maureen always did with unpleasant feelings: squashed them down, then buried them under a gloating layer of her triumphs.

Duff wasn't in the library, or the drawing room, and Maureen paused to think where she should try next. For once there were no guests at Clandeboye – everyone Maureen asked had said no, they didn't feel it was a good time to travel, and Duff's friends were all swarming around Westminster, like wasps round jam, she thought, drawn by the hint of growing unrest. Duff himself was back for a rare few days. She opened the door to his study and looked in. The room was empty and cold. The fire hadn't been lit and it smelled of wet dog and rubber galoshes. Closing it, Maureen turned towards the back door. She would try the stables.

She wanted to be with him. To hear him breathe, to feel the strong thump of his heart vibrate in the air around him, to look up from whatever she was doing and catch his deep brown eyes resting on her face. She wanted to think of excuses to pass close by him wherever he sat, so close that she smelled the way his cologne mingled with leather, horse sweat, wood smoke – those smells of Clandeboye that he put on like an old jacket when he was here and that were uniquely his. She quickened her pace.

'Is it the boy you're looking for?' Lady Brenda drifted towards her. At least she was wearing shoes, Maureen thought. 'The boy' was what she called Duff, so Maureen, who usually avoided talking to her, said yes.

'He's upstairs. In the attic.'

'What's he doing up there?' Maureen said patiently. She assumed Lady Brenda was mistaken, lost in one of her fairy dreams.

'Hiding.' Lady Brenda smiled, showing dimples like a child.

'What attic?'

'Follow the music.' More fairy nonsense, Maureen presumed, but nonetheless she went up, past her own room, to the nursery floor, and along the dark passageway that led to the attic. Around her, the house was cold and sullen and she was about to turn back when she heard something. Music. Could Lady Brenda be playing some kind of mean trick? Maureen wouldn't have put it past her. The music, indistinct and out of place, was so eerie that she had to remind herself firmly that what Lady Brenda believed was nonsense.

She followed the ghostly sounds ahead of her, around corners and along dirty passages. She was now in a part of the house she had never been to before, a place even servants didn't much come by the look of the dust that lay low and thick, like early-morning fog across a stubbled winter field.

After a while she realised it was one of Bach's Brandenburg Concertos. Not fairies, she thought ruefully. Then, with the music, came a smell. Cigars. Definitely not fairies. She kept moving, tracking. Who else but Duff would smoke a cigar?

Sound and smell came together at a half-open doorway at the end of a poky corridor tucked under the roof. Tin buckets were placed along it at intervals, presumably to catch drips. Looking into one, she saw it was half full with dirty water. So much for the roof repairs.

She stood outside the door for a moment, listening. The music was incongruously rich and jaunty, heard in this mean little place. She pushed the door further open. Inside, Duff had his feet up on a carved wooden chest, smoking a cigar – not his first judging by the thick blue haze that filled the room. He had a book in his hand and a decanter by his side. He lay back in the chair at his ease, the hand holding the cigar moving briskly back and forth in time to the music.

'What are you doing?'

He jumped, and looked momentarily guilty, before smoothing his expression. 'Reading.'

'What is this place?' Maureen looked around. The room, for all that it was untidy and needed a good clean, was cosy. A worn Persian rug covered the floor; the chairs were a mismatched lot, chosen for comfort, judging by their ample seats and sturdy arms; a chest of drawers and a small table held books, magazines, newspapers, some yellowed and curling at the edges, some fresh. Someone had even tacked a piece of red material across the grimy windows so the late-afternoon light came through with a rosy hue, and had stuffed newspaper into the loose window frames to silence them. Oil lamps stood on every surface and although they were unlit, under the thick smell of cigars Maureen caught the sour tang of animal fat.

'Just an old hidey-hole,' Duff said. 'I had a sudden whim to see it again.'

'Several sudden whims by the looks of it,' Maureen said sharply. 'Those newspapers can't be more than a few days old, and I see this month's *Economist*.'

'Let's go down,' he said, standing and coming towards her.

But Maureen wasn't to be moved. 'I say,' – she was accusatory now – 'is this where you used to come with Betjeman and Churchill and those fellows when you were on vac from Oxford?'

'Yes.'

'To hide from your mother?'

'Yes.'

'And now you're here again.'

'I have an affection for the place.' He looked tired, she saw. Dark rings under his eyes, his face puffy. There was a bottle of crème de menthe on the floor by his chair, hidden while he had been sitting down. It was empty.

'Because it has no one in it but you?'

'Partly. It's a quiet place to read.'

'You have a library, a study, several drawing rooms, rooms I don't even have names for, a bedroom and dressing room.' Maureen was furious.

'But all of them are likely to have someone in them. Here, I know there will be no one except me.'

'Especially not me, is that it?'

'Maureen, please.' He put up a hand and rubbed his eyes.

'Why couldn't you read in your dressing room?' she demanded. 'No one would look for you there.'

'The sound of Caroline's crying disrupts me.'

'I can have Nanny take her elsewhere. We can move the nursery entirely, into another wing, and you won't have to hear her at all.'

'God, no, don't do that. The poor child sees little enough of us as it is.' Angry though she was, Maureen chose to stay clear of that particular argument.

'Manning knows, doesn't he?' she asked suddenly.

'He has sometimes carried a tray up here for me.'

'So, as well as shunning me, you make a fool of me in front of the servants.'

'I don't shun you.'

'Clearly, you do.'

'Maureen, I cannot keep arguing as we do. It's wearing me out.'

'We don't argue so very much,' she said mechanically. It wasn't true: they did. She knew it. And she knew that she was the cause of the arguments. But how else was she to feel the full force of his attention, the way it had been in the early days of their marriage when there had been no one else for him in any room but her? Better to argue than be ignored. She was about to say that perhaps there was a way to argue less, when he continued, his voice unbearably flat, 'I love you Maureen, but I don't have energy enough for the job I must do, not the way the world is going, and to keep you happy. Not the way you choose to be happy.'

What did that mean? she wondered. But didn't ask. 'So, I'm just another thing for you to do, another thing on a list?' she demanded. If only he would tell her that he cared nothing for his work, that he did it only because he must. That he cared nothing for his friends and saw them only because they insisted. Then she could have been content. But he didn't.

'That's not what I said. But I have duties. Responsibilities. You know that.'

'What job is it you do, anyway? Not even secretary. An under-secretary. Like an undergarment, or an under-housemaid.' He sighed again, too used to her baiting to respond. 'And, anyway, you don't keep me happy,' she said. She turned and marched back the way she had come, listening to the sound of her heels striking the dusty wooden floors, listening for the sound of Duff coming after her. But there was nothing except the accusing sound of drops falling into one of the tin buckets, like a finger pointing, she thought. *Plonk. Plonk. Plonk.* It had started to rain again.

Chapter Forty-Seven

Rutland Gate, London

Oonagh still hoped that somehow all would yet come right: that Philip would wake to the knowledge that he did, after all, love her. But then two things happened, close together, that took hope from her hands. The first was that Violet had her baby – a boy, exactly as she had expected, named Julian Henry Peter – in October and, after an easy birth, was very much back to her social life, spotted and written about in all the society columns so that Oonagh could track her progress across the hotels, parties and night-clubs of London. She could also track that Victor was never with her, and Philip often was.

The second was more tragic. In November, Philip's younger brother Richard, 'Daring Dick', was killed while travelling on top of a moving train. 'It's what he did,' Oonagh said, when Kathleen asked how on earth such a thing could happen. 'He called it "train jumping", something he picked up from travelling in America where they don't have so many tunnels, and he did it so often that Philip believes he must have grown careless because this time, it seems, he was caught by a bridge. In any case, his body was found on the roof of a carriage when the train arrived in Farnham station.'

'And Philip?'

'Awfully cut up. Says he sees now that he can't continue living the way he has been, and must make changes.'

'What changes?'

'I suppose we'll find out,' Oonagh said wearily.

And when she did find out, there was so little surprise that she knew she had simply been waiting. Waiting for proof. Waiting for them to get sloppy and be caught. Waiting for them no longer to care that she knew.

'Look,' she said, one morning a few weeks after Dick's death, handing a magazine to Kathleen. The *Tatler*. On the cover was a photograph of Jeanette MacDonald, who had left Hollywood and was performing at the Dominion Theatre on Tottenham Court Road.

'She's beautiful.' Kathleen said.

'Not that, open it. Go to the diary.' Kathleen flicked through to the pages and pages of photographs – parties, openings, race meetings, the Prince of Wales playing golf in Biarritz. 'Stop,' Oonagh said, 'there,' and she pointed to a photograph of Philip and Violet: *At the Savoy, where they ordered the famous soufflé, Mr Philip Kindersley and Violet, Lady Brougham*, the caption read.

'When?' Kathleen asked.

'I don't know. What does it matter? Look at what she's wearing.'

'What is it?'

'A dress I paid for, is what it is. If she is willing to go out with him and be photographed wearing a dress that is more than three years old, the very dress she wore as bridesmaid at our wedding,' she stabbed a finger onto the picture of Violet, 'well, what point is there in this pretence any longer?' She buried her face in her hands, and then started to laugh.

'How is it funny?'

'Oh, I suppose it's not really. Just, you know, the look on Philip's face when I said that to him and he realised that Violet knew very well what he had no idea of – that I would instantly recognise the dress, and that wearing it was a gauntlet I could not ignore. She must have had no end of a time fitting back into it. One almost admires her dedication . . .' She laughed again. 'Philip did look cross for a moment when I told him,' she continued, 'but then he said there must have been a mistake and she would never do something like that deliberately. He will hear no bad of her.'

'Will he not give her up? Even now, when there are Gay and Tessa? And her little boy too?'

'She has appealed to his chivalrous side – she a damsel in distress, with her gambling husband who will lose the very house from under them, and me, in contrast, so secure and needing nothing.'

'It's not true that you need nothing.'

'No. But Philip does not see that, and I cannot seem to show him. I'm not sure he understands much beyond money,' she said thoughtfully. 'And so he understands that Valsie needs him because she is about to be poor, and he thinks that I, because I have money, do not.'

'Can you not tell him?'

'No, or rather, no more than I've already tried.'

'So what will you do?'

'I think I'll go away for a while, to Ireland. I wish to be at Luggala. I think there I will understand what I need to do. Without the endless noise and rush of London, all those parties, the people in the streets who look at one with such angry eyes as one goes by . . .'

'What people?'

'All of them, now. It's as if they're sizing one up. Calculating how much one must have spent on clothes and, you know, hair and such, and that for the first time they know, to the pound, and that they hate one for it. I see them as I go by in the motor-car, and it makes me positively afraid. Your friend Ned is right. Ernest is right too. Things are changing.'

'Will you ask Philip to go with you?'

'No.' She shrugged. 'I cannot see the point of that. I'm going to ring up Aileen right now and tell her I'll be coming over.'

Peters brought in the telephone once the call had been put through, and Oonagh explained her plan, holding the heavy Bakelite receiver at a distance from her ear so that Aileen's voice floated out clear and distinct.

'Whatever will you do in Ireland?' Aileen demanded, between the click of a cigarette lighter and the sound of a long exhale. 'I warn you, I'm not terribly social just now. Rather ill, actually.' She paused for Oonagh's congratulations. 'Yes,' she said, 'Brinny is terribly pleased,' and then, more bashfully, 'I suppose I am too. Funny to think that a third time could be so exciting . . . I thought I was done with babies, and when I found I was not, well, I was happier than I could have imagined. This time will be different, I'm sure. But meantime, I warn you, without me to amuse you, you will be horribly bored.'

'There are other people in Ireland, Aileen,' Oonagh said patiently.

'What other people?'

'Well, Dominick and Mildred have said I must visit Castle MacGarrett.'

'Have they indeed? Careful, Oonagh.' Aileen started to laugh.

'Yes, he's NST – think what he'll be like in his very own castle,' Oonagh said. 'So terribly attractive, though. One wouldn't mind so much if he did . . .'

'Wouldn't, or doesn't?' Aileen asked.

'Both. Neither.' She giggled a little, the first happy sound Kathleen had heard her make in days.

'I see. That's how the wind is blowing, is it? Well, come if you must.'

'Who are Dominick and Mildred?' Kathleen asked, once Oonagh was off the phone.

'Lord Oranmore and Browne. Mildred is his wife.'

'And what's NST?'

'Not Safe in Taxis. Meaning he makes the most frightful passes.' And she began to hum quietly to herself, taking a gold compact from her handbag and powdering her face with brisk energy.

Chapter Forty-Eight

London

When Oonagh talked seriously of returning to Ireland, Kathleen was glad. This was the spur she needed, she decided. This was the thing that would force the conversation with Ned. What they were to one other now – well, it was different, very different, from what they had been when she'd gone to Clandeboye. His answer, now, would be different. Surely it would.

Kathleen knew Ned cared for her – he told her so, and proved it with the enthusiasm of his attention, the way his face lit up when he saw her, the compliments he gave that no one else could have given: 'I love the shininess of your hair,' he would say, stroking the brown curls that he said were the colour of teak oil, 'and I love the liveliness of your mind. I love that you are curious and decisive, and I have never yet known you afraid to speak up.' Anyone else, she thought, would have stopped at the hair. 'I admire you,' he said, again and again. And if he didn't say he loved her, well, maybe he just didn't know how.

'Oonagh will move to Ireland,' she told him, as they walked through Regent's Park, kicking at the dried leaves underfoot and watching children gather conkers. Beside them, a fountain sent up a spray of stinking water and Kathleen saw the bottom was clogged with rotting leaves.

'Without Philip?' Ned knew all about the return of Violet, and Philip's gradual withdrawal.

'Without Philip.'

'Marriage is a only a bourgeois creation anyway,' he said. 'And she's rich. She doesn't need him.'

'Is that meant to be comforting?'

'Yes. Isn't it?'

'Not very. I'm not sure she sees it quite like that.'

'And you?' he asked, but only after so long that she feared he wouldn't ask at all. 'What will you do?'

'I don't know,' Kathleen said. 'Oonagh expects me to go with her.'

'Of course she does. By now she expects that you will be with her for ever, smoothing the way for her every move. But what do you want?'

'I know. But I need to go back. I want to see my da, my sisters. I can get a position teaching now, a decent one.' She didn't like the way he was nodding thoughtfully at her, when she was saying these things only because he hadn't said anything. She was throwing words into the gap left by the words he hadn't said. Words that should have been: *Stay here, with me.* 'What about you?' she asked, to bring him into this talk of her plans. 'Do you ever think of going back?'

'I do not,' he said firmly. 'Why, this city is ready to go up like a tinder box.' He sounded pleased. 'The showdown comes closer every day. Now that Mosley has organised fully, we have a visible enemy to fight, and because of that, more men flock to us every day.' As always, a conversation she hoped would be about them, the two of them, had become about Ned's ideas, his Comrades, his obsession with Mosley.

'But don't you think it's time . . .'

'Time for what?'

'Well, time to settle,' she said. 'Now that you have a job writing for *The Times*—'

'A few pieces here and there,' he said. 'Don't forget that my job is to unload boats, Kathleen. Guinness boats.'

'But you could write more for *The Times*. You're clever.'

'Maybe. But what else?'

'Well, settle.' He stopped then and looked at her. A long time. She couldn't meet his eyes. Not after that *settle*. As well have got down on one knee and begged him to marry her.

'Come and sit down,' he said, leading her to a bench. They sat side by side and Ned, looking straight ahead rather than at her, said quietly, 'When you say "settle", I think I know what you mean.' She stirred beside him and he said, 'Don't worry, I won't make you say it . . . But I think I understand, and, Kathleen . . .'

He paused so long she was forced to say, 'What?'

'That kind of settling isn't for me. It never has been. I'm sorry if you thought otherwise.'

'But . . . We . . .'

'I'm sorry if you thought otherwise,' he said again. 'I like you very well. Very well indeed. I cannot imagine any other girl than you. But even so, that life is not for me.'

'But why?'

'There is too much to do.'

'But why must it be you who does it? Or why you all the time? Why can't you do other things as well? With me.' She forced herself to look at him, even though he wouldn't look at her.

'It isn't only me. There are many of us. You've met some of them. Wintringham, all those others. But while there are men like Mosley around, we need everyone, all the time.'

'You think about that man even more than Diana does,' she snapped. She left then, saying she had to get back, and walked slowly alone through Regent's Park wondering why she was surprised when what she had always known to be true was indeed true: that Ned, as his mother had said, supped sorrow with a long spoon. That he was a person given to life at a fast pace. Not the pace of marriage and slow contentment and families. Wondering, too, why she was so unhappy when she had warned herself a thousand times that Ned was wed already, to a cause and a group of men who sought that cause like he did.

And yet she found in the days that followed that she had known, and not known. That somewhere she had counted on a different answer from him without admitting to herself that she counted on it, and now that he had said no or, if she was fully accurate, not said yes, she found all her usual energy deserted her. She no longer knew what to do. Her plan, to move home to Dublin when Oonagh went to Wicklow to see her family and find a position in one of the bigger schools teaching girls – teaching them everything she had learned, not just English composition and maths – all that, so sure in her mind, vanished, and she had nothing to put in its place.

She didn't hate Ned. She couldn't. Not when honesty forced her to admit that the plans she had made were hers, not his. That never once had he spoken of their future together. Only of the future he saw for other people.

When Oonagh carried on making her arrangements to leave London, in the assumption that Kathleen would come with her, Kathleen said nothing and let her. She would go with Oonagh. She would give her a little more, even though she had already given so much. How she had become caught up in their lives, these Guinness girls, and the never-ending needs of those lives, she thought. Always a new baby, a drama, trouble of some kind, in their marriages and in themselves, in the way they were more and more at odds with a changing world. But Oonagh needed her. And that was a comfort.

'I would like to turn the page of my life and begin again, crisp and new,' Oonagh said, one afternoon a few days later, as she looked through the clothes Burton had assembled for her to take. Sensible tweeds, warm knits, stout walking shoes: all reminders that Dublin was not London.

'That isn't what happens,' Kathleen said. 'You just have to keep going with everything you have and try to do better.'

'How exhausting you make it sound.' Oonagh was petulant and Kathleen, because she felt the very same, snapped, 'It is exhausting, Oonagh, but that's the way it is. You can't just fly up, like a butterfly or a bumblebee, and land somewhere else. In any case, even bumblebees have specks of pollen clinging to their feet that weigh them down.'

'Why are we talking about wildlife?' Oonagh looked limpidly at her, and Kathleen gazed back, unsure if Oonagh was being deliberately obtuse, or if she truly didn't understand what Kathleen had meant. With Oonagh, either of those things could be true.

Part Four

1934–1936

Chapter Forty-Nine

Luggala, Co. Wicklow

'**Mamma?**' Gay had been standing by the nursery window for nearly an hour, looking impatiently up the long, narrow track that led from the valley to the main road above, waiting for Oonagh to return. Around them, the sloping mountains came to a gentle stop beside the peat-black Lough Tay; its sliver of beach gave the place the look of a spilled pint of Guinness, dark water lapping against the white of the sand that was brought there in trucks from a beach in Wexford. Luggala might have been a small house, a cottage, by Guinness standards, with just seven bedrooms – seen from the road above, it was a gleaming white pebble lying at the edge of a brackish pool – but was as neat and trim and cosy as the house of Beatrix Potter's Mrs Tittlemouse. Ernest had bought it years before, but it had stood empty while Oonagh was in London.

It was a blessed spot, Kathleen thought, and the year they had spent there on and off had been among the happiest of her life, even if at first it felt as though they were running away – all of them – leaving a London that had become uncomfortable and hostile.

She had seen her family – many times now – sometimes spending days with them. And if at first she had been secretly shocked by the pokiness of the rooms above the ironmonger's shop, by the way her father struggled to put his thoughts into words and how fast her sisters finished the food on their plates, she had quickly learned to laugh at her own surprise, and had settled back into the ease of their old ways.

'What do you intend to do?' Peggy asked her, and when Kathleen, at a loss for what exactly to say, answered, 'Save my wages for a little longer,' Peggy had nodded and said, 'Sensible. Then you can make your own future,' so that Kathleen felt as though she had some sort of a plan.

'Mamma?' Gay asked again.

Tessa pulled herself up behind him, holding tight to the hem of his navy shorts. 'Maaa,' she said in imitation. She was two and a half, still the same sunny child who took the world at a generous rush.

Oonagh had been away for almost a week and had been expected since lunchtime. It was almost time for nursery tea, and she was not yet there. But that was no wonder, Kathleen thought. All that time in London, she had forgotten the state of Irish roads. Many of them were barely roads at all, and scarcely improved by the gangs of men with shovels and trucks of tarmacadam who were everywhere, leaning on the handles of their implements and smiling as the car went by.

Oonagh had been on a visit to Luttrellstown, where Aileen had gathered a party that included the actor Douglas Fairbanks Jr, now living apart from his wife Mary Pickford, along with others of her London friends, then telephoned and demanded Oonagh's presence. 'You have to,' she said peremptorily. 'I need you to distract everyone so, you see, you must.'

'As if I were a *conjurer*,' Oonagh said. 'But very well.' Aileen had another baby – yet another girl, Marcia, born in March the previous year, a delicate wisp with grey eyes, the 'reconciliation baby', Oonagh called her – but Aileen was not, Kathleen thought, noticeably more content after all, despite her hopes. She filled the castle nightclub and bedrooms with guests in the way a farmer might fill a barn with hay for winter: anxiously, relentlessly, driven by the threat of lean times.

Oonagh herself, ever eager to please, had become horsy too. 'It's all there is in this country,' she said, when Kathleen teased her. She went to race meetings, point-to-points, hunt balls, to stay with various friends for hunting, although she didn't ride out, and had even let her hair go a soft mousy brown that she styled casually, rather than her usual shining golden crop. 'It's easier,' she said, 'and anyway,' – looking up through her eyelashes – 'some people prefer it.'

'Some people', Kathleen knew well, meant Lord Oranmore and Browne, Dominick – or Dom, as Oonagh now called him. And while Kathleen had no idea whether he preferred Oonagh's hair brown to blonde, it was obvious that he preferred her company to anyone else's. He and Lady Browne, Mildred, had visited Luggala enough, and they themselves had been guests at Castle MacGarrett, their ugly, shabby but friendly house in Mayo, near Ashford Castle, enough for Kathleen to have seen this. This Dom was a man quite unlike the others in Oonagh's life. He was not a businessman, like Ernest, or debonair in the way that Philip was, not a brilliant politician such as Duff. Despite a sensual face with sleepy eyes and a soft, full mouth, he was a man of the outdoors, active and energetic, with a booming voice, constantly raised as he called to dogs, horses, servants, children – there were four, two girls followed by two boys, aged from eight to three, and Mildred was expecting another in just a matter of months.

But for all that he was so surrounded by evidence of domesticity, he was captivated by Oonagh in a way that must, Kathleen thought, have been humiliatingly obvious to his wife. There were times he looked at her as if she were something shiny in a piece of barmbrack. His eyes followed her as she moved around, and he took every chance to touch her – help her on with her coat, pull out a chair for her, take her elbow getting in and out of the motor-car. When they danced together – and, those days, the drawing room at Luggala was full of music, the gramophone playing constantly, the chairs pushed back to make space for dancing – he held her as though he had been handed something that might shatter at the slightest impact.

In his company, Oonagh was animated in a way Kathleen had never seen her. She was witty, because although he was no great wit himself, Dom laughed at everything she said. Beside his pronounced maleness, she became even more feminine, at ease with herself in a way she had never been with Philip. And she was constantly good-humoured, busy at some scheme or another, and full of energy for the round of activities that seemed to take them all over the country, from the horse show in Dublin to the Tramore races, trips on Ernest's yacht, the *Fantome* that was moored in Killary harbour beyond Ashford Castle.

And even though Mildred was always, or mostly, with them, they behaved as if it were just the two of them, making plans that were theirs alone, into which others fell by chance. Mildred was not beautiful, Kathleen reflected, but she had a face full of character and a direct nature that, alas for her, suffered when set against Oonagh's fey charm. Her pleasant forthrightness seemed dull and even coarse in comparison, and what should have been an impressively practical mind appeared trivial and humourless when set against the elusive sparkle of Oonagh's.

There were letters from London – from Philip, Mary, at times even Ned, although they never contained anything but talk of his Comrades, and Kathleen didn't answer them. She didn't know what to say, nothing in her life had changed, and she couldn't admit that to him. The letters seemed to make very little impact on their lives, like missives from somewhere half remembered. Philip's were short, dashed off in an impatient hand, and read by Oonagh even more quickly. They arrived by the morning post and Kathleen carried them up to her with her tea while she was still in bed. She would scan the contents in a matter of moments, then say, 'Papa sends his love,' to Gay and Tessa. 'He says he will see you soon.' He never telephoned, and neither did she ring him.

Mary, Kathleen learned in one letter, had been let go by Diana. Shortly after Diana moved to Eaton Square, to cheer Jonathan up because he was fretting about the whereabouts of his papa, Mary told the boy that Bryan had done nothing wrong and was a kind and good father. But Jonathan repeated what she had said to Diana, so Mary was told, 'I think it best if you go, and I will give you a week's wages for notice.'

I wasn't allowed say goodbye to the boys, she wrote, *which fair broke my heart because now they will think that I have abandoned them too and that is something I never would.* Kathleen had thought of Mary – *in truth, if he knew, it's the job of a mother I do* – and felt a terrible pang.

'Mamma!' Gay shouted then. He was right. Kathleen could see the afternoon sun glinting off the silver body of the motor-car as it wound its way downhill towards them. He ran outside to greet her, dogs at his heels, while Kathleen followed with Tessa and Nanny.

'Darlings!' Oonagh cried, getting out of the motor. She looked tired, with purple shadows under her eyes – Aileen's parties went on very late – but threw her arms around Gay, then lifted Tessa from Nanny's arms and kissed her. 'Did you miss me?' she asked, and, when they had all chorused yes, she said, 'Let's have tea, and I'll tell you all about it.' Gay took her hand, so that she had to shift Tessa to the other arm, and towed her into the house.

'Well, I don't think Aileen need have worried,' Oonagh said, when they were seated with tea, plates of scones and dishes of whipped cream and jam. She leaned back and put her feet up on a footstool. She had become, Kathleen thought, far more casual in everything of late, including the way she sat and stood. Cloé would certainly have been appalled and called it 'slouching', but to Kathleen, Oonagh looked comfortable. 'I don't know how Aileen does it. Gives the most *rackety* parties, and yet somehow stays tucked out of sight. Fairbanks and Sylvia Ashley-Cooper were like a couple on honeymoon. Sylvia was a chorus girl before marrying Lord Ashley. Does that mean she will be a chorus girl again, when she marries Fairbanks, who is an actor?'

The French windows were open so that they heard the sound of waves on the surface of the lake drifting in on the late-afternoon air. The sun retreated from the valley early so although the tops of the mountains were bright the lower slopes were already falling into golden shadow.

'We are invited to Castle MacGarrett for the beach races at Bertra in September. All of us, Gay and Tessa too,' Oonagh continued. 'Dom says not to bring Nanny, that two more in the nursery will hardly be noticed. And Papa will be close by at Ashford, Mamma too. Aileen will come up and even Maureen may visit.' Maureen had had her second baby, a girl called Perdita, in July and had been mostly in London so that Oonagh had seen very little of her. 'Any letters?' Oonagh said then.

'Yes, here, from Philip.' Oonagh cut along the top edge of the cream envelope with a sharp silver letter opener and scanned the contents.

'Well?'

'Nothing much. He says he has been to a party at Ivor Novello's flat and that Tallulah Bankhead, who is back in London, arrived unexpectedly and danced with Prince George who is now the Duke of Kent. He doesn't say he attended the party with Violet although I know he did because Maureen made sure to tell me. And he says Lady Furness is back in England from America, and in a terrible temper because of Mrs Simpson.'

'So, Violet . . . ?'

'They go about everywhere together now. Even the *Bystander* has taken to referring to her as my "erstwhile friend".' She made a face that was almost a smile, without any real humour, but also without the sadness that would have been there a year ago. Then, 'We'll need to set off early for Castle MacGarrett. Even if we break the journey, it's still terribly long and poor Tessa will be miserably sick.' She began to buff her nails. 'I wonder Diana isn't more cross that she and Mosley aren't married yet,' she said, head bent over her small white hands. 'After all, it's over a year since poor Cimmie died. And more since she divorced Bryan.'

Mosley's wife Cynthia had died so unexpectedly after an appendix operation, just a few months after Diana's divorce, that for a while the malicious said she must have been ill-wished. The credulous still did. Bryan, of course, did exactly as Oonagh had predicted – hid his sorrow beneath a veneer of perfect manners, and allowed Diana to divorce him uncontested, citing adultery. And yet for all the path had been cleared – miraculously – of all obstacles, still they weren't married.

'Apparently,' Oonagh said, 'Mosley has been putting it about that Duff's great-grandfather – Viceroy Frederick's father – was actually Benjamin Disraeli, that Helen played poor Price Blackwood false, and that Duff is therefore one-eighth Jewish. Maureen is so furious, she says she wishes she'd given him more than a black eye when she had the chance. But Diana doesn't care what Maureen says. She doesn't care what anyone says. She and Unity have been hanging about in Berlin, making friends with high-up Nazis, and hoping to meet Hitler. Can't you just imagine Unity jackbooting about? Remember how we used to say she was a gruesome child? Well, she's grown into an even more gruesome adult. And aren't you glad we're here, far away from it all?'

And yet Kathleen noticed that these days Oonagh was not so unforgiving of Diana as she had been. She talked far less about her 'faithlessness' and even, sometimes, allowed that 'the call of love' could trump other calls, and persisted with that even when Kathleen said, 'Nonsense. What she did to Bryan was unforgivable.'

'I must lie down,' Oonagh said then, with a yawn. 'Such a long drive. Nanny, you may take the children.' Her confidence, Kathleen reflected, was now visible in all things – in how she expressed her wishes as much as in the way she dressed and wore her hair. Without Philip to contradict her or tell her not to be a fool about her children, Oonagh no longer looked over her shoulder when she gave orders or second-guessed what others might think of them. She stood straighter and her voice, always soft, was decisive now. And if the new confidence came with a little less gentleness, then, Kathleen thought, perhaps that was only as it had to be.

Chapter Fifty

Castle MacGarrett, Co. Mayo, Autumn 1934

The journey to Castle MacGarrett was indeed long, and despite a night in Tullamore along the way they were all tired and the children cross by the time they arrived in the early evening. The castle was a higgledy-piggledy collection of pinkish buildings built around and between each other so that, Oonagh thought, it was almost like a tiny town of terraced houses. Except, of course, this was all one house, although parts of it were closed off and unused. It was hideous, architecturally, with rooms that were as damp and mouldy as a labourer's cottage, shut up and left to rot, like a limb that has developed gangrene and will eventually infect everything around it, yet to her it was somewhere merry and welcoming, like no other house she had ever known. The tumble of children, and the dogs, rabbits, ponies, toys and picture books that accompanied them, was as intoxicating to her as a stirrup cup before hunting.

The minute they arrived, while Oonagh still stood on the dirty gravel of the front yard, the house rising abruptly in front of her out of the dank pebbly ground, the Browne children rushed down to greet Gay. The two oldest girls, Patricia and Brigid, who were eight and seven, took him by a hand each and helped him into the house, and Oonagh heard Patricia say solemnly, 'We will show you what will be your room while you are here. You will share with Dominick and Martin and they have made space for your things.'

Dominick stood in the doorway to welcome her, thumbs hooked through the side pockets of his tweed jacket. He had the posture of a guardsman still, she thought, standing so upright under the austere stone porch, even though he had been bowler-hatted years before. His face was both pompous and sensual, with fine bones and a full mouth, until he smiled, which he did now, and the pomposity melted instantly into mischief. She could always make him smile like that, she thought, giving him her hand.

'You're late,' he said warmly. 'Or maybe it's just that I've been waiting since early morning.'

Inside, they gathered in the largest of the drawing rooms with some friends of Dominick's, all dressed to go out except Lady Mildred, who sat on a long chair with a rug tucked over her. She was by then very large with pregnancy, her normally lively eyes made small and dull by the puffiness of her face and her slightly protruding teeth clenched against fatigue.

Someone handed Oonagh a glass of whiskey punch, and she looked around. The room was untidy – piles of newspapers on every surface, a bunch of wilting flowers on a table that had several ring-shaped stains from wet glasses – and the people dowdy. But somehow everything was laid over with the excitement of Dominick's presence, the woody smell of his cologne, the sound of his voice and ready laugh. A woman she thought might be called Catherine came over and said abruptly, 'Will you be at the Curragh for the races?'

'I will,' Oonagh said. 'My sister has a horse running in the Derby. Millennium, he's called.'

'Not expected to win,' the woman said.

'No, but he's very young, and is expected to race well,' Oonagh said gently. She knew how much store Aileen set by this horse.

'I hear Aileen entertains Edwina Mountbatten in that basement nightclub. They say she will be cited as co-respondent in the Fairbanks-Pickford divorce.'

'They say that of every woman who has two legs and isn't yet ninety,' Oonagh retorted. She looked over to where Dominick was pinching lemon rind into the silver punch bowl. Immediately he came over. 'I must just run up and see are the children settled,' she said.

'They are in the nursery,' Mildred interjected. She must have been listening carefully, Oonagh thought, because the room was full of talk. 'They are perfectly all right, you know.'

But Oonagh insisted – 'I would just like to see them settled. Gay will expect it.' She knew that Dominick was entranced by the open, affectionate way she behaved with her children, so unlike Philip, who could barely conceal his irritation, and so, in his presence, under his adoring eye, she became even more affectionate, more playful.

'I'll take you,' he said instantly, offering his arm.

'Dominick, Oonagh knows where the nursery is,' Mildred said impatiently. 'If she really must go.' But Dominick ignored his wife, taking Oonagh's hand and pulling it tight through his arm. Upstairs, they went to the large shabby room overlooking the tangled gardens that was the nursery. There, with the Browne nanny knitting comfortably in front of the fire, Gay and Tessa sat on the floor with the Browne children, noisily playing Go Fish. Tessa was on Patricia's knees, and Patricia had wrapped her arms around the child's waist, holding her tight. 'I thought she might be lonely, because this isn't her home,' Patricia explained, when they came in.

'How kind you are,' Oonagh said, and smiled at the girl, who beamed back and said, 'Would you like to play?'

'I'd adore to,' Oonagh said, laughing, 'but I promised your papa that I would go out with him. Maybe when I come back.'

'Yes, please,' Patricia said. 'You are much the nicest of Mamma's friends.'

'She's not Mamma's friend, she's Papa's friend,' Brigid said.

'I'm everyone's friend,' Oonagh said gaily. 'You must all think of me as your friend,' and she saw how Dominick smiled at that.

On the way back down to the drawing room, he held her hand, stroking the palm over and over with his thumb, kneading the fleshy parts below her fingers, until her hand felt weak and boneless. 'We mustn't,' she said.

'We must,' he insisted, interlacing his fingers with hers. And even when the woman called Catherine stepped out of the drawing room below them and called up, 'We must leave or we'll miss the first race,' he let go only slowly.

'How shall we travel?' Catherine demanded, when they were downstairs.

'I'll take Oonagh and we'll meet you directly there,' Dominick said.

'But if Matthew takes four, and Mark and I take two, then the rest can go in the Bentley with George,' said Catherine.

'Doesn't make sense,' Dominick said. 'I will take Oonagh, and George may squeeze in with Matthew.'

Oonagh said nothing, content to let him battle for the right to drive her. 'Kathleen, will you come?' she said, and when Kathleen said she wouldn't, Oonagh said, 'Maybe it's just as well. Papa is coming over for dinner and I know he will be early, as always, so if you're here you may entertain him.'

'I'm sure I can manage that,' Mildred said, stirring irritably beneath the rug.

'But of course!' Oonagh said quickly. 'I only thought you might be *tired*.'

'I'm not so tired I cannot do my duty as hostess and wife,' Mildred responded.

Once her directness – she was Scottish, and did not mince her words – would have discomfited Oonagh. But not now. Oonagh smiled vaguely, charmingly, and murmured, 'But of course,' laid a tiny hand on Dominick's arm, and said, 'Shall we go?'

When everyone had left, Kathleen asked Mildred if she would like to be read to, but Mildred snapped, 'No, thank you,' and left the room. Kathleen heard her walking heavily upstairs – the ceiling shook so that the crystal drops in the squat chandelier danced – and she hadn't come back down by the time Ernest arrived, early, exactly as Oonagh had predicted, so that Kathleen was the only one to greet him.

'I don't like what I'm hearing,' he said abruptly, direct as he ever was with her. 'My daughter and Dominick. Is it true?'

'It might be,' Kathleen said, equally direct. 'Although, if you ask me, it's as much the abundance of his family life that Oonagh is drawn to. The busy nursery with four children tumbling about, watching him play cricket and rounders with them. The way this is a house for a family and not a house for show. All of that appeals to her right now, perhaps more than she understands. It is what she always wanted for herself, which did not come about with Philip.' And indeed, Oonagh, Kathleen reflected, wanted the life she glimpsed through Dominick, the very life she had once described as the one she dreamed of – and didn't seem willing to understand that someone else was already living that life with him. But it wasn't just that, she thought, although she didn't know how to describe to Ernest what else she had noticed: the rapt look on Oonagh's face when she gazed at Dominick, the way she leaned towards him when he touched her. But perhaps Ernest understood.

'The man is like a stallion,' he said. He frowned. 'I hope this will run its course quickly. It's not at all the thing. Why, his wife is about to have another baby any day. I must speak to Oonagh.'

'I'm not sure it will do much good,' Kathleen said.

'By which I gather that you have tried already?'

'I have. She told me not to fuss.'

'Oonagh's gentle way of telling you that she won't put up with any interference,' he said with a reluctant smile. Oonagh could ever twist him to her way of thinking, unlike Aileen, who made him impatient, and Maureen, with whom he was more likely to clash openly. 'But I fear Diana's divorce has done a great deal of harm.'

'How so?'

'She and Mosley are far more respectable than they should be, considering the lack of restraint both have shown. Theirs will be a bad example. Bad, but popular, as so much, now, that is bad is popular.'

'Does it not seem as though the Fascists have won what you called "the allegiance of all those men who are desperate"?'

'Nothing is won yet,' he said. 'Or lost, for that matter. Many of those who salute under Mosley's flag are like underdone beefsteak.' Kathleen looked blank, so he explained: 'Brown on the outside, red in the middle. They could, even now, declare for the other side. What motivates them is anger at what they do not have, and a desire for change, not Mosley's talk of "the Jewish interests", and certainly not his admiration of Hitler and Mussolini.'

'Maybe. But it has gone on a long time now, this restlessness.' Kathleen changed the subject. 'How is Cloé?'

'She has been better recently, under the care of a new doctor. She is going out more. In fact, she will join us later this evening.'

That evening, Oonagh sat beside Dominick at dinner, and neither tried to hide the way they whispered to one another, laughing at jokes they would not share. Even the presence of Ernest, opposite Dominick, did not restrain Oonagh, although Kathleen noticed that when Cloé joined them in the drawing room after dinner was over, Oonagh left the photograph album she had been poring over with Dominick – snatches of 'I'm sure I was at that very same dancing party. Look, isn't that me, under all those frightful curls?' drifting towards the rest of them – joined the women around Mildred, and talked politely about fashions and the difficulty of keeping cooks.

The next morning, Kathleen knocked on Oonagh's door once she had seen her morning tea go in. She was awake and alone – the children were breakfasting in the nursery – the sash window pulled up to let in the morning sun. Kathleen could hear the diligent sound of a tractor in the distance and, close to, the cawing of the rooks who lived in such numbers about Castle MacGarrett.

'Oonagh, what is it you're doing with him?'

'With whom?'

'You know very well.'

'Dom?'

'Yes.'

'Must I be doing something with him?' She looked out from under her lashes.

'Plainly you are, but what, I don't know.'

'Well, can't you guess?'

'But he's not yours.'

'No. Not yet. But don't you see? This answers everything. Dom and I are happy together, and Philip and Valsie, now that she is divorced from poor Victor, will be happy too. In fact, the whole thing has worked out jolly well.'

'Not for Mildred.'

'No. Rather hard on her, I suppose.' She did not, Kathleen thought, sound much as though she meant it.

'And the children?'

'Oh, but the children will still come for holidays and for them it will be like nothing has changed.'

'But this is their home.'

'And when they come and visit it will still be their home. If you're here to scold, Kathleen, don't. It is the first time I have been happy in a long time. Certainly since Gay was born. And why should I not have happiness?' She looked mutinous, refusing to meet Kathleen's eye, pretending to examine something on the side of her teacup.

'He is someone else's husband.'

'But I love him.' It was, Kathleen saw, all the justification she needed. Love must be made to conquer all. Even those who did not want to be conquered. 'I know it's hard on Mildred,' she said again, 'but he loves me, and I love him, and when everything is settled we will be happy together for ever and all will be well. Sometimes one takes a wrong turn at first, but then, if one can take the right turn, why, one can stay on the path for ever.'

'I hope you're right.' Kathleen didn't say what she thought – that Oonagh sounded like a child telling a fairy story.

A month later, they all went on holiday together – Oonagh, Dominick, Philip and Violet – to the west of Ireland. To Tramore in Waterford, for the races, then on to Kerry. 'Such a civilised arrangement' was the general verdict, and just like Oonagh, no one seemed to think of Mildred or the four – soon to be five – children she and Dominick had together.

Chapter Fifty-One

Hans Crescent, London

Lond, Maureen reflected gloomily, was different. Quieter, yes, but not just that. It felt, she thought, like a city flayed, stripped raw of everything that had been opulent and grand, as though battening itself down in conscious preparation for hard times. What even a year ago had been vague whispers – used, often, simply as seasoning for entertainment – had now lumbered close so that she could feel grim news in the streets, see it on the faces of the people, in the way they spoke to each other and looked around them.

The first thing London had stripped itself of, she thought, was fun. The chimneypiece at Hans Crescent was almost bare of the crisp cards of invitation once pegged to it like laundry on washing day, and nights out in town were furtive. Once, she thought, that might have been amusing, adding secrecy to the itinerary. But not now. Not when there was Duff to come home to, always asking her disapprovingly where she had been and who with, to say that she would be better at home, at Clandeboye with Caroline and the new baby, Perdita, now two months old. Saying all these things, but not the way he once would have, with the heady energy of anger. Now, he just sounded tired. He no longer came to her room at night, or if he did, he didn't stay until morning. She would wake to find herself alone, the connecting doors closed tight between them, and would listen to him get up, move about his own bedroom, get dressed and leave for the day.

But where others had become fretful and timid, Maureen was ferocious. If others chose to hang back, she thought, she would have her own parties. Evenings at Hans Crescent began to involve the same hard-drinking crowd night after night, those who knew to gather there, and in the houses of one or two others. These people were minded, as Maureen was, to ignore bad news and keep late hours; a disordered crew, a mix of the foolish, the brave and the arrogant; those who would not, could not or did not see how much trouble was coming.

'Like a shipwreck,' was how Nancy described it, popping in reluctantly to one of these evenings and looking around disapprovingly. 'The hardy few, clinging together amid the wreckage.' She was married at last – a man called Peter Rodd 'who talks about nothing but turnpikes', according to Diana.

'Better a hardy few than a feeble many,' Maureen snapped.

'Even when the hardy few includes Elizabeth Ponsonby?' Nancy asked, watching Elizabeth dance past, eyes as huge and round as saucers.

'She's not invited, she simply shows up, and, really, what can one do?'

Elizabeth danced past the other way then, on her way back to the drinks table, singing scratchily in time with the Billie Holiday record on the gramophone, something about 'your daddy' being rich and 'your ma' good-looking, turning to glare at Maureen as she sang.

'I see she is divorced now too,' Nancy said.

'Yes, and has a job in a *nightclub*. So riddled with debt, you can hear the wind through her.'

'She doesn't look well,' Nancy said. 'Sort of sad and desperate and terribly tired.'

'Tiring, more like.'

'And Chips?' Nancy asked, watching him dance with Elizabeth, all the while scanning the room for who came and went.

'He needs to escape hearth and home,' Maureen said ironically. 'Especially since Honor had the baby. And I don't mind at all helping him do that. A man must have his outlet and there are only so many hours he can spend at the Turf Club pretending to be a Duke of the Blood.'

'Does Duff still think he's a spy?' Nancy drew closer and murmured discreetly.

'He's positive. But says it's better to have him close where we can keep an eye on him. Besides, he's screamingly funny – did you hear how he described Mrs Simpson? "Like a ferret that has got loose in Cartier" – and he does mix the most *lethal* cocktails.'

'What's so lethal about them?' Nancy wanted to know.

'A secret ingredient, shall we say?'

'Which is?'

'A new kind of uppy called dexie that Chips gets from an American doctor he knows here in London. The doctor, who is a positively grisly fellow, puts it into cunning little bottles to be added, a drop or two, to cocktails.'

'And I suppose you and Chips turn a drop or two into three or four?'

'I suppose we do.'

'Well, I wish you wouldn't. The last thing you – either of you – needs is more energy. Already you run the rest of us ragged.'

Maureen grinned.

'You have lipstick on your teeth,' Nancy said thoughtfully. 'You look as though you have bitten something bloody.'

Maureen would never have said so, but she felt burdened with responsibility to make these evenings fun, so she stepped up her capering and practical joking, even though she knew well that her sisters and husband now considered this bordered on the vulgar. Duff was mostly away from home, and when he did attend these parties, he talked less and drank more than formerly, bottles of crème de menthe disappearing with his usual brandy. They fought less, much less, and Maureen told her sisters this as though it were something good, but she knew it was not. She said she didn't care that he was never at home but always 'in a huddle' with Mr Churchill and others, but for all that, she tracked his movements continually, as someone will consult a watch when they know they are late: constantly, anxiously, reflexively.

If a door banged in the house, her head would snap up. A tread in the hallway or on the stairs would send her to the door to look out. Never would she say what – who – she looked for, but she wasn't easy unless he was with her, and often not even then. Instead, she was restive and angry, because between them there was neither harmony nor the blistering rows she once could provoke so easily. Now, he was like the water in the bathroom tap at Clandeboye – a thin, tepid trickle.

'I wish you would put half as much energy into your children,' Duff muttered to her then, as she flew about the drawing room getting up an entertainment in which her guests shouted lines from a play by Mr Coward at each other. The drawing-room furniture had been cleared, pushed back around the edges so that the small sofa where he sat was hemmed in on one side by the spindly backs of several chairs and on the other by a round marble-topped table.

'The place for them is in the country.'

'Perdita has barely seen you, while Caroline just turned three, and she hardly knows you. I thought we could go for a visit. I've found a most charming pony for her. The prettiest beast imaginable.'

'So you go and give it to her.' Maureen paused in her arranging and stood close by him. 'At least it might stop her reading. She's far too shy and altogether too much like Oonagh. She must be brought out of herself.'

'Does she wish to be brought out of herself?'

'I don't know and I don't care. She must be made to

be less shy, whether she wants it or not. Her life will be intolerable otherwise. An unattractive girl is a dreadful thing to be.'

'You see the same sort of life for Caroline, and Perdita, that you and your sisters had?' he asked, standing up. 'Balls? Coming-out, being presented at court? Needing to attract, like a bright flower that must compel bees or die?'

'What else?'

'God knows amid what rubble you think these things will happen, Maureen. There is war coming to Spain. They call it a civil war, a matter only for Spaniards, but I fear it will drag us all towards it. But you always were blind to anything you don't like. It's a strength, I suppose, for ever to make the world exactly as you wish it to be, in defiance of all evidence that would say it otherwise.'

'I know what I want,' Maureen said defiantly.

'I know you do. And it's a strange kind of a gift, but gift it is. Or so it seems to me. I am the very opposite. I cannot shut my eyes to anything, or make it small and safe because I want it to be so. And I am haunted by the dreadful possibilities that may unfold – of what may happen, and what will be required of us all.'

'Well, then, we're the balance of one another, either end of a scale?' she said hopefully, looking up at him, willing him to look down at her in the way he used to. But he didn't.

'I fear your side will always weigh more heavily,' he said, staring over her head into a distance that contained things she didn't understand.

'Do you remember you once said I was like Salome? That I wanted your head on a plate?' She hoped to remind him of how they had been with one another, where to say such things was a passionate game between them.

But he just sighed and said, 'I wonder would even that satisfy you now?' He inclined his head then to look at her, and she, meeting his gaze, opened her mouth to say something – anything – that might draw them together.

But Chips interrupted, brandishing a cocktail shaker. 'Try one of these,' he said to Duff. 'I made 'em special. Then sit down and tell me what you've been doing with the wonderful Mr Churchill.' Duff drew his eyebrows in and down in one small quick movement, then shook his head. Immediately Chips moved off. 'Another time,' he said expansively, 'another time.'

'Maureen, it's your turn,' someone called, so she drained her glass and went to take her part in the entertainment. She began to sing a comic song, one of Mr Coward's, 'Mad Dogs and Englishmen', kicking her legs up, slow then fast, as she sang. She paused when she got to the bit about Rangoon and the heat of noon that makes the inhabitants put their Scotch or rye down.

'I say,' she called suddenly. 'Rangoon, isn't that the capital city of Burma? Duff, you'll know.'

'It is.'

'And, of course, the Kingdom of Ava is in Upper Burma? From where your grandfather, Frederick, took his title?'

'Yes. And?'

'Well, I was just wondering if you were going to put your Scotch or rye down. But I suppose that isn't at all likely.'

Her friends roared, as if she had told a great joke, but she saw Duff's face – the twitch of anger, but also the flicker of humiliation, and knew that she had reached him at last. And if the reaching was done with a weapon, the weapon of her wit, still, she thought defiantly, it was better than nothing.

A minute or two later he got up to leave, and Maureen watched him go and said nothing, although regret pulled at her mouth just as clearly as her eyes shone glassy with defiance.

Chapter Fifty-Two

Luggala, Co. Wicklow

'Mildred has had a baby. A girl called Judith. Dom just rang.'

'That's nice,' Kathleen said. 'Three girls and two boys.'

'Yes. I suppose.' Oonagh fidgeted with one of her rings, twisting it about on her finger. 'But you don't think . . . Well . . . Now that there is another baby, and Mildred will be slim again . . . She is such a horsewoman when not in pig.'

'Oonagh! What a disgusting expression! Anyway, what are you trying to say?'

'Oh, you know exactly.' She flared up. 'That Dom will forget about me, now that he has a sweet new baby, and Mildred can exert herself to fascinate him again . . .'

'But he loves you. You said he did.'

'And he said he did. But will he still? That's what I'm asking.'

'I have no idea.'

'He said he wouldn't see me for a while, that he couldn't leave Mayo . . . I know!' she said suddenly. 'We'll go to Ashford. Maureen and Aileen are both visiting this weekend. Papa has guests, his cousin Bertie Kerr-Pearse staying with his daughter Elizabeth, some other people. It will be delightful to see them all.'

'And Ashford is so close to Castle MacGarrett,' Kathleen said wryly.

'If we leave early and don't bring the children we can journey up in one day,' Oonagh said, ignoring that.

They set off the next morning and arrived at Ashford Castle in the late afternoon. Aileen was sitting on the stone steps, waiting for them. She stood up when she saw the car and waved. 'I heard you were coming,' she called out. 'Come and chat.'

'I must make a telephone call first,' Oonagh said.

'How you do carry on,' Aileen said. 'I can't imagine the children miss you half as much as you imagine.' But it wasn't to Luggala that Oonagh telephoned, or not first anyway. She did indeed telephone home, but only after she had spoken to Dominick and made a plan to meet him the next day; a plan in which it seemed to her that she pressed forward, for once, while Dominick hung back a little. She would drive to Ballinrobe, less than halfway between Ashford and Claremorris, and he would meet her there.

'Mamma says it's time to change for dinner,' Aileen said, when she had finished. 'And Maureen has arrived, so come to my room and have a drink before we have to face them in the drawing room.'

'Was it a terrible journey?' Oonagh asked Maureen when they had shut the door of Aileen's bedroom. They sat on Aileen's bed while Aileen sat in an armchair pulled close, her feet propped up on the bed beside them.

'No worse than any other, although it's so long since I've been in Dublin, I'd forgotten how shabby it is. Even just driving through from the station. All those filthy little streets.' She was, Oonagh saw, stouter, her make-up wilder, and under the thick dusting of powder, her complexion was mottled. Close to, she smelled hot and frantic, like a cat kept too long in a cage.

'But now you are here, and can breathe all the lovely fresh air,' Oonagh said comfortingly.

'We have air in London, Oonagh. Tell me the news. How is the Great Oouja?' Maureen asked, but the mocking way she normally used Brinny's nickname was absent, Oonagh noticed. Almost, she sounded a bit sorry for him.

Aileen began to tell some story of complaint about Brinny, then moved straight into another, smooth as the water that seeps through boggy ground, silently filling footprints from below and honeycombing what looks like solid ground so it becomes treacherous. Brinny seemed disappointing to her, in ways she could not articulate, instead complaining fretfully about his 'dullness' and slowness of wit. She was thin – thinner than Oonagh had ever seen her – and sat in a cloud of discontent that hummed about her head. She was so smartly dressed that she might have been on her way to a party, rather than a quiet country evening with her sisters.

She fell silent at last, the litany of Brinny's minor faults worn out. 'How's Duff?' Oonagh asked then, and Maureen, instead of smirking and showing off, was sombre in a way that was not like her. 'He's very often away,' she said. 'In London when I'm at Clandeboye, at Clandeboye when I'm in London. I hear rumours of his gambling debts, which are said to be enormous, but he no longer comes to me with them.'

'How does he settle them?'

'I don't know. It used to be I who settled them, but now . . .'

'I suppose you raged at him once too often,' Aileen said wisely, 'so he stopped telling you.'

'Something like that,' Maureen admitted.

'And I suppose you were harsh and cutting, more than you knew, and then couldn't take it back?' Oonagh said sympathetically.

'I suppose I was. And now I hear nothing. He's become . . . rather unreachable.'

'Well, couldn't you say you didn't mean it?'

'I couldn't.'

'No, I suppose not. You're like a person bewitched sometimes, Maureen. As though goaded ever on by some violent creature that is your very own nature.'

'In any case, there's no point when I did mean it, and he knows that. If he would only apologise, I could forgive him. But he never will.'

'I've heard he drinks a lot,' Aileen cut in bluntly.

'Everyone drinks a lot,' Maureen responded, lighting a cigarette with a hand that shook slightly. She emptied the decanter into her glass and said, 'So what will you do?' She didn't say about what, but Aileen seemed to understand.

'There must be other ways to be happy,' she said. 'I think of going to America. Everything here is growing so dreary. Each time I talk to Papa he warns me about something that I must do or not do. About deflation and devaluation of the pound. About unrest and anger that I must try to avoid or deflect. Places I should avoid, people I shouldn't see. He's become as fussy as an old hen, and the way he talks, you'd swear we're living in a tinder box that's been put too close to an open fire.'

'Would you really?' Oonagh asked, looking impressed at Aileen's bravery. 'It's so very far . . .'

'I would. And it isn't far at all any more, not really. Certainly not when you feel, as I do, that I cannot stay here any longer.'

'I thought Marcia would be the saving of everything,' Oonagh said.

'How naïve you are,' Aileen said. 'Always thinking more children are the answer. Has Tessa saved you and Philip?'

'No, but . . .'

'And do you expect Mildred's baby to save her and Dom?'

'Well, no. But . . .'

'Well, then. Brinny couldn't dote on anyone the way he dotes on Marcia. She is our reconciliation baby, our best chance, but even so, it may not be enough.'

At dinner, in the rather gloomy dining room used for smaller parties where the wood was too heavy, too highly polished, the curtains too thick, there was a great deal of family talk and brewery business. Cloé questioned Bertie Kerr-Pearse closely on the more distant family members with whom he was in touch, while Ernest and his brewery men – Osmond Baker and Edward Peake, the latter one of the new brewers just down from Cambridge – talked about their plans for the move to Park Royal in London. Elizabeth Kerr-Pearse seemed intelligent and well-educated, Oonagh thought. She made thoughtful contributions to the disentangling family discussions and had a long conversation with Kathleen about a book they had both read, but neither Ernest nor Cloé wished to prolong the party and it broke up early. Oonagh was relieved. The strain of meeting Ernest's questions about why she planned to go to Ballinrobe the next day, Cloé's raised eyebrows and considering gaze disconcerted her more than she wanted to say.

Maureen tried to persuade the Cambridge graduate, Edward, to join her for a drink and, when he politely declined, she turned to Oonagh and Aileen. When they both said no, she said, 'In that case, have Lapham send a nightcap to my room. In fact, have him send two.' Cloé and Ernest looked appalled, but said nothing. Late that night, Oonagh heard her gramophone playing loudly into the early hours, and wondered at the way so much had changed that, where once her parents would have demanded every detail of the Ballinrobe plan and forbidden it, where they would have told Maureen smartly that, no, she couldn't have the decanter sent to her room, now they looked on, disapproving, yes, but silent. It was a relief, and yet, she found, she missed the firm weight of their acceptance or refusal; the known heft of the boundaries they set.

Chapter Fifty-Three

Ashford Castle, Co. Mayo

Staying at Ashford Castle was always tiring, Kathleen reflected, as she got dressed early the next morning. Mostly, it was the way she preferred to be out of the house than in it – anywhere Cloé wasn't.

That morning, she had eaten and taken a short walk by the time Ernest and his guests were down. As she came in, he was announcing a plan to take them to Killary harbour, for a turn on his new speedboat. 'She will do fifty miles an hour. A beauty,' he said. 'The *Fantome* is moored there so we might board and have lunch. I'll send a message. Who will come?' The men immediately said they would – Bertie Kerr-Pearse, Edward and Osmond – and Elizabeth, after some persuasion, said she would join them. She was, Kathleen saw, carefully solicitous for her father Bertie's comfort, telling him please to be sure to wear something warm as it was likely to 'blow terribly' on the boat, 'and

Mother will never forgive me if I bring you home with a cold'. He laughed, and patted her cheek, and said to Ernest, 'Is a man not blessed to have daughters?' to which Ernest, Kathleen thought, agreed more cautiously.

The girls all declined to go. Oonagh said vaguely that she 'must do some things'. Aileen announced her intention to 'read and walk about', and Maureen, who hadn't emerged from her room, sent a message to say, 'Lord, no, you couldn't begin to persuade me.' Kathleen found being on a boat made her sick, but said she would like to come for the drive, if she could watch them from the shore. The idea of being left behind at Ashford with Cloé was too unappealing.

'We'll take two cars,' Ernest said. The drive was almost two hours and the day was fresh as though newly washed and put out to dry. Clear and bright with a pale blue sky and a brisk wind that ordered puffs of white cloud on and off stage in succession. They reached Killary before midday and made for the tiny stone pier where Ernest's boat was tied up with two crewmen from the *Fantome* waiting, and a fisherman slowly gathering his lobster pots.

The speedboat was as beautiful as Ernest had promised. Rich reddish wood varnished to a high shine that reflected the sunlight with glossy delight, and red leather seats set deep into it. The steering wheel was compact and upholstered in cream leather, stitched as carefully as a handbag. Kathleen was almost tempted in that moment to go with them, but there wasn't room for her. Indeed, it was already a squash with seven.

Far out in the mouth of the harbour, which was long

and narrow, she could see the masts of the *Fantome* reaching spidery to the sky. Without her sails she was much reduced – like one of Oonagh's dogs when they had been clipped – but the elegance of her lines, even so far away, gave her poise. She could see Ernest look fondly at her, and then he began disposing people, 'Elizabeth, if you sit here . . .' and saying, 'I will drive,' to the crewmen.

Kathleen took up a spot on the stone wall facing the sea, a rug from the motor-car over her knees, another under her, and a thermos of tea Ernest had insisted on bringing for her. Behind her she could hear all the busy sounds of a hillside – grass and brambles stirring idly in the breeze, insects that hummed and buzzed, the deeper noises that told her the earth, too, was breathing: slow, profound breaths. She watched the boat bounce playfully on the surface of the water, which was broken by small choppy waves. The eager chug of the engine drifted back to her for a time, before wind and distance drowned it out. The sun was no stronger and the wind brisker there so that soon she put the rug around her shoulders. It was hopeless to think she could tie her hair back so she left it to whip about her face.

The boat was far out in the harbour now, moving towards the *Fantome* and she imagined Ernest's delight at the wide open space. In all that wide expanse of sea and sky, the boat was the only thing that moved with purpose. The fisherman had at last stowed his pots to his liking and left and no one else was near.

They were perhaps halfway between the pier and the *Fantome* when the speedboat stumbled. It lurched first to the left, then sharply to the right, then seemed to sit suddenly down, nose pointing towards the air, like a duck come to a rapid skidding halt after flight. Kathleen watched, confused, as it sank lower into the water, and lower again. She was so far away that there was no sound, no sense of urgency, just the boat slipping smoothly below the water. Even as she began to understand that this wasn't right, two smaller craft set off from the *Fantome*, and she knew there was urgency to that. From where she sat, these small boats seemed to move with trickling slowness, specks in all that blue. She watched because there was nothing else to do. She couldn't see the detail of what took place, only that soon – so soon that she wondered was there some mistake and was this planned after all – the speedboat had disappeared, gulped down by the smooth blue water. But what now went on out there in the water where it had been, she could not see. She stood and stared, and only her heart understood that there was an emergency she couldn't respond to. It thudded and lurched and her ears were full of the sound of it so that even had they been close enough to call out she didn't think she could have heard them.

After an agony of time, the tiny yacht craft reached the place where the speedboat had been swallowed, and stopped there, bobbing nauseatingly. Kathleen thought of running up the road, shouting, to see whom she might raise, but it was an isolated spot without houses. There were the motor-cars, but she couldn't drive, and neither could she tear herself away. In any case, what could anyone she might find do, trapped on land, while the drama unfolded far out in that unstable sea? Help had been sent, by the *Fantome*, and the best she could do was watch.

Her hand where she held the rug around her was blue, and when she first tried, she couldn't release the fingers that had been clutching too hard. Her jaw hurt where she had been clenching it. The two *Fantome* craft separated. One headed back to the yacht, and the other made its way towards the pier where she now stood at the very edge, waiting. The sky was turning from pale to deeper blue and the wind had dropped so the afternoon was still, and it seemed improbable that anything very terrible could have happened. A spill, she thought. A wetting. Something they would laugh about over dinner. That would provide more and livelier conversation than last night's genealogy and brewing. She knew the giddiness that came with disaster averted – an accident that, after all, was not so bad – and how it infected everyone with the energy of relief, the wild consciousness of their own invincibility, and she looked forward to it. She imagined Ernest's face – the rueful look he got when something went wrong and he feared it was his fault. He was driving the boat, so whatever happened, he would be certain it was his fault.

The craft arrived beside the pier and she counted the people in it over and over, sure that she had missed one. But there were only four, and two of those, in front, were crew from the *Fantome*. In the back, Elizabeth was huddled under a pile of oilskins, her face the powdery grey of milled oats, and Osmond cradled his arm that sat at an awkward angle.

'Ernest?' she asked the crewman, when the two had been helped up towards where a small crowd was now gathered. Someone must have radioed from the yacht because there were policemen there, and cars.

'On the *Fantome*.'

'The others?'

'One of the crew is there too. We pulled him out, but he was already gone.' They paused in their speaking. 'We couldn't bring him back on this run.' They could not, they meant, mix the living with the dead.

'The others?' she said again.

He stared at her as though she was stupid. 'We'll go back out now,' he said, 'and keep looking. We've a few hours before it's too dark.'

Someone drove her home. She didn't know who he was and they didn't talk so she never found out. Elizabeth and Osmond had been taken to Westport to the hospital. Someone must have telephoned ahead because Cloé and the girls were waiting for her, standing at the bottom of the front steps, the castle spread behind them, like something skinned and pegged out to dry. But when she tried to tell them what she had seen, Cloé cut her off. 'That's enough,' she said sharply, as though Kathleen had been displaying something unseemly, a ghoulish curiosity. 'We know enough.'

The next morning brought little news – the three men were still missing – and by the time they left, Oonagh and Kathleen to Luggala, Maureen and Aileen home to their houses because Cloé said there was 'no need or indeed sense' in them remaining at Ashford, they still had not seen Ernest, who remained aboard the *Fantome*. He wouldn't come off, and Kathleen didn't know if it was because there was something amiss with him that they hadn't been told, or because he felt he must remain there until the other men – Bertie Kerr-Pearse, Edward Peake, the lively graduate from Cambridge who wouldn't have a drink with Maureen, and the seaman, whose name was White and who had a family – were found.

After a week there was an inquest and Ernest gave his evidence from the *Fantome*, where he was still in bed, so that the coroner had to go out to him. That very morning, the body of Edward Peake was discovered. They said he had died from a blow that fractured his neck. All this they were told in the daily telephone calls with Cloé, who relayed the news in a voice so flat and sentences so short that Kathleen could feel the effort with which she kept herself in check as clearly as though she had put her hand on the lid of a pot and felt the water boiling hard within.

Kathleen didn't know when Ernest finally came off the *Fantome*, or what was required to persuade him, but then she heard that his doctor had ordered him into hospital in London 'for an operation'. What the operation was, or why it needed to be carried out just then, was not revealed. Only that he would be obliged to recover for 'quite some time,' said Cloé, who herself was 'going away' to a different place, a sanatorium. 'For my nerves,' she said, and her voice was like a grass stalk that had been peeled right down to the pale, tender inner stem. 'You cannot imagine what it has been like, caring for Ernest at this time.'

'It's the first time she's had to look after him,' Oonagh said bitterly, 'and she cannot even do that.' She twisted the lid of the jar of face cream she was holding violently, and, when it would not open, slammed it down hard on the dressing-table so that everything there jumped. But Kathleen thought how terrifying it must be for Cloé, always the one to be minded, to be suddenly required to mind the man who had always looked after all of them, with his boundless energy and good sense. As though she had put her foot confidently down on something plain and solid, only to find it going through, and down and down into nothing.

Chapter Fifty-Four

London, Spring 1936

Kathleen hadn't planned to go to Oonagh's wedding, although Oonagh had tried to coax her: 'I know you disapprove, but it is my wedding day. Please come.' She and Philip had been divorced nearly a year now, on the same day and in the same court as Dominick and Mildred. Oonagh and Philip had suggested lunch afterwards at the Ivy, and been surprised when Mildred refused.

'How *civilised*,' their friends had said, just as they had said all along, 'how tidy,' relieved to find that, after all, under the surface of civilisation there was nothing more terrible than more civilisation.

'I don't disapprove, Oonagh,' Kathleen said then. 'That is altogether too simple a word for what I feel.'

'I will be a good mother to those children,' Oonagh said. 'They adore me.'

'Because you indulge them shamelessly – with gifts and treats and games. I overheard Patricia say that you are "nothing at all like a grown-up". And, anyway, they have a mother, even if she does now live in rooms in Marble Arch and not in a castle in County Mayo. Honestly, Oonagh, you're so greedy for children, even when they're not your own.'

'It will all come right,' Oonagh said. 'You'll see. Dom feels just as I do. A nursery full of little ones tumbling about. More darling babies, now that Tessa is already four.'

'Little Judith is just a year and a half,' Kathleen said.

'I'm sorry you disapprove of me so much,' Oonagh said.

'Oh, I know you're sorry. You've always been far too concerned with what other people think,' Kathleen said, but her voice was softer. And when Ernest called shortly after Oonagh had left for Marylebone Register Office, she tied a scarf around her hair, promised Gay she would bring him back two sugar almonds – one pink and one white – and got into the motor-car with him.

Outside the register office, a knot of news reporters had already gathered, packed close together and avid. 'It's a circus out there,' Ernest said.

'Apparently the papers are looking for something new,' Kathleen said, taking off her headscarf and folding it into a small square. 'Good news of some kind, I suppose. An antidote to all the bad.'

'If that's how they look at it,' Ernest said, lighting one of the thin cigars he had taken to smoking and blowing out a dense blue cloud.

'How do you look at it?'

'A failure. Followed, I hope, by no more failures.' He

sounded irritable, almost querulous. Kathleen was reminded again that he was not himself. Had not been since the accident in Killary harbour. It was nothing, she reflected, watching him chew the end of his cigar, that you would see immediately – although he now had a slight limp, which had never been explained to them beyond that it related somehow to the accident and the operation – and there was a groove in his forehead so deep it was like a second mouth. Mostly, it was in his demeanour. He had not the same energy, the same certainty as before, and she missed it. He was more often displeased, complained of what he saw but without his old knack for instantly putting to rights what he didn't like. Almost, he seemed fearful of what was around him now, drawing himself in and away from things only he could see that distressed him.

She didn't know what was wrong with him. Indeed, no one had even admitted aloud that there was anything wrong, until Cousin Bryan said it. Kindly, but clearly: 'Ernest has lost his nerve, his faith in himself, like a bad fall from a horse. He will be all right, but it will take time.'

How much time, no one asked, and still they didn't know, because now it was nearly two years after that terrible day, and still he was not who he had been. And because of that his daughters had all grown around him to hide the place he no longer occupied, the way shrubs in a garden would grow around a great tree that had been uprooted. And even so, they were all conscious of the gap still: the solid thing they had leaned against was gone. They were louder in his presence now: Maureen more decisive, Aileen more demanding, Oonagh more childish, because they were frightened by his absence, and sought to hide it, even from themselves, to cover it with noise and activity.

Ernest fidgeted with his coat – there was plenty of winter still in the April wind – and seemed unable to adjust it to his liking, twitching at the collar and sleeves until Kathleen longed to reach out and button it for him, but knew he would not like her to. 'I suppose Aileen will be next,' he said. 'She says nothing to me, but her actions speak clearly. All those rubbishy people she entertains. Far too many of them remnants of that Fort William set. Riff-raff, friends of Mrs Simpson,' he continued. He was becoming worked up now – any mention of Mrs Simpson did this. He was dismayed at how long it was taking the new king, Edward VIII, to put away the childish things that had preoccupied him before his father's death in January – chief among them, his American friend. 'Every day that liaison persists, he damages the monarchy, and it is not a good moment for damage. There will be sides to be chosen,' he continued darkly. 'And I wouldn't be altogether sure which side that king of ours will take.'

He fidgeted some more with his sleeve, trying to pull it down further than it wanted to go and the groove, the mouth, cut in his forehead deepened. 'There's the Stallion now,' he said, as Dominick pushed his way through the crowd, hat pulled low over his eyes. The rapid-fire of the cameras, like so many aggressively snapped fingers, grew loud, then quiet as the doors swung closed behind him.

'Does Oonagh know you call him that?' Kathleen said.

But Ernest paid no attention. 'I'll go,' he said. 'No need for me to hang about.'

There were more people than ever now – most of them newspaper men who shouted and shoved – but some bystanders too, the idle and curious. The newsmen pushed up against the steps and entirely filled the pavement outside. Kathleen tried to find a way in, thinking she might duck beneath their arms as they held their cameras up high above their own and each other's heads, with gloating cries, like seabirds that circle upon a shoal of mackerel. But she couldn't, and realised her mistake clearly when she was roughly elbowed by the man beside her. She stumbled, and was afraid that, if she lost her footing, she would be trampled.

'Here.' Someone thrust a hand in front of her and she grabbed it gratefully. She was pulled clear of the crowd, to the outskirts, and looked up. It was Ned.

'What are you doing here?'

'I read that Oonagh was to be married and I came to see. I didn't realise so many others would come. What can they be interested for? And I thought I'd see you . . .'

'Well, I never thought I'd see you.' She wanted, she realised, to laugh and grin, like a person possessed, as though his presence were the answer to a question she hadn't even known she was asking, had been asking for three years now.

He burst out laughing. 'No, I can imagine that's true. But I'm glad you're here. Did you get my letters?'

'Yes.'

'But you didn't answer them?'

'I didn't have much to say.'

'What have you been doing?'

'Not much, the same.'

'Teaching?'

'No.'

'I see.' He looked kindly at her, as though he did see. 'I think we need to do something about that. I saw Ernest just before I saw you. I waved, but I don't think he saw me.'

'Maybe not. He isn't quite himself . . .' and she told Ned about the accident, and the way Ernest was now.

'It's a pity,' Ned said. 'He will be needed.'

Oonagh and Dominick emerged then, and the roar of clicks and shouts around them intensified. The couple almost immediately retreated. Three times they tried to exit, and twice they ducked back inside the register office, as around the low building with its one tall and strident tower, men pressed forward and shouldered one another. On their third attempt, Kathleen watched as Dominick put his arm protectively around Oonagh, both lowered their heads into their coat collars, and rushed to the waiting motor-car. They drove off, followed by the newsmen, who leaped into their cars in pursuit so quickly that soon the road was empty, except for a small woman who picked up one of the flowers that had fallen from Oonagh's bouquet.

'Come for coffee?' Ned said. Kathleen opened her mouth to say no, and then closed it. Suddenly, she was sick of being the one to hang back, to say no, to wait and fear. If the whole world could go mad, and talk of war, if a king could refuse to give up his divorced mistress and newsmen chase people down streets, if the whole country could divide into two camps and stare across at one another with hatred, why was she, Kathleen Murphy, holding back, living by rules that were old and bound no one any more?

'I will,' she said.

Chapter Fifty-Five

London, Autumn 1936

Autumn came, and with it, the return of London's fogs from wherever they had been banished for the summer. They crept out through cellar gratings and up from manhole coverings as if on the summons of a silent whistle, consuming everything they touched, rolling over buildings and lamp posts and trees and cars, spiriting them all away. That year was particularly bad, Kathleen thought. Or perhaps it was just that the feeling of waiting had intensified, so that it seemed as if, now, everything was held at bay by uncertainty, made indecisive by delay: a city that had yet to take form – vague shapes beneath the misty covering – waiting for something to happen that would solidify it.

Aileen came back to London saying she would go to Paris but she never did, just hung around the city. Maureen stopped giving parties 'because no one will come', and Oonagh continued to deliberate over what to do with Rutland Gate. The feeling of waiting lay heavy on all of them.

And maybe the something they waited for would be war, Kathleen thought. Just as Ernest had predicted, there was civil war in Spain and men had started to travel from all across Europe, drawn to it like iron filings to a magnet. 'This is our fight,' Ned said to her. 'It's the very same as the battle of Hyde Park, only bigger and more vital. Don't you see? It's not about Spain, Republicans against Nationalists, it's a fight for all of Europe. The question is, do decent, honourable people triumph, or brutes like Franco and Mosley?'

His cough was back – it returned every year: 'Like a Brent goose, it winters close to home,' he joked, when he could get his breath back – and they met, indoors more often than out, in his room, which was more cheerless than ever now that the sun had been dragged earthwards and could no longer breach the tops of the line of houses opposite. Without light, the room drew in upon itself as though it, too, were sick.

They huddled under his thin blankets and there was little left of the laziness of summer – days they had spent there, talking, laughing, sharing peaches and small pastries from the market barrows. Now, she thought, it was like a game of hide-and-seek where they had crept into a place together to hide, but at any moment a cry of 'Found you!' would come to eject them.

'Will you not move?' Kathleen asked him. 'There are better rooms than this that you could afford.'

'I won't be here much longer,' he said.

'You will move?' He nodded, and she made him

promise, because when it came to practical matters like
that, he was inclined to be forgetful.

'I promise,' he said.

Rutland Gate was to be sold. 'There cannot be a point
in keeping it,' Oonagh said, 'for Dom says we will be
at Castle MacGarrett, and if we do come to London,
it will be without the children so there is no need for
such a big house.' They were looking through her things,
making piles of what she no longer wanted and would
send to the jumble sale, against those clothes that would
travel to Ireland. The portrait by de László was to go
to Luggala. 'It's a pity,' she said. 'I'll miss it. But I can't
have it looking down every day on Dom, as though
Philip himself were peeping through the eyeholes,
watching us.'

'Will you be happy at Castle MacGarrett?'

'The children will be. It will be such a merry place,
for Gay and Tessa, and Dom's children when they
visit,' Oonagh continued. 'Think how lovely, Kathleen,
seven children and maybe more. It will be as I have
always imagined I would be – surrounded by little
ones.' It was not the question Kathleen had asked, but
she knew better than to pursue it. 'I met Unity this
morning, going on and on, all fervent and self-
important, and I said to her, "I suppose you think we
are like the lilies of the field,' as a sort of joke, and
only guess what she said?'

'What?'

'She said, "You're not lilies, you're weeds. You choke
everything. You may hate what I believe in, but at least

I believe in something. You, what do you believe in? Practical jokes?" So I said, "That's Maureen," because indeed it is, and Unity just looked at me. As though I were a – a – I don't know, a *door* that wouldn't open properly. Now, try this on.' She handed Kathleen a coat from the wardrobe, a brown houndstooth check with broad collar and full skirt. 'Let's see if it suits.' Like a hare that had reached its den, she had twisted herself free of the conversation.

Kathleen shrugged the coat on. 'Turn to the side. And now the other. And turn to me again.'

Kathleen stretched her arms out to the sides then raised them above her head. 'Tight,' she said. 'Everywhere.'

'You're fatter,' Oonagh said consideringly.

It was true. Kathleen could no longer wear Oonagh's cast-off clothes because they didn't fit. Always they had been too short – Oonagh, in her stocking feet stood only to her shoulder – but there were hems to let down, sleeves to sew a band to. Now the clothes didn't fit at the waist or at the bust. It was only by a little so that Kathleen, who had no eye really for fashion or the cut of a garment, had been slow to notice. But now, trying to button the coat, she realised she was growing bigger, and thought with regret of all the lovely things Oonagh had given her that she wouldn't be able to wear.

'Turn to the side again,' Oonagh said. Kathleen did so. 'How is Ned?' she asked then.

'He is well.'

'And do you see as much of him as ever?'

'I do.'

'I see. And what does he think of this?' Oonagh raised

her hands into the air in front of her and sketched a vague shape with them.

'Of what? The coat? He hasn't seen it yet.' Kathleen was confused.

'Not the coat, silly. The baby.'

'What baby?' But, of course, as soon as she said the words, she understood – the turning her this way and that, the careful scrutiny, the too-tight clothes. But still she said, 'What baby?' again, more in panic this time, in the hope that Oonagh would say, 'Aileen is to have a new baby.' Or Maureen, or Violet. Or anyone at all.

'Your baby,' she said gently. 'I wondered did you know. I'm not in any doubt but, still, you had better see my doctor.' Kathleen's breath came out in hard, sore gasps because her heart had moved from its home and lodged in her throat so that she had to try to breathe around it. 'Sit,' Oonagh said firmly, 'sit down. Breathe, Kathleen, breathe properly. And be calm. I will help you through this.'

Through what? Kathleen thought. There was no 'through' this thing. This baby. Because a baby, for her, was an end. A solid brick wall of an end that couldn't be got over. All her grand recklessness was gone now. The way in which she had gone to Ned, thrown away caution so decisively, giddy at her own daring, in thrall to some fantastical future she had invented. All that, she saw now, was idiocy, foolishness of the worst kind. There wasn't any fantastic future – no future at all, barely even a life – for a woman like her with a baby and without a husband. Her hands shook and bright spots danced in front of her eyes.

'Breathe,' Oonagh said again, more sharply. 'Sit, Kathleen. Now. I will help you through this. If there is one thing I am good at, it's babies. You know that. Be calm.' She forced Kathleen down to sit on her bed, to bend over so that her head was closer to her knees and to take deep breaths even though Kathleen had to fight the tightness in her chest to do so. When she was better, and the shakiness had passed, Oonagh let her sit up. 'First,' she said, 'you must tell Ned. Until you know what is in his heart, you cannot know what to do.'

'Not yet,' Kathleen said.

'No. Not yet. I understand that. But soon, Kathleen. Now, tidy your hair and come with me to see Aileen, who is having fittings at Lachasse, and see if you can't help me cheer her up.'

How like Oonagh to say that Aileen needed 'cheering up', Kathleen thought, a few hours later, as if she had a headache or was momentarily mopey. In fact, watching Aileen issue detailed instructions as to the precise finish of the many tailored suits she ordered, wearing a dress identical to one Kathleen had seen on Mrs Simpson in the pages of a magazine recently, what she seemed was thin and wintry, a frozen version of herself that was elegant, precise and unreachably cold. The skin of her face was stretched tighter over the fine bones, as if it had found there wasn't enough to go round. Her collar-bones were sharp as a hare's, jutting against the black satin of her neckline. Beyond her carapace of diamonds and jewels in the outrageous colours of a reptile, behind the exquisite clothes and expensive handbags, she was smaller than she should have been and discontented.

She bought clothes, Kathleen thought, as some children gather sweets, stuffing them into their pockets and even into socks, to carry away and eat later.

But Kathleen paid only half her attention to Aileen, because the other half was turning over and over the same ground: *I have a baby. I will have a baby.* All the things that that meant came at her in quick succession: *What must I do? Where can I go?* What did Oonagh mean when she said, 'I will help you through this'? But in the end, when she was done sifting through all the frightened visions – herself alone and poor and friendless with a child, no husband, no work – she found a tiny kernel of something stouter: *I am thirty-one years old, and I am to have a baby.* She sat up a little straighter.

Late that afternoon, she went to find Ned. As well tell him soon as late, when the telling filled her with such dread. Coming out at Green Park she found the fog was massing, and was thicker again by the time she got to Berwick Street. The street was emptier than she had ever seen it, although it was not late. No children played or chased each other, and she thought of them, kept indoors, the windows of their bare rooms stuffed with rags to keep out the creeping fog that choked them. Did Ned do the same? Or did he not, and was that why his cough was bad? She must remind him of his promise to leave this place, she thought. The door was open and she walked up the scuffed staircase. The banister was wet to the touch, as though the fog had draped itself across it. At Ned's room she knocked and called his name. And again. He did not answer. There was no noise at all from behind the door. She knocked, and called out again. Nothing.

She heard a noise behind her and turned to see a young man walk from the far end of the dark hallway towards her. As he came closer, she saw it was the boy with the torn shoe sole who once asked her had she "anything" for him. She wondered would he speak, ask her for something, and was already turning over in her mind what she might give him. But he didn't, only passed her and went on towards the stairs. He was, she saw, taller and broader, moving with purpose. But still with the same face pinched by hunger. His boots sounded quick and hollow on the stairs, and she waited til the sound had quite died out before following him down.

Back on the street, she looked up at Ned's windows, which were flat and black and hostile. The street was still empty, filled with thick fog that turned back light as surely as a blanket might. It was like the screen against which something might be projected – a film or image. Except that in a fog like this, there was no projection, and no audience to watch, just the screen itself, repeated and repeated, wrapped around so that everyone in it was lost inside their own cocoon, woven from damp layers of obscurity. She thought of calling Ned's name in case he was nearby, but dared not because she feared her voice would not be enough to force a path through. That it, like the light, would be thrown back to her, and she would have to hear how pitiful it was.

He is not there, she told herself. I will find him tomorrow. She knew where he would be the next day, because he had told her. 'Mosley's Blackshirts are meeting at the Tower and will march to the East End where they will try to occupy the streets and get rid of the Jews and Communists. We will set up barricades and stop them.' His eyes had gleamed, exactly as if he were planning a game, Cowboys and Indians, perhaps. But this was real.

'Those men will hurt you,' Kathleen had said, when he told her.

'Not if we hurt them first,' he'd replied.

Chapter Fifty-Six

The next day she got to the East End early because she hoped to find Ned, tell him what had happened, what she was, and leave before anyone marched anywhere. She had been to those streets before, many times, with Ned, but that day was immediately different. There was no idle flow of people, coming and going from their work on the docks, shopping, trading, loitering outside the public houses. Today all was purpose, and a steady stream of men and women, children too, moved towards a barricade set up where Christian Street met Cable Street. Someone had parked a dirty cream truck across the entrance to the street, and around it was a perilously ramshackle mass made up of packing cases, mattresses, pallets, old chairs, broken furniture: a game of fort made large and dangerous. It was towards that that the people moved, carrying more to reinforce it – she saw two men go by with an iron bedstead slung between them – to build it high and deep, and keep Mosley's Biff Boys out.

Someone had scrawled 'Smash Fascism Forever, Long Live the Jews' on a wall in white paint, while on the pavement was daubed 'They Shall Not Pass'. She saw children gleefully gathering bricks and bottles, bringing these to the men at the barricades, while more brought their marbles, clutched in hands and carried in handkerchiefs. 'For the horses,' one shouted at her over his shoulder when she asked what they were doing. 'For rolling under their 'oofs.'

It was like the preparations for Oonagh's twenty-first birthday party, Kathleen thought: such busyness, such sense of purpose, a million tiny tasks in service of one great event. Except this was done with a different urgency. She watched a thin-shouldered man with wire-rimmed spectacles stuff screws of newspaper into the gaps between shutters and window frames beneath a shop sign that read 'S. Gronofsky Suits Made to Measure. Misfits a Speciality'. He worked fast and smoothly, as if preparing his small shop for assault was something he had done before.

She kept moving, looking for Ned, or anyone who knew him, trying to go against the tide of people that she might be better able to spot him. It was barely ten o'clock and the streets were full. Some of those who passed her were dressed in their finest clothes as though for a day out, and there was a carnival air. Sunday dinners must be cooking early – roast beef, boiled potatoes – yet below that was something else, a smell like rust, that she was afraid of, just as she had been taught to be afraid of a rusty nail or jagged piece of metal as a child.

She couldn't see anyone she recognised, and the streets became more and more full, with news now being passed up and down – 'They have left the Tower and begun to make their way' . . . 'Mosley in an open-topped Rolls-Royce surrounded by his marching men' . . . 'Six thousand police are with them, many on horseback.' She thought of the children and their gleeful hoards of marbles, the damage they would do to the horses, causing them to slip agonisingly on their great hoofs. She couldn't stay. For all the swirl of excitement, she could sense what was coming, and it was not, as Ned would have it, a game. She went home to wait. As she walked away, the noise and urgency gathered behind her.

Hours, almost the full day later, Ned arrived at Rutland Gate. The house was sold but not yet packed up. He stood on the steps outside while Peters hung back behind Kathleen in the doorway so she couldn't tell if he would bar Ned's way or ask him to step in. Ned's face was dirty and the collar of his shirt torn. There was a red swelling high on his cheekbone that would surely bruise. 'Come inside,' she said.

'Not a bit,' he said cheerfully. 'Tom says he saw you this morning on Whitechapel Road but couldn't make you hear when he called out, so I came to see that you got home safe. What were you doing there, Kathleen? Come to show solidarity?' He grinned.

'I came to find you. Do come in. We can talk in the library.' Now that Philip no longer lived there, the room was scarcely used and she knew they would not be interrupted. And this way she would not have to bring Ned through the house and risk Oonagh, or indeed

Aileen or Maureen who were with her, seeing him and trying to offer him beer or talk.

In the library, she shut the door on Peters, who was hovering. 'What happened to your cheek?'

'It's nothing, a tussle with a policeman.' He touched it briefly, indifferent. 'They are calling it "the battle of Cable Street" on the news reports, and such a battle it was.' He was triumphant. 'Now, why were you walking the wrong way down Whitechapel Road this morning?'

'I was looking for you.'

But instead of asking why, he asked, 'What did you think?' as though showing her something he had made. Kathleen tried to tell him how it had all seemed to her: the parade-like atmosphere thinned by a sense of urgency, the dull rumble of men's boots, the threat of violence that left marks in the air, like the screech of car tyres will leave on a road. But it was as if he couldn't hear her. He nodded eagerly and began relaying numbers that made no sense to her – five thousand Blackshirts, six thousand policemen, six and a half thousand protesters, thousands of this and thousands of that. She could see that now he knew her to be safe, he longed to be off, to be back with Wintringham and the others who were there so they could talk and talk, talking their story of the day into being. There was no sense in trying to tell him anything, Kathleen realised, not then. She resolved to wait, and was about to ask him to go, to meet her tomorrow instead, when he said, 'I'm going to Spain, Kathleen.'

'Why?'

'To fight. Tom is going, as a journalist, but he plans

to join the International Brigades. And I will join with him. There are clear choices now – anyone can see that.'

'When will you go?' As with the baby, she found she couldn't understand how she hadn't expected this. Prepared for it as one prepares for bad weather by closing windows, securing shutters, testing weak spots and shoring them up.

'Soon. Tom leaves next week. We go to France first, then over the mountains, the Pyrenees.' And the way he said 'Pyrenees', with a rolling sound of joy, Kathleen knew he was gone already in his heart.

'Would you not wait till you're better?' He was still coughing, a great deal.

'Wintringham said the same, but I won't. The sun will do me good, I'm sure. But no matter if it does or not, I will go, Kathleen, and nothing must stop me.'

And so she said nothing. Or nothing of that, anyway. She let him talk, and watched his blue eyes crinkle at the corners with the laughter that came so naturally to him, and she nodded and smiled and pretended to listen, and stayed silent.

What could she say? She had no way to tell him his plan was more dangerous than he had any idea of. If Ernest were himself, she felt certain he would have been able to do something. He would have stopped Ned leaving on what was a child's mission. Or far worse. A child's mission was one that ended in a scraped knee, a tumble, tears. This – this would end in pain and hurt, maybe death. But Ernest wasn't himself, and maybe never again would be, and she had no idea at all what to say.

'There is something I must know, before I go,' he said then, looking seriously at her. 'When I come back, will you marry me? I have thought so much of you, the years you were in Ireland, and I know I was wrong when I said I couldn't settle. I can settle, Kathleen, with you. Once I have this done. And then together, we will do more.'

Now was the moment to tell him – to give him the news that might keep him from going, that would make his promise of return unnecessary. Tell him, and they could be married straight away. But she didn't. His *once I have this done* was too strong, a solid barrier against his intentions, one that couldn't be dissolved.

And so 'Maybe,' she said. 'Come and find me when you're back, and ask me then.' The more she said 'when you're back', the more she could believe it. She needed to believe it. The leap of her heart demanded it.

'I will,' he said. 'And I'll tell you something else before I go.' He gave a wide grin. 'Something you'll find funny. Mosley and Diana are to be married, tomorrow, in Germany, at Joseph Goebbels's house. Diana is there already and Mosley goes straight to join her.'

'How on earth do you know that?'

'We have spies in their ranks. They say that's why he didn't get out from his Rolls-Royce and fight today – afraid he'd have a black eye for his wedding.' He touched his own eye briefly, reflexively. 'They hope Hitler will attend, and he wants to look his best.' The petty vanity of the man, even while he orchestrated grand and terrible doings, astonished her.

Ned was clearly ready then to be gone, telling her he

would see her to say goodbye before he went. Already his mind was far away from there, from her. So she told him he would have too much to do to think of seeing her again, and that they should say their goodbyes now. She asked how she might find him, to write, and he said he would send an address as soon as he had one.

When Ned had gone she went back upstairs. She planned to go to her room, to lie on her bed and think more about what she must do, but the drawing-room door was open and Oonagh called, 'Kathleen, is that you?' so Kathleen knew she had been waiting.

'It is.'

'What did Ned say?'

Peters must have told her he had called. Kathleen went into the drawing room, where all three Guinness girls were gathered. The fire was lit, the dogs dozing in a warm heap before it. The thick curtains were drawn against the darkening evening, although she could hear a brisk wind rattling at the windows. 'Well?' Oonagh demanded, scanning Kathleen's face. She was sitting close to her Tiffany lamp, the one with stained glass patterned with dragonflies, so her face was greenish in its glow.

'Well . . .' Kathleen said. She didn't know what else to say. Had Oonagh told her sisters?

'Did he propose marriage?' Oonagh demanded. She must have told them. Still Kathleen didn't say anything, and after a minute, Oonagh made an exasperated face. 'You didn't tell him, did you?'

'I couldn't.'

'Honestly, Kathleen. I should have come with you. Give me his address and I'll go and see him now.'

'No, he's leaving for Spain. To fight the Fascists. He must be allowed to go, Oonagh. There will be time enough to tell him later. They say it will be a quick war.'

'They always say that about wars,' Maureen said sombrely. 'And what if something happens to him?'

'He'll be all right,' Kathleen said. She had to believe it. 'He's always all right.'

'It's a war, Kathleen,' Aileen said, but gently, 'not a skirmish in the East End where he might get a black eye.' Peters must have told them everything he could.

'Even so. I have to let him go. I can't keep him. He'll stay if I tell him. If I ask.' She didn't know that to be true, but tried to assume it was. 'But I don't want that. I'll tell him when he comes back.'

Maureen opened her mouth and Kathleen knew she was going to say, 'If he comes back,' but Oonagh shook her head firmly and Maureen stayed silent. And as long as no one said it, as long as she did not hear or say the word 'if', Kathleen felt she could believe. That he would return. And that when he did, she would be able to tell him that there was a baby, that she loved him and needed him. All the things she couldn't say to him in the library. And he would listen to them, and be glad, and say the same to her.

'What will you do?' Aileen asked.

'There's plenty of room in the nursery at Castle MacGarrett,' Oonagh said, and Kathleen could see she was pleased at the idea of another child there.

'And in Luttrellstown,' Aileen added, which was kind, because Kathleen knew she didn't really wish it. Kathleen looked at Maureen, who grinned at her, knowing perfectly well that Kathleen would put no child of hers into the nursery at Clandeboye.

'That's very kind,' she said, 'and maybe for a while I will say yes. But, actually, I've had an idea.' And she told them the things she had been thinking since the day before, when it came to her that, yes, this baby was the end of her life. But also the start of a new, different life, and that she didn't need Ned's answer to the question she hadn't asked him.

'I'm going to be a teacher,' she said. 'Ernest sent me to teacher-training college, and it's time I became what I'm trained to be. It's a fine thing to be. I think about politics just as Ned does, you know.' Almost, she was afraid to say this to them, but they nodded, all three of them. 'I see the unfairness, just as he does. I don't have any stomach for fighting or marching or shouting. But I should like well enough to teach, and maybe change the way things are like that.'

'And the baby?' That was Oonagh, face screwed up in concern.

'Who better to bring up a baby than a teacher?' she joked feebly.

'Well, you'll need money, at first anyway,' Maureen said, ever practical.

'I have some. My wages, all these years, that I have hardly spent.'

'Wages?' Aileen asked.

'Yes. Every Friday. In my bedroom. I have been putting them by so there is a tidy sum now.'

'Did you . . . ?' Maureen asked Oonagh.

'No.' Oonagh looked shamefaced. 'It never occurred to me.'

'Typical!' Maureen said. Then, 'Papa, I suppose.'

'I wasn't quite sure,' Kathleen said. 'I never asked.'

'How very like him,' Maureen said, and her face was sad.

Would any of them speak of the difference in Ernest, the absence in him and around him? Kathleen wondered. For a moment she thought Oonagh would say something. But the moment passed, and she didn't.

Peters brought in the cocktail tray, put it down beside Oonagh and stirred up the fire to a bright blaze. There would not be many more such evenings.

When Peters was gone, closing the door softly behind him, Kathleen said, 'All the same, why must Ned go looking for trouble?'

'He doesn't see it as trouble,' Maureen said.

'No, I suppose he doesn't.'

'And I'm not sure it matters what he does. Trouble will find him, same as it will find all of us,' Oonagh said then. 'At night I hear the sounds of marching men, of boots ringing on cobblestones in unison. I suppose it's in my dreams but it isn't always easy to tell. I'm glad I'm moving to Ireland. Aileen, you must be glad to be there too. Maureen, wouldn't you prefer it? Out of the way and safe?'

'I'm not so feeble as that,' Maureen said. 'Out of the way is rather out of the way, isn't it? And that's not for me. Anyway, I rather thought Aileen had had enough of Ireland and was looking to America.' She gave Aileen a sly smile.

'Perhaps.' Aileen huddled further back into her chair, as if to remove herself physically from the conversation. 'Don't you long to get away from all this too?' She jerked an arm out and sketched a swooping shape through the air, taking in the cocktail tray, her sisters, the sleepy dogs by the fire, and on towards the windows, with curtains drawn tight over, and whatever lay behind them. 'But, as it happens, I've decided not to. Not yet, anyway.'

'Giving it another go?' Maureen asked. '*Another* other go?'

'Yes, and don't be catty. Now doesn't seem the time to be setting off on new adventures, when everywhere is so full of uncertainties, and one's chums all busy and bothered and making dire predictions.'

'Does Brinny have any say in all this? Or does he just await his instructions, like the good soldier he is?'

'I know you're trying to be nasty, Maureen, and perhaps I deserve it, but I think Brinny will be jolly pleased. He is a good soldier, just as you say, and that isn't a slight, though I know you try to use it as one.'

'Of course he will be,' Oonagh rushed to say.

'If I'm honest with myself as I suppose one must sometimes try to be, all this restlessness isn't Brinny so much as it's me,' Aileen continued. 'I don't seem able to be content, as he is, with what we have and do. I find myself wondering if there isn't more, or better, or just something else I could be doing. A way to break up all those days, always the same, coming one after another after another, in a non-stop procession, like watching the Horse Guards.' She sighed. 'And you know how deathly that is after the first ten minutes.' Oonagh and Maureen both nodded thoughtfully. 'I suppose I thought I could find some excitement, anything to liven things up a little. But now that everything is getting so horribly lively everywhere else, I find I'm not so keen. And the girls are such darlings now. Neelia is starting her schooling, Doon will be five in three days, so pretty and funny, and Marcia at three is a perfect poppet. I almost see, Oonagh, why you spend so much of your time playing nanny. Maybe, you know, all that hearth-and-home carry-on mightn't be so feeble after all.' She sounded to Kathleen as though she was trying, hard, to persuade herself. But maybe that was the best thing she could do. 'And I have promised to get Annie a job. She speaks jolly good German, you know. Surely that must be useful now, when there is so much interest in Germany. I must ask Papa if he knows someone I could talk to about her.'

'If he doesn't, Duff will. But why would you help her? I thought you found her a frightful bore?'

'Not for a long time now. She's really rather good fun. And frightfully clever. She says she doesn't wish to marry. And even though at first I thought that an affectation, well, now I think I understand better . . .'

'Not wanting to be married?' Oonagh sounded surprised.

'Yes. All those single gels one felt so sorry for, with their *jobs* and their dreary little *interests*, well, I see them differently now.'

'Would you really?' Oonagh demanded. 'Get a job?'

'Oh, not I. I don't know how to do anything except

be married.' She sounded, Kathleen thought, rather sad. 'But I understand better why others might want to look elsewhere for what to do with their lives. There certainly seem to be more possibilities than Mamma or Gunnie ever let on . . . So I plan to help Annie with a career if she doesn't want a husband, and that way she won't have to have one.'

'Well, I don't know . . .' Oonagh began.

'Of course you don't. You've swapped one husband for another,' Aileen said.

'It's not like that.'

'Isn't it?'

'No,' Oonagh insisted.

'So, you're staying put, Aileen, is that it?' Maureen, ever practical, said.

'Yes,' Aileen said. 'And you?'

'Oh, yes. Duff may be sick of me, but I shan't be going anywhere.' She said it defiantly. 'He once told me I was like Salome, wanting his head on a plate.'

'And do you, still?' Aileen asked.

'Yes,' Maureen said viciously. 'I do. He was joking, I think, but he was right. It's worse than he knows. If I was to sit in judgement like Solomon, I'd rather see him dead than give him up.' The blaze Peters had stirred up had settled into a hot red glow that seemed, to Kathleen, to mirror the intensity of Maureen's words. Outside, the wind tested the windows more urgently.

'The children—' Oonagh began, but Maureen cut her off.

'No, Oonagh. They are not the answer. They do not

dilute what I feel for him at all. If anything, it's worse now, because I know that, no matter what one feels for them,' – she did not, Kathleen thought, try to describe what she felt for them – 'it takes none of the madness from my feelings about him. I still want every shred of him and cannot be content with less.'

'How uncomfortable that sounds.' That was Oonagh, Kathleen thought, always trying to tame Maureen's wilder impulses, drag them downwards from where they ballooned savagely in the high wind of her personality and tether them to something civilised and reasonable, something merely *uncomfortable*; *unfortunate*; *inconvenient*.

'It is. But it's no good talking about it.' And it wasn't, Kathleen could see that. Maureen would continue to fight with Duff as long as he allowed it, hurling the sharp demands of her nature against the deep implacability of his. 'Something will have to give eventually,' she said. 'And then there will be a change, whether I want it or not. Because even I know we cannot continue as we are.'

'No,' Aileen agreed. 'I imagine not.'

'Shall I mix a cocktail?' Maureen asked then, keen to change the subject, getting up and moving towards the tray.

'Do. But none of Chips's little additions. How is he anyway?'

'Too grand even for me now. He and Honor have moved in beside the Duke of Kent. In fact, Chips has rather surpassed us all. Terribly pally with Mrs Simpson, and therefore with the King. He's hosting a party for them both in a few weeks, along with Prince Paul of

Yugoslavia and Princess Olga of Greece. He drips HRHs these days.'

'Just what he always wanted,' said Oonagh.

'Yes. And he's close to Mr Chamberlain too. Last time I saw him, he told me in high delight that he had "backed the winning side" and said it was a terrible pity Duff hadn't seen which way the wind was blowing. As if Duff would do anything so feeble as blow with the wind,' Maureen said indignantly. 'But, oh, how I hate being on the losing side,' she finished crossly.

'Nothing is won yet,' Kathleen said. 'Or lost.'

'And don't pretend any of it will touch you anyway, Maureen, because it won't,' Aileen said. 'Nothing ever really does, does it? Any of us, I mean.'

Almost, Kathleen thought, she sounded sad. As though the smooth impenetrability of their lives, the way they were protected but also isolated, was something she had learned to mistrust. And as though she might have liked to be less remote, if only she knew how.

Kathleen looked at them then, the three Guinness girls: Oonagh humming quietly to herself as she stroked the edge of a child's blanket with her finger; Maureen pouring a measure of gin into a glass and throwing it back in one gulp; Aileen staring into the fire as if the answers to her questions lay in its hot heart. So assured, so sought-after, so protected and, beneath that, every bit as uncertain, hopeful and fearful as she was herself.

'Don't pretend you want to be *touched* by things.' Maureen sounded revolted.

'Maybe every once in a while,' Aileen said. 'Just to know how others feel.'

'Better not,' Oonagh said, with one of her funny gleams of wisdom. 'We haven't been brought up to it. Kathleen, what do you think?'

'I think I wouldn't like to be adrift from all my fellows when I could be close with them,' Kathleen said. 'But maybe those are Ned's words more than mine. Now that he's gone, I suppose I'll have to find out.'

'I suppose we all will,' Maureen said, and she tilted her chin in silent defiance towards the window, beyond which lay troubles that were new and strange and only half imagined.

They were, Kathleen thought, like characters in a play, sitting in their allotted places, waiting for the curtain to go up that they might assume their roles and begin. Except that the curtain was already up, and they had missed the moment of its rising.

Afterword

Aileen's daughter Marcia died in an accident that I have never heard explained, very shortly after I ended this book, on Christmas Day 1936. Aileen and Brinny separated within a few years, and divorced in 1940. Brinny died on active service during the Second World War in 1941 aged thirty-eight.

Maureen had a third child, a boy called Sheridan, in 1938. Basil Blackwood – 'Duff' – died on active service in Burma, near the city of Ava, in 1945, aged thirty-five. Maureen went on to marry twice more.

Oonagh had three boys with Dominick Browne. One, named just Baby Browne, died within a few days of birth in 1943. Oonagh's daughter, Tessa, died aged fourteen in 1946 after an allergic reaction to a diphtheria inoculation. Her youngest son, Tara, died in a car accident aged twenty-one in 1966. Oonagh and Dominick divorced in 1950. She married once more, adopted two children from Mexico and, after Tara's death, gained custody of his two children.

The point at which I have ended this book is, I think, historically interesting because of how much the political landscape of Britain changed immediately after it.

When Maureen says of Duff, in the final chapter, that he hadn't backed the winning side – that seemed true when she said it. Appeasement, as it became known, was the policy of the British government in the first part of the 1930s. Driven by the recollected trauma of the First World War peace, even at a heavy price, was considered attractive. It reached a peak in September 1938 when Neville Chamberlain signed the Munich Agreement that allowed Hitler to annex the Rhineland, on the understanding that Germany's expansion was then complete. But the policy ended abruptly in March 1939 when Hitler occupied the rest of Czechoslovakia, and then invaded Poland. On 3 September 1939, Britain declared war on Germany, and the side Chips had aligned himself with – Chamberlain, Edward VIII, appeasement – was discredited.

On 10 December 1936, King Edward VIII abdicated, saying, 'I have found it impossible to carry the heavy burden of responsibility and to discharge my duties as King as I would wish to do without the help and support of the woman I love.' He was succeeded by his brother, who became George VI. That ended a period of pro-Nazi sympathies among the British aristocracy, led by Edward VIII.

During the Second World War, Sir Oswald Mosley was interned at Holloway Prison, Diana with him, from May 1940 to November 1943.

Author's Note

When I left the Glorious Guinness Girls at the end of the first book about them, they were all newly married, and about to set off on a new decade – the 1930s – with the excitement and hope that comes with new circumstances.

It seemed a good place to leave them, hovering on the brink of what they believed would be wonderful things. I wanted them to pause there for a while, because I already knew that the next decade wouldn't be especially kind to any of them.

Between them, the three Guinness girls married eight times. Oonagh married first at nineteen, to Philip Kindersely, and that marriage was over by 1935. Aileen struggled on a little longer but she and Brinsley Sheridan Plunket were separated by the late 1930s and divorced in 1940. Maureen and Duff stayed married until his death in 1945, but their rows were legendary. The story I have included here – of Duff cutting up Maureen's clothes – is true. The fact that both drank at this time

(Randolph Churchill, who described Blackwood as 'the most lovable man I met at Oxford', also said of him 'an undue addiction to drink blighted what might have been a fine political career') didn't help the harmony of their marriage.

Throughout the 1930s, the girls' expectations of marriage and motherhood were tested: by infidelity, boredom, feelings of inadequacy and bereavement, and all the other ways in which harsh reality butts up against happy fantasy, particularly for a generation of women who were brought up to believe that marriage was their best – sometimes their only – option.

After writing *The Glorious Guinness Girls*, I realised that with a book like this, readers really want to know what is real and what is not. So, how much of this book is 'true'? The answer is, a great deal, but not all.

Many of the specific details are correct – dates of marriages and births of course – but also parties, holidays and appearances in gossip columns.

It is true that Oonagh and Philip lived on the same street as the Mitfords, at Rutland Gate. That was a detail that influenced my image of the friendship between these two sets of sisters. The idea that Oonagh, from her windows, could watch the comings and goings of all the Mitford children was irresistible, especially during the times that she was pregnant and housebound.

Philip did indeed commission a portrait of Oonagh, by Philip de László, a Hungarian painter very much in vogue then (who happened to be married to a cousin of Oonagh's, Lucy Guinness).

This portrait, by the by, was sold some time after Oonagh's death in 1995, and remained 'lost' for several decades, only to reappear unexpectedly at an auction in Atlanta, Georgia in 2020. It was bought for nearly $325,000, around ten times what it guided at.

It is also true that Oonagh was frequently warned by her doctors to have no more babies, but such was her love for children that she didn't listen. The end of her marriage was precipitated by her seeing a photograph of Philip and Violet in a society magazine, and spotting that Violet was wearing the dress Oonagh had bought her to be bridesmaid at Oonagh's wedding to Philip three years previously. In a society where women changed their wardrobes seasonally, a three-year-old dress was almost certainly a statement; a coded message sent by one woman to another. Or so I believed when I found that detail in Paul Howard's wonderful book *I Heard The News Today Oh Boy*, about the life of Oonagh's son, Tara Browne.

Violet's husband, Lord Brougham and Vaux, gambled heavily, just as I have recounted here, losing most of his money and having to auction, first the contents of Brougham Hall, and then the house itself.

The affair between Philip Kindersley and Violet Valerie French, then Lady Brougham, is also true, as is the fact that Philp's brother, Dick, died in a bizarre accident involving something called 'train jumping', when the train he was on top of went through a tunnel. Violet, Philip, Oonagh and Dominick Browne did indeed all go on holidays, to Wexford, in 1934. And a year later, in November 1935, Philip and Oonagh divorced on the same day and in the same court as Dominick and his first wife Mildred. Those sorts of details are well beyond anything most writers would feel were credible if they invented them.

The party held on 7 July 1932 at Cheyne Walk by Diana Mitford, then Guinness, as a coming-out for her younger sister Unity, is also a real event, as is the detail that Diana wore a dress of grey tulle and 'all the diamonds I could lay my hands on'. It was after that party that Diana left Bryan Guinness for Oswald Mosley, whom she nicknamed Kit.

Nancy Mitford's suicide attempt is also true – as is her comment that 'it's a lovely sensation just like taking anaesthetic'.

One of the best things that happened during the writing of this book was the publication of the first volume of diaries of Henry 'Chips' Channon, edited by Simon Heffer. This, covering the years 1918–38, was a rich source of material. Channon was a brilliant and perceptive diarist – in recording everything he did, but also given to very full descriptions of how he felt about people, their personalities and appearance. Chips, who makes various appearances in this novel, was an American from Chicago, married to Honor Guinness, cousin to the Guinness girls. He was an unashamed snob and a bon viveur, who seems to have gone everywhere, known everyone and viciously sketched most of them. Here is his entry on Oonagh and Philip, which I read halfway through writing this book:

January 17 1935

The Kindersleys are separated and perhaps drinking . . .
He, Phil Kindersley, is a good-looking, almost dashing
'Ya-Hoo' – common as clay; I thought him terrible [on
holiday in Austria in 1933] – very common naked,
which is such a test. He looked like a handsome
policeman. For two years now he has had a liaison with
Lady Brougham and Vaux, a moron and half-tart . . .
Oonagh K has always pretended not to mind, but her
fair, stupid little heart was breaking.

My own research had led me to very similar conclusions,
but he is far, far more cruel than me.

Chips' diaries give no account of how he met Honor,
and nothing seems to be known about that, so I've
given my version of that event in this book.

Also true are the boating accident I describe when
Ernest Guinness' speedboat overturned and four people
died, and the Battle of Cable Street, in which I have
Ned participate. This took place on 4 October 1936,
and was a clash between Mosley's British Union of
Fascists and a mix of anti-Fascist demonstrators,
including Communists, trade unionists, anarchists, Irish
dockers, British Jews and socialist groups. It always
sounded to me like an exhilarating, vital event and I
wanted to include mention of it.

Finally, Maureen's own daughter Caroline once said
that her childhood was too painful to speak of, but in
this book I hope I go some way to representing Maureen
as the complex person that she was.

So, the pillars of this book are largely true. The story I have created between these pillars is not. These are my imaginings and interpretations of those facts that are still available, ninety-odd years after the time during which the novel is set. This is a novel, not a history book, but for me, the fun of the whole thing is to stick closely to the facts, and use them as structural foundations for an invented story.

Kathleen is not a real person, nor is Ned. In telling the story of the Guinness girls and the 1930s, I wanted someone who could bring the reality of that turbulent decade, when Communism and Fascism battled for the hearts and minds of millions of unemployed and badly paid men and women, many of whom were driven to join the large Hunger Marches that took place throughout the early 1930s, some involving tens of thousands of people, marching many miles, to protest the miserable circumstances of their lives.

None of the Guinness girls involved themselves in politics or any sections of society beyond their own privileged circles, but I wouldn't have felt I had done the decade any kind of justice if I had ignored all that side of it. And so, Kathleen is a go-between, someone who moves between the world of the Guinnesses and the world of working people, cross-pollinating as she goes, taking bits from one and bringing them into the other.

She is also a reminder of Ireland, and the reality of lives there – dominated by the Church and narrow social expectations in the decade in which the Irish Taoiseach Éamon de Valera (who was indeed Professor of Mathematics at the Carysfort Teacher Training College early in his career, a few years before I sent Kathleen there) embarked on a protectionist economic policy that left Ireland very isolated.

Ireland doesn't feature as heavily in this novel as the last, nor does Irish history, but neither was far from mind as I wrote it.

Acknowledgements

Writing in a pandemic – like everything in a pandemic – is a series of challenges, physical and psychological. There's home-schooling, isolation, never having an empty house, a dearth of inspiration, an excess of generalised anxiety and some moments of highly specific anxiety. Like life really, except writ large, and small.

So first I want to thank the people who kept me sane, chiefly David, as always. You must be so sick of being the level-headed one. My children, for their wonderful company during the long locked-down months. My mother for being, in a crisis (as she is in every crisis) incredibly calm and resilient. My siblings and friends for taking every opportunity no matter how windswept and cold, to meet and bump elbows, and thereby keep me going. Just about.

This book went through a number of incarnations as I tried to find a way to continue telling the story of the Guinness girls, but in a way that felt different to the first book, and that took into account that they are now adults, and their lives have taken them to three separate houses in three very different places. There were several false starts, and I want to thank my ever-wonderful editor, Ciara Doorley, for bearing with me while I worked through these, and for her vital readings of early drafts, and the incisive comments that helped forge the direction the book took.

Thank you to everyone in Hachette Ireland – particularly Joanna Smyth – for their help with getting the book right, visually and every other way. Hazel Orme for a vigilant and meticulous edit. Sherise Hobbs and everyone at Headline UK for being lovely to work with, and Beth de Guzman, Kirsiah McNamara, Kamrun Nessa and Tiffany Porcelli for the truly wonderful journey that being published in the US has been.

Thank you to Ivan, who has the *mot juste* for so many things, and a great ability to help/force me to really refine my sometimes vague ideas.

And most of all, thank you to the wonderful, amazing readers who were so enthusiastic about the Guinness girls, finding them as gloriously fun as I do.

Bibliography

There were a great many books that came with me on my research travels for *The Guinness Girls: A Hint of Scandal*. In particular, Maureen Guinness's daughter Caroline Blackwood's Booker-nominated novel *Great Granny Webster*, which gave me wonderful insight into life at Clandeboye.

Joe Joyce – *The Guinnesses*
Frederic Mullally – T*he Silver Salver: The Story of the Guinness Family*
Michele Guinness – *The Guinness Spirit*
Jonathan Guinness & Caroline Guinness – *The House of Mitford*
Claud Cockburn – *The Devil's Decade*
Paul Howard – *I Read the News Today, Oh Boy*
Bryan Guinness – *Diary Not Kept: Essays in Recollection*
Andrew Barrow – *Gossip 1920–1970*
Robert O'Byrne and his brilliant The Irish Aesthete website, theirishaesthete.com, as well his fantastic book

Luggala Days: The Story of a Guinness House
D.J. Taylor – *Bright Young People*
Nancy Schoenberger – *Dangerous Muse: The Life of Caroline Blackwood*

I'd like to thank Beth Gormley and Irene Ward at UCD, and Marianne Cosgrave, Archivist for the Sisters of Mercy, who were so helpful getting me information about the Carysfort Teacher Training College in the 1920s.

Just as useful as books of history, are novels from the time. And the 1930s was a rich time for novelists. Patrick Hamilton, Stella Gibbons, Virginia Woolfe, Aldous Huxley (*Brave New World* was published in 1932, can you believe…), George Orwell, Evelyn Waugh, Daphne Du Maurier, and yes, PL Travers' *Mary Poppins*; all these were my companions while I researched and wrote this book.

The Glorious Guinness Girls are the toast of London
and Dublin society. Darlings of the press, Aileen,
Maureen and Oonagh lead charmed existences
that are the envy of many.

But Fliss knows better. Sent to live with them as a child,
she grows up as part of the family and only she knows of
the complex lives beneath the glamorous surface.

Then, at a party one summer's evening, something happens
which sends shockwaves through the entire household. In
the aftermath, as the Guinness sisters move on, Fliss is
forced to examine her place in their world and decide if
where she finds herself is where she truly belongs.

Set amid the turmoil of the Irish Civil War and the brittle
glamour of 1920s London, *The Glorious Guinness Girls* is
inspired by one of the most fascinating family dynasties in
the world - an unforgettable novel of reckless youth,
family loyalty and destiny.

Available in print, audiobook and ebook

HACHETTE
BOOKS
IRELAND